T0363200

MEDICS

Down

Under

MARION
LENNOX

MEREDITH
WEBBER

SUE
MacKAY

MILLS & BOON

CONTENTS

Stormbound Surgeon

Marion Lennox

Dear Reader,

We have our summer holidays at a remote little fisherman's cottage where only a tiny strip of land connects us to the mainland. While snoozing on the beach (my major holiday occupation), I thought, wouldn't it be fun to wipe out the road and lock two completely disparate people together? Before I knew it, I wasn't on holiday anymore—I was plotting like crazy. Joss and Amy are the result.

I hope you enjoy the outcome of my snoozing!

I'd love your feedback. Contact me through my Web site at www.marionlennox.com.

Happy reading!

Marion Lennox

PROLOGUE

THE LAWYER CLEARED his throat and looked miserable. This was nothing short of blackmail, and the girl before him deserved so much better.

But the old man finally had her where he wanted her. Robert Fleming had manipulated people all his life. The only person who'd broken free had been his stepdaughter, and now he was controlling her from the grave.

The will was watertight. Fleming would succeed and there wasn't a thing the lawyer could do about it.

'Just read it,' Amy said, stony-faced. The lawyer collected himself. And read.

'To my stepdaughter, Amy Freye, I leave my home, White-Breakers. I also leave her the land on Shipwreck Bluff and sufficient funds to build a forty-bed nursing home. The home is to be built in the style of a resort, to ensure resale is possible, and I set aside the following to be invested for maintenance...

The above bequest is conditional on Amy living permanently in Iluka for at least ten years from the time of my death. If she doesn't fulfill this condition, White-Breakers and the nursing home are to be sold and my entire estate is to be divided evenly between my nephews. The nursing home is to be sold as a resort for holiday-makers who'll appreciate Iluka. As Amy never has.'

CHAPTER ONE

'IF IT DOESN'T stop raining soon I'll brain someone.' Amy put her nose against the window and groaned. Outside it was raining so hard she could barely see waves breaking on the shoreline fifty yards away.

'Great idea. Brain Mrs Craddock first.' Kitty, Amy's receptionist, was entirely sympathetic. 'If I hear "Silver Threads" one more time I'll do the deed myself.'

It was too late. From the sitting room came the sound of the piano, badly played, and Mrs Craddock's warbling old voice drowned out the television.

'Darling, we are getting old,
Silver threads among the gold...'

Murder was looking distinctly appealing, Amy decided. 'Can you taste arsenic in cocoa?' she muttered. 'And just what are the grounds for justifiable homicide?'

'Whatever they are, it can't be more justifiable than this. A week of rain and this lot...'

It was the limit. Nothing ever happened in Iluka, and this week even less than nothing was happening. The locals jokingly called Iluka God's Waiting Room and at times like this Amy could only agree.

It did have some things going for it. Iluka was a beautiful sea-side promontory with a climate that was second to none—apart from this week, of course, when the heavens were threatening another Great Flood. It had two golf courses, three bowling greens, magnificent beaches and wonderful walking trails.

On the cliff out of town was Millionaire's Row—a strip of outlandishly expensive real estate. At the height of summer the town buzzed with ostentatious wealth.

But the rest of the time it didn't buzz at all. Iluka was a retiree's dream. The average age of Iluka's residents seemed about ninety, and when the rain set in there was nothing to do at all.

Nothing, nothing and nothing.

Card games. Scrabble. Hobbies.

Lionel Waveny had made five kites this month and he hadn't flown any of them. The sitting room was crowded at the best of times, and if he made one more kite they'd have to sit on them.

From the sitting room came excited twittering. 'Amy... Bert's won.'

Great. Excitement plus! Summoning a smile Amy headed into the sitting room to congratulate Bert on his latest triumph in mah-jong. She stepped over Lionel's kites and sighed. She really should stop him making them but she didn't have the heart. They were making him happy. *Someone* should be happy. So...

'Great kite,' she told Lionel, and added, 'Hooray,' to the mah-jong winner. 'Bert, if you win any more matchsticks you can start a bushfire.'

Despite her smile, her bleak mood stayed.

Oh, for heaven's sake, what was wrong with her? she wondered. What was a little rain? This was a decent sort of life—wasn't it? The nursing home she'd set up was second to none. Her geriatric residents were more than content with the care she provided. She could start a cottage industry in knitwear and kites, she had a fantastic home—and she had Malcolm.

What more could a girl want?

Shops, she thought suddenly, and a decent salary so she could enjoy them. She stared down in distaste at the dress she'd had for years. What else? Restaurants. A cinema or two, and maybe a florist where she could buy herself a huge bunch of flowers to cheer herself up.

Yeah, right. As if she'd ever have any money to buy such things.

She looked out the window at the driving rain and thought… What?

Anything. Please…

Amy wasn't the only one to be criticizing Iluka. Five miles out of town Joss Braden was headed for the highway and he couldn't escape the town fast enough.

'It's the most fantastic place,' his father had told him over the phone. 'There's three separate bowling greens. Can you believe that?'

'Yes, but—'

'Now, I know bowling doesn't interest you, boy, but the beaches are wonderful. You'll be able to swim, catch lobster right off the beach and sail that new windsurfer of yours. Go on, Joss—give us a few days. Get to know your new stepmother and have a break from your damned high-powered medicine into the bargain.'

He'd needed a break, Joss thought, but five days of rain had been enough to drive him back to Sydney so fast you couldn't see him for mud. For the whole week his windsurfer had stayed roped to the car roof. The seas had been huge—it would have been suicidal to try windsurfing. His father and Daisy had wanted him to spend every waking minute with them; they'd been blissfully and nauseatingly in love, and medicine was starting to look very, very good in comparison.

So this morning, when the newsreaders were warning of floods and road blockage, his decision to leave had bordered on panic. Now he steered his little sports car carefully through the rain and crossed his fingers that the flooding wasn't as severe as predicted.

'Ten minutes and we're on the highway and out of here,' he told his dog. His ancient red setter, Bertram the Magnificent, was belted into the passenger seat beside him, staring through the windscreen with an expression that was almost as worried as his master's. If they were stuck here...

'We'll be right.'

They weren't.

'Amy, love, we need a fourth at bridge.'

'I'm sorry, Mrs Cooper, but I'm busy.'

'Nonsense, child. We know you always go for a walk on the beach mid-morning. You can't walk anywhere now, so come and join us.'

'But I can't play.'

'We'll give you hints as we go along. You'll be an expert in no time.'

Aargh...

Once they reached the highway it'd be easier.

The road into Iluka from the highway twisted around cliffs along the river. It was a breathtakingly scenic route but it was dangerous at the best of times, and now was the worst possible time to be driving.

Joss's hands gripped white on the steering-wheel. He leaned forward, trying to see through the driving rain, and his dog leaned forward with him. Bertram's breath fogged the windscreen and Joss hauled him back.

'There's no need for both of us to see.'

It'd be better once they were on the highway, he told himself. Just around this bend and across the bridge and...

His foot slammed hard on the brake.

Luckily he was travelling at a snail's pace and the car's brakes responded magnificently. He came to a halt with inches to spare.

But inches to what? Joss stared ahead in disbelief. He had to be seeing things.

He wasn't. Ahead lay the bridge. The water was up over the timbers in a foaming, litter-filled torrent, and the middle pylon was swaying as if it had no base.

And as Joss stared, there was a screech of tortured metal, a splintering of timber and the entire bridge crumbled and buckled into the torrent beneath.

'I can't play bridge. I've promised to help Cook make scones.'

'Oh, Amy...'

Beam me up, someone. Please beam me up...

Joss opened the car door with caution. He was safe enough where he was but seeing a bridge disappear like that made a man unsure of his own footing. Thankfully the ground underneath felt good and solid, even if a relentless stream of water began to pour down his neck the minute he opened the door.

Before him was a mess. The entire bridge was gone. In the passenger seat Bertram whimpered the unease of a dog in unfamiliar territory, and Joss leaned in to click the seat belt free.

They weren't going anywhere fast, Joss thought grimly. Bertram was a water dog at heart, and if Joss was going to drown out here at least he'd have happy company.

'Stupid dog. You can't possibly like weather like this.'

He was wrong. Joss even managed a grin as Bertram put his nose skywards, opened his mouth and drank.

But his humour was short-lived. How was he to get back to Sydney now?

First things first, he told himself. Before he started to panic about escape routes, he needed to do something about oncoming traffic. He didn't want anyone plunging unaware into that torrent.

He bent into the car again and flicked his lights to high beam.

The river wasn't so wide that oncoming cars wouldn't see his warning. Then he flicked on his hazard lights.

But his warning was too late. A truck came hurtling around the bend behind him and it was travelling far too fast. Above the roar of the river Joss hardly heard it coming, and when he did he barely had time to jump clear.

The smash of tearing metal sounded above the roar of the water. There was a crashing of broken glass, a ripping, tearing metallic hell, and then the sounds of hissing steam.

Joss backed away fast and Bertram came with him.

What the…?

His car had been totalled. Just like that.

He swallowed a few times and laid a hand on his dog's shaggy head, saying a swift thank you to the powers who looked after stupid doctors who ventured out in sports cars that were far too small. In a world where there were trucks that were far too big. In weather that was far too bad.

Then he took in the damage.

The other vehicle looked like an ancient farm truck—a dilapi-dated one-tonner. If Joss's sports car had been bigger it would have fared better, but now… His rear wheels were almost un-derneath his steering-wheel. The passenger compartment where Joss and his dog had sat not a minute before was a mangled mess.

Hell!

'Stay,' he told Bertram, and thanked the heavens that his dog was well trained. He didn't want him any closer to the wreck than he already was. The smell of petrol was starting to be overpowering…

He had to reach the driver.

Damage aside, it was just as well his car had been where it was, Joss thought grimly. Coming with the speed it had, if Joss's car hadn't been blocking the way the truck would now be at the bottom of the river.

If anyone else came…

There was another car now on the other side of the river, and it also had its lights on high beam. Joss's lights were still working—somehow. The lights merged eerily through the rain and there was someone on the opposite bank, waving wildly.

They'd all been lucky, Joss thought grimly. Except—maybe the driver of the truck.

The smell of petrol was building by the minute and the driver of the truck wasn't moving. Hell, the truck's engine was still turning over. It only needed a spark...

The truck door wouldn't budge.

He hesitated for only a second, then lifted a rock and smashed it down on the driver's window. Reaching in, he switched off the ignition. The engine died. That'd fix the sparks, he thought. It should prevent a fire. Please...

Were there injuries to cope with? The driver was absolutely still. Joss grabbed the handle of the crumpled door from the inside and tried to wrench it open. As he worked, he lifted his phone and hit the code for emergency.

'The Iluka bridge is down,' he said curtly as someone answered, still hauling at the door as he spoke. 'There's been a crash on the Iluka side. I need help—warning signs and flashing lights, powerful ones. We need police, tow trucks and an ambulance. I'm trying to get to the driver now. Stand by.'

'If you won't play bridge how about carpet bowls?'

'That's a good idea.' At least it was active. Amy was climbing walls. 'Let's set it up.'

'But you'll play bridge with us tomorrow, won't you, dear? If it doesn't stop raining...'

Please, let it stop raining.

'You're wanted on the phone, Amy.' It was Kitty calling from the office. 'It's Chris and she says it's urgent.'

Hooray! Anything to get away from the carpet bowls—but the local telephonist was waiting and at the sound of her voice, Amy's relief disappeared in an instant. 'What's wrong?'

'I don't know.' Chris was breathless with worry. 'All I got was that the bridge is down. There's been a crash and they want an ambulance. But, Amy, the ambulance has to come from Bowra on the other side of the river. If the bridge is down... If there's a medical emergency here...'

Amy's heart sank. Oh, no...

Iluka wasn't equipped for acute medical needs. The nearest acute-care hospital was at Bowra. The nearest doctor was at Bowra! Bowra was only twenty miles down the road but if the bridge was down it might just as well be twenty thousand.

'I don't know any more,' Chris told her. 'There was just the one brief message and the caller disconnected. I've alerted Sergeant Packer but I thought...well, there's nowhere else to take casualties. You might want to stand by.'

It was a woman and she was in trouble.

Joss managed to wrench the door open to find the driver slumped forward on the steering-wheel. Her hair was a mass of tangled curls, completely blocking his view. She was youngish, he thought, but he couldn't see more, and when he placed a hand on her shoulder there was no response.

'Can you hear me?'

Nothing. She seemed deeply unconscious.

Why?

He needed to check breathing—to establish she had an airway. He stooped, wanting to see but afraid to pull her head back. He needed a neck brace. If there was a fracture with compression and he moved her...

He didn't have a neck brace and he had no choice. Carefully he lifted the curls away and placed his hands on the sides of her head. Then, with painstaking care, he lifted her face an inch from the wheel.

With one hand holding her head, cupping her chin with his splayed fingers, he used the other to brush away the hair from her mouth. Apart from a ragged slash above her ear he could feel no bleeding. Swiftly his fingers checked nose and throat. There was no blood at all, and he could feel her breath on his hand.

What was wrong?

The door must have caught her as it crumpled, he thought as he checked the cut above her ear. Maybe that had been enough to knock her out.

Had it been enough to kill her? Who knew? If there was internal bleeding from a skull compression then maybe...

She was twisted away from him in the truck, so all he could see was her back. He was examining blind. His hands travelled further, examining gently, feeling for trauma. Her neck seemed OK—her pulse was rapid but strong. Her hands were intact. Her body...

His hands moved to her abdomen—and stiffened in shock. He paused in disbelief but he hadn't been mistaken. The woman's body was vast, swollen to full-term pregnancy, and what he'd felt was unmistakable.

A contraction was running right through her, and her body was rigid in spasm.

The woman was in labour. She was having a baby!

'Amy?'

'Jeff.' Jeff Packer was the town's police sergeant—the town's only policeman, if it came to that. He was solid and dependable but he was well into his sixties. In any other town he'd have been pensioned off but in Iluka he seemed almost young.

'There's a casualty.' He said the word 'casualty' like he might have said 'disaster' and Jeff didn't shake easily. Unconsciously Amy braced herself for the worst.

'Yes?'

'It's a young woman. We're bringing her in to you now.'

'You're bringing her here?'

'There's nowhere else to take her, Amy. The bridge is down. We'd never get a helicopter landed in these conditions and Doc here says her need is urgent.'

'Doc?'

'The bloke she ran into says he's a doctor.'

A doctor… Well, thank heaven for small mercies. Amy let her breath out in something close to a sob of relief.

'How badly is she hurt?'

'Dunno. She's unconscious and her head's bleeding. We're putting her into the back of my van now.'

'Should you move her?'

'Doc says we don't have a choice. There's a baby on the way.'

A baby.

Amy replaced the receiver and stood stunned. This was a nursing home! They didn't have the staff to deliver babies. They didn't have the skills or the facilities or…

She was wasting time. Get a grip, she told herself. An unconscious patient with a baby on the way was arriving any minute. What would she need?

She'd need staff. Skilled staff. And in Iluka…. What was the chance of finding anyone? There were two other trained nurses in town but she knew Mary was out at her mother's and she didn't have the phone on, and Sue-Ellen had been on duty all night. She'd only just be asleep.

She took three deep breaths, forcing herself to think as she walked back out to the sitting room.

Thinking, thinking, thinking.

The vast sitting room was built to look out to sea. Mid-morning, with no one able to go outside, it held almost all the home's inhabitants. And they were all looking at her. They'd heard Kitty say the call was urgent and in Iluka urgent meant excitement.

Excitement was something that was sadly lacking in this town. These old people didn't play carpet bowls from choice.

Hmm. As Amy looked at them, her idea solidified. This was the only plan possible.

'I think,' she said slowly, the solution to this mess turning over and over in her mind, 'that I need to interrupt your carpet bowls. I think I need all hands on deck. Now.'

* * *

Fifteen minutes later, when the police van turned into the nursing home entrance, they were ready.

Jeff had his hand on his horn. Any of the home's inhabitants who hadn't known this was an emergency would know it now, but they were already well aware of it. They were waiting, so when the back of the van was flung wide, Joss was met by something that approached the reception he might have met at the emergency ward of the hospital he worked in.

There was a stretcher trolley rolled out, waiting, made up with mattress and crisp white linen. There were three men—one at each side of the trolley and one at the end. There was a woman with blankets, and another pushing something that looked blessedly—amazingly—like a crash cart. There was another woman behind…

Each and every one of them wore a crisp white coat and they looked exceedingly professional.

Except they also all looked over eighty.

'What the…?'

He had barely time to register before things were taken out of his hands.

'Charles, slide the trolley off the wheels—that's right, it lifts off. Ian, that's great. Push it right into the van. Push it alongside her so she can be lifted… Ted, hold the wheels steady….'

Joss glanced up from his patient. The efficient tones he was hearing weren't coming from a geriatric. They came from the only one in the group who didn't qualify.

She was a young woman, nearing thirty, he thought, but compared to her companions she was almost a baby. And she was stunning! She was tall and willow slim. Her finely boned face was tanned, with wide grey eyes that spoke of intelligence, and laughter lines crinkled around the edges that spoke of humour. Her glossy black hair was braided smoothly into a long line down her back. Dressed in a soft print dress with a white coat covering it, she oozed efficiency and starch and competence. And…

Something? It wasn't just beauty, he thought. It was more…

'I'm Amy Freye,' she said briefly. 'I'm in charge here. Can we move her?'

'I… Yes.' Somehow he turned his attention back to his patient. They'd thrown a rug onto the van floor for her to lie on. It wasn't enough but it was the best they could do as there'd been no time to wait for better transport. The thought of delivering a distressed baby in the driving rain was impossible.

'Wait for me.' Amy leaped lightly into the van beside Joss. Her calm grey eyes saw and assessed, and she moved into action. She went to the woman's hips and slid her hands underneath in a gesture that told Joss she'd done this many times before. Then she glanced at Joss, and her glance said she was expecting matching professionalism. 'Lift with me. One, two, three…'

They moved as one and the woman slid limply onto the stretcher.

'OK, fit the wheels to the base,' the girl ordered of the two old men standing at the van door. 'Lock it into place and then slide it forward.'

In one swift movement it was done. The stretcher was on its wheels and the girl was out of the van.

'Take care of the dog, Lionel,' she told an old man standing nearby, and Joss blinked in astonishment. The top triage nurses in city casualty departments couldn't have handled things any better—and to even notice the dog… He opened his mouth to tell Bertram things were OK, but someone was handing towels to the man called Lionel, the old man was clicking his fingers and someone else was bringing a biscuit.

Bertram was in doggy heaven. Joss could concentrate on the woman.

'This way,' Amy was saying, and the stretcher started moving. Doors opened magically before her. The old men beside the stretcher pushed it with a nimbleness which would have been admirable in men half their age, and Joss was left to follow.

Where was he? As soon as the door opened, the impression of a bustling hospital ended. Here was a vast living room, fabulously sited with three-sixty-degree views of the sea. Clusters of leather settees were dotted with squashy cushions, shelves were crammed with books, someone was building a kite that was the size of a small room, there were rich Persian carpets...

There were old people.

'Do we know who she is?' Amy asked, and Joss hauled his attention back where it was needed.

'No. There was nothing on her—or nothing that we could find. Sergeant Packer's called in the plates—he should be able to get identification from the licence plates of the truck she was driving—but he hasn't heard back yet.'

She nodded. She was stopping for nothing, pushing doors wide, ushering the stretcher down a wide corridor to open a final door...

'This is our procedures room,' she told Joss as she stood aside to let them past. 'It's the best we can do.'

Joss stopped in amazement.

When the police sergeant had told him the only place available was the nursing home he'd felt ill. To treat this woman without facilities seemed impossible.

But here... The room was set up as a small theatre. Scrupulously clean, it was gleaming with stainless-steel fittings and overhead lights. It was perfect for minor surgery, he realised, and his breath came out in a rush of relief. What lay before him started looking just faintly possible.

'What—?'

But she was ahead of him. 'Are you really a doctor?' she asked, and he nodded, still stunned.

'Yes. I'm a surgeon at Sydney Central.' But he was focussed solely on the pregnant woman, checking her pupils and frowning. There didn't seem a reason for her to be so deeply unconscious.

He wanted X-rays.

He needed to check the baby first, he thought. He had two patients—not one.

'You can scrub through here.' Amy's face had mirrored his concern and she'd followed his gaze as he'd watched the last contraction ripple though her swollen abdomen. 'Or…do you want an X-ray first?'

'I have to check the baby.' She was right. He needed to scrub before he did an internal examination.

'I'll check the heartbeat. The sink's through here. Marie will help.'

A bright little lady about four feet high and about a hundred years old appeared at his elbow.

'This way, Doctor.'

He was led to the sink by his elderly helper—who wasn't acting elderly at all.

There was no time for questions. Joss was holding his scrubbed hands for Marie to slip on his gloves when Amy called him back.

'We're in trouble,' she said briefly, and her face was puckered in concern. She'd cut away the woman's smock. 'Hold the stethoscope here, Marie.' Then, with Marie holding the stethoscope in position over the swollen belly, she held the earpieces for Joss to listen.

His face set in grim lines as he heard what she'd heard. 'Hell.' The baby's heartbeat was faltering. He did a fast examination. The baby's head was engaged but she'd hardly dilated at all. A forceps delivery was still impossible. Which meant…

A Caesarean.

A Caesarean here?

'We don't have identification,' Amy was saying. 'Will you…?'

That was the least of their worries, he thought. Operating

without consent was a legal minefield, but in an emergency like this he had no choice.

'Of course I will. But—'

'We have drugs and equipment for general anaesthetic,' she finished, moving right on, efficient and entirely professional in her apology. 'The Bowra doctor does minor surgery here, but I'm afraid epidural is out of the question. I... I don't have the skills.'

After that one last revealing falter her eyes met his and held firm. They were cool, calm, and once again he thought that she was one in a million in a crisis.

'What's your training?' he started, hesitating at the thought of how impossible it would be to act as anaesthetist and surgeon at the same time—but she was before him there, too.

'Don't get the wrong idea. I'm not a doctor,' she said flatly. 'I'm a nurse. But I'm qualified in intensive care and I spent years as a theatre nurse. With only one doctor in the district, I've performed an emergency general anaesthetic before. That's why we have the drugs. For emergencies. So if you guide me, I'm prepared to try.'

He stared at her, dumbfounded by her acceptance of such a demand. She was a nurse, offering to do what was a specialist job. This was a specialist job for a qualified doctor!

But she'd said that she could do it. Should he trust her? Or not?

He hardly had a choice. He'd done a brief visual examination on the way here. The baby was still some way away—the head wasn't near to crowning—and now the baby's heartbeat was telling its own grim story. If they waited, the baby risked death.

He couldn't do a Caesarean without an anaesthetic. The woman was unconscious but the shock of an incision would probably wake her.

He needed a doctor to do the anaesthetic, but for him to perform the Caesarean and give the anaesthetic at the same time was impossible.

Amy wasn't a doctor. And she was offering to do what needed years of medical training.

But... 'I can do this,' she said, and her grey eyes were fearless.

He met her gaze and held it.

'You're sure?'

'Yes.'

'You realise insurance...'

'Insurance—or the lack of it—is a nightmare for both of us.' She nodded, a decisive little movement of her head as though she was convincing herself. 'But I don't see that we can let that worry us. If we don't try, the baby dies.'

It went against everything he'd ever been taught. To let a nurse give an anaesthetic...

But she was right. There was no decision to be made.

'OK. Let's move.'

It was the strangest operation he'd ever performed. He had a full theatre staff, but the only two under eighty years old were Amy and himself.

Marie stayed on. The old lady had scrubbed and gowned and was handing him implements as needed. Her background wasn't explained but it was assumed she knew what she was doing, and she handled the surgical tray with the precision of an expert.

And she had back-up. Another woman was sorting implements, moving things in and out of a steriliser. A man stood beside her, ready with a warmed blanket. Every couple of minutes the door opened a fraction and the blanket was replaced with another, so if—when—the baby arrived there'd be warmth. There was a team outside working in tandem, ferrying blankets, hot water, information that there was no chance of helicopter evacuation...

Joss took everything in. He checked the tray of instruments, the steriliser, the anaesthetic. He measured what was needed, then sized Amy up.

'Ready?'

'As ready as I'll ever be.' Still that rigid control.

He looked at her more closely and saw she was holding herself in a grip of iron. There was fear...

It would help nothing to delay or probe more deeply into her fear, he decided. She'd made a decision that she could do it and she had no choice. There was no choice!

'Let's go, then.'

Amy nodded. Silently she held her prepared syringe up so he could check the dose. He nodded in turn and then watched as she inserted it into the IV line.

He watched and waited—saw her eyes move to the monitor, saw her skilfully intubating and inflating the cuff of the endrotracheal tube, saw her eyes lose their fear and become intent on what they were doing.

He felt the patient's muscles relax under his hand.

She was good, he thought exultantly. Nurse or not, she knew what she was doing, which left him to get on with what he had to do.

He prepped the woman's swollen abdomen, lifted the scalpel and proceeded to deliver one baby.

CHAPTER TWO

IT WENT LIKE CLOCKWORK.

This team might be unusual but their competence was never in question. As he cut through the abdominal layers the old woman called Marie handed over instruments unasked. When Joss did need to ask, her responses were instantaneous.

And Amy's anaesthetic was first class.

All this was—had to be—ancillary to what he was doing. He was forced to depend on them: his attention was on the job. The anaesthetic was looking fine. All he knew was that he had what he needed and the woman's heart rate was great.

If only the baby's heartbeat held...

This was the moment of truth. He looked up to ask, but once again his needs were anticipated. The second of the older women stepped forward to push down on the uterus, giving him leverage as he slid one gloved hand into the incision.

Please...

'Here it comes.' He lifted the baby's head, turning it to the side to prevent it sucking in fluid. 'Yes!'

It was a perfect little girl.

Joss had only seconds to see that she was fine—the seconds while he scooped the baby free. As soon as she was free of her mother—before he'd even tied off the cord—hands were reaching for her, the sucker was in her mouth and they were removing mucus and freeing her to breathe. These people knew what they were doing! The old man behind Marie ducked in to scoop the infant into the waiting blanket as the elderly nurse cleared her airway.

'We'll be fine with her.' Amy motioned him back to the wound. 'She's looking good.'

He had no time to spare for the baby. He turned back to deliver the placenta, to swab and clamp and sew, hoping his geriatric helpers were able to clear the baby's airway in time.

Amy would supervise. He knew by now that she was a brilliant theatre nurse. She was acting as a competent anaesthetist. Apart from a couple of minor queries about dosage, he'd rarely had to intervene.

And as he began the lengthy repair process to the uterus there came the sound he'd been hoping for. The thin, indignant wail of a healthy baby.

The flattening of its heartbeat must have been stress-induced, he thought thankfully. A long labour and then the impact of the crash could have caused it.

How long had the girl been in labour?

A while, he thought, glancing to where Amy still monitored the intubator. The new mother was as white as death and the wound on her forehead still bled sluggishly. He'd suture it before she woke.

If she woke.

Why was she unconscious?

Hell, he needed technology. He needed to know if there was intracranial bleeding.

'We can do an ordinary X-ray here,' Amy said, and his eyes flew to hers. Once again she was thinking in front of him. 'We have the facilities. It won't show pressure if there's a build-up, but it'll show if there's a fracture.'

'Is there no way we can we get outside help?' He wanted a CT scan. He wanted his big city hospital—badly.

'Not until this rain eases.' Outside the window, the rain was still pelting down. 'Given decent conditions, a helicopter can land on the golf course, but not now. There's too many hills. The country's so rough that with visibility like this they'd be in real trouble.'

So they were still on their own.

'We'll be OK,' she said softly as he worked on. Their eyes locked and something passed between them. A bonding. They were in this together...

Joss felt a frown start behind his eyes. He didn't make contact like this with theatre staff. He didn't make contact with anyone. But this woman... It was as if she was somehow familiar...

She wasn't familiar at all. 'We're not finished yet. Let's get this abdominal cavity cleaned and stitched,' he said, more roughly than he'd intended, and bent back over his work.

Finally the job was done. Under Joss's guidance, Amy reversed the anaesthetic, concentrating fiercely every step of the way. At last, still rigid with anxiety, she removed the endotracheal tube and the woman took her first ragged breaths.

Amy had done it, and until now she hadn't known she could. She closed her eyes, and when she opened them again Joss was beside her, his hands on her shoulders and his face concerned.

'Are you OK?'

'I... Yes.' She tried to draw back but his eyes were holding her in place as firmly as his hands were holding her shoulders.

'Exactly how many anaesthetics have you given in your professional career?' he demanded, and she gave a rueful smile.

'Um...one,' she confessed. 'A tourist who had penile strangulation. The doctor from Bowra was here seeing someone else when he came in, screaming. I had no choice there either. If I hadn't given him the anaesthetic he'd have been impotent for life.'

'But...that's a really minor anaesthetic.'

'I know.' She took a deep breath. 'And, of course, as you reminded me, the insurance is a nightmare and if anything went wrong I could get sued for millions. So I shouldn't have done it, nor should I have done this one. But I've seen it done and, the way I figured, I didn't have a choice. Bleating to you about my lack of training wasn't going to help anything.'

She was amazing, he thought, stunned. Amazing!

'You were fantastic,' the woman called Marie said stoutly. 'To give an anaesthetic like that... She was wonderful, wasn't she, Doctor?'

Joss looked around at them all. He had four helpers in the room. Three geriatrics and Amy. And he had one live and healthy baby and one young woman whose colour was starting slowly to return to normal.

Because of these people, this baby would live and the unknown woman had been given a fighting chance. Because Amy had been prepared to take a chance, prepared to say to hell with the insurance risk, to hell with the legalities; because these old people had been prepared to shake off their retirement and do whatever they could, then this baby stood a chance of living. Living with a healthy mother.

'I think you're all wonderful,' he told them. He smiled at each of them in turn, but then his gaze returned to Amy's. And there was that jolt of...something. Something that he didn't recognise.

Whatever it was, it would have to wait. Now was not the time for questioning. 'I think you all deserve a medal,' he said softly. 'And I think we all deserve a happy ending. Which I think we'll get.'

He lifted the baby from Marie's arms and stood looking down at her. The tiny baby girl had wailed once, just to show she could, but she was now snuggled into the warmth of her prepared blanket and her creased eyes were blinking and gazing with wonder at this huge new world.

'You need your mum,' Joss said, and as if on cue there was a ragged gasp from the table. And another. Amy's eyes flew from the baby back to her patient.

'She's coming round,' she said softly. 'It needs only this to make it perfect.'

The woman was so confused she was almost incoherent, but she was definitely waking.

Joss took her hands, waiting with all the patience in the world for her to recover. When this woman had lost consciousness she'd been in a truck heading out of town. Now she was in hospital—kind of—and she was a mother. It would take some coming to terms with.

'You're fine,' he told her softly, his voice strong and sure, and Amy blinked to hear him. Joss looked decisive and tough but there was nothing tough about the way he spoke. He was gentleness itself. 'My name is Joss Braden. I'm a doctor and you're in hospital.' Of a sort. There was no need to go into details. 'Your truck crashed. You were in labour—remember?' And then at her weak nod, he smiled. 'You're not in labour any more. You've had a baby. The most gorgeous daughter.'

He held the child for her to see.

There was a long, long silence while she took that on board. Finally she seemed to manage it. She stared mutely at the softly wrapped bundle of perfect baby and then tears started trickling down her cheeks.

'Hey.' Joss was gentleness itself. One of his elderly nurses saw his need and handed him a tissue to dry her tears. 'There's not a lot to cry about. We're here to take care of you. We had to perform a Caesarean section but everything's fine.'

Her tears still flowed. Amy watched in silence, as did her three geriatric nurses.

There were more outside. The door was open—just a crack. How many ears were listening out there? Amy wondered and managed a smile. Well, why shouldn't they listen in to this happy ending? They'd worked as hard as she had, and they deserved it.

'Can you tell me your name?' Joss was saying.

'Charlotte…' It was a thready whisper.

'Charlotte who?'

Silence.

Her name could wait, Amy thought happily. Everything could wait now.

But Joss kept talking, assessing, concerned for the extent of damage to the young mother now that the baby had been delivered safely.

'Charlotte, you've had a head injury. I need to ask you a couple of questions, just so I'm sure you're not confused.'

She understood. Her eyes were still taking in her baby, soaking in the perfection of her tiny daughter, but she was listening to Joss.

'Do you know what the date is today?'

'Um...' She thought about it. 'Friday. Is it the twenty-fifth?'

'It sure is. Do you know who won the football grand final last week?'

That was easy. A trace of a smile appeared, and the girl shed years with it.

'The Bombers,' she said, and there was an attempt at flippancy. 'Hooray.'

'Hooray?' She was a brave girl. Amy grinned but Joss gave a theatrical groan.

'Oh, great. It's just my luck to bring another Bombers fan into the world.' Then he smiled and Amy, watching from the sidelines, thought, Wow! What a smile.

'And your surname?'

But that had been enough. The woman gave a tiny shake of her head and let her eyes close.

Joss nodded. He was satisfied. 'OK, Charlotte.' He laid a fleeting hand on the woman's cheek. 'We'll take some X-rays just to make sure there's no damage, then we'll let you and your daughter sleep.'

'So is anyone going to tell me what the set-up is here?'

With the young mother tucked up in a private room, her baby by her side and no fewer than two self-declared intensive-care nurses on watch by her side, there was time for Amy and Joss to catch their breath.

'What would you like to know?' Amy was bone weary. She felt like she'd run a marathon. She hauled her white coat from her shoulders, tossed it aside and turned to unfasten the strings of Joss's theatre gear. They'd only had the one theatre gown, so the rest of their makeshift team had had to make do with white coats.

But making do with white coats was the last thing on Joss's mind. 'Tell me how I got a theatre staff,' he said. 'It was a miracle.'

'No more than us finding a doctor. That was the miracle. Of all the people to run into...'

'Yeah, it was her lucky day.' He gave a rueful grin and Amy smiled back. He had his back to her while she undid his ties and she was catching his smile in the mirror. He had the loveliest smile, she thought. Wide and white and sort of...chuckly. Nice.

In fact the whole package looked nice.

And as for Joss...

He stooped and hauled off the cloth slippers from over his shoes and then rose, watching while Amy did the same. Underneath her medical uniform Amy Freye was some parcel.

She was tall, maybe five-ten or so. Her tanned skin was flawless. Her grey eyes were calm and serene, set in a lovely face. Her hair was braided in a lovely long rope and he suddenly had an almost irresistable urge to...

Hey. What was going on here?

Get things back to a professional footing.

'What's someone with your skills doing in a place like this?' he asked lightly, and then watched in surprise as her face shuttered closed. Hell, he hadn't meant to pry. He only wanted to know. 'I mean... I assumed with your skills...'

'I'd be better off in a city hospital? Just lucky I wasn't,' she retorted.

'We were lucky,' he said seriously. 'We definitely were. If you hadn't been here we would have lost the baby.'

'You don't think Marie could have given the anaesthetic?'

'Now, that is something I don't understand.'

'Marie?'

'And her friends. Yes.'

She smiled then, and there were lights behind her grey eyes that were almost magnetic in their appeal. Her smile made a man sort of want to smile back. 'You like my team?'

'It's...different.'

She laughed, a lovely low chuckle. 'Different is right. An hour ago I was staring into space thinking, How on earth am I going to cope? I needed an emergency team, and I had no one. I thought, This place has no one but retirees. But retirees are people, too, and the health profession's huge. So I said hands up those with medical skills and suddenly I had an ambulance driver, two orderlies and three trained nurses. I've even got a doctor in residence, but he's ninety-eight and thinks he's Charles the First so we were holding him in reserve.'

She was fantastic. He grinned at her in delight.

This felt great, he thought suddenly. He'd forgotten medicine could feel like this. Back in Sydney he was part of a huge, impersonal team. His skills made him a troubleshooter, which meant that he was called in when other doctors needed help. He saw little of patients before they were on the operating table.

His staff were hand-picked, cool and clinically professional. But here...

They'd saved a life—what a team!

'I wouldn't ask it of these people every day,' Amy told him, unaware of the route his thoughts were taking. 'Marie's had three heart pills this morning to hold her angina at bay. Very few of my people are up to independent living but in an emergency they shine through. And even though Marie's heart is thumping away like a sledgehammer, there's no way she's going for a quiet lie-down now. She's needed, and if she dies being needed, she won't begrudge it at all.'

It was great. The whole set-up was great, but something was still worrying him. 'Where are the rest of your trained staff?'

That set her back. 'What trained staff?'

'This is a nursing home. I assume you have more skilled nurses than yourself.'

'I have two other women with nursing qualifications. Mary and Sue-Ellen. They do a shift apiece. Eight hours each. The three of us are the entire nursing population of Iluka.'

He frowned, thinking it through and finding it unsatisfactory. 'You need more...'

'No. Only eight of our beds are deemed nursing-home beds. The rest are hostel, so as long as we have one trained nurse on duty we're OK.'

'And in emergencies?'

'I can't call the others in. It means I don't have anyone for tonight.'

'What about holidays?'

'I do sixteen hours if either of the others are on holidays,' she said, with what was an attempt at lightness. 'It keeps me off the streets.'

She was kidding! 'That's crazy. The whole set-up's impossible.'

'You try attracting medical staff to Iluka.' She gave a weary smile. 'You try attracting anyone under the age of sixty to Iluka. Both my nurses are in their fifties and are here because their husbands have retired. Kitty, my receptionist, moved here to be with her failing mother, my cleaning and kitchen staff are well past retirement age, and there's no one else.'

'The town is a nursing home all by itself.'

'As you say.' She shrugged, and there was a pain behind her eyes that he didn't understand. 'But we manage. Look at today. Weren't my oldies wonderful?'

'Wonderful.' But his mind was on her worries, not on what had just happened.

'So the two looking after the baby...'

'Marie and Thelma, and they're in their element. Both are trained nurses with years of experience. Thelma has early Alzheimer's but she was matron of a Sydney hospital until she retired and there are some things that are almost instinctive. Marie's with her, and her experience is in a bush nursing hospital. She's physically frail but mentally alert so together they'll care for the mother and baby as no one else could. And I'm here if they need me.'

Joss looked across at her calm grey eyes. *'I'm here if they need me.'* It was said as a matter of course.

How often was she needed?

What was her story?

'Don't look so worried.' Her smile was meant to be reassuring. 'If I didn't think they'd manage—and love every moment of it—I'd be in there, helping. I'm only a buzz away.' Her smile faded as his look of concern deepened. 'What's worrying you? Charlotte's showing no sign of brain damage. The baby looks great. All we need to do is find out who she is.'

'Now, that's something else I don't understand.' His frown deepened. 'Jeff says she's not a Iluka resident and no one here recognises her.'

'No.' It had surprised Amy that she hadn't recognised the girl. She knew everyone in Iluka.

When she'd thought about it she'd even figured out where Joss fitted in. David and Daisy Braden had been speaking of nothing but their wonderful surgeon-son's visit for weeks. The whole town had known his exact arrival time, what Daisy was going to cook for him every night, where David intended to take him fishing and...

'What?' Joss asked, and Amy's lovely smile caused a dimple to appear right on the corner of her mouth.

It made him need to struggle hard to concentrate on what she was saying.

'Sorry. I was just thinking we should set the town onto finding out about our mystery mother. They told me all about you.'

'Did they?' He was disconcerted. He was trying really hard not to look at the dimple.

The observations that were happening were mutual. He looked nice when he was disconcerted, Amy decided.

Nice.

There was that word again but it described him absolutely. The more she saw of him the more she liked what she saw. Joss was taller than she was by a couple of inches. He had deep brown hair, curly, a bit sun-bleached and casually styled. His skin was bronzed and he had smiling green eyes.

And his clothes... He'd hauled off his sweater before they'd gone into Theatre but she'd been too rushed to notice, and then he'd put on a theatre gown. Now she was seeing his clothes for the first time.

They were...unexpected, to say the least. He was wearing faded, hip-hugging jeans and a bright white T-shirt with a black motif. The motif said:

'You've been a bad, bad girl. Go straight to my room.'

She blinked and blinked again. Then she grinned. This wasn't her standard image of a successful young surgeon. It was a rude, crude T-shirt. It shouldn't make her lips twitch.

'What?' he demanded, and her smile widened.

'I was thinking I shouldn't be in the same room as you—with that on.' She motioned to his T-shirt.

Damn. He'd forgotten he was wearing it. His father had given it to him for his birthday... Good old Dad, still trying to get his son moving in the wife department...

Fat chance.

But Amy had moved on. 'I need to talk to Jeff,' she said, and crossed to the door.

Joss frowned. 'I need to find him, too. He's looking after my dog. Or did one of your residents take him?'

'Lionel has him.' Her eyes creased into the smile he was starting to recognise. 'I saw him. Actually, I've heard about him, too. I thought he was much larger than he really is.'

'Have you been talking to my stepmother?'

Amy assumed an air of innocence. 'I might have been.'

He sighed. 'According to Daisy, he's the size of an elephant. That's because Bertram takes exception to anyone else sitting on my knee—and her dratted Peke decided it would grace me with its favours.'

'Lucky you.'

'As you say.' He shook off the light-headedness he was feeling. Was it the crash? Or…was it just the way she made him feel? Like he ought to get the conversation back to medicine—fast.

'Sergeant Packer and I could find no sign of identification at all in the mother's truck. But he is able to run a plate check. We're hoping we can find out who she is that way.'

She nodded. 'And I guess we need to fully examine the baby.'

'I'll do that now.'

'Thank you.'

Joss nodded, aware that he was retreating. He'd come out of his shell a little—a very little—but he didn't want to stay out.

He had to leave.

'I'm going to have to figure out how I can get away from this place,' he said.

Her brows rose at that. 'You're leaving?'

'I was. Until my car was totalled.'

'Your father said you were here for two weeks.'

'Yeah, well…'

'The honeymoon couple were a bit much for you, were they?' Her eyes danced in sympathy, demanding that he smile in return.

'You know my father and Daisy?'

'I certainly do.' She grinned. 'Until she met your father, Daisy had her name down here as a potential resident.'

'Oh, yeah.' Right.

'They're very happy,' she said—and waited.

And out it came. 'They're always happy.'

'Excuse me?'

'My father's been married four times.' It was impossible to keep the bitterness from his voice.

She thought about that. Looking at his face, she saw the layers of pain behind the bald fact.

'Divorce?'

'Death. Every time.'

That made it so much worse. 'I'm sorry.'

'Yeah.' He gave a laugh that came out harsher than he'd intended. 'You'd think he'd learn.'

'That people die?'

'Yes.'

'You can be unlucky,' Amy said softly. 'Or you can be lucky. I guess your dad has had rotten luck.'

'He keeps trying to replace...'

'Your mother?'

He caught himself. What was he saying? He was talking as if she was really interested. As if he wanted to share...

She was a nurse. A medical colleague. He didn't get close to medical colleagues.

He didn't get close to anyone.

But she'd seen the expression on his face. She knew he needed to move on.

'But you *do* have two weeks' holiday, right?' she probed. 'Being stuck here isn't a disaster.'

'I'll get out.'

'How?'

That stymied him. 'I guess...when it stops raining...'

'If it stops raining.'

'There's no need to sound like a prophet of doom,' he snapped. 'It'll rain for forty days and forty nights so collect your cats and dogs and unicorns and build a boat...'

She chuckled. 'OK. *When* it stops raining. But it'll take some time to get the bridge repaired. Maybe we can get a ferry working.'

'I could get out by helicopter.' But he sounded dubious and for good reason.

'Even when it stops raining I doubt you'll persuade one to land here unless it's an emergency. Being weary of watching your father and his new wife cuddle each other might not fit into the category of emergency.'

'The sea…'

'Have you seen the harbour? There's no way a boat's putting to sea until this weather dies.' She shrugged. 'Sure, there are boats which will bring supplies when the weather backs off but until then… I'm afraid you're stuck with us, Joss.'

He liked the way she said his name, he decided. It was sort of lilting. Different.

But he had more important things to think of than lilting voices. His own voice took on a hint of desperation. 'I can't go back to stay with Dad and Daisy. I'm going around the twist!'

'That bad?'

'They hold hands. *Over the breakfast table!*'

Amy choked on laughter. 'So you're not a romantic, Dr Braden. Well, I never. And you with that T-shirt.'

He had the grace to grin. 'OK. Despite the T-shirt, I'm not a romantic. Is there a hotel in town?'

'Nope.'

Sigh. 'I don't suppose there's a room available here.'

'You don't suppose your father would be mortally offended if you stayed in a nursing home rather than with him?'

He would. Damn.

But she was thinking for him. 'What excuse did you give— when you left so suddenly?'

'That I had to prepare a talk for a conference. It was worrying me so I thought I'd get back early to Sydney to do some preparation.' Then, at her look, Joss gave an exasperated sigh. 'It's the truth. I do.'

'I believe you.' Another chuckle. 'Though thousands wouldn't. But you've solved your own problem.'

'I have?'

She hesitated, and then said slowly, as if she wasn't sure she was doing the right thing but wanted to anyway, 'If you need privacy then maybe you can stay at my place. It's a great isolated spot for writing conference material.'

'Don't you live here?'

'Are you kidding?' She smiled, and he thought suddenly she shed years when she smiled. She really was extraordinarily lovely. 'Give me a break. I'm twenty-eight years old. I'm not quite ready to live in a retirement home full time.'

Twenty-eight... What was a twenty-eight-year-old incredibly skilled theatre nurse doing in a place like Iluka?

Caring for a husband? For parents? Unconsciously he found his eyes drifting to the third finger of her left hand. Which was tucked in the folds of her dress. Damn.

'Um...so where do you live?'

'Millionaire's Row.'

'Pardon?'

'Didn't your father show you round the town?'

'Yes...' He thought back and then his eyes widened. 'Don't tell me you live in one of *those*.'

There could be no mistaking his meaning. Amy chuckled again and shrugged. 'Of course. I live in the biggest and the most ostentatious mansion of them all, and I do so all on my lonesome. I have nine spare bedrooms and three whole spas you can choose from. You can have one and your dog another. You can tell your father that you need to be alone to write—and you can be. You can sit and write conference notes to your heart's content and we need never see each other. If that's what you want.'

Of course it was what he wanted. Wasn't it? But...that smile...

Damn, there was so much here that he didn't understand.

'Tell you what,' she said. 'I have heaps to do and you have a baby and a dog to check, and maybe you need to see Sergeant Packer about your car—or what's left of it. Lunch is at twelve and you're very welcome to eat with us. I'm off at two. If you can keep yourself amused until then, I'll take you home.'

'You make me sound like a stray puppy,' he complained, and her smile widened.

'That's how you sound.'

'Hey...'

Her grey eyes twinkled. 'I know. Nurse subordination to doctors has never been my strong point. Dreadful, isn't it? Are you sure you don't want to reconsider?'

But Joss was sure. He definitely didn't want to spend any more time with his father and Daisy.

And the more he saw of Amy Freye, the more he thought a few days in the same house wouldn't be such a bad idea.

Was he mad? What on earth was he thinking?

'Um...no, I won't reconsider,' he told her, and she laughed. It was as if she knew what he was thinking, and the feeling was distinctly disconcerting.

'Until two o'clock,' she told him—and left him to make of her what he would.

CHAPTER THREE

THE HOUSE WAS STUNNING.

Amy drove Joss and Bertram out to Millionaire's Row and turned her car off the road into a driveway leading to a mansion. As she had said, it was the most ostentatious house on Millionaire's Row. Which left him more confused than ever. Amy's car looked as if her next date was with the wrecker. Her dress was faded and shabby. She looked as if she hadn't a penny to bless herself with, yet the house she lived in was extraordinary.

Or maybe extraordinary was an understatement.

It was set back from the beach but it had maybe a quarter of a mile of beachfront all of its own. The house was two storeys high and huge. It was built of something like white marble and the entire edifice glistened in the rain like some sort of miniature palace.

Or maybe not so miniature…

'Wow,' he said, stunned, and Amy looked across at him and smiled.

'Welcome to my humble abode.' Her smile was mocking.

'It's…'

'Ostentatious? Over the top? Don't I know it.' She pulled into one bay of what appeared to be an eight-or ten-car garage and switched off the engine. The car spluttered to a halt, and a puff of black smoke spat out from under the bonnet.

'Um…about your priorities…'

'Yes?'

'You don't think you might do with one bedroom less and get yourself a new car?'

She appeared offended. 'What's wrong with my car?'

'Er…nothing.' He hesitated and then decided on honesty. 'Well, actually—everything.'

'Bertram likes it.' She swung herself out of the car and opened the rear door for Bertram. She ran a hand under the silky velvet of his ears as he nosed his way out of his comfortable back seat, and the big dog shivered with pleasure. Amy grinned. 'If your dog likes it, who are you to quibble? He's a gentleman of taste if ever I saw one.'

Joss smiled in return. Her grin was infectious. Gorgeous! 'Bertram likes smells and there'd be enough smells in your car to last a dog a lifetime. I reckon there are four or five generations of smells in that back seat.'

But she wasn't listening to criticisms of her ancient car. She was intent on Bertram's wonderful ears. 'He's lovely.'

'You don't have ten dogs of your own?'

'No.' Her voice clipped off short at that, as if collecting herself, and Joss gave her a strange look. There were so many things here that he didn't understand.

'Come through.' She flicked a switch and the garage doors slid shut behind them, and then she walked up the wide steps into the house. 'Welcome to my world.'

It grew more astonishing by the minute.

The house was vast but it contained barely a scrap of furniture. Joss walked through a wide passage leading to room after room, and each door led to a barren space. 'What the…?'

'I only live in the back section of the house,' she told him over her shoulder as she walked. 'Don't worry. There's a spare bed.'

He was staring around him and he was stunned. 'You own this whole house?'

'Sort of.' She was leading the way into a vast kitchen-living area. Here was a simple table and two chairs, two armchairs which had seen better days and a television set. Black and white. Nothing else.

It grew curiouser and curiouser. *He* grew curiouser and curiouser.

'You'll have to explain.'

'Why?'

Why? Of course she didn't need to explain anything. He was her guest. She was doing him a favour by putting him up. But...

'I'm intrigued,' he admitted, and she grinned.

'Good. I like my men intrigued.'

He was more intrigued by the minute, he thought faintly. She was a total enigma. And when she smiled... Whew!

'Will you tell me?'

'It's a long story.'

'By the look of the weather I have forty days and forty nights to listen.'

'I need to go back to work.'

'I thought you were off duty.'

'I have paperwork to do, and I don't want to leave our new mother for too long. Mary's there now but I don't like to leave her on her own. I'll stay for an hour but...'

'Then we have an hour. Tell me.'

Amy made a cup of tea first. Hell, she really did have nothing, he thought as he watched her spoon tea leaves into a battered teapot and pour the tea into two chipped mugs. Nothing.

Poor little rich girl...

'This house was my stepfather's,' she told him.

Joss took his mug of tea and sat, and Bertram flopped down beside him. It seemed almost ridiculous to sit in this vast room. Somewhere there should be a closet where this furniture should fit.

It wouldn't need to be a very big closet.

'Was?'

She sank into the opposite chair and by the look on her face he knew she was very glad to sit. Once more there was the impression of exhaustion. She looked like someone who had driven herself hard, for a very long time.

'Was?' he said again, and she nodded.

'Yes.'

'And now?'

'It's mine—on the condition that I live in it for ten years.'

He stared around in distaste. 'He didn't leave you any furniture?'

'No.'

'Then...' He hesitated. 'You haven't thought of maybe selling the place and buying something smaller?'

'Didn't you listen? I said I had to live in it for ten years.'

He thought that over. 'So you're broke.'

'Yes. Absolutely. It costs a fortune to keep this place.'

'Maybe you could take in lodgers.'

'Lodgers don't come to live in Iluka.' She hesitated and then sighed. She sat leaning forward, cradling her mug as if she was gaining warmth from its contents. As indeed she was. The house was damp and chill. It needed heating...

'Don't even think about it,' Amy told him, seeing where he was looking. The central-heating panels almost mocked them. 'Have you any idea of what it costs to heat this place?'

'Why don't lodgers come to live in Iluka?'

'The same reason no one comes to live in Iluka. Except for retirees.'

'You'll have to explain.'

'The town has nothing.'

'Now, that's something else I don't understand,' he complained. 'My father's married Daisy and seems delighted with the idea of coming to live here. There's a solid residential population...'

'On half-acre blocks which are zoned residential. We have

a general store, a post office and nothing else. No one else has ever been allowed to build here.'

'Why?'

'My stepfather owned the whole bluff and he put caveats on everything.'

'So?'

'So there's no land under half an acre available for sale. Ever. That means this strip along the beach has been bought by millionaires and it's used at peak holiday times. The rest has been bought by retirees living their rural dream. But for many it's turned into a nightmare.'

'How so?'

'There's nothing here.' She spread her hands. 'People come here and see the dream—golf courses, bowling clubs, miles and miles of golden beaches—so they buy and they build. But then they discover they need other services. Medical services. Entertainment. Shops. And there's nothing. There's no school so there's no young population. No land's ever been allocated for commercial premises. There's just nothing. So couples retire here for the dream and when one of them gets sick...' She hesitated. 'Well, until I built the nursing home it was a disaster. It meant they had to move on.'

'That's something else I don't understand,' he complained. 'You built the nursing home? How did you do that when you can't even afford a decent teacup?'

Amy rose and crossed to a kitchen drawer, found what she was looking for and handed it over.

He read in silence. 'To my stepdaughter, Amy Freye, I leave my home, White-Breakers.

'I also leave her the land on Shipwreck Bluff and sufficient funds to build a forty-bed nursing home...'

He read to the end, confusion mounting. Then he laid it aside and looked up to find her watching him.

'Now do you see?'

'I do—sort of.'

'This place was desperate for a nursing home. There's been huge numbers of couples for whom it's been a tragedy in the past, couples where one has ended up in a nursing home in Bowra because they were too frail to cope at home but the other was stuck here until the end. And each time, as isolation and helplessness set in, my stepfather would offer to buy them out of their property for far less than they'd paid. He did it over and over. He found it a real little gold mine.'

He was struggling to understand. 'Surely they didn't have to sell their properties back to him. Surely they could have sold on the open market?'

'With the restrictions on the place? No. It's better now, but then... Then it was impossible.'

'So where do you fit in?'

'I don't.'

That made Joss raise his eyebrows. 'I beg your pardon?'

'My stepfather and I...didn't get on.'

'Why doesn't that surprise me?'

Amy gave a mirthless laugh, then stooped to give Bertram a hug. Like she needed to hug someone. Something.

She hadn't had enough hugs in her life, Joss thought with sudden insight and he put a hand out as if to touch her...

It was an instinctive reaction and it didn't make sense. She looked at his hand, surprised, and he finally drew it away. It was as if he'd surprised himself. Which he had.

'So tell me why he's left you this—and tell me why you're in trouble.'

She blinked and blinked again. The concern in his voice was enough to shake her foundations.

No one was concerned for her. No one. Not even Malcolm.

'I... I need to get back.'

'No.' He stood and lifted the mug from her hands, placed it on the sink and then put his hands on her shoulders. Gently he pressed her into the opposite chair, then sat down himself. His eyes didn't leave hers. They were probing and caring and kind—

and she felt tears catch behind her eyes. Damn, she never cried. It must be the pressure and the emotions of the morning, she thought. Or…something.

But Joss was still watching her. Waiting.

'I… It's just… I'm fine. The terms of the will…'

'Are draconian.'

'I guess.' She shook her head. 'You have no idea.'

'So tell me.'

She shrugged and then settled in for the long haul. 'My mother married my stepfather when I was nine years old. We came here. But we soon learned that my stepfather was a control freak. He was…appalling. My mother's health was precarious at the best of times. He bullied her, he manipulated her—and he hated me.'

'Because you were feisty?'

'Feisty?' Amy looked startled and then gave a reluctant chuckle. 'Well, maybe I was. I only know that my own father had taught me that the world was my oyster, and here was my stepfather drilling into me that I was only a girl, and I wasn't even to be educated because that was such a waste. There wasn't a school here so I had to do my lessons by correspondence but he took delight in interrupting. In controlling, controlling, controlling.'

Joss thought it through—to the obvious, but dreadful next step. He thought about it for a moment and then decided, hell, he'd risk it. In his years as a doctor he'd learned it was better to confront the worst-case scenario head on. So he asked.

'He didn't abuse you?'

That shocked her out of her introspection. She took a deep breath and shook her head. She might be shocked by the bluntness of his question, but the idea wasn't incredible. 'No,' she told him. 'Apart from hitting me—which he did a lot—he didn't touch me. But…' She shuddered then, as if confessing something that had been hidden for a very long time. 'The awful thing is that it's not such a stupid question. I'm sure he wanted to. The way he looked at me. It was only…that was the only matter in which my mother stood up to him. If he ever touched me—like that—she'd have gone straight to the police, she told him, and she meant it. So he hated me from a distance. Oh, he hated me.'

'So you left?'

'As soon as I was fifteen I was out of here. Somehow I ended up in a city refuge, I met some great people and I managed to get myself educated. There's help if homeless kids want it badly enough. Which I did. I would have liked to have done medicine but that was impossible so I made it nursing. But my mother… she wasn't allowed to contact me, and she was getting worse. Medically there was nothing here for her. So my mother and many more of the population here were being screwed by my stepfather for everything they had, and there wasn't a thing I could do about it. I wasn't allowed home unless I promised I'd give up nursing and stay here permanently.'

'The man was a megalomaniac,' he said, stunned, and she nodded.

'He was.' She shrugged. 'Maybe I should have come home but I didn't know—couldn't guess—how ill my mother was. When my mother died I was so angry… But at least, or so I thought, I'd never have to have anything more to do with my stepfather. But my independence still rankled. It must have, because when he died he left this crazy will.'

'Leaving you the lot.' Joss frowned. 'Maybe because he felt sorry for the way he treated you.'

'No.' Anger flashed out then. 'Not because he felt sorry for me. No way. It was a last gesture to get at me. He knew I'd come. Because of my mother's distress and because her friends here were in such trouble, he knew the idea of setting up a nursing home would be irresistible. But he and his nephews after him have made sure that I haven't a cent other than what was put into the terms of the will.'

'He's left you nothing else?'

'He's left barely enough to cover the running costs of the

home—though we do get government subsidies now and it's improving. But still... I'm allowed to take out my nurse-manager salary and that's it. Even that often has to be ploughed back to make up shortfalls. The nephews removed the furniture—everything that wasn't nailed down. Their plan is to make me as uncomfortable as possible so I'll leave, because if I go before the ten years is up they'll have the lot.'

'And how many of your ten years have gone?'

'Four.'

'Six years to go?'

'Six years of purgatory,' she said—lightly, but he knew it was just that.

'Is there any relief?'

'I... Yes.' Amy sighed and then managed a smile. 'Oh, of course there is. Heck, in six years' time I'll be fabulously wealthy.'

'Is that why you're doing it?' Somehow he didn't think it could be, and her answer was no surprise.

'No.' Her response was fierce. 'I'd walk away if I could, but the covenants he's put on this place are unbelievable. People like your stepmother moved here in all faith but they found they've done their money cold. There's nothing here for them. The nursing home is their only hope for future support.'

'I don't understand.'

'Talk to the lawyers,' she said wearily. 'They'll tell you. The place is a disaster and if I walk away there'll be three or four hundred couples who'll have to walk away with me. They'll lose everything they own.'

'As bad as that?'

'As bad as that.'

Silence. Then: 'Do you have any support at all?'

She caught herself then. 'I... Of course I do. There's Malcolm.'

'Malcolm?'

'My fiancé.'

Her fiancé.

Of course. There had to be a fiancé. For the first time he concentrated on her hands and there it was, a diamond solitaire, declaring to the world that she was taken.

Well. That was fine. Wasn't it?

Of course it was. There was no reason in the world for his gut to wrench.

But she'd risen and was laying her coffee-mug on the sink, intent on the next thing. 'I need to go.'

'Yeah?'

'Yeah. I'll call you if I need you.'

'Did you come home just to offload me?' he asked, and she grinned.

'Of course. Why else would I come home in the middle of the day?'

'Because you're off duty?'

'There is that. But I have paperwork to do, and I really would like to be there for our new mum.'

'You'll ring me the minute you're worried?'

'The minute I'm worried I'll be here in my wreckage-mobile to cart you back to the hospital so fast you can't blink.'

'Wreckage-mobile permitting?'

'Wreckage-mobile permitting.'

'You realise if you leave then I'm stuck?'

Amy thought about that. 'Do you want me to drop you off at your father's?'

'No!'

'There you go, then.' She smiled. 'A willing captive. My very favourite sort.'

Humph.

Willing captive or not, as soon as she left that was how Joss did feel. Trapped.

He explored the house—sort of—but a proper tour could take days. He figured out which bedroom Amy used. That'd be the room with blankets on the single bed and one ancient and overflowing dresser.

Then he figured out his bedroom—the one with the single bedstead and nothing else—though surprisingly there were blankets and linen folded at the end. It seemed as if Amy did have guests.

Guest, he corrected himself. One guest and one guest only sometimes. Not often.

'So where's this Malcolm?' he asked, and was surprised to hear the note of anger in his voice.

But there were no answers.

Bertram was loping along by his side and he apologised in advance for the sleeping arrangements. 'This is a single bed,' he told his dog. 'That means me. On my own. No bed-sharing with you!'

The dog looked at him mournfully and Joss folded his ears back. In truth he liked the dog sleeping with him as much as Bertram liked obliging.

Sleeping by himself was the pits.

'Can you tell me where this fiancé comes in?' he asked of Bertram, and Bertram cocked a head to one side as if thinking about it. 'Yeah, like me, you don't understand. If he's such a hero, why doesn't he loan her some furniture? If she was my girl...'

Now that was not a thought worth pursuing.

Damn, what was he going to do with himself? Isolation was all very well, but...

He needed things. Like a razor. Like a spare shirt. He thought about his belongings. They'd been in the trunk of his car and the trunk had been mangled into the steering-wheel. Any razor would be matchsticks.

His laptop had been sitting on the floor of the front passenger seat. Maybe it was OK. Please...

He could ring the police sergeant and find out if anything was salvageable. Jeff would probably still be out at the wreck, clearing debris and making the roadblocks safe.

But he'd quite like to return to the hospital. Charlotte's head injury was a worry. In her condition, not to have a doctor on standby seemed downright dangerous.

There was only one solution.

Sighing, he lifted his phone from his belt and called his father.

'So tell me about Amy Freye.'

He was still sitting at Amy's kitchen table while his father and his father's new wife clucked their concern about his accident and stared around them with open-mouthed astonishment. It seemed they'd never been in Amy's home and they were stunned. 'No, Daisy, I don't want another cup of tea. I want some gossip.'

But he wouldn't get gossip from this pair. He'd get nothing but praise.

'Amy's wonderful,' Daisy declared. 'She's saved this town single-handed.'

'Explain.'

And he got the story again—the same story Amy had told him, embellished with gratitude.

'The old man robbed us blind,' Daisy told him, easy tears appearing in her eyes at the memory. 'We—my late husband and I—moved here because we were stupid, and as soon as we bought we were stuck fast. Oh, we thought it was fantastic when we first arrived but then John got sick and there was nothing. Not even a pharmacy. I spent my life on the road between here and Bowra, and then when John got worse he had to go into the Bowra Nursing Home. I figured that I'd have to sell—but people had woken up by then that there was never going to be any commercial development.'

'No commercial development at all?'

'No.' She sighed and shook her head. 'There's one general store and a post office—that's it. During the height of the season there's supplies from Sydney delivered to the millionaires, but that style of shopping is out of the range of ordinary people like us. The wealthy like their isolation but for us...it's the pits.

So I was stuck. I couldn't get a buyer at half the price we paid. Then John died. And fortunately so did Amy's stepfather. Then Amy arrived and it's all different.'

'How is it different?'

'Every way you can think of,' Daisy said roundly. 'She's built the home but she's done so much more. She runs meals on wheels to take decent dinners to the old folk stuck at home. She runs shopping rosters so we're not always in the car to Bowra. The nursing home's set up so the Bowra doctor can visit and do minor procedures here. She's organised pharmacy supplies so we can get urgent medicine. Everything. Half the people in Iluka are still in their homes today because of Amy.'

'I could never have moved here without her,' his father told him. 'I met Daisy when I came to play an interclub bowls match and it felt like heaven. But then Daisy told me the problems she's been having… We still couldn't sell her place, but with Amy we're safe for another six years.'

'For as long as she's stuck here,' Joss said thoughtfully.

'Yes. And even after that. As long as she puts up with us for the legal ten years, then the nursing home will be a going concern for ever.'

'There's a lot riding on her staying.'

'She has a good heart,' Daisy said roundly. 'She'll stay.'

'And she's engaged to a local man.'

'Sort of. Malcolm is an accountant in Bowra and his dad's a lawyer. He met Amy when his father was looking after Amy's legal affairs and…well, there's a bit of a dearth of young men around here.'

'He doesn't look after her very well.'

'Well, they're not married.'

'If I was engaged to Amy…'

'Yes, dear, but you're not,' Daisy said patiently. 'And, of course, Malcolm can't move here. His practice is in Bowra and when it rains it floods and the road's cut. Though not always as spectacularly as it is now.'

There was a lot he still didn't understand but it was time to move on.

'You guys have two cars, right?'

His father and stepmother looked at each other. 'Yes, but...'

He saw where their thoughts were headed. 'No, I'm not planning to try a stunt jump over the river. I know I'm stuck here.'

'You're very welcome to stay with us for as long as you like,' Daisy told him, and his father beamed his consent. They'd come out to Amy's practically twittering with excitement, and now they were aching to take him home.

'I'm happy here,' he told them, and Daisy looked around and shuddered.

'Yes, dear, but it's hardly cosy.'

'And that's something else I wanted to talk to you about. Look at this place.'

They looked—and they could only agree.

'We didn't think she lived like this,' Daisy told him. She was clearly puzzled. 'We thought...well, she lives in such a huge house we thought that her clothes and her car were a sort of eccentric choice.'

'She has no money.'

His parents looked shocked at the thought. 'Of course she has money. She lives in this place...'

'Which is costing her a bomb, but she can't even afford to heat it. I gather she has no money at all.'

'She told you that?'

'Yes.'

'But you've only just met her.'

'I have a very confiding nature,' Joss told them, and got an odd look from his stepmother for his pains.

'She really has nothing?'

'So I gather. The old man left everything but the house and the nursing home to his nephews.'

They practically gaped. And then Daisy moved straight into the organisational mode Joss was starting to dread. 'Well! I'm sure we could find all sorts of furniture to give her and so could half the population of Iluka. If we'd had any idea… Most of us are in a position to give. We think so much of Amy…'

'It wouldn't work.' Joss was doing some on-the-spot thinking. 'She'd sell it. She's strapped for cash and the nephews are breathing down her neck for more. But if you lent her things…'

'Lent?'

'Like, for six years. Would you do that?'

He watched their faces and saw the measure of respect and affection in which Amy was held. There was no hesitation at all. 'Of course we would.'

'We'll get onto this straight away,' his father told him. 'It'll be a pleasure to do it. If the town had known… I know Jack Trotter—he's Shire President. I'm sure there's things we can do. This town's coffers are very healthy indeed—there's not a lot of traffic lights that need maintaining around here. Come to think of it, there's not a lot of anything that needs maintaining. Now, how about you, lad? You don't want to stay here, I assume?' He looked around the barren room in distaste. 'It puts a man off money, seeing the place like this.'

'It does.' But Joss hesitated. 'If it's all the same to you, Dad, I might stay on. If you can lend me one of your cars…'

'Surely.' But his father's face was a question. 'But why?'

'It's just… The reason I was leaving was to get down to work on this conference paper. That still applies. This place is quiet…'

'And you need to be here as our furniture arrives.' Daisy was smiling in a way Joss didn't like. It meant his stepmother was reading far too much into his intention to stay. 'You leave the boy be, David. He doesn't want to be staying with a couple of oldies like us when he could be staying with Amy.'

'Amy's engaged,' David said, surprised. He'd caught the gist of where Daisy was headed but he didn't follow.

'Yes, she is,' Daisy muttered, and Joss raised his eyebrows.

'You don't like this Malcolm?'

'No.' Daisy was blunt and decisive.

'That's not really fair.' Joss's father was frowning. 'You hardly know the man.'

'I know that he's wishy-washy.'

'He's a decent bloke.'

'He's never going to set the world on fire,' Daisy retorted. 'He's an accountant in Bowra and he's the sort of man you'd know from five years old that was where he'd end up.'

'That's a bit harsh. Amy must like him,' Joss said mildly, and Daisy snorted.

'Yeah. Like she had a choice. He's a presentable young man and presentable young men are a bit thin on the ground here. And as for Malcolm... He's onto a very good thing with Amy Freye and he's enough of a money manager to know it.'

'In six years, maybe.'

'Would you take great trouble to hold onto a gold mine even though you knew it wouldn't pay out for six years?'

He thought that through. 'I guess I would.'

'There you go, then,' Daisy said triumphantly. 'He's wishy-washy and a gold-digger. I rest my case.'

CHAPTER FOUR

JOSS RETURNED TO the hospital to find Charlotte was sleeping. Amy was taking her obs as he walked into her room. She had her white coat on over her clothes again and he thought again how strikingly attractive she was. Once she was out of those dreary clothes...

Maybe he could get Daisy onto that, too.

But Amy was smiling and he thought, Why bother? She was gorgeous enough as she was.

Luckily, Amy wasn't into mind-reading. She was concentrating on her patient. 'She's hardly stirred.'

'She's due for some pain relief.' He took the chart and wrote up what was needed—and then he hesitated. 'I suppose we have the necessary drugs...'

'Because we're isolated I have permission to run a limited pharmacy. I have what's needed.'

He shook his head in appreciation. 'This is an amazing nursing home.'

'It is,' she said without any false modesty. 'But didn't I have you trapped at home?'

'My father and Daisy came to the rescue. I am currently driving Daisy's pink Volkswagen.'

She grinned. 'I bet your dad's relieved. He might be in love but even he blanched when she had it spray-painted pink.'

'Bertram took one look and elected to stay at home.'

'Wise dog.'

'But I thought I might be needed here.'

'So you decided to brave even a pink Volkswagen. What a man!'

She was laughing at him. He liked it, he decided. He definitely liked it.

'Maybe I'm not needed,' he said, moving on but not without a struggle. 'Things are looking good here. The baby's still fine?'

'Yep. She's in the sitting room with the oldies. My nursing staff decided that while her mother slept they could babysit.'

'So we have…twenty babysitters?'

'At least. Charlotte will be lucky if she gets her daughter back. Talk about a case of collective cluck.'

'I wonder who she is.'

'I wonder.' Amy followed his gaze to the sleeping mother. 'She looks exhausted.'

'But she's not a local?'

'I'd reckon every single one of our residents managed to get a look at her on the way in and no one recognises her.'

'Her truck looks like a farm truck.'

'And that's what she looks like. A farmer. Her hands…they're work hands.' She lifted the girl's fingers gently from the counterpane. Joss saw and thought that they had matching hands. The stranger's hands were work-worn but so were Amy's. Both women knew how to work hard.

'She'll tell us soon enough when she wakes.'

'I'm not sure.' Amy was still watching the girl's face. 'She woke for a little but she seems…she seems almost afraid.'

'There's nothing to be afraid of here.'

'Apart from being cosseted to death. What a place to have a baby. There are no fewer than five sets of bootees and matinée jackets being knitted as we speak.'

'Fate worse than death.'

'As you say.'

* * *

They left Charlotte sleeping and made their way to Amy's office. Charlotte was nicely stable and the baby was doing beautifully. There was no reason for him to stay, but Joss made no move to leave.

There wasn't a good reason for him to leave, Amy figured, remembering where he was going home to. So she might as well make use of the man.

'How do you feel about checking Rhonda Coutts's lungs?'

'Rhonda Coutts?'

'I think she might be building up to pneumonia. She had a fall last week and spent a few days on her back. She's up now but she's coughing and she's weak. As the Bowra doctor can't get through...well, would you check her?'

'Sure.' Rhonda Coutts's lungs. Well, well.

He was a surgeon—one of the top in his field. It had been a long time since he'd been called on to advise about the possible pneumonia of an elderly patient with no surgical background.

She sensed his hesitation. 'Would you feel competent...?'

He bristled. 'Hey, of course I'm competent.'

'I only thought...well, with you being a surgeon you might have...'

'Forgotten?'

'I'm sorry.' She gave a rueful smile. 'Insulting, huh?'

'No. It's fine.' He was still bristling. 'Lead the way to Mrs Coutts.'

'I have a real live doctor on tap. For a week, if I'm lucky. What I won't be able to achieve in a week...'

Kitty, Amy's secretary, was staring at her as if she was demented as Amy danced in to fetch Mrs Coutts's medical records. 'What on earth are you talking about?'

But Amy was practically whooping on the spot as she planned ahead. 'Mr Harris's ingrown toenails. Ethel Crane's eczema. Martin Hamilton's prostate. They can all be seen here. Now.'

Martin's prostate was the best one. The Bowra doctor was a middle-aged woman and Martin wouldn't consent to speaking to her about his prostate, much less let her examine him. 'With a doctor right here, I can solve all these problems in one fell swoop.'

'But he's here on holiday,' Kitty said doubtfully. 'Do you think he will?'

'He's staying at my house.' Amy's jubilation faded a little when she thought of that—she'd felt embarrassed to ask him out to the shambles that was her home but the upside was that it put him nicely in her debt. 'And he's proud, Kitty. I only have to suggest to the man that he can't and he will. The man's a renowned surgeon after all, and he's a walking ego if ever I saw one, so I don't see why we can't use him.'

'He seems...nice.' Kitty was still doubtful.

'He's a man, isn't he?' Amy demanded. 'Therefore he's here to be used. And use him I will, for however long I have.'

All the signs were that Mrs Coutts did have pneumonia and as Joss put away his stethoscope she burst into tears.

'I'm not going to hospital,' she sobbed. 'I should never have let you examine me. I'm not leaving here.'

'You have the odds in your favour,' Amy said wryly. She sat on the bed and took the elderly lady's hands in hers. 'Rhonda, remember the bridge?'

Her sobs arrested as the old lady looked up at Amy—and then burst into tears again.

'But I'll die. If I can't go to hospital...'

Amy gave Joss a rueful grin and hugged the old lady. 'You know, there is a third choice.' As Rhonda sobbed on, Amy put her away from her and forced her wrinkled face up so her eyes met her own. 'Rhonda, look who we've got. Our very own doctor, for however long the rain takes to subside. We have a really extensive drug cupboard—all the supplies we need we have right here—and you have your own personal physician.'

Rhonda stared. She hiccuped on a sob, then sniffed and looked up at Joss.

'He's as stuck as we are,' Amy told her, and grinned.

And finally Rhonda smiled.

'Really?'

'You'll look after Rhonda, won't you, Dr Braden?' Amy asked submissively, but there was nothing submissive in her twinkle as she looked up at him.

And there was no choice.

'Yes,' he said, goaded, but then he looked at the old lady in the bed and thought, Damn, they were all in this together. They were all stuck. And he was sure the X-ray he intended to take would verify she had pneumonia.

'Of course I will,' he said in a voice that was much more gentle. 'How can you doubt it?'

After that he saw Mr Harris's ingrown toenails, Ethel Crane's eczema, Martin Hamilton's prostate and Kitty's splinter under her thumbnail just for good measure.

'I've been meaning to do something about it for a few days but it's such a hassle to go to Bowra,' the secretary told him, blushing as he held her hand and gently examined her inflamed finger. 'And now Amy says you're here to be used... I mean she says you don't mind being doctor...'

Joss caught Amy's eye—and there was laughter there! She looked like a child caught out in mischief.

She was enchanting, he thought. Enchanting! The more he saw of her the more she had him fascinated.

She was using him for all she was worth.

But even her effrontery had its limits. She helped administer a local anaesthetic to Kitty's thumb, then watched as he cut a tiny section out of the nail to remove the splinter—he really was an excellent operator, she thought with satisfaction—and then she decided it was time he was dismissed. After all, he'd had a rough day—and she had plans for him in the morning.

'Maybe it's time you finished for the day,' she told him. 'You've been very useful.'

'Gee, thanks.'

'Think nothing of it.' She glanced at her watch. 'There's not much to eat at home but if you don't want to eat with your parents maybe you could grab yourself something from the general store. They're open until six so you have half an hour.'

Wow, that sounded exciting. He didn't think.

'And you?'

'I'll eat here.' It didn't cost her to eat at the hospital—but she wasn't admitting that.

'Do you need to stay here?' he demanded. By now he'd met Mary—Amy's second in charge—and had been impressed. Mary was bustling around with starched efficiency, slightly miffed that she'd missed the day's excitement. She was delighted with the opportunity to be used as an acute nurse and Amy would have no problem leaving all her patients in her charge.

'I have some office work to do...'

'No, you don't,' Kitty said blithely, as Joss fastened a dressing over her thumb. 'Amy works too hard, Dr Braden. Make her go home.'

'Tell you what,' he suggested. 'I'll stop at the store and cook for both of us.'

'You?'

'Me.' Once again she'd caught him unprepared and he reacted with ego. 'I can cook, and I need to do something to pay for my lodging.'

'I think you've done enough. One Caesarean. A healthy mum, a gorgeous baby and four treated residents...'

And one secretary minus her splinter—who was match-making for all she was worth. 'I'll donate a bottle of wine,' Kitty said blithely, beaming from Amy to Joss and back again. 'Mum gave it to me because she doesn't like it—and I can't think of an occasion more splendid.'

'Kitty—'

'More splendid than a welcome to Iluka's new doctor.'

'Hey, I'm only here until it stops raining,' Joss said uneasily, and Kitty beamed.

'Then long may it keep raining.'

'Keep your wine to stop you thinking about your thumb,' Amy suggested, and Kitty shook her head.

'Nope. I've been thinking about my thumb for four days now and suddenly it's better.'

'The anaesthetic hasn't worn off,' Joss warned, but Kitty would have none of it.

'Go on. Shoo, the pair of you. Have a wonderful night.' And as she pushed Amy out the office door and closed it after them she was crossing every finger and every toe. 'For a change,' she said.

Amy didn't go home at once. 'I'm not travelling in a pink Volkswagen even if you are,' she told Joss. 'And besides, I want my car at home. I'm not leaving it here.'

She wanted her independence. She certainly didn't want to be stuck out at White-Breakers with no way of getting back here but to be driven by Joss. So she sent him homewards and did a bit of busy work around the place—and finally popped in to see Charlotte.

The young mother was just waking. Marie was still on watch, and Mary was hovering nearby. Amy signalled them to disappear for a while. Charlotte should be up to talking but the last thing she wanted was a crowd.

'Feeling better?'

Charlotte gave her a wan smile. Her baby was sleeping beside her in a makeshift cot made out of a filing cabinet drawer and a television stand. It served the purpose, however. The little one looked blissfully content.

'I am...a bit.'

Amy pulled up a chair and smiled sympathetically at the new mother. 'You can say you feel lousy if you feel lousy.'

'OK, then. I feel lousy.'

'Dr Braden's written you up for pain relief. You can have something now.'

'I'll wait a while. I'm having enough trouble as it is, getting my head around...what's happened.'

'Is there someone you'd like us to contact?' Amy asked her gently. 'Someone must be worried about you?'

'No.'

That was blunt. 'You're really on your own, then?'

'Yes.'

Amy hesitated but then pressed further. There was a pallor about the girl's face that spoke of deep-seated misery—not just the shock of the day's events. 'Charlotte, can I ask why you were in Iluka?'

'I came here...looking for someone.'

'And did you find him?'

'Her.' She closed her eyes. 'And yes. Yes, I did.'

'So you do know someone in Iluka.'

'No one who wants to know me.'

'Charlotte, can I help you?' Impulsively Amy reached out and took the girl's hand. No one should be alone like this—especially when she was hurting so badly. And the pain wasn't just from the head wound and the effects of the Caesarean. The pain was soul deep. 'Let me close,' she urged. 'Tell me what's going on.'

'No.' The girl's face was shuttered and closed and she pulled away her hand.

Amy backed off. The last thing she wanted was to put more pressure on her. 'OK. I'm here if you want me.'

'How long am I stuck?'

'The river's in full flood. It may be up to a week before there's access, but you need a week in bed anyway. For now you must lie back and let your body recover—for your daughter's sake if not for your own.'

The girl looked down at her sleeping baby and her face

twisted in something that was close to despair. 'She is beautiful, isn't she?'

'Yes, she is.' Amy looked down at the perfect little girl and she could only agree. 'Have you thought of what you might call her?'

'I… I need to speak…'

'To her daddy?'

The girl's face closed and she bit her lip. 'No. I don't need to speak to him. I can make up my own mind.' She chewed her lip for a little and then looked again at her daughter. 'What do you think of Ilona?'

'Ilona?'

'It's Hungarian for beautiful.'

'Then it's perfect.' Amy put a finger down and traced the soft curve of the baby's cheek. 'Ilona. It's just right.'

'It's sort of… I mean, she was born in Iluka. Iluka—Ilona.'

'Then it's even more perfect.'

The girl's face flushed with pleasure and she smiled. For the first time Amy saw her as she could be—a truly beautiful woman. 'You really think so?'

'I really think so.' She rose. 'You need to sleep now but, before you do, can I bring you the telephone? Isn't there someone you want to contact?'

'I don't—'

'I'll bring you the phone anyway,' Amy told her, stepping in before she refused entirely. 'Then when there's no one else around, you can make up your own mind who you want to tell about Ilona.'

Amy came out of the room and found Joss waiting. He was leaning against the wall of the corridor with his arms crossed, looking like a man prepared to wait for however long it took. He looked like a man waiting for his wife to try on a dress, she thought suddenly. He had just that proprietorial air.

The thought was stupid. Nonsense. She brought herself up with an inward jolt. 'I thought I sent you home.'

'I don't always go when I'm sent.' He grinned down at her and another image sprang to mind—a half-grown Labrador who'd just brought her the next-door neighbour's newspapers. He was pleased and guilty all at the same time.

He made her want to smile.

'You realise we don't have anything to eat now,' she said, trying to sound cross. 'The general store closes at six and there's nowhere else.'

'Hey, I've been and come back,' he told her, wounded. 'I have a car full of supplies. I'm not silly. And I am hungry.' Then his smile faded and he looked toward the closed door of Charlotte's room. 'Any joy?'

'She's not saying anything.'

'Her name's Charlotte Brooke. The police sergeant got that from her plates. He just rang in with the information. She lives on the other side of Bowra.'

'She's a long way from home, then.'

'Sergeant Packer wants to know whether he should check out the address—just in case someone's frantic about her.'

'She doesn't want anyone told.'

'And if someone reports her missing?'

'We'll worry about it then.' Amy frowned. 'But what do you think? Do we respect her need for privacy?'

'It seems to me,' Joss said slowly, 'that if she wants privacy and a few days' thinking time—time out to come to terms with everything that's happened to her—then maybe we should respect that. It might be just what she needs. She's not suicidal?'

'No.' Amy thought back to the girl's face as she'd looked down at her little daughter. 'She's falling deeper in love with her daughter every minute. I don't think she's making any plans to abandon her. She's named her Ilona.'

'Ilona…' Joss ran it over his tongue and smiled. 'I like it.'

'So do I.' Amy smiled up at Joss and suddenly thought, *Wow!* This felt good. It felt right—that she should smile up at him.

There was some connection… Something she didn't really understand.

And she liked it that he'd come back. He was as concerned as she was about Charlotte, she thought, and that felt good, too.

But what on earth was she thinking of? She had no links to this man. As soon as the weather eased he'd be off.

She didn't want friendship.

Or rather—she did but she knew only too well that it'd hurt when it finished. As it had hurt leaving every friend she'd ever made outside the tiny population of Iluka.

'Are you ready to go home?' he asked. He was still smiling. She had to give herself an inward shake to escape the vague feeling of unreality. The feeling that here was sweetness she could sink into…

'Um… I'm still not travelling in your pink Volkswagen.'

'Daisy will be hurt.'

'Daisy will never know.'

'That you chose your wreckage-mobile over her fine automobile?'

'There are some choices that are easy,' she retorted, and turned her back on him to head for the car park. But part of her was thinking, Some choices are way too hard.

Joss followed her out to White-Breakers and she was aware of him following her every bit of the way.

Why on earth had she asked him to stay? she wondered. She could have insisted he stay with his father and stepmother. It would have been far less complicated.

But then he might not have felt obligated to donate his professional services…

He would have stepped in anyway, she thought. Joss wasn't a man to stand back and watch while the likes of Kitty suffered with a splinter under her thumb.

He was a thoroughly nice man.

No. He was a darned sight more than that.

He was gorgeous!

Oh, for heaven's sake. She was engaged, she thought savagely. Malcolm was in the wings. OK, Malcolm lived at Bowra and she didn't see him all that often but that didn't leave her any less engaged. Any less committed.

She was committed to Malcolm. She was committed to Iluka. Sometimes she was so darned committed that she wanted to scream.

Amy drove into her nine-car garage and Joss drove in beside her. The two crazy little cars looked incongruous in such a setting. This garage had been built to house stretch limos or Mercedes at the very least. Not one Just-On-Wheels and a pink Volkswagen.

At least it was better than empty, she thought. She found she was looking forward to tonight. Sharing the kitchen—such as it was—with Joss and his lovely dog.

Maybe she should get a dog.

Yeah. And buy dog food with what?

Six more years...

'Damn you,' she told her departed stepfather for what must be the thousandth time. 'But I'm sticking with this. You won't win completely.'

Then Joss was climbing out of his Volkswagen, his arms laden with carrier bags, and she forgot all about her stepfather. Because who could think of a mean old man while Joss was here?

'Do you want help to carry them?' she asked. Food. Real food! No soup and toast tonight. How wonderful!

Joss looked at her face and he grinned. Taking a woman out to a five-star restaurant had never felt so good.

'I'll carry them,' he told her. 'Otherwise I have a feeling they might be demolished by the time they reach the kitchen.'

She'd offered to help carry the bags. Joss had refused her offer and it was just as well. She'd have dropped the lot when she saw what was in front of her. She led the way, pushed open the kitchen door and stopped dead.

What...?

Daisy was some organiser, Joss thought with wry appreciation as he looked around the transformed kitchen. Wow!

Before it had seemed empty. Now it was almost too full.

Amy had given Joss a key and Joss had left it with Daisy when he'd returned to the hospital. In the time he'd been away it looked as if the whole town had paid a visit.

With furniture.

There was a dining table and twelve chairs. An overstuffed settee. About five squashy armchairs. A huge rich Persian carpet. A colour television, a stereo, a couple of standard lamps. A wide oak desk.

The room was enormous and now it looked as it should. The furniture was old-fashioned and mismatched but it was comfortable and good quality. Daisy had chosen with care and she'd obviously had a lot to choose from!

'What...?' Amy was practically speechless. She walked forward in disbelief.

'I wonder if they've done the bedrooms yet,' Joss mused. He walked out along the corridor, opened the doors and checked. 'Yep.' Two of the bedrooms—the one Amy had been using and the one she'd designated his—were now fully furnished. They both had new beds, complete with luxurious bedclothes. More armchairs. Dressing-tables, wardrobes, bedside tables...

There was even a big squashy dog-bed at the foot of his bed. Bertram was already ensconced, looking up with doggy satisfaction as Joss entered. He rose and waggled his tail, but his sleepy demeanour said he'd been entertained very well—he'd had a very busy afternoon supervising all this activity.

'This is fantastic.' Joss smiled his appreciation as his dog loped over for a pat. '*They're* fantastic.'

'Um...' Amy had walked into the bedroom behind him. She

looked as if she'd been struck by a piece of four by two and hadn't surfaced yet. 'Who's fantastic?'

'The combined residents of Iluka. When I told Dad and Daisy how you were living...'

'You told them?'

'Of course I told them.'

'You had no right,' she said, distressed. 'Joss, this is my business. How I live.'

'You spend your time looking after the town. It's about time the town looked after you.'

'But this furniture... I can't keep it.'

'Of course you can.'

'You don't understand.' She was close to tears, he thought. Her hands were pressed to her cheeks, as if fighting mounting colour. 'Trevor and Raymond and Lysle...'

'Who are Trevor and Raymond and Lysle?'

'My...my stepfather's nephews.'

'Ah.'

'I can't accept this,' she told him. 'I can't keep anything.'

'I don't understand.'

'The nephews... My stepfather left me nothing. Have you any idea what the land tax is on this place?'

'I can guess.' In truth, he knew. Thanks to his father. The phones in Iluka had been running hot all day.

'And the land tax on the land beneath the nursing home?' she was saying. 'The overheads?' Still she was pressing her face. 'The nephews took everything I didn't own personally, and anything I do own has to be sold to keep the bank happy.'

'So what does that have to do with this?'

'I can't accept. Even if I did I'd have to sell—'

'This isn't a gift,' he said gently. He took her shoulders and steered her back to the kitchen. Bertram was shifting his sleepy body to the rug before the range and she thought suddenly, It's warm. It's warm!

But Joss was still speaking. 'Everyone at Iluka has moved

here from somewhere else,' he told her. 'It's a retirement village so most people have built houses that are smaller than they're used to. Daisy says there's hardly a retiree who doesn't have something that they can't bear to sell but that doesn't fit easily into their new home. So this furniture is on loan. For as long as you need it.'

'But I can't—'

'You can. Hell, Amy, you work your butt off for these people. Allow them to repay it a little.'

'But…' She stared wildly around and focussed on the stove. There was a kettle on the hob, gently hissing steam. 'How long have you had the stove on? And the heating? I can't afford to pay for all this.'

'The heating's my lodging fee,' he told her. 'It's self-interest on my part. I have a conference paper to write and I don't like being cold. So I rang up the gas board and gave them my credit-card details. There's at least a six-month supply of gas been credited to your account. You can't use my rent to pay unimportant things like land tax. Oh, and speaking of land tax…'

'Yes?' She was so dazed she could hardly speak.

'My father's been on to Jack Trotter, the Shire President. The councillors had an emergency meeting this afternoon—in your kitchen.'

'Here?'

'Yes.'

'I don't believe this.'

'You should have let them know. Amy, they were horrified to see how you were living. The whole district wants to help. They voted unanimously to waive land tax on White-Breakers and the nursing home for the next six years. Retrospectively. They can't backdate it any more than a year but last year's tax will be refunded.'

Amy was practically speechless, but she was becoming angry. 'Joss, this is none of your business. I should never have let you near the place.'

'Then that would have been a great shame. I'm sorry to have to tell you this but your time as a martyr is over.'

He was enjoying this, she thought. A genie granting three wishes couldn't have looked any more placid than Joss Braden.

'You can't...'

But he was smiling. 'I already have.' He pulled a cheque from his pocket and handed it over. 'Mrs Hobbs from the general store asked me to give this to you. I gather she's the Shire treasurer.'

She looked down at the figure on the cheque and gaped. 'This is crazy. And as for you paying the gas... You know I didn't intend charging you rent. You mustn't.'

'It's been done,' he said virtuously. 'You try getting refunds from the Gas Corporation. Good luck is all I can say.'

Heat. She had heat. She had furniture. And enough money for essentials.

She had Joss, and a dog.

'Now to dinner,' he told her, lifting her chin with one long, strong finger. 'Bertram's hungry, even if we're not. Are you hungry?'

She couldn't take it all in. All she could absorb was the question.

Was she hungry?

'I'm starving,' she told him and it was the truth. She was.

'Good. Let's eat.'

It was the strangest meal. Joss had brought one of Mrs Hobbs's famous beef pies, and he had side dishes to match. Amy ate as she hadn't eaten for months—no, years—and all the time Joss watched her with that curious look of complacency.

'You look like a Scout who's just received his knot certificate—and I'm your very tricky knot,' she complained, and he grinned.

'I can see that. A knot, huh? Would you like some lemon meringue pie? Mrs Hobbs threw it in free.'

'Does the entire population of Iluka see me as their do-a-good-deed-to-Amy project?' she asked cautiously, and his grin widened.

'Don't knock it. It'll be a damned sight more comfortable than the way you've been living for the last four years. Why no one did anything about it...'

'Yeah. You come sweeping into town—'

'Guns blazing.'

'Ego blazing,' she retorted, and he chuckled.

'Egos are good for something. Does Malcolm have an ego?'

'Malcolm?'

'Your fiancé.'

'I know who Malcolm is,' she snapped. 'And, no, as a matter of fact, he doesn't have an ego.'

'That's why he hasn't come to the rescue of his maiden in distress.'

'I'm not in distress.'

'You are. Or you were. You know, a knight in shining armour with ego to match can sometimes be a very good thing. He gets things done.'

'Because he rides roughshod over people.'

'I haven't ridden roughshod over anyone,' he said gently, and her indignation took a step back. OK, he hadn't. Or...he had but in such a way...

'Um...'

'Wrap yourself around your lemon meringue pie,' he told her kindly. 'We don't want to upset Mrs Hobbs, now—do we?'

'No.' Of course she didn't.

But it wasn't Mrs Hobbs she was thinking of.

CHAPTER FIVE

AFTERWARDS JOSS HELPED Amy with the dishes and then settled himself down at the table with his briefcase and laptop.

'Sergeant Packer rescued these, but the rest of my luggage is matchsticks,' he told her sadly. 'All I'm wearing is courtesy of my dad.' He looked ruefully down at the splendid example of Daisy's handiwork on his chest. 'Fair Isle sweaters aren't really my thing.'

'I think you look very...fetching,' she managed, and he glowered.

'Fetching what?'

'Fetching not very high stakes in fashion contests?' she ventured, and ducked as a wad of paper sailed across the room and hit her on the forehead. 'Ow.'

'You asked for that.'

'Hey, I like your sweater,' she said, laughing, and his glower deepened. But he didn't want to glower. She was smiling across the room at him and he wanted...

Damn, he knew exactly what he wanted, but the lady was engaged to be married. He was a guest in her house.

He couldn't.

'At least Sergeant Packer retrieved my briefcase,' he managed, and he wondered if she'd heard that his voice sounded odd. For heaven's sake, what was the matter with him? He was behaving like a schoolboy.

'You really do have a conference to prepare for?'

'Hey, that's what I told Dad and Daisy. Do you think I'd lie?'

'Only if you couldn't get what you want any other way.'

He tried a glare but it didn't come off. She was gorgeous! But he had to stay serious. He had to concentrate on something other than that beautiful smile. 'She's maligning me, Bertram.' Joss bent and fondled his dog's velvety ears. 'You hear that? I cook her a meal to die for and she maligns me.'

'There you go again. Who cooked the pies?'

'Mrs Hobbs might have,' he admitted grudgingly. 'But who fetched them. At great personal cost.'

'Personal cost?'

'I had to drive a pink Volkswagen.'

'There is that.' Then she frowned as the front doorbell pealed. 'Who on earth…'

'Maybe it's another sofa,' Joss told her. 'Daisy told me there was more to come.'

'Another sofa? How many do you think I need?'

It wasn't another sofa. It was a crate of good china, with a problem attached.

'I thought I'd drop these in and ask…'

Amy knew Marigold Waveny well. Her husband, Lionel, was the kite builder in the nursing home, and since Lionel and his kites had removed themselves from her ultra-neat home she'd never been happier. Neither had Lionel. Sometimes Amy wondered whether he'd feigned his senility to get more room for his kite-making. He and Marigold were still happily married—possibly much happier apart than they'd ever been together. Marigold spent her days at the nursing home, admiring kites, but at night she returned to her immaculate little home where there wasn't a kite in sight.

'I would have brought these earlier,' she told them, handing over her box to Joss with gratitude. 'But I was... I wasn't very well. I had my phone switched to the answering machine so I didn't hear about what Daisy was organising until just now.' She gave Joss a shy smile. 'Then I thought, Of course, I have all this china that I don't even like.'

Amy lifted a cup and gasped. 'Marigold! It's Royal Doulton. It's beautiful.'

'You enjoy it. Heaven knows, you do enough for my Lionel.'

'I wouldn't be brave enough to use it,' Amy told her, and Marigold shook her head.

'I have Royal Doulton, too,' she told them. 'But not such a loud pattern. This belonged to Lionel's mother, and if you dropped it I'd be very pleased. And I thought...' The voluble little lady faded to silence for a minute and then worked up courage. 'I thought...if I brought something...a gift...while the doctor was here...'

'Yes?' Joss was ushering her into the kitchen while she was speaking. His eyes were twinkling and he was smiling at Amy over the top of the elderly lady's head. He'd been a doctor for long enough to know what was coming. 'You didn't need to bring a gift to speak to me.'

'No, but I thought...'

'Tell us, Marigold,' Amy prodded, and Marigold took a deep breath and started.

'Well...'

'Well?'

'I think... I think I'm dying.'

Joss blinked. He set down the carton of china and thought about it. 'You what?'

'I just...' She shook her head as if trying to get rid of something. Get rid of terror? 'My heart's failing,' she whispered. 'It's going to stop. I can feel it. I'm dying and who cares about fancy china then?'

She stared wildly from Joss to Amy and back again—and burst into tears.

* * *

Finally they got it out of her—the reason for her terror. She was sitting in one of Amy's new chairs while Amy knelt before her, holding her hands, and Joss listened. And watched.

'I've been so tired,' she told them. 'For weeks I've been so tired I feel like I'm about to fall over. But when I go to bed at night I can't sleep. I just lie there and my heart hammers and hammers and I get so upset... I have thumping in my chest—it's thumping now. The palpitations are awful. I can't seem to get enough breath. Everything's just too much effort. I try... I've been going into the nursing home every day to see Lionel but it's been too much. Today I felt so dreadful I didn't go.' She looked distressfully at Amy. *I didn't go!*'

She should have realised, Amy thought ruefully. Marigold spent every day at the nursing home and today Amy hadn't even missed her. It was just...well, today had been different.

Lionel hadn't realised—but, then, Lionel had been taken up by a new kite and Joss's dog.

'I stayed in bed,' Marigold told them. 'But it didn't help. My heart's thumping just the same. And it hurts. I thought... I thought I might die carrying that box but then I thought at least I'd die on the doctor's doorstep and not at home by myself.'

Gee, thanks, Amy thought wryly. Just what every home needs—a corpse on the doorstep.

But Joss kneeled beside her, and his expression said he was taking this deadly seriously. He took Marigold's wrist loosely between thumb and middle finger, counting her pulse as he glanced at his watch. His brow was furrowed in concentration.

'Do we have a stethoscope, Amy?' he asked, and she nodded and rose. Her bag was by the door—she acted as district nurse so she always had her bag handy.

'Am I going crazy?' Marigold whispered.

'I don't think you're going crazy.' Joss was watching her closely, his mind obviously in overdrive. 'You're very thin. Have you always been this thin or have you lost weight recently?'

'I've lost a bit,' she admitted, looking fearfully up at him. 'I'm so tired. I can't be bothered cooking.'

'So you've lost weight and you're constantly tired?'

'I *am* seventy-three, dear.'

'You're a spring chicken compared to those in the nursing home.' He tilted her chin and ran his hand down her throat, gently feeling. 'Mrs Waveny, do you have any family history of thyroid trouble?'

'I...' She thought about that and finally nodded, not sure what he was getting at. 'Maybe I do. My mother had to take iodine for something. Would that be it?'

'Maybe it would.' Amy handed Joss a stethoscope, and he held it to Marigold's chest and listened. There was silence. Bertram wuffled and snuffed beside the fire, a dog at peace, but there was no peace on Marigold's face.

'It's bad, isn't it?' she whispered as Joss finished listening.

Joss hesitated, thinking it through. He wasn't a physician. He was a surgeon, for heaven's sake—but he was practically sure he was right.

'Marigold, you have what we call atrial fibrillation,' he told her. 'It's a fast, irregular heartbeat.'

She gasped. 'Is that bad?'

'It's not good. But I don't think you're dying. I suspect...' Once more he ran his hands down her throat, feeling the swelling. 'I suspect you have an overactive thyroid. I can't be sure until we run a blood test—which I'd imagine we can't do here—but for the moment I'm going to assume that's the case.'

'I... The thyroid is causing heart failure?'

'You don't have heart failure. Your heart isn't failing—it's just running on overdrive. Now, I'm not certain, but you have all the signs. You're tired, your neck seems a little swollen. You're short of breath, you're agitated, you have pains in the chest and you have a fast, irregular heartbeat. If I'm right—if this is just an overactive thyroid—then it can be controlled with tablets.'

She stared, torn between disbelief and hope. 'You're kidding.'

'I'm not kidding.'

There was a silence while she took that on board, her face lighting up by the moment.

'I'm not mad?'

'You're not mad.'

'Then what do I do about it?' She gazed from Joss to Amy and then back again. 'I guess…forget about it until I can see the doctor from Bowra?'

'No.' Joss shook his head. 'Marigold, we can't completely rule out heart disease, and until we do then we assume the worst. If you had someone living with you, maybe you'd be OK, but as it is you need to stay at the nursing home until we have some answers.'

'But…' Her distress level was rising again. 'I *will* be able to go home again?'

'Of course.' He rose and took her hand, pulling her up after him. 'If you like, I'll drive you home now. We'll pick up a nightie and a toothbrush and I'll take you in to hospital. I'd imagine Amy has Lanoxin in the drug cupboard? Am I right, Amy?'

'Sure.' She was almost as dumbfounded as Marigold.

'Great. Lanoxin slows your heart rate, Marigold. It'll make you feel a whole heap better—and we'll give you some sleeping pills, too, so you can get a decent sleep tonight. The combination will make you feel fantastic. Is it OK with you if you leave your car here? There's a bed available, isn't there, Amy?'

'I…yes.' Amy felt as stunned as Marigold looked at the speed with which things were being organised.

'There's no need—' Marigold started, but Joss shook his head.

'There is a need,' he said firmly 'Amy, will you ring Mary and let her know we're coming? Let's go now.'

Just like that…

Amy was left staring out at the departing pink Volkswagen feeling hornswoggled.

She would have coped.

Maybe she would have coped. If Marigold had come to her, she would have popped her into hospital and rung the doctor in Bowra. But Marigold wouldn't have come to her.

There was a huge difference in people's attitudes to a nurse and a doctor. The locals knew Amy was overworked and they knew she only had nurse's training. If Joss hadn't been here, Marigold would have waited. If it had been heart disease...

It could well have been a disaster.

Iluka needed a doctor.

It was never going to have one, Amy thought sadly. Joss would leave and they'd be back to where they'd started. But for now...

But for now, she'd eaten better than she had for months, she had a warm, comfortably furnished house, a doctor caring for her patients.

She felt so good she could almost burst.

'Let's go for a walk,' she told Bertram, picking up pad and pencil and scribbling Joss a note. She needed to walk some of this happiness off before Joss returned.

It was still raining.

'That's what raincoats, galoshes and umbrellas are for,' she told Bertram. She looked at the dog's eager face and knew without being told that Bertram was as eager for a walk as she was.

'Then what are we waiting for?' She took a deep breath. 'I need to get rid of some energy. Get rid of... I don't know. Something. Because otherwise your master's going to walk in the front door and I'll kiss the guy.'

And that would never do. Would it?

Joss returned to find Amy gone.

'Bertram and I are at the beach,' the note told him. He stared at it for a while as if he didn't know what to do with it.

He had work to do.

He'd just done some work. Marigold was nicely settled in a room next to Lionel. She felt wonderfully at home, she had a diagnosis that she could cope with, her husband was by her side and she was with friends.

Would that city hospitals could be this good.

Could he ever be happy as a country doctor? He thought about it. Tonight had felt good. The whole damned thing. Hospitals where everyone knew each other...

But this would be an impossible place to set up a practice.

Whoa! What was he thinking about? Setting up here as a country doctor? He was a surgeon. He lived in the city.

Amy was here.

Amy was engaged to be married.

The whole damned thing was a figment of a stupid fancy. Get a grip, Braden, he told himself. What the hell was happening to him?

Amy was happening to him. Quite simply she was the most gorgeous woman he'd ever met. She affected him as no one else had ever done.

He didn't react to women this way.

Women were ancillary to his life. He'd decided that long ago. He liked having women around but he didn't do the love thing. The commitment. He had his father's example of what happened with commitment and there was no way he was travelling down that path.

So, tempting as it might be to commit himself to some woman—a house, babies, a mortgage, country practice...

No. It wasn't tempting in the least. So why was he thinking about it?

Maybe it was because Amy was so patently unavailable.

That was it, he decided, and he was a bit relieved to discover a reason. She was engaged to another man. She couldn't leave this place if she wanted to, so she was absolutely unattainable. Which was probably the reason he wanted her.

But that nice sensible reason didn't help much at all. He flicked on his laptop and stared down at his conference notes.

Life-threatening haemorrhage can be caused by aortic dis-

section extending into the media of the aorta following a tear in the intuma, resulting in true and false lumina separated by an intimal flap...

What the hell was he talking about?

He'd written this a week ago. A lifetime ago. Tonight it wasn't making any sense at all, because tonight all he could think of was Amy.

She was down on the beach. With his dog. While he was sitting up here like a fool with some stupid conference notes that no one wanted to hear.

'They're important,' he told himself. They represented work he'd been committed to for the last three years.

'I'll worry about them when I get back to Sydney.'

'You told Dad and Daisy you needed to stay here to get them written.'

'So I lied. I stayed here to be near Amy.'

'Amy's engaged to another man.'

Damn.

He was going nuts, he decided. With a groan he pushed away his laptop, grabbed a coat that he'd seen hanging in the back porch and headed out the front door toward the beach.

The beach was wonderful. She always loved it. The seashore here was wild and windswept. In the summer millionaires parked their sunbeds here and concentrated on their tans but in winter she had it all to herself. The sand stretched away for miles in either direction. Her beach.

And tonight she had Bertram. That was special. The rain had eased a little—it was still stinging her face but not so much that she minded. She'd jogged down to the beach, Joss's dog loping beside her, and by the time she reached the sand she was warm and flushed and triumphant.

It had been a truly excellent day.

She'd helped deliver a baby. The weight of her financial need had been lifted by magic. She had furniture, she had heating, she had enough to eat...

'He's solved all my problems in one fell swoop,' she told Bertram, hurling a stick along the sand and watching in delight as the big dog went flying through the rain to fetch it back for what must surely be the hundredth time.

He loved it as much as she did.

Maybe she could get a dog.

Did Malcolm like dogs? She thought about that and decided probably not. Bertram hurled himself into the waves after another stick and came lunging back up the beach to her, then shook himself, sending seawater all over her.

No. Malcolm would definitely not like dogs.

Malcolm...

He hadn't rung tonight, she thought, frowning. He always rang, at seven every night. If he didn't find her at home he rang her at the nursing home.

Maybe the flooding had caused problems. Maybe the Bowra line was out of order.

She'd ring him when she got in. Or then again, maybe she wouldn't, she decided. It was ridiculous to speak to him on the phone every night. It was just a habit they'd got into.

Malcolm was just a habit.

No. Malcolm was just... Malcolm.

As opposed to Joss?

Now, that was a stupid way of thinking. When the rain ceased and a ferry could be established, Joss would be gone. Malcolm was all she had, so she should take care of the relationship.

She'd phone tonight.

Or tomorrow night.

Whatever.

She was a dark shadow outlined against the sea. The moon was struggling to emerge from behind clouds. There were faint glimmers breaking through, sending shards of silver light across the waves. Amy was tossing sticks for Bertram and Bertram was running himself ragged, wild with excitement.

Joss stayed where he was among the dunes, watching woman and dog. They made a great pair, he thought. Amy was enjoying herself. Her body language as she bent over the dog, as she stooped to lift his stick and throw…she was soaking in every minute of this.

She should have a dog of her own.

Where could he get her one?

That was a crazy thought. For heaven's sake, he didn't *know* that she liked dogs. Maybe she was just being polite.

He didn't think so.

She was…lovely.

But he was being stupid. Fanciful. This was a Cinderella type of situation, he told himself harshly. He was attracted to Amy because she was deserving and she was beautiful and she was unattainable. Would he be as attracted if she was available? Surely not.

She was committed to living in this dump for the next six years. What man would go near her knowing that?

Malcolm would. Obviously. And it wasn't such a dump.

'It's the ends of the earth.'

'This beach is lovely.'

'Look around,' he told himself harshly. The rain had stopped momentarily and the moon was full out. The beach stretched away for miles, as far as the eye could see. The moonlight played over the sodden sand, the wind whipped the waves into a frenzy and…

And nothing and nothing and nothing. There was only Amy and his dog. There was nothing else for miles.

Why would anyone ever come to this place through choice?

The millionaires did, he thought, looking back up the beach to the show of ostentatious wealth lining the foreshore. But the houses obviously belonged to those who valued their privacy. The millionaires came through choice. The elderly retirees who lived behind the sand dunes had come because they'd been conned.

This isolation must have been why Amy's stepfather had built the place, Joss decided. It would be why all these mansions had been built. There were no shops to speak of and even the retirees who lived here weren't provided for. Here there was absolute seclusion.

There'd be no children here spoiling the sand on sunny days—imposing their noisy presence on this super-wealth. In Australia, where it wasn't possible to own a private beach, this was the best this tiny pocket of elite millionaires could do. They'd built their houses and they were screwing the rest of the population to maintain their fabulous lifestyle. For six weeks a year.

He was getting bitter.

He was also getting cold, he thought, and gave himself a mental shake. He had better things to do than stand here and think about Amy's problems. He had a conference paper to write.

Ha!

The conference paper could wait. He took a deep breath and turned his face into the wind. Digging his hands deep into his pockets, he went to join his dog.

And Amy.

She saw him coming.

Joss was hunched into an ancient overcoat, and for a moment as he came down the sand hill toward him she had a vision of her father. The man who'd loved her and died, leaving her to her dreadful stepfather.

She'd loved her father. He'd been one special man.

'What?' He reached her and found she was smiling, but it was an odd sort of smile, tinged with sadness. 'You look like you've seen a ghost.'

'Maybe I have.' She pulled herself together. 'It's that coat.' She thought about not saying anything but then decided to tell him anyway. 'It was my father's—not my stepfather's but my father's. My mother kept it and then loaned it to Robbie. Robbie was our gardener.'

'You were fond of Robbie?'

'He's a lovely old man. My friend. I had to let him go—there's no money to keep him. One of the local farmers puts a couple of sheep on my grass now and that's the extent of my gardening. Meanwhile, Robbie's living in a council flat in Bowra and I know he's miserable. I tried to make him keep the coat but he wouldn't.' She gave a twisted little smile. 'He said to keep it until I can have him back again. As if... But I know he misses me as much as I miss him. And he's so broke. My stepfather should have set up a superannuation fund for him, but loyalty to his staff wasn't his style.'

'You don't sound like you spend much time polishing your stepfather's headstone.'

'I leave that for the nephews.'

'They loved him?'

'They loved his money.' She grimaced. 'Anyway, it's too good a night to think about my stepfather. Isn't this fabulous?'

Fabulous?

It had started to rain again and there was a cold trickle running down his nose. The wind was making a mockery of his hood—it had blown back and his hair was damp and windblown. The smell of the sea was all around them and the breakers were roaring into the night.

It was fabulous, he decided, and he glanced down at Amy and found her smile had changed.

'You like it, too,' she said on a note of satisfaction. 'I thought you would.'

'It's great.'

'There was no need for my stepfather and his cronies to make this beach so exclusive,' she said reflectively. 'You could have thousands of people here and still find a spot where you can be alone. There's miles and miles of beach...' She put back her arm and tossed Bertram's stick with all her might along the beach.

The dog put back his ears and flew. 'And it's all ours. Some-times...sometimes I feel rich.'

'Hmm.'

'How can you bear to go back to Sydney?'

'I can't,' he said promptly. 'I think I'll stay here.'

'And become a beachcomber?'

'There are worse fates.'

'You wouldn't miss your surgery?'

Of course he would. They both knew it. Beachcombing was a dream. Beachcombing with Amy.

'Do you want to walk out on the rocks?' she asked, seeing Joss's face and having enough sense to change the subject. 'It's great—though you might get your feet wet.'

'Wetter,' he muttered. His shoes had sunk into the wet sand and he could feel the damp creeping into his socks. 'Well, why not?'

'Excellent.' Amy grinned and grabbed his hand. 'Follow me.'

The feel of her hand changed things.

Follow her...

She was leading him to a rocky outcrop which spiked up out of the breakers. 'It's a bit dangerous,' she warned. 'If you don't know where you're going, you can get into trouble. So hang on.'

How could he do anything else?

A bit dangerous...

She needed her head read, he thought as she clambered over the first of the rocks, towing him behind. There were breakers smashing over the rocks in force. Back on the beach Bertram stood and looked on in concern. There was no way he was fol-lowing and the look on his face said they were crazy to try.

But she'd done this a thousand times before.

The first few rocks were the worst—the foam from the break-ers was surging over the slippery surface and they had to time their way between waves. Even then they didn't quite make it—Joss ended up on the other side with shoes full of water.

'Don't tell me. It's low tide now and the next wave will carry us off to our doom. Or we'll be trapped with the tide rising inch by inch.'

'You've been reading too many adventure novels,' she said severely. '"The moon was a ghostly galleon, tossed upon stormy seas…" With moonrakers, pirates, chests and chests of jewels, and a heroine chained to the rocks as the tide creeps higher… higher.'

'I seem to remember,' he said faintly, 'that "The moon was a ghostly galleon" started a tale of a highwayman.'

'Same difference,' she said cheerfully. 'Same criminal hero and a dopey heroine abandoning all for love. But don't worry. The tide's full now so it doesn't get any worse than this, and I'm not about to end it all for anything. Look. Clear rock.'

It was, too. The outcrop of rock stretched right out into the bay, a breakwater in its own right. And where she was leading him now… It was a channel of rock. The rocks on both sides formed a barrier.

'It's like Moses and the Red Sea,' he said, stunned, and she grinned.

'Yep. The parting of the water. This is my very favourite place in the whole world and I love it best when it's just like this. Wild and stormy and wonderful.'

Joss didn't answer. He couldn't. Maybe it was because he was concentrating on keeping his footing on the slippery rocks—or maybe it was that he was just plain bemused.

Finally they reached the end—a vast flat rock perched high above the breakers. Amy released his hand to scramble up the last few feet, leaving him to follow. When he found his feet she was standing right at the end, staring into the moonlight.

The shafts of moonlight were playing over her face. She looked up and he thought that he'd never seen anything so lovely.

'He makes bright mischief with the moon…'

Where had that come from?

Wherever—from a poem deep in the recesses of his school-boy reading—it suddenly seemed apt.

Only the pronoun was wrong.

She makes bright mischief with the moon.

Amy would be happy wherever she was, whatever she did, he thought. She made the most of her life. She cared.

She was soaked to the skin. Her braid had come unfastened and her curls were a tangled riot around her face. She was wearing a coat that was too small and clothes that were too old—and she was turning her face into the wind as if she'd been given the world.

It was too much. It would have been too much for any man.

He took her hands in his as if to steady himself, and when her body twisted toward him he pulled her close.

He kissed her.

Of course he kissed her. There was a compulsion happening here that he had no hope of controlling. He couldn't even try.

She was so desirable. So beautiful. So...

He didn't know. But there was a damp tendril coiling down her forehead that he had to push softly away. There was salt water on her face that he had to taste... And her lips were soft and pliant and...and waiting.

Waiting for him.

She was so lovely.

His woman...

'Lady, by yonder blessed moon I swear...'

Moon madness. That's what this was—the same blessed moon that had caused Romeo to forsake all for his Juliet.

For heaven's sake, he was a surgeon—not a poet!

But he was a poet tonight. Who wouldn't be with such sweetness in his arms.

Amy was so right for him. It was as if a part of him had been missing and had found its way home. Each curve of their bodies fitted together as if they knew each other through and through.

Joss held her close and deepened the kiss—because nothing, ever, had felt so right before.

And Amy?

What was she doing? she thought wildly. She'd taken this man to her very special place—her place—the place where she'd sobbed her heart out as a child or come when life had been just too bleak for words. It was a place of sanctuary and of healing.

She hadn't expected this to happen.

To fall in love...

Because that was what was happening. As though responding to a force beyond her control, she opened her lips to the man who held her. More. She opened her heart.

It was so right! Her body was melting into his—aching—wanting and welcoming.

She felt herself sinking into him. Desperate to deepen the kiss. Desperate to grow closer. Though how could they be closer than they were at this minute? Two halves of one sweet whole. They'd been torn asunder by some mystery of fate and could now come together for always.

Always.

Joss's hands were pulling her body ever closer. His kiss deepened and deepened again—and so did the wonder.

She was like no woman he'd ever kissed, he thought, dazed with the sensation of what was happening to him. And why? She was sodden with sea spray. She wore no trace of make-up and her clothes were shabby and her hair was blown every which way. There were trickles of rainwater running down her nose, merging with the rain on his face where their lips met. She looked about as far from his ideal woman as he could possibly imagine any woman being.

So how could she be meeting this need—this desperate desire—that until now he'd never known he had?

He didn't know. All he knew was that she was... Amy.

And that was enough.

* * *

And finally—*finally*—they pulled away, as pull away they had to. The waves were sloshing over their shoes, they were sodden and back on the beach Bertram was starting to bark his anxiety for the world to hear.

'We're worrying Bertram,' Amy managed, and her voice was a husky whisper, full of uncertainty.

'Worrying Bertram!' Joss tried to smile down at the confusion on her face. 'I'm worrying me.'

That worked. 'Hey, I don't have any infectious diseases.'

He smiled—but only just. 'Amy...'

But she put a finger on his lips to stop him saying more. 'Don't.'

'Don't what?'

'Apologise. It was a magic night. It *is* a magic night, and I always think magic nights should be sealed with a kiss. Don't you?'

'I don't understand,' he said, dazed. 'Amy, what the hell happened there?'

'An electric charge?' Her smile was returning. 'Moonbeams and water. They pack a lethal charge.'

They certainly did. 'Amy, I never meant...'

'Of course you didn't,' she said cordially. 'And neither did I. But Bertram thinks we did and seeing as he's acting as our chaperon I think we should go back to him. Don't you?'

'Yes.' Of course he did. After all, he was cold and he was wet. Why on earth would he want to keep standing here?

He did. Badly.

But she was more in control than he was. 'Let's go,' she told him, her voice firming as she took his hand to lead him back to the beach. 'I have a fiancé to telephone and you have a conference to prepare for.'

Right. Right!

Bertram was waiting for them to return to the beach. His conference paper was waiting to be written. The unknown Malcolm was waiting in Bowra.

His life was waiting for him to get on with it.

But how the hell was a man to concentrate on writing a conference paper after that? Joss showered and changed into more of his father's clothes—he'd kill for another pair of jeans, he decided, and wondered for about the thousandth time how Amy put up with no shops. Dried and warm, he returned to the kitchen to find Amy had disappeared.

'I've gone to bed,' the note on the table read. 'Make yourself some cocoa.'

Right. Cocoa. When what he needed was...

Sex?

No. Not sex. Or not just sex.

He wanted Amy.

It was nine o'clock. After the day he'd had he should be exhausted. Maybe he should go to bed, but as he wandered down the passage he heard the shower running in Amy's bathroom. A vision appeared unbidden...

Whoa. Unless he was careful here, he'd have to take another shower. This time cold.

Bertram was nosing at Amy's bedroom door, whimpering to be let in to visit someone he'd decided very firmly was a friend, and Joss took his collar and pulled him away.

'No. We're not wanted, boy. She has a fiancé.'

It was just as well she did, he decided. The last thing he wanted was a tie that could hold him to Iluka. It was bad enough that he had a father here and he'd have to visit every few months.

But Amy was here.

The sound of the shower ceased. She'd be drying herself.

'Oh, for heaven's sake, Braden, get a grip. You're a grown man.'

'Yeah, with grown man urges.'

'She doesn't want you.'

'I could just towel her back...'

He was a guest in her house. He wasn't wanted. He had a bed of his own to go to.

The phone rang and he hesitated, half expecting—half hoping—Amy would open the door and come out to the kitchen to answer it. And then he realised it was ringing in her bedroom. Damn, she had an extension. What business did she have, having an extension when she was broke?

He was losing his mind.

But he didn't move. He sort of listened—just for a minute.

And from the other side of the door he heard, 'Malcolm. How lovely. I was worried about you.'

Damn.

He took himself firmly in hand and took himself off to his bed. Alone. She was worried about Malcolm?

He was worried about himself!

Amy had herself under control—sort of—and was answering the phone to her fiancé. What had gone on tonight with Joss was an aberration, she told herself firmly. It had nothing to do with her or with her future. It had only been a kiss.

Which was why she'd made a dash to her bedroom and had locked the door, thankful that her room had an *en suite* bathroom so she didn't have to face Joss again tonight.

It was only a kiss, she said to herself like a mantra. A kiss with no future.

Her future was here in Iluka. Her future was with Malcolm. Now he'd phoned, as she'd known he would—though it was really unusual for him to ring two hours late.

'I was worried,' she told him, striving to keep her voice light. 'When you didn't ring I thought the telephone lines might be down.'

'No. The lines are fine. But I hear you've lost the bridge.' Malcolm sounded strained, she thought. Unlike him.

'Yes. We're stranded but we're fine. Though there was one casualty…'

'A casualty?' Still that note of anxiety.

'No one we know. A young woman crashed her truck and she was in full labour. She ended up having her baby here in the nursing home.'

'A baby?' His voice rose in disbelief and Amy thought, He really is worried. For some reason he sounded terrified.

'She's fine, Malcolm. We all are. David Braden's son is here and he's a doctor. He was trapped when the bridge came down and Joss is a fine surgeon. He did a Caesarean, delivering a beautiful little girl, and now he's on the spot for any medical needs we might have.'

There was a silence while Malcolm thought that through, then he said, 'So…the woman's fine. And the baby?'

'Great. Malcolm, is there anything wrong?'

'No. No. Did the woman say…who she was?'

Amy frowned. Charlotte hadn't exactly given permission for her name to be broadcast. If it hadn't been for the policeman tracking of her licence plates, they still wouldn't know it. 'For some reason I don't think she wants her identity known.'

'Oh.'

'But I'm afraid she's as stuck here as we all are. I guess they'll organise a ferry over the river soon.'

'Yeah.'

'You sound…odd.'

'Do I?' There was another lengthy silence from the end of the line then he added, 'It must be the distance or something. Water in the line.'

'Is everything OK at your end?' she asked.

'Why wouldn't it be?'

'No reason.' But still she had this niggle of a doubt. He sounded distracted.

'You're OK yourself?' He still sounded strained.

'I'm fine,' she said gently. 'Just a bit tired. It's been a long day. Goodnight, Malcolm.'

For some reason he was as eager as she was to end the conversation. 'Goodnight,' he told her, and hung up—leaving her staring at the receiver.

What on earth was going on?

Amy went to bed but she didn't sleep. She lay awake and stared at the ceiling, thinking of a kiss.

This didn't make any sense. The kiss and how she was responding to it didn't make sense at all.

When Malcolm kissed her it didn't feel like this.

Maybe it was because Joss was forbidden fruit, she thought bleakly. You always wanted what you couldn't have—and she couldn't have Joss.

Maybe she could open her bedroom door...

Oh, yeah, great. What was she thinking of? A spot of seduction?

'I wouldn't mind,' she told herself honestly and then bit her lip. Where would that lead her? To a broken engagement and desperate unhappiness when Joss left.

As he surely would.

'But I could just have fun—for a while. For a few short days while the bridge is down...'

Fun? She'd never had fun. She'd forgotten the meaning of the word. From the time her father had died the world had become a dangerous and threatening place, where the only way to survive was sheer, grinding hard work.

She had six years to go.

And after that? Marriage to Malcolm...

They might even marry earlier, she thought, and there was a note of desperation entering her thoughts now. Malcolm had been pushing for them to marry straight away. He'd have to stay in Bowra as his practice was there, and she was stuck at Iluka, but he could come at weekends. A weekend marriage...

It didn't excite her at all.

Malcolm didn't excite her.

'It's because he's familiar,' she told the dark. She knew him as well as she knew a pair of old socks. But... She thought about it. Tonight he'd been different. Not different in the way Joss was different but different all the same.

She didn't know what had got into Malcolm tonight.

'Maybe I don't know all there is to know about him. Maybe he'll turn into a James Bond in disguise. Or a Joss...'

The thought made her smile.

But it didn't make her go to sleep—and it wasn't Malcolm she was thinking about as she tossed and turned in the night.

It was very definitely Joss.

Joss had had a huge day. He'd almost been killed, he'd almost been swept away in the river, he'd fallen in love...

Hey! Where had that come from?

'You're imagining things,' he told the dark. Love? What did he know about love?

He only knew that Amy was the most beautiful woman he'd ever met.

But she wasn't beautiful, he decided, trying to see things dispassionately. Not in the conventional way. She was too careless of her appearance to be classed as beautiful.

But when she smiled...

'Beautiful,' Joss told his pillow, and he groaned as he turned over yet again and tried for elusive sleep. 'Just beautiful.'

At two in the morning the phone rang. Joss was still awake, so he heard it, and he heard Amy's soft voice answering. Something at the hospital? By the time Amy knocked at his door he was already reaching for his father's spare dressing-gown.

'Problems?'

It was hard to concentrate on problems. He didn't have his lamp on and Amy was lit by the hall light. She was wearing a long nightgown, trailing down to bare feet. It was cut low in the front and her curls were wisping down to her breasts. It was the first time he'd seen her with unbraided hair and the sight almost took his breath away. She looked sort of ethereal. Gorgeous...

But she was already hauling her hair back into a knot, ready for what lay ahead. 'Joss, can you help?'

That was what he was there for. He was almost grateful to be asked. Any more staring into the dark and he was in danger of losing his mind.

Any more staring at the woman in front of him and he'd definitely lose his mind.

'What's wrong?'

'A child. A little girl...'

He stared at that. 'A child? In Iluka?'

'We do have them. Just not many. Margy Crammond has her granddaughter staying with her. Emma's six years old and she's woken feeling dreadful. Margy says she can't walk.'

'Yeah?' He tossed aside his dressing-gown, hauled off his pyjama jacket and reached for his dad's Fair Isle sweater. His mind shifted straight into emergency mode. He was already sifting and discarding diagnoses, so much so that he didn't even wince as the amazing patterned sweater slipped over his head. Joss was a doctor first and foremost, and an emergency had him putting everything else aside.

Or almost. Amy's damned negligee was almost transparent... Concentrate!

'What do you think the options are?' he asked. 'Hysteria?' Paraplegia in children was so unusual the first suspicion was a psychological diagnosis rather than a physical one.

But Amy was shaking her head. 'Margy seems to think it's something more serious. Hysteria would be unusual at two in the morning—though she is homesick. She's been staying with her grandparents for a week and was supposed to be going home today. She's a bit upset that she can't. But Margy said she was sound asleep a couple of hours ago when they went to bed and she's woken in trouble.'

Hell! He thought about the possibilities—in a place where there were no acute facilities—and he didn't like them one bit. 'I'll go. Where is she?'

'We'll go,' Amy told him. 'This is my town. My people.'

'And you have work tomorrow.'

'We'll go,' she said again in a voice that told him he might as well save his breath. She wasn't listening to arguments. 'Half a minute while I pull on some jeans.'

CHAPTER SIX

This was not hysteria.

Emma Crammond was one sick little girl. By the time they reached Margy and Harry Crammond's house, the girl's grandmother was beside herself with worry and her grandfather was coming a very close second.

'She can't make anything work,' Margy told them as she led them through the house. She glanced up at Joss with gratitude. The whole town knew who Joss was now. News travelled fast in a small community. 'Oh, Dr Braden, thank heaven you're here. She looks just awful.'

She did.

The child was still in bed, but she was wide-eyed and frantic. Her breathing was fast and furious—as if she'd just run a marathon—but by her skin pallor Joss could see that she wasn't getting enough oxygen no matter how hard she breathed. Even from the doorway he could see that she was cyanosed, her skin taking on the tell-tale bluish tinge arising from inadequate oxygen.

What on earth was wrong?

They'd travelled in Amy's car. Joss usually travelled with a basic medical kit but it had been pulped along with the rest of the rear of his car. So he was dependent on Amy. 'Do we have oxygen?' he asked, expecting the worst, but Amy was nodding, moving already back to the front door.

'Yes. I'll get it.'

She had more than just oxygen. She had a complete and extensive medical kit.

She was back in seconds, handing Joss a stethoscope as she hauled out the oxygen mask to attach to the cylinder by her side. Whew, Joss thought—and then reminded himself that he should have expected no less. Amy obviously acted as district nurse and was first port of call in emergency for Iluka's elderly. Oxygen would be something she needed all the time.

So he had what he required. Now he could concentrate on the child. He needed to concentrate. Her illness was frightening.

'I can't...' The little girl was frantic. She was tossing wildly on the bed—as if trying to escape some unknown demon—and her grandfather was vainly trying to restrain her. 'My legs... I can't move them... Oh, I want my mummy.'

'Her mother's in Bowra.' Beside the bed, her grandmother was sobbing with fear. 'Dear God, what's wrong?'

'Emma, you must hush and keep still while the doctor works,' Amy told the little girl. She signalled to Harry to stand clear and sat on the bed. 'I'm fitting a mask over your face to help you breathe. But if you fight it, it won't help. You must keep still. Do you hear?'

The little girl nodded, but her terror was still almost palpable.

'We don't know what's wrong with you yet.' Amy was already sliding the mask over the little girl's face. 'But here we have Dr Braden who's stuck in Iluka like you are, because the bridge fell down. So we have our very own Iluka doctor. Isn't that lucky?'

Lucky? Yeah, great. Except he didn't know what was wrong with her. Hell, he was a surgeon, not a physician.

But he had gone through basic medical training. He'd worked for two years in an emergency department of a busy city hospital before he'd specialised—but this wasn't fitting into anything he'd ever seen.

The child was badly cyanosed. Her skin was growing more

blue by the minute, which meant she still wasn't getting enough oxygen. Her heartbeat was rating 170 beats a minute and her breathing was far too fast. Yet she wasn't running a temperature. She was completely afebrile and both lungs sounded normal.

The oxygen didn't seem to be making a difference.

'What's she eaten tonight?' Joss asked. This wasn't making any sense.

'Just what we ate. Roast beef and veggies. Apple pie. Nothing else.'

'You're sure?'

'Yes.'

They'd have three patients here in a minute, Joss thought grimly, and sent an unspoken message to Amy with his eyes. They had to get the pressure off the elderly couple before they collapsed.

'We need to get Emma to hospital,' he told them. 'I want a chest X-ray. There must be something going on.'

But what?

'She's asthmatic,' Harry told Joss. He took that on board but still it wasn't making sense. 'It's only mild...' The old man gulped and swallowed a couple of times. 'I thought—I thought you should know.'

Asthma he could deal with, but this wasn't asthma. Still, it was something... 'OK. Amy, do we have salbutamol?'

'Sure.' Amy was already preparing it. She was a fine nurse, Joss thought. A wonderful team member. He could work alongside her any day.

'We'll give her salbutamol just to make sure,' Joss said, looking at the little girl's frantic eyes. He shook his head. 'But asthma...it doesn't make sense.'

Nothing did.

They drove Emma to the hospital in Amy's wreckage-mobile with Joss cradling the child in the back seat as he held the oxygen mask in place. They'd left her grandparents collecting her night things and contacting her mother—and pulling themselves together. The old people were shocked and shaky, and Amy rang their neighbours, asking them to drive the couple in. The neighbours just happened to be Joss's father and stepmother.

Amy didn't refer to Joss before she rang them. Joss had enough to worry about keeping Emma alive. David and Daisy were dependable and solid; she could rely on them to look after Emma's grandparents and she didn't want any more casualties tonight.

One was enough—and maybe even one was too many to save. By the time they reached the hospital things were deteriorating even further.

Amy found herself making silent pleas as she drove, and as she helped Joss lift Emma out of the car her pleas grew more desperate. Were they going to lose her?

Why? This was no asthma attack. What was going on?

Joss was agreeing with her. 'There's no way this is just asthma,' Joss muttered as they carried her swiftly through to X-Ray. The nursing home was settled for the night. It was darkened and at peace, and Sue-Ellen, the night nurse, emerged from the nurses' station, shocked at the startling interruption to her night.

Sue-Ellen, like Amy, had done her training in an acute hospital and she switched to acute care without a murmur. Joss couldn't have asked for a better team as they set up the drip, monitored the oxygen flow and organised the child for an X-ray.

Emma was still terrified. The most important thing had to be reassurance—but how to do that when they didn't know what they were dealing with?

The X-rays told them nothing. The X-rays were normal.

Hell, what? *What?*

Joss was raking his hair as he looked helplessly down at the child on the bed. 'We need blood tests. I don't suppose you have the facilities here...'

Amy shook her head, knowing what he needed was beyond

them. 'We can do blood sugars and we have an oxi-meter to measure oxygen levels.'

'I want to do blood gases.'

'We can't.'

Hell!

He wanted his teaching hospital, he thought desperately. He wanted a specialist paediatrician and a pathologist. He wanted some answers...

The child was slipping into unconsciousness and he'd never felt so helpless.

'Joss?'

'Mmm.' He was holding the child's wrist, feeling her racing pulse. His mind was turning over and over. What...?

'Joss, the swab...' Amy sounded hesitant—unsure—and she caught Joss's attention.

What was she looking at? He followed her gaze.

He'd set up a drip before the X-ray, thinking that they might need adrenalin at any minute. The child couldn't keep this pulse rate up for ever, and the cyanosis was at dangerous levels. So he'd inserted a drip and placed tape over the back of Emma's hand to hold it steady. But the insertion site had bled a little. Amy had swabbed the blood away and the swab lay in a kidney dish. Sue-Ellen had lifted the dish out of the way but Amy was reaching to grip her hand.

Sue-Ellen paused, the dish with the swab held before her. The light was directly on it.

'It's brown,' Amy said stupidly, and she looked up at Joss. 'Surely that can't be right?'

He stared. There it was. The bloodstained swab had turned to a deep, chocolate brown colour.

No, it wasn't right, but there it was. Unmistakable.

Where had he read about that? Joss closed his eyes, his mind racing. Where...?

And there it was. An article studied for a long forgotten exam. Useless information suddenly resurrected.

'Methaemoglobinaemia.' Joss could hardly frame the word. He could barely remember it. But it must be. He stared at the swab as if he couldn't believe his eyes.

Amy was still confused. 'What?' She'd never heard the word. 'Methaem—'

'Methaemoglobinaemia. It's a type of acute anaemia caused by exposure to some sort of poison.' Joss could hardly take his eyes off the swab. 'I've never seen it before—I've only read about it. But some chemicals—some poisons—oxidise the iron in the blood, meaning the blood can't carry oxygen. That describes exactly what we've got here. Chocolate brown blood. I must be right. I can't think of anything else. Amy, get me Sydney Central. I want to talk to a haematologist. Tell them we want an expert in poisons—the best they have—and I don't care if you have to wake him up to speak to him. This is urgent.'

His mind was whirring over half-forgotten textbook cases. 'I'd guess activated charcoal or...' The article was becoming clearer in his mind as he spoke, forgotten texts somehow dredged up into memory. 'Do we have any methylene blue?'

'Methylene blue?'

'It's used to treat methaemoglobinaemia—when the blood can't deliver oxygen where it's needed in the body. It's also used as a dye to stain certain parts of the body during surgery.' What was the chance of having it in Iluka? Damn, why didn't they have a pharmacy? Though even a normal city pharmacy might not stock this.

Amy shook her head, dazed by the speed and certainty of his diagnosis. 'Methylene... I'll check. We're set up with emergency supplies so if the Bowra doctor's here she has everything she needs in the drug cupboard.'

'I think we might have something called that,' Sue-Ellen said diffidently. 'If I remember right. Dr Scott—the doctor from Bowra—gave us a list when we opened four years ago. She put all sorts of weird things on the list. I remember the pharmacist who supplied us scoffing and saying she was way out of date, and I think it was the methylene blue he was talking about when he said it.'

Please… 'Let's hope you're right,' Joss told her. 'But even if you are, I don't know the dosage. Amy, get onto the phone. I need a haematologist with paediatric back-up. Now!'

What followed was an example of a medical community at its best.

Within five minutes Amy had a telephone link set up—a conference line with a paediatrician, a haematologist and a pathologist for good measure. They'd all been woken from sleep but their concern was audible through the teleconferencing link from Sydney.

They were fascinated as well as concerned. If we have to have a dangerous illness maybe it's as well to have an interesting one, Amy thought ruefully. All doors were open to a case of a perilously ill child with an unusual diagnosis.

The case conference was swift, intelligent and concise, and by the time Sue-Ellen had located a dated bottle of methylene blue from the back of the drug cupboard Joss was ready. While everyone held their breath—including the three specialists on the end of the phone—Joss administered fifty milligrams.

Then they waited. They all waited, and the specialists from Sydney stayed on the phone and waited with them. There was no appreciable change but at least Emma didn't get worse. She was drifting in and out of consciousness, fighting the oxygen mask every time she surfaced. More and more Amy wanted her mother to be there. In her mother's absence she cuddled the child herself.

After twenty minutes the combined opinion was to wait no longer. Thanking his lucky stars for a comprehensive drug cupboard—and that methylene blue didn't suffer a use-by date—Joss administered another twenty-five milligrams.

Then they stood back and waited again, and it was the hardest thing—dreadful—to do. To watch and wait as a child fought for life.

And then results.

At first they thought they were imagining it. There was a combined holding of breath, and then they were almost certain. The awful blue was fading. The cyanosis was easing—just a bit, but enough to think that maybe...

Maybe was right. Another few minutes and they were sure. Emma was improving while they watched. The specialists on the end of the phone were jubilant, and so was everyone in the room. Sue-Ellen burst into tears, and it was all Joss and Amy could do not to join her.

Still they watched, but the child's agitation was settling. Her colour was improving by the minute. Her breathing was easing as the oxygen was finally reaching her blood. The danger was over.

'Look for a poison,' the haematologist growled, before disconnecting and returning to his bed. He was a gruff man but there was emotion in his gruffness. 'She must have eaten something that oxidises the ferrous iron in the blood. Sodium nitrate, maybe? Don't let the kid go home until you discover the source or you'll have her back in with another episode, and next time you mightn't be so lucky. And if anyone's eating where she's been eating, get them out of the house until you know where the hell it came from.'

He left them to it and went back to his bed.

There was the sound of a patient's bell from somewhere else in the nursing home. Life went on. Sue-Ellen made her escape, weeping audibly into her handkerchief, leaving Joss and Amy staring at each other in disbelief.

'Oh, thank God,' Amy murmured. Emma was drifting into an exhausted natural sleep, and her colour was almost back to normal. Amy had been cradling her to comfort her distress. Now the child's lashes had fluttered closed. Amy laid her back on her pillows and gently tucked her in.

'Do you want to tell her grandparents the good news?' Joss asked, and by his voice Amy could tell he was as shaken as she had been. Margy and Harry Crammond hadn't come into the room. They'd stayed out in Reception and panicked in isolation. Their distress had just upset their granddaughter more.

'You tell them.' Amy was smiling and smiling. 'You made the diagnosis.'

'You noticed the swab.'

'Together we make a great team.' Amy's eyes were bright with unshed tears. She was still holding Emma's hand but the little girl was slipping into a deep and natural sleep. 'Off you go. Tell her grandma and grandpa while I watch over her. And, Joss?'

'Yes?' He paused at the door and looked back.

'Thank you.'

'Think nothing of it.' His chest was expanding by the moment. The child would live, and it felt great! 'What else is a doctor for but to save lives? Given nursing staff with the power of observation you seem to have…well, as you say, we make a great team.'

He looked down at Amy and the child. They looked…magnificent. He closed the door behind him before she could see that his own eyes weren't exactly dry.

There were four people in Reception—Emma's grandparents, Joss's father and Daisy.

'We drove them here,' David told his son. 'And then we stayed. Did you really think we could go home before knowing the little one was safe?'

Joss looked at his father with affection. No. He didn't.

He operated with his heart, did his dad. It got him into all sorts of trouble. He'd buried three wives! His heart had been broken so many times, Joss thought, and each time he surfaced again to set himself up for more heartbreak.

Joss had never understood, but tonight, as he watched his father embrace his friends and celebrate this wonderful news—tonight he saw where his father was coming from.

Sure it hurt to give your heart. But now... This was such jubilation. Maybe...

Maybe what? What was he thinking of?

Was he thinking of giving his heart to Amy?

It wasn't wanted, he told himself savagely. Amy had a fiancé. She had a life. She had nothing to do with him.

'Can you put Mr and Mrs Crammond up for the night? Give them a bed?' he asked his father, but he knew before he answered what the response would be.

'Sure. But why?' The four elderly people were looking at him now with varying degrees of confusion.

'Emma ate something she shouldn't have,' he told them. 'You said she had roast meat and veggies and apple pie for dinner. Is that all? Did she eat anything that you didn't eat?'

Her grandparents were shaking their heads. 'No. She didn't.'

'And you're both feeling fine now?' They looked fine, he thought. Stressed but fine. Emma's illness had been dramatic. If they'd eaten the same thing they would have been ill by now.

'We're good.'

'Then I want you to stay that way. There's something that's contaminated Emma and until we know what it is I want you out of your kitchen. I don't want you to make so much as a cup of tea there before everything's tested. I'll ring Sergeant Packer and we'll go through the kitchen first thing in the morning.'

'She wouldn't...' Margy Crammond was becoming distressed. 'She wouldn't have eaten anything she shouldn't. Sergeant Packer... The police... You're not suggesting we poisoned her?'

'I'm doing no such thing.' Then, because it seemed the right thing to do—even though such a thing was unheard of in his professional life—he reached out and gave her a hug. 'Sergeant Packer's better at investigating than me. He's trained to figure out unusual circumstances, which is the only reason I suggested

I'd call in his help. By tomorrow Emma should be up to answering questions and we'll sort out what happened in no time. But for now you should phone her parents and tell them she's fine. Then go to bed. And don't worry.'

He pulled back and lifted the old lady's face so she was forced to meet his smile. 'Can you do that?'

She nodded and gulped.

His father was watching with a strange expression on his face. 'Do you want Daisy and me to stay awake and watch them—just in case they're poisoned and it takes longer to take effect in adults?' Joss's father asked his question idly, as if it'd be no more than a mild inconvenience to stay up all night, and Joss thought, Yeah, he'd do that, too. He wore his heart on his sleeve did his father. He loved...

May Daisy live for ever. But if she didn't...

Loss wouldn't stop his father loving again, he thought. Loving was a part of the man he was.

And all of a sudden—for the first time in his life—he was jealous. Ever since his mother had died he'd thought his father was a fool to love. And here he himself was, being jealous.

He needed to go take a cold shower. He needed to go home. To bed.

In the room next to Amy. Yeah, right.

He took a deep breath.

'OK. We've had enough for tonight. Dad, don't worry about checking. If the Crammonds are sleeping in the same room they'll wake if either becomes ill, and I know they'll have enough sense to wake you. But if they had been poisoned by what they ate for dinner, they'd be ill by now. So relax. It's time for bed.'

They nodded and turned wearily away, but before David left, he gripped Joss's hand. 'Thanks, Joss,' he said softly. And then his grip hardened. 'I'm proud of you.'

CHAPTER SEVEN

THEY DROVE HOME in the wreckage-mobile. It had started raining again—hard—and Amy had to concentrate on the road. Maybe that was why they were silent for the entire journey.

Or maybe...maybe it was that Joss's life had subtly changed, and it occurred to him to wonder—had Amy's world changed, too?

No. The emotions that Joss was feeling were just that, he told himself savagely. *His* emotions. And stupid emotions they were at that.

They were silent because of what had just happened. They'd saved a life. A child's life. It felt good.

But it didn't override this strange new feeling that was flooding through him. Like life was opening up. It was a life he hadn't known existed or if he had, he'd thought it was stupid until now.

The world of loving.

They pulled into the garage. Bertram came lolloping out to greet them and Joss was relieved by the noisy welcome. He'd been trying to train the dog to be a bit more sedate, but tonight it eased the tension.

Why should there be tension? He and Amy were medical colleagues who'd just achieved a very satisfactory outcome. There shouldn't be any tension at all.

But...

'Goodnight, Joss. And thank you.' Before he knew what she was about she'd taken his face in her hands and she'd kissed him.

It was a feather kiss. A kiss of gratitude and goodnight.

There was no reason at all why he stood in the garage and stared stupidly after her as she disappeared into her house.

No reason at all.

Dawn saw them heading for the Crammonds' house.

'I'm coming, too,' Amy declared when Joss emerged from his bedroom. He'd rung Jeff the night before, emphasising that he didn't think this was a crime but that there was certainly something in the Crammond house that shouldn't be there. The Sergeant had suggested meeting at seven o'clock and Joss rose at six to find Amy bundled into jeans and a sloppy Joe sweater— looking absolutely delicious—and right into detective mode.

'OK. What should I take? A microscope? I don't have skeleton keys and I'm sure they're necessary.' She looked thoughtfully down at Bertram—who was looking thoughtfully up at her toast. 'Can we bring our sniffer dog?'

'He's not just a sniffer dog,' Joss told her, taking a piece of toast she'd prepared for him. Damn, why didn't toast taste this good when he made it himself? But somehow he made himself focus on Bertram. 'He's an eater dog. If he sniffed out poison he'd eat it straight away. He demolishes everything on the assumption that if it's not digestible he can bring it back up later.'

'That's an intelligent dog.' Bertram was promptly handed a piece of toast and he demonstrated his consumption ability forthwith. The toast disappeared with a gulp and he was wagging his tail for more. 'That's enough, Bertram. We have serious work to do. Do you think I should wear my raincoat with my collar turned up like they do in detective movies?'

'If movies were made in Iluka—yes, you should.' He stared out the window with morbid fascination at the sheets of rain pelting against the glass. 'I could be stuck here for months.'

'It suits me,' Amy said, but she'd turned back to the toaster and he couldn't see how serious she was. Or if she was serious at all.

* * *

The Crammonds' home was certainly not like a crime scene. It was the comfortable home of a cosy pair of grandparents and there was nothing suspicious at all.

Joss had been given the key the night before. Now the three of them, the policeman, Amy and Joss, pulled the kitchen apart.

'It'd help if we knew what we were looking for,' the policeman complained. 'You don't think they're into illicit substances—heroin or the like?'

'It crossed my mind last night,' Joss admitted. 'Not heroin, no. The symptoms of heroin overdose are very different to what happened to Emma. But I did wonder if they might be manufacturing amphetamines.'

'The Crammonds?' Amy's eyes widened in disbelief. 'You have to be kidding.'

'The strangest people are into drugs,' the policeman told her. He was inspecting canisters, one after another, poking his finger in and sniffing. 'One of our local grannies had a quarter of an acre of cannabis planted in her vegetable patch. I only found out about it when husband became fed up with her pulling out his tomatoes. They had a full-scale domestic, the neighbour got worried and I was called.'

'Here?' Amy shook her head in disbelief. 'In Iluka? Why did I never hear about it?'

'Because I sprayed the lot with weedkiller and told her to make a donation to the Salvation Army's drug rehabilitation programme,' Jeff said dourly. 'She was only growing it for herself—in fact, I suspect she hardly used the stuff and I didn't see much point in sending her to prison.'

'No.' Amy was still stunned.

'So Iluka's a hotbed of vice.' Joss was intrigued. 'I thought nothing ever happened in Iluka.'

'It's precisely because nothing ever happens that things do happen,' the policeman told him. 'People get bored.'

'Murder and mayhem?'

'You'd be surprised.'

'Yet you keep it under wraps.'

'If I can,' the policeman agreed. 'No sense in airing dirty linen in public.'

Amy was sifting through the cooking cupboard, peering into packages. 'So if they're into amphetamine production...'

'They'd need equipment and there's no sign of it. And they'd be nervous. The Crammonds weren't. They were quite happy to let us search the house and the garage.'

'Do we know what we're looking for?'

'No.'

'Great.'

But Joss was sorting through the clutter on the bench and he'd lifted the lid of the sugar bowl. Without really expecting anything, he'd taken a tiny pinch of sugar and placed it on his tongue. His face stilled.

'Jeff...'

'Mmm?' The policeman crossed to his side and peered into the bowl. 'What? It looks like normal sugar to me.'

'Taste it.'

'Yeah?' He did—though the look on his face said that he might as well be eating cyanide. 'Ugh. It's bitter. That's not sugar!'

'No.' Joss was gazing thoughtfully into the jar. 'It's not. They had apple pie and maybe Emma sprinkled it with what she thought was sugar. She might not have tasted it like that, and maybe her grandparents didn't use it.'

'But what is it?' Jeff was poking into the white substance with his finger. 'It's a bit finer than sugar but...well, you wouldn't notice it.'

'Where do they keep the packet?' Joss asked, and Amy poked around in the grocery cupboard under the bench until she found a half-empty sugar packet. She opened it and tasted.

'Sugar. It's fine.'

'Then what...?'

'What's nearby?' Joss knelt beside her—it felt good to kneel beside her, he thought, and then gave himself a mental shake. He was losing his mind here. He should be concentrating on things that were important and all he could focus on was how good Amy smelled. Fresh and clean, and there was some lingering perfume about her. It was faint—as if it was in her soap, and not applied out of a bottle—but it was unmistakable. Lily of the valley? Gorgeous.

Groceries. Poison. Get a grip, Braden.

And there it was.

The packet was white with blue lettering. It was smaller than the sugar packet, and its lettering was clear.

Speedy Cure.

'What the heck is Speedy Cure?' he demanded, and rose, opening the packet as he did.

It was a white powder, slightly grainy. If you didn't know better, you could mistake it for sugar.

'What is it?'

'My mum used to use that,' the policeman told them, taking the packet away from Joss and staring down at it in recognition. 'It's used to cure corned meats. I seem to remember it makes a great corned silverside.'

'But what is it?'

The sergeant was turning over the packet.

'Sodium nitrate,' he read. 'Could that be it, Doc?'

'It certainly could.' Joss stared from the packet to the sugar bowl and back again. 'Maybe...if the sugar bowl was empty Mrs Crammond might have asked her granddaughter to fill it.'

'And if she said the sugar's in the cupboard...' Amy was way ahead of him. 'Emma would have grabbed the first package that looked like sugar.'

'Problem solved.' Joss grinned. 'How very satisfactory. And you won't have to arrest anyone, Jeff. Not that you would have, anyway.'

'I would have at this,' Jeff told them. 'If a child was hurt because of drug dealing...' He held up the packet and grimaced. 'Mind, they should have known better than to keep this where kiddies can get near it.'

'I think they'll have learned their lesson.'

'I'll go across to your dad's and tell them.' Jeff grinned at them both. 'Well done, the pair of you. You make a good team, you know.'

You make a good team...

It was a throwaway line. There was no reason for it to reverberate in Joss's head like a vow.

Amy was taking it lightly, which was just as well. 'We know we're a great team,' Amy said smugly. 'I'm thinking of talking to the weather bureau. Arranging it so that it keeps raining and Joss will have to stay.'

'Put in a word from me, too, then,' Jeff told them. 'If it meant we'd get a permanent doctor for this town then I'm all for it.'

'Why can't you get a doctor?'

'Are you kidding? Bowra has enough trouble keeping Doris, and she's impossible. There's no specialists this side of Blairglen—the place is a desert.'

'But it's a beautiful place to live.'

'Yeah. It is,' the policeman said dourly. 'But the only land without legal building caveats—bans on commercial building— is the land under the nursing home. The old man screwed up our lives when he set this place up and we were all too stupid to see it.'

There followed a horrid interlude with Emma's grandparents, who were overwhelmed with guilt.

'I asked her to fill the sugar bowl,' Margy Crammond sobbed. 'How could I have been so stupid? I hadn't realised how poisonous Speedy Cure is. Harold loves his corned beef and the general store only stocks the really basic meats...'

Here was another example of how isolated this place was, Joss thought grimly. The old man really did have a lot to answer for.

'With this population, surely there's a way you can get shops?'

'On what land?' Amy shook her head. 'No. He cheated a whole town of retirees out of a great place to live.'

'Hmm.'

The more he saw the more it intrigued him—and the more the girl by his side intrigued him. They drove back to the nursing home in silence, both deep in their thoughts.

'When are you and your Malcolm planning on getting married?' he asked as they pulled to a halt in the hospital car park. She looked at him, startled.

'What on earth...?'

'Does that have to do with me? Nothing.' He grinned with his engaging grin, which could get him anything he wanted. Almost. 'But I want to know. Are you waiting for six years?'

'Maybe.'

'How often do you see each other?'

'He comes every second weekend—except when there are floods.'

'Do you ever spend time at Bowra?'

'I can't leave Iluka.'

'The old man's will stipulated that you live here,' Joss objected. 'It didn't say you could never leave.'

'But with no doctor here...' She spread her hands in a gesture of helplessness. 'Mary and Sue-Ellen don't accept much responsibility and there are always crises.'

'What's the population here?'

'About two thousand.'

'And in the district?'

'You mean—once the bridge is rebuilt?'

'Yes. How many live in a twenty-mile radius?'

She thought about it. 'A lot,' she said at last. 'The farms here are small and close together—the rainfall's good and farmers can make a living on a small holding.'

'And all those farmers go to Bowra with their medical needs?'

'You're very curious.'

'Indulge me.'

She gave him an odd look—but what was the harm after all? 'They go to Blairglen mostly,' she told him. 'There's no specialists at Bowra—only Doris.'

'But Blairglen's more than a hundred kilometres away.'

'People travel. They must.'

She sounded odd, he thought. Strained. Well, maybe he'd asked for that. He'd kissed her. She was a perfectly respectable affianced woman. She had nothing to do with him—and he'd kissed her.

He'd really like to do it again.

Instead he sighed, climbed out of the car and walked around to help her out. She'd waited—as if she knew that he'd come and she welcomed the formality of what he intended. It was a strange little ritual and it had the effect of heightening the tension between them.

Help. When would the rain stop? When would they organise a ferry across the river? An escape route?

He needed it—because he wasn't at all sure what was happening here. Or maybe he was sure and he didn't know what the heck to do with it.

Their lives were worlds apart and that was the way they had to stay.

So somehow—*somehow*—Joss kept his hands to himself as she rose from the car and brushed past his body.

Amy was a practical, efficient, hardworking and committed nurse, he thought desperately. She wasn't wearing anything to entice. Right now she had on faded jeans, a soft cotton blouse and a pair of casual moccasins.

She was dressed for hard work. She was dressed in clothes so old no woman of his acquaintance would have been seen dead in them!

So why did he really badly want to...?

What?

He didn't know.

Or he did know. He just didn't want to admit it.

* * *

The Iluka nursing home was looking more and more like an acute hospital. It was busy, bustling and alive with a sense of urgency that had never been there before. Even the front of the nursing home had more cars than usual—this was the scene of the only action in Iluka and no one, it seemed, wanted to be left out. If they didn't have family here, the residents had friends—or maybe even just a sore toe, and maybe this charismatic young doctor could be persuaded...

This charismatic young doctor was feeling more and more out of his depth by the minute.

Bertram bounded out of the wreckage-mobile as the car drew to a halt in Amy's parking bay. They'd collected him on the way because of the residents' delight in him the day before, and he was greeted with even more pleasure than they were.

'Bertram.' Lionel Waveny's old face creased in delight as the dog appeared, and he put a hand proprietorially in his collar. 'Come with me, boy.' He was grinning like a school kid given a day off. 'Marigold's here,' he told them. 'She tells me she's probably got an overactive thyroid and she's sleeping in the room next to mine. She's feeling a lot better this morning but what she really needs is a visit from Bertram to cheer her up.'

'Go right ahead,' Joss told him, and Amy could only stare.

'I swear... Joss, yesterday that man could hardly remember his wife's name.'

'Dogs do that to people.' Joss looked at the old man's retreating back and Bertram's waving plume of a tail with satisfaction. 'Pet therapy. It's well documented. You want me to order you a dog or two as resident therapy?'

'You're kidding.'

'Just say the word.'

It was too much for her. Amy subsided into silence—which was just as well. They opened the doors to the sitting room and anything they said would have been drowned out straight away by baby screams. Ilona was being washed in preparation for her morning feed, and she was objecting in no uncertain terms to the violation of her small person.

The day took over.

Sue-Ellen greeted them as they walked in the door with a request for Joss to ring Emma's parents. To have their child so ill with no way of reaching her was making them feel desperate, and they wanted their daughter's progress given to them by a *real* doctor. Then Sue-Ellen handed over medical reports of all acute patients. All five of them.

This felt terrific, Amy thought contentedly as Joss read through Sue-Ellen's change-over notes. She stared around at the buzzing sitting room. Three of her oldies were helping bathe the baby and there were a couple more looking on with pleasure. One of those watching was Jock Barnaby. Jock had stared at the floor and nothing else since his wife had died two years ago!

Amazing!

What else? The knitting club—five ladies and one gentleman in their eighties—were trying to outdo each other by finishing the first matinée jacket. Through an open door she could see a couple of her inmates sitting by Emma's bed, just watching. Marie and Thelma were clucking over their pneumonia patient.

The place had come alive.

It could be like this all the time, she thought, dazed. It would be. If she had a doctor here. But how on earth could she ever attract anyone to practise here?

She couldn't. In a few days Joss would leave and it would go back to being same old, same old.

But meanwhile…she was going to soak it up for all she was worth, she decided. As she looked around her, her eyes danced with laughter and delight. 'This is great,' she said happily. 'Don't you think so, Dr Braden?'

'Just great,' he agreed weakly, and thought, Hell, it really is, but why?

* * *

Emma was recovering nicely.

Rhonda Coutts was looking good and her breathing had eased. Her pneumonia seemed to be settling.

Marigold's heart rate had settled after a good night's sleep. Joss needed a blood test to be sure, but he was more and more certain that his thyroid diagnosis was right. Marigold and Lionel had Bertram on her bed and the pair were petting and cooing over the big dog like first-time parents with their baby. Bertram was soaking it up with the air of a dog who'd found his nirvana.

This was a really strange ward round, Joss thought as he went from patient to patient, and it took an effort to keep his thoughts on medicine. He must—any of them could have a significant need that might be missed if he didn't treat this seriously—but with a nursing staff whose average age was about ninety it was a bit hard.

Amy didn't help. She couldn't disguise the fact that she loved what was happening around her, and her dancing eyes and bright laughter were enough to distract him all by themselves.

These people loved her. But she deserved better than to be stuck here for ever, Joss thought.

What did she deserve? A job in the city?

She'd do well in a city hospital, he decided. She was a magnificently skilled nurse, and she had the intelligence to be even more, given the right training. If she'd had the opportunity, she could be working alongside him as a fellow doctor, he thought, and the thought made him feel...odd.

All the thoughts he was having were odd. Stupid! It was increasingly obvious that by leaving her he'd be abandoning her.

It was no such thing, he reminded himself sharply. His life wasn't here. For heaven's sake, he couldn't set up medical practice in a town of geriatrics. He'd go nuts within a week.

As Amy was going nuts.

Amy had nothing to do with him.

He had one patient left to see—the new mother. By the time he reached Charlotte's room he was so confused he didn't know how to handle it, but somehow he put it aside. His examination of the young mother must be careful and thorough. Charlotte needed him. She was only one day post-op, and she was still suffering from her battering in the car crash.

'Talk to her by herself,' Amy said, leaving him at her bedroom door. 'She's traumatised and I don't know why. Maybe she'll be more willing to speak to you if you're alone.'

Amy was sensitive as well as competent, Joss thought, watching her retreating back.

She was a woman in a million.

She had nothing to do with him, he told himself for what was surely the twentieth time this morning. Concentrate on Charlotte!

Physically Charlotte was recovering well. His medical examination finished, he replaced the dressing over her wound and hauled over a chair to the bedside. Charlotte eyed him with caution as he sat.

'Hey, I'm not about to bite,' he told her, and she managed a smile.

'I didn't say—'

'No, but you looked.' He'd asked for her baby—Ilona—to be brought back into the room. Now he looked into the makeshift cot and smiled. 'Ilona's just right for a name. She's definitely beautiful.'

'Yes.'

'Does she have a surname?'

'I... I haven't decided yet.'

'Whether you'll use your name or her father's name?'

'That's right.'

'Are you going to tell me your surname?' Jeff had given him her surname but he wanted it to be the girl herself who gave it to him. The last thing he wanted was for her to think he'd instigated a police investigation.

She hesitated but Joss's hand came out and caught hers. 'I'm not sure what you're running from,' he said gently. 'But whatever it is, I'm not about to hand you over.'

'I'm not running.' She hesitated. 'My name...my name's Charlotte Brooke but... There's people I don't want to know...'

'That you're here?'

'That's right.'

'You need a bit of thinking time?'

'I do,' she said gratefully. 'I know it's messy, with medical insurance and things...'

'We can do all the paperwork when we discharge you,' he told her. 'That'll give you the time you need.'

'You won't tell Amy? Who I am?'

Joss frowned. Amy already knew but Charlotte's name had meant nothing to her. 'Is Amy one of the people you're hiding from?'

'No.' She bit her lip. 'But you won't tell her?'

'No.' But he was still frowning.

'I just want to do what's best.'

'Don't we all,' he managed. He was still holding her hand and now he looked down at the coverlet at her fingers. They were work-worn and there were traces of soil in her fingernails. She was used to hard physical labour. There was no ring on her finger. Nothing.

'Charlotte, if I can help...'

'You've done enough. You've given me my baby.'

'Amy did that.'

'That's what I mean.' Charlotte sighed and withdrew her hand. 'Before...it all seemed so easy. So possible. But now...'

'Now what?'

She turned away, wincing as the stitches caught. 'Now it just seems impossible,' she said.

'Did she tell you who she was?' Amy asked as he gently closed the door behind her. Joss had given Charlotte something to ease the pain and she should sleep until lunchtime.

'Yes.'

She caught his look and held. 'But she still doesn't want everyone to know?'

'Now how did you know that?'

'I'm a mind-reader.'

She was laughing at him. Her eyes were so disconcerting. They danced, he decided. She really did have the most extraordinary eyes.

'She told me who she was and she asked me to keep it to myself. I agreed. It means we can't bill her through Medicare until she allows us to, but she's agreed to let us use her name at the end of her stay.'

'It doesn't make any sense.'

'No.'

'But you agreed?'

'I agreed.'

She looked at him for a long moment. And then the smile returned to her eyes. 'You really are a very nice man, Joss Braden.'

It threw him. It was all he could do not to blush.

'I know,' he managed, and she grinned.

'And modest, too.'

'I can't deny it.'

'I've put you down as a fourth at bridge,' she told him, and that shut him up entirely.

'You haven't.'

'Someone had to do it,' she said demurely. 'My oldies tell me it takes brains to play bridge so who am I, a mere nurse, to take the place of a specialist?'

A mere nurse. She was no such thing.

She was enchanting.

'I was planning on...'

'Yes?' She fixed him with a challenging gaze. 'You were planning on what?'

'Doing more of my conference notes.'

'There's the whole afternoon to do that,' she told him. 'And tonight. And tomorrow morning and—'

'Whoa!'

'There's no urgency about this place,' she told him. 'Haven't you realised that yet?'

'Yes, but—'

'There you go, then.' She smiled her very nicest smile. 'Bridge, Dr Braden.' She pointed to the lounge. Looking through the glass door, he saw three old ladies clustered around a bridge table. Waiting.

When they saw him looking they smiled and waved.

'You've set me up.'

'Yep.' Her grin broadened. 'You've done your ward rounds and you're cadging board and lodging from yours truly. You have to pay some way.'

He had to pay.

The thought stayed in his mind while he learned the intricacies of bridge.

It stayed while he took Lionel and Bertram for a walk in the rain and listened to Lionel tell him a long and involved joke— four times. What was that joke about Alzheimer's? You can tell the same joke every time and get a laugh. You needn't bother getting fresh whodunits from the library—because you never remember whodunit. And you can tell the same joke every time and get a laugh.

Very funny.

He checked Marigold's heart and did some adjusting of the Lanoxin, checked on Rhonda's lungs, and that was it. It wasn't exactly intense medicine.

Amy was busy during the day but it was mostly administrative stuff. Organising meals on wheels. Sorting out the myriad problems of an aging community. She was wasted in this job, he thought. Her medical skills were far too good.

It wasn't worth saying that to her.

The whole set-up was a trap, he decide bitterly, and it was

Amy who was trapped. He was here for a few days. Amy would marry her Malcolm and be here for life.

With no excitement at all.

Saturday rolled on. Joss found himself making kites with Lionel and wishing the weather would ease so he could try them out. They really were excellent kites.

He thought of what he'd be doing in Sydney now. He was a workaholic. Saturday afternoon he'd be coping with accident victim after accident victim, most of whom he never saw again after he left Theatre. The comparison with what he was doing now—keeping one old man happy by talking about kites and dogs—was almost ludicrous.

It was still medicine. He conceded that and wondered—how happy could he be in such a life?

He couldn't be happy. He needed acute medicine. He needed more doctors around him.

Iluka needed those things!

Amy didn't go home. Well, why should she? For once the nursing home was buzzing and vibrant and happy. Even with her new furniture, White-Breakers seemed dismal in comparison.

Bertram took himself for a run along the beach and came back soaked. Kitty stoked up the fire to a roaring blaze, and Bertram lay before the flames and steamed happily. Cook made marshmallows for afternoon tea and Amy helped the residents toast them in the flames. Thelma and Marie coaxed Joss into learning the basics of mah-jong.

If anyone had said a week ago that Joss could enjoy a day like this he'd have said they were nuts. Now... He put down his tiles, ate his marshmallows, watched Amy's flushed face as she held the toasting fork to the flames and thought...

His world was tilting, and he didn't know how to right it again.

He wasn't even sure that he wanted to try.

* * *

David and Daisy came by at dinnertime and firmly took Joss home with them for the evening.

'You can't impose on Amy for every meal,' his father told him and Joss waited for Amy to demur—to say she really liked having him.

But she didn't.

She'd started to grow quieter as the afternoon had progressed. He'd look up to find her watching him, and her face seemed to be strained.

'Amy...'

'I can't keep you from your parents,' she told him. 'You have a house key to White-Breakers. I'm a bit tired after last night so I'll probably be asleep when you get home.'

Damn.

And when Joss woke the next morning she was already back at the nursing home.

'Have a good day writing your conference paper,' the note on the kitchen table told him. 'I'll ring if we need you but barring accidents you should have the day to yourself.'

Humph. He didn't want the day to himself.

He couldn't stay here. He was going nuts.

He drove to the nursing home—to see his patients, Joss told himself, but it was more than that and he knew it was.

He wanted to see Amy.

Sunday. The day stretched on, interminably, and wherever Joss went, Amy wasn't. Hell, how big was this home anyway?

The rain was easing, but the wind was still high. The talk was that as soon as the wind dropped they could get a ferry running. He could be out of here by tomorrow.

He might not see Amy again.

Why was she avoiding him?

* * *

Amy was going nuts.

Everywhere she tried to go there was Joss. He was larger than life, she decided, with his gorgeous smile and infectious laughter. He had the residents in a ripple of amusement, and she'd never seen them look so happy. Every single one of them seemed to have found a reason why they should be in the big living room.

She had a few residents who kept to themselves—who hated being in a nursing home and who showed it by keeping to their rooms.

Not now. Not when Joss and his big dog and his air of sheer excitement were around. With Joss here you had to think anything was possible. Something exciting might happen.

Exciting things didn't happen to Iluka, Amy thought drearily, and tried to imagine how she could sustain this air of contentment after Joss left.

She couldn't.

Exciting things didn't happen in Iluka.

But something exciting did.

'There's a boat hit the harbour wall.'

'What?' Amy had lifted the phone on the first ring and Sergeant Packer was snapping down the line at her.

'Of all the damned fool things, Amy. A speedboat tried to come in the harbour mouth—in this wind! It's come through the heads and nearly got in but it smashed into the middle island. Tom Conner was down there, trying to fish. There's someone in the water. Can you come?'

'Joss?'

'Yeah?' He was admiring Myrtle Rutherford's knitting and quietly going stir crazy. 'Trouble?' Amy's face said there must be—and it was serious.

'Possible drowning. Can you come?'

CHAPTER EIGHT

IT WAS AS bad a situation as Joss could imagine.

The harbour entrance was formed by two lines of rock stretching out from the river mouth. In calm water boats could slip through with ease, but this wasn't a fishing port. It was a fair-weather harbour, maintained by the millionaires to house their magnificent yachts in the summer season. In winter the yachts were taken up to the calmer waters of Queensland where the élite could use them at their pleasure.

Now the harbour was empty, and with good reason. The rain had stopped but the wind was wild. Surf was breaking over the entrance. There were occasional clear gaps as waves receded but they were erratic. The rocks were jagged teeth waiting for the unwary, and what had come through...

It was certainly the unwary.

Jeff was there, and Tom Conner. The old fisherman and the policeman were identically distressed—and identically helpless.

'I've rung the Bowra coastguard,' Jeff told them. 'But it looks hopeless. We can't get a boat out there and it'll take a couple of hours to get a chopper here. If a chopper can operate in this wind...'

'Where...?' Amy was trying to see through the spray being blasted up by the wind. When she did she gasped in horror.

Right in the neck of the harbour was a tiny rocky outcrop.

It formed a natural island, forcing boats to fork either right or left. Normally it was a darned nuisance but nothing more. If the harbour had been used for commercial fishing it might have been dynamited away but because this was a fair-weather harbour built for pleasure craft only, it wasn't worth the expense to remove it.

'It almost got through.' Tom Conner was literally wringing his hands. 'I saw him come and I was yelling, "Damned fool, go back" but he didn't hear. Then a wave picked him up and threw the boat like it was a bath toy. I still thought he was going to make it but the wave surged into the island and it hit hard and the guy was thrown out. He's still there.'

He was. Horribly, he was.

The boat was a splintered mess, half in and half out of the water. Its glossy red fibreglass hull was smashed into three or four pieces and as they watched it was being sucked down into the water.

There was a body on the rocks.

'He's been thrown further up,' Tom told them, and the old man was close to weeping. 'He hasn't moved.'

The man—whoever he was—looked like a limp rag doll. He was wearing yellow waterproofs and he was sprawled like a piece of debris across the rocks. While they watched, a wave smashed across the tiny island. The water surged almost up to his neck, shifting him, and they thought he'd slip.

He didn't. He must be wedged.

'Hell.' Joss said what they were all thinking. The island was about two hundred yards out. Impossible to reach him.

'He'll drown before the chopper reaches him,' Jeff said, and he sounded as sick as they all felt. 'That is, if he's not dead already.'

'Was he the only one on board?' Joss asked, his eyes not leaving the limp figure.

'Yeah,' Tom told him. 'The boat didn't have a cabin, and

it was him doing the steering. I would have seen if there was someone else.'

Another wave crashed into the rocks and Amy's hand went to her mouth as the body shifted slightly in the wash. She felt sick. 'I can't bear this.'

'We need rope,' Joss said, and they all stared.

Jeff was the first to recover. He shook his head. 'Rope? No way. You go in that water and you're a dead man. You can't swim against that current.'

'I'm not going in that water,' Joss snapped. 'How much rope can we find? I want a rubber dinghy and I want five hundred yards of rope—or more—and as many able-bodied people as we can find. Are there any families living within calling distance on the other side?'

'There's a few farms,' Jeff told him.

'Contact them and tell them I want as many people as possible on the opposite shore. Then I want Lionel and his biggest kite.'

'Lionel's kite...' Amy stared at him, seeing where his thoughts were headed. 'But...'

'But what?' His eyes met hers, challenging her to find objections.

She was starting to see what he was thinking. 'The wind's a south-easterly,' she said slowly. 'It'd take a kite straight across the river.' Her eyes widened. 'Maybe it could carry a rope. Maybe.' Despite the drama of the situation Amy felt a twinge of pleasure. Using Lionel's kites for such a plan... The old man would be delighted.

If it worked.

'Will a kite hold that weight?' Jeff sounded as if he thought the idea was crazy, but Amy was nodding.

'I bet it will. Lionel reckons a big box kite would hold a man, and in this wind...well, maybe the wind can work for us rather than against us.'

And at least it was a plan. It was something! Better than sitting waiting helplessly for the body to slip.

Jeff needed no more telling. Like them, he was desperate for action. Any action! He was already reaching for his phone.
'Great. Let's move.'

One thing Iluka was good at was mobilising. It was a small community. Most people were indoors because of the filthy weather. Jeff made one call to Chris and in ten minutes the telephonist had organised half the population of Iluka at the river mouth with enough rope to fence a small European country. Plus there were three rubber dinghies, one enormous box kite—Lionel attached—and ten or so men and women standing on the other side of the river.

'How much weight can that kite hold?' Joss demanded, and Lionel scratched his chin and looked upward. There wasn't a trace of his dementia.

'In this wind? As much rope as you like. I reckon it could lift me.'

'That's what I'm counting on,' Joss told him, and he managed a grin. 'No, Lionel, I'm not planning to sky-ride on your kite. But I'm depending on it just the same.'

There was a delay of a few minutes while ropes were securely knotted together—a delay where all eyes were on the prone figure sprawled on the island rocks. Maybe he was already dead. Maybe this wasn't worthwhile.

But... 'I think I saw him move.' Someone had brought binoculars and Amy was focussing on the yellow waterproofs. 'I think his hand moved.' She couldn't see his face. She could see very little but a mass of yellow.

It was enough. 'Then we try,' Joss told her. He'd been deep in discussion with Lionel. Lionel had shed his years like magic and was talking to him as an equal.

Amy was still confused. 'I don't know how...'

'Just watch. Lionel and I have it under control.' He hesitated and then conceded a doubt. 'I think.'

The kite was launched. In this weather it was dead easy. Lionel and a couple of his mates simply held it to the wind and it lifted like magic, its huge trail of rope acting as if it were a piece of string. It soared skyward, a dozen men feeding the rope out. Lionel held a lighter string, as if he needed to anchor it to himself.

They needed a stronger anchor than Lionel. They'd fastened the end of the heavy rope to rocks—just in case the men couldn't hold it. In weather like this they could end up with the kite sailing on to Sydney.

'How do we get it down?' Amy asked.

But Joss and Lionel had the operation under control. The kite was over the river now, sailing past the heads of the crowd gathered on the other side. Lionel motioned to the lighter cord he was holding—a cord that on closer inspection turned out to be a loop. 'We tug hard on this and she collapses,' he said diffidently. 'Watch.'

They watched. He pulled the cord and the fastening on the kite came unclipped. The box kite soared upward—next stop Queensland—and the snake of rope and the looping cord crumpled across the river, the ends coiling downward to be seized by the people on the opposite bank.

They had a rope bridge now, with men and women on either end pulling it tight.

'With teams holding the rope over the island, I reckon I can reach him,' Joss told them. At Amy's horrified look he shook his head. 'I'm not swinging Tarzan style. I might be brave but I'm not stupid. Lionel and I worked it out. I fasten the dinghy using a slider that moves along with me. I loop a slider around my belt and I fasten the dinghy to me. The lighter cord Lionel was holding forms a loop so we can use it as a pulley, with the teams at both ends controlling as I work myself along the heavier rope. Easy. When I reach the rocks I haul whoever he is into the dinghy. I take a couple more ropes with me to make him safe on the way and Bob's your uncle.'

Amy was just plain horrified. 'And if you fall in?'

'I told you,' he said patiently. 'I'm attached to the rope and I'm attached to the dinghy. If worst comes to worst I can come back hand over hand—but if it's all the same to you I'll stay in the dinghy.'

'If it's all the same to me, you'll stay here.'

'And let him drown? I can't do that.' He stared into her appalled eyes, and something passed between them. Something.

That something was deeper than words. He put out a hand and lifted her chin, forcing her eyes to meet his. Their gazes locked for a long, long moment. Someone was looping a rope through Joss's belt but he had eyes only for Amy.

'I'll be fine.'

'You'd better be.' Her voice was choked with emotion and he thought, What the hell—if he was going to be a hero, surely he was allowed to kiss a fair maiden?

In truth he didn't feel all that brave.

But he was here. The body on the rocks was about to be swept out to sea. The average age of those around him was about seventy or maybe older—even the policeman was over sixty—so he was the youngest man there by almost thirty years.

And he knew damned well that if he didn't go then it'd be Amy who roped herself to the dinghy. She was accustomed to taking the weight of the world on her shoulders.

This time it would be him. If this was all he could do for her—then so be it.

He had no choice.

He bent and he kissed her, a swift demanding kiss that was more about grounding himself, somehow, making sense of what he was about to do.

A month ago, maybe he would have thought what he intended was madness—risking himself for someone who might even now be dead. But Amy was watching him with eyes that shone. Amy was holding him. Amy's mouth was pliant and soft under his and she knew what he was doing. She might hate it but she expected it because he knew without doubt that if he didn't go then she would.

Amy, who gave her all.

He...loved her?

Now was not the time for such crazy thinking. Now was the time to put her away from him and loop the rope at his waist around the massive rope that now swung across the river.

They were waiting for him.

'Let's go,' he said. He gently put his hands on Amy's shoulders and put her away from him. It was like a physical wrench.

As it was for Amy. She lifted her hand and touched his cheek—one fleeting touch—and then stood back.

Her life had been about hard choices and she knew more than most that Joss didn't have a choice at all.

He had to go.

There was nothing for her to do but watch.

The dinghy was fastened to the stronger cable so it couldn't be pulled off course, and they'd attached the dinghy to the looping lighter line so those on either side could pull. Joss, therefore, had only to keep his little craft stable.

It was easier said than done. The water was a maelstrom of surging surf. He lay back in the boat to give him maximum stability, his hands holding the thicker cable as he was pulled carefully, inch by inch, across the river. Each time a breaker surged he stopped and concentrated on keeping the boat upright. It was a mammoth task.

A couple of times the breakers almost submerged the boat but Joss emerged every time. He'd done his preparation well. The two teams had control of the boat as much as they could, and Joss was attached to the boat and to the cable. He had the best chance...

He just had to keep upright.

Amy's heart was in her mouth. There wasn't a word from the team on her side. Joss's father was here—he was head of the team feeding out rope after the dinghy, helping to guide it.

Daisy was in the team holding the main cable. Margy and Harry Crammond were here, and with a shock Amy recognised at least eight inmates from her nursing home.

They might be old but when there was work to be done they weren't backward in coming forward.

They were her people.

She loved them so much. She looked out to where Joss was fighting the waves and the impossibility of what she was thinking broke over her yet again. She was falling in love—no, she'd fallen in love—but her choice was bleak indeed.

No. She had no choice. Her place was here, with her people. Joss belonged to another place. Not Iluka.

He was not her man.

But...dear God, she loved him.

All Joss could think of was staying afloat. Of staying alive. But he wasn't alone.

The teams on either side were manoeuvring his boat, trying as best they could to keep it steady as they inched it toward the island. He was alone, but not alone.

They had another dinghy and he didn't need to be told that if he fell someone else would try.

Maybe Amy...

No! He had to reach the island.

Somehow he did. The dinghy reached the island just as the waves had backed off. Those holding the ropes had timed it brilliantly. He unfastened himself—even that was hard—and stepped out onto solid rock. The boat was immediately dragged away. For a moment he panicked—but only for a moment. Of course. They'd drag it away from the rocks to keep it from being punctured. Another wave broke and he had to kneel and cling to keep a foothold.

As the wave receded, he looked up. The figure was still

sprawled face down on the rocks. As Joss scrambled to reach him, he stirred and moaned.

He was alive!

Just. He'd come close to drowning, Joss guessed. His eyes were glazed and not focussing. He was barely conscious.

Joss worked fast. The guy was trying to breathe but it was shallow and laboured. Was the airway clear? Carefully he manoeuvred the injured man onto his side, conscious all the time of the damage he could do himself. It was no use making the man's breathing easier if he destabilised a fractured neck in the process.

Another wave surged but the man's head was just above the water line. Joss moved his own body to take the brunt of the wave's force. The guy muttered and groaned again.

'You're OK, mate,' he told him. 'Just relax.'

There was no response.

The man was about Joss's age, he guessed—in his early thirties, maybe? He was dressed in waterproofs but his clothes underneath were neat and almost prim. He wore a white shirt and smart casual trousers—or they had been smart. They were smart no longer.

This was no fisherman.

Of course it wasn't a fisherman. A fisherman would have known it was crazy to take a boat out on a day like today.

With Joss's body deflecting the water from his face, the man's breathing was deeper, his colour returning. Joss took a quick blood pressure and pulse reading—blood pressure ninety, heart rate a hundred and twenty.

Why the low blood pressure? Was he bleeding?

He'd groaned. He must be close to surfacing. What else?

Swiftly Joss ran his hands over his patient's body, doing a fast physical examination. There seemed little to find on his upper body. He'd copped a blow to his head—there was a haematoma already turning an angry red-purple on his forehead but it didn't look too bad. The bone structure seemed intact. If there were fractures, they were minor.

His hands moved lower. The guy's waterproof pants had been ripped and his knee was bleeding sluggishly. He lifted the leg and a gush of blood met his hand from below.

Hell.

With the man's breathing stable, this was a priority.

Joss grabbed a pressure bandage, pushed it down hard until the bleeding eased and then taped it into position, but the pool under the man's leg was bright with blood. He must have lost litres.

There was nothing he could do about it here. The waves were still surging over him. He had to get the man back into the dinghy but he was trying to assess if anything else needed urgent attention before he did.

One leg seemed shorter than the other.

Joss frowned and did a visual measurement, but it wasn't his imagination. He was sure.

The hip was either fractured or dislocated—or both. The blow to the leg must have shoved the femur out of position. Joss flinched again as he saw it.

He had to move fast. Dislocated hips were a time bomb. The muscular capsule, the lining inside the cup holding the major bone to the leg, should provide blood to the ball of the thigh joint. Disrupt that for too long and the head of the femur would begin to die. He had a couple of hours at most.

He couldn't do anything about it here. He needed help. An orthopaedic surgeon? An anaesthetist?

Amy.

He'd make do with what he could get and Amy was a darned sight better than nothing. He glanced toward the shore and he could see her. She had on a pale blue raincoat and she was staring at him through the spray…

Amy. It was enough to give a man strength to move on to the next thing.

These rocks were sharp! They were stabbing into him as he knelt.

He needed to get them both out of here.

He moved back to the guy's head. He was breathing in fast, jagged rasps. His eyes were starting to open, confusion and pain making him struggle.

Joss held him still. 'It's OK. You're fine.'

Well, sort of fine. But it seemed a good thing to say, as much to reassure himself as his patient.

And maybe it was the right thing to say. The guy's eyes opened a bit more, as if the light hurt at first, and then they widened.

'What…?'

'You've had a spot of an accident,' Joss told him. *A spot.* There was an understatement. 'Your boat hit a rock.'

'Who…?'

'I'm Joss Braden. I'm the doctor at Iluka.'

'I'm Malcolm,' the guy said. His eyes widened and Joss saw agony behind them before he passed out.

Malcolm?

Amy's Malcolm?

Maybe he'd been desperate to see his love, Joss thought, but as he looked down at the guy he knew that it didn't make sense.

He'd passed out from the pain, he thought. His breathing was easier now. It'd be his leg…

If you were measuring pain levels, dislocated thighs would take you off the scale. If he regained consciousness he'd be a basket case.

Once more he checked the guy's breathing and then he signalled to the teams to bring in the boat.

This was the hardest part of all, but it had to be done now. If Malcolm had been conscious he'd have been screaming in agony. He had to try while the guy was out of it. Waiting wasn't going to make this easier.

Swiftly he tied a rope, harness fashion, around Malcolm's

chest and shoulders, then attached it to the cable that the teams
had manoeuvred above his head. It meant if Malcolm was to
fall from the dinghy he'd be swinging head up from the cable
until somehow Joss could haul him in again. Joss flinched at
the thought of it. Maybe it wasn't satisfactory—there was an
understatement again—but it was the best he could do.

Then he had to drag the inert man into the dinghy—which
was probably the hardest thing he'd done in his life. The term
dead weight meant something, and Malcolm was just that. A
dead weight. Joss slipped a couple of times, crashing into the
rocks as he hauled Malcolm into the water. He'd hurt his own
leg, he thought grimly, feeling the warmth of his blood dripping
down his sodden leg.

But finally he had Malcolm in the bottom of the dinghy, and
he was pushing the craft away from the rocks while the guys
with the cables pulled him outward.

He was still thinking, his hectic brain in overdrive. Maybe
he could signal them to haul the dinghy to the mainland side
of the river. That side meant expert help. An ambulance ride to
Blairglen and specialist orthopaedic surgeons, who were what
this guy needed.

But on that side lay a reach of jagged rocks, both submerged
and out of the water. The men on the mainland side were having trouble holding the cable free of the rocks. He didn't like
their chances of getting the boat over them.

On the Iluka side the breakwater rose steeply out of deep
water. It was much, much safer.

So...back to his prison?

Back to Amy.

Fine. He held up his hand to signal that he was ready to go,
and they started to pull.

It was a nightmarish journey but somehow he did it. With Malcolm crumpled in the base of the dinghy Joss somehow kept
the boat stable as the men on the bank hauled him in. Often the

breakers surged over the boat. Each time he had to lean over and make sure Malcolm was still breathing. He hadn't gone to all this trouble to let him drown!

Finally the dinghy was nearing the rock face of the harbour wall. There were men clambering down the rocks. Eager hands were reaching out to hold the boat steady—old hands, but willing.

And Amy.

'Joss,' she said as she took his hand and helped haul him up onto the safety of the rocks. She held him for just a fraction of a second too long. A fraction of a second that said she'd been scared out of her wits.

He held her, too—to draw comfort and give it.

Amy. His home...

But she was already turning away to look at the man in the bottom of the dinghy. They were lifting him up the rock wall, using the dinghy as a stretcher, and her eyes widened in stunned amazement as she saw who it was.

'Malcolm?'

There was no time for questions.

'I want him back at the nursing home—fast,' Joss snapped as he helped haul the boat up the rocks. 'I need to get the hip X-rayed. What's the story with the helicopter?'

'The wind's too fierce to bring the chopper in. The forecast is for it to ease. Maybe in a couple of hours...'

'That's too long. Amy, I probably need to operate. Can you...?'

She took a deep breath.

'Of course I can.'

'Amy...' Malcolm was drifting in a pain-induced haze but as they loaded him into the back of Jeff's police van he seemed to focus. Joss had administered morphine but with that hip the pain would still be fierce.

'Malcolm.' Amy took his hand and Joss was aware of a stab

of…what? Jealousy? Surely not. He had nothing to be jealous of. This guy was Amy's fiancé. He had every right to hold her hand. Even if he had the brain of a smallish newt.

'What on earth were you doing out in the speedboat?' Amy asked.

And Joss thought, Maybe she's thinking the same thing. Brain of a newt. The thought gave him perverse satisfaction.

Malcolm was struggling to speak. 'Wanted to see…' he whispered, and closed his eyes.

'I'm here.' She stroked back the wet strands of his blond hair. The man was seriously good-looking, Joss decided—not entirely dispassionately.

He ought to be. If Amy loved him.

'Hush,' she was saying. 'Just relax. We've given you something to help the pain.'

'My leg…'

'It'll be fine. Don't try and fight it. Close your eyes and see if you can sleep.'

Malcolm seemed to think about that for a while as Jeff eased the van onto the main road. Then his eyes widened and he stirred, fighting the fog of pain and morphine and shock.

'I crashed my boat.'

'Mmm.' Amy was still holding him.

'What…what are you doing here?'

'You're in Iluka,' she told him. 'You tried to bring the boat into the harbour. Can you remember?'

He frowned in concentration. 'I wanted… I wanted to see…'

'It doesn't matter now,' Amy told him, wiping a trace of blood from his forehead. 'You've hurt your leg and we need to fix it. Just lie back and relax and we'll get you to sleep.'

Moving back into medical mode was a relief. Joss was more confused than he cared to admit. It must have been the danger of the whole thing, he decided, but he was having trouble concentrating on what needed to be done. It was a relief to pull up at the hospital.

No. It wasn't a hospital. It was a nursing home, he reminded himself, but the way it was going they'd need to apply for twenty beds of acute care. Maternity, orthopaedics, kids' ward—take your pick.

Iluka Base Hospital. It had a good ring to it.

It had a crazy ring. He was trying to think about something other than the way Malcolm's hand was gripping Amy's.

He was losing his mind!

CHAPTER NINE

ONCE BACK AT the nursing home they concentrated on medical matters—much to Joss's relief. He could function as a doctor. It was this interpersonal stuff that he couldn't handle.

It was the way he felt about Amy!

The inmates of the nursing home were back in medical mode as well, and Joss looked at his crazy medical team and saw that they were really enjoying this. The drama had lifted them all out of themselves. Maybe next week they'd go back to being senior citizens but for now they were needed and useful, and they'd never been happier. They helped Malcolm out of the police van with the same expertise as they'd unloaded Charlotte two days ago.

Marie even put a detaining hand on Joss's arm and said, 'Doctor, you're dripping blood. You come with me and I'll dress it before you start looking after anyone else.'

Bemused by the old lady's starched efficiency, he let her apply a fast dressing—enough to stop blood staining the carpet—and then he followed Amy to where she'd organised X-rays.

This place was running like a well-oiled machine and he thought, What a waste for it to turn back into a nursing home... For now, however, it was an acute-care hospital and he could treat it as such. He turned his attention to the X-rays.

Much to Joss's relief, the contusion on Malcolm's forehead

didn't match a skull fracture. The skull was fine. There was only the hip. Which was bad enough.

To Joss's huge relief there was little bone damage. The force of the impact on the rocks had punched Malcolm's femur out of the rim of the cup, but the cup itself was intact. There'd be nerve damage, Joss thought as he studied Amy's pictures. The sciatic nerve would be traumatised and that could well mean months of pain before it resettled. But for now there was only the matter of getting the femur back in place before the hip was irretrievably damaged.

'Can we organise helicopter evacuation?'

'Kitty checked while you were doing your hero stuff,' Amy told him. 'The weather reports are saying the wind's dying and the rain has cleared. The place where they've landed before is deep mud but Jeff's organising gravel to be laid now. It should be possible to bring in a machine by this evening.'

'Not until this evening?' He winced, staring at the X-ray. 'This won't wait.'

'Can you do it?'

'With your help. Are you willing to do the anaesthetic?' It wasn't fair to ask her but he must.

Her gaze was untroubled. 'Yes. It has to be easier than Charlotte. Doesn't it?'

He gave her a faint grin of reassurance. 'Yes, it does. But contact the helicopter people and tell them we do need an evacuation, even if it's late. With a hip dislocation there may well be nerve damage. He'll need specialist assessment for long-term care. But the first thing to do is get the ball back into the socket. I'll ring the orthopod at Sydney Central and run this by him, but I think he'll tell me what I'm already guessing. This can't wait until this evening. We need to do it now.'

Amy gave the relaxant anaesthetic almost without guidance. She was getting to be an expert, she thought grimly. Joss was setting himself up for the procedure ahead and, while Malcolm slipped under the anaesthetic, she had a moment to think.

What on earth was Malcolm doing here? This was so out of character for him that it was crazy.

It didn't make sense—but a moment's thought was all she had. Joss was ready.

'We'll administer suxamethonium as well,' he told her. They'd stripped off their outer gear and scrubbed, but there was time for no more. 'The muscle will have seized up as the hip wrenched out of place.'

Mary was in Theatre as well this time, so he had two trained nurses—or rather, two trained nurses under eighty, with Marie and Thelma still acting as back-up. Mary was beginning to think she'd missed out on the excitement of Charlotte and if there was any more excitement to be had she'd like a hand in it, too, please. From nurses who'd been willing for Amy to shoulder total responsibility, she and Sue-Ellen were now both actively looking for ways to help.

The hospital was seeming more and more an acute-care facility and all the staff were stepping up a notch in their expectations of themselves.

Amy could only be grateful. Her hand might be rock steady as she administered the anaesthetic, but inside she was jelly.

This was Malcolm.

Or...maybe it wasn't just that. Maybe part of it was reaction. To watching Joss haul himself up those damned rocks. To seeing the water wash over him...

'Ready?' Joss asked and she took a deep breath.

'Ready.'

In the end it was fast. Joss had done this once before as a surgical registrar, but he'd done it then under supervision. It wasn't the same as doing it alone. More than anything, he wanted a skilled orthopaedic surgeon to be present—but it was himself or no one.

What was the old adage? See one, do one, teach one? If that

was the case, he'd be ready for a teaching job tomorrow. With that wry thought he started.

The moment the muscle relaxant took hold, Joss placed his knee up on the table to give him greater leverage. Once in position he took hold of Malcolm's upper thigh. While the two nurses watched in astonishment—this wasn't like any surgery they'd ever seen—he lifted his other knee until he was kneeling completely on the table. Now he was gripping Malcolm's right leg, the lower leg at ninety degrees to the upper.

This didn't look like any operating scene you'd see in the movies, Amy thought, stunned. This was a real manipulative nightmare, where what was called for was a mixture of brute strength and skill. And courage.

'Can you lean in and push down on each side of the upper pelvis?' Joss demanded. He was breathing hard—what he was attempting took as much strength as skill, and it wasn't a job for weaklings. He needed Amy to do this. In truth, he needed another strong male, but once again Amy was the best that he had.

'Here?'

'Yes. Right. Both hands flat and push as hard as you can. Mary, take over the monitor for a moment. Right, Amy. Now!'

She pushed. Joss pulled, smoothly but sharply and with all his force.

The joint slid back with a sound somewhere between a dull pop and the clunk of two pieces of wet timber being knocked together.

The thing was done.

'Fantastic,' Joss said. He climbed off the table, found a chair and put his head between his knees. And stayed there.

Amy stitched Malcolm's leg—and then she stitched Joss.

'Because the doctor's leg really needs stitches, Amy,' Marie had started scolding the minute they came out of Theatre. 'If you don't do it,' the old nurse added, 'then I will, and my eyesight's not all that good.'

So while Mary supervised a recovering Malcolm, Amy took Joss into her office, closed the door and demanded he remove his still damp clothes. When he demurred she simply pushed him into a chair and removed his trousers for him. Plus the rest of his wet clothes. She handed him a hospital gown and barely waited for him to be respectable before she hauled off Marie's makeshift dressing over the gash on his leg.

'I'm a grown woman,' she told him. 'Plus I've been a trained nurse for years. There's nothing I haven't seen so let's get on with it. Modesty's for sissies.'

'I'm not—'

'Moving. No, you're not. If you try, I'll fetch half a dozen senior persons and we'll tie you down.'

'Amy...'

'Shut up and let me do what has to be done.'

It was a jagged tear, not so deep as to be serious but ragged enough to definitely need stitches. Joss sat on the day-bed in her office while she applied local anaesthetic, cleaned and debrided the edges and then set herself to the task of sewing him up.

It was a weird sensation, Joss decided as he sat and let her suture. It was a sensation of being completely out of control.

It was a feeling to which he was growing more and more accustomed.

'What do you reckon Malcolm was trying to do?' he asked, more to keep his mind off what she was doing than anything else. He could feel her pulling his skin together but it wasn't the feel of her stitches that was the problem. It was the feel of her, period. Her touch against his skin. The way her braid fell forward over her shoulder while she worked. The way those two little concentration lines appeared on the bridge of her nose and her tongue came out—just a peek. She was concentrating.

She was gorgeous!

Yeah, right. The lady might be gorgeous but she had a fiancé who was recovering in the next room. Her fiancé was a man who'd risked his life to see her.

Dopey git!

And Amy's words echoed his thoughts.

'It does seem a little over the top.'

He agreed entirely. 'Even Romeo wouldn't have been so daft.'

She thought about that and applied a couple more stitches. 'Romeo was pretty daft.'

That pleased him. He wasn't quite sure why, but it did. 'You mean your own personal Romeo's act of devotion doesn't meet with your unqualified approval.'

'He could have picked up the telephone and called with much less dramatic effect.'

'Where's the romance in that?'

'The rain's almost stopped and the forecast is for decent weather at last. The ferry may well be up and running by to-morrow. Surely he could have waited.'

'So you're going to be…how sympathetic?'

Amy thought about it. 'I guess I'd better be a bit sympathetic. Though if he thinks I can help with the repayments on a splintered speedboat…'

'It was his speedboat?'

'Yeah, but he only uses it on the river. I've never known him to take it out to sea. It just doesn't make sense.'

'He must be missing you enormously.'

'And that doesn't make sense at all.'

'Why not? Isn't the man in love?'

She thought about that. She looked like a sparrow, Joss thought, with her head to one side, thinking while concentrating at the same time. She was using tiny stitches—this would be the prettiest scar known to man.

He'd be able to look at it and remember Amy…

And that was truly ridiculous.

'I guess he must be,' she said, and he had to think about what he'd asked. Right. Isn't Malcolm in love?

Of course. He had to be.

But Amy was still considering. 'It's so out of character.'

'He's not prone to over-the-top declarations of passion?'

'He's sensible.'

'Well, what he did today wasn't sensible in the least.' He felt peeved, he thought, and he couldn't figure out why. She'd tied off the last stitch and had lifted a dressing from the tray. 'Leave this,' he told her. 'I'll do it.'

'I—'

'You go back to Malcolm,' he said, and if he still sounded peevish he couldn't help it. 'He needs you.'

'Nope.' She had herself back in hand. 'I'll dress this and then I'm putting you to bed.'

'Pardon?'

'You're having a sleep.'

'I am not.'

'You've risked life and limb, your leg's sore, you've got half a dozen nasty bruises that I can see, and if I peered closer I bet I'd see more.'

'You would not.' He hauled his hospital gown closer.

'And don't tell me you didn't nearly pass out in Theatre.'

'I didn't.'

'Marie, Mary and I all reckon you did. That's three against one. And we hold the ace.'

'I beg your pardon.'

She swooped and lifted the bundle of still damp clothes from where he'd dropped them. 'I'll take these to the laundry, so if you're going anywhere you go in your hospital gown. And I'd check the mirror for your view from behind before you take that option. You'd be shocked to the core! Meanwhile...'

'Meanwhile?' He sounded stunned. He *felt* stunned.

'Meanwhile, we've put Malcolm in the bedroom at the end of the hall. It's a double room with a spare bed. You take yourself down there and get between the covers. Marie's asked Cook to make you an omelette and a cup of tea and then the order is to sleep for the rest of the afternoon.'

He was eyeing her cautiously. She was one bossy woman and he was a man who didn't like to be bossed. By anybody.

But this was Amy and she was laughing at him, and he was…

Damn, she was right. He was shell-shocked. He'd thought it was just his emotions but it was more than that. He tried to stand but his legs felt distinctly odd.

Maybe he quite liked to be bossed.

Maybe the order was changing.

'You've had enough,' she said, and she moved to support him. His arm came around her and he held on.

He held on for too damned long—but neither wanted to let go.

This was crazy. She was engaged!

'I'll go,' he said at last.

'You'd better,' she whispered, and they both knew what she meant by that.

He'd better—or they weren't prepared for the consequences.

Lunch—or maybe it was dinner, it was halfway between the two—was great, but by the time he'd finished eating his head was heavy on his shoulders and he was prepared to concede that Amy knew what she was talking about.

Mary was watching over Malcolm, who lay in the bed beside him. Damn, why wasn't it Amy? It wasn't and he had to be content with Mary clearing his plate and tucking him in. Like he was a four-year-old.

'Now, you sleep,' she said sternly—and, like it or not, he slept.

When he woke it was dark and someone was in the room.

For a moment he was confused, trying to remember where he was. The room was in darkness. A nightlight was shining from under the bedhead, and he could just make out someone framed in the doorway.

A woman?

Charlotte.

What was Charlotte doing here?

He opened his mouth to speak but her whisper cut across the room. This must be what had woken him.

'Malcolm?' It was an urgent whisper and brought a whisper in response.

'Charlotte.'

Charlotte glanced at Joss but he didn't stir. As far as she was concerned, he was one of the several old men in the nursing home, settled down early for his routine bedtime.

Joss wasn't settled at all. *Charlotte knew Malcolm?*

The plot thickened…

He fixed his eyes firmly shut, told himself to ignore the itch on the end of his nose—itches only seemed to happen when you had to be still—and strained to listen.

'Are you OK?' She was shuffling forward. She'd only been out of bed a couple of times since the Caesarean and her stitches would be pulling. She moved awkwardly forward with another nervous glance toward Joss.

Joss tried an obliging snore and wuffled a bit, like he was eighty.

'No.' That was Malcolm from the next bed and Joss could hear the pain in his voice. 'I'm not OK. Hell, it hurts. I damn near killed myself. Of all the…'

'Why did you come?'

'I had to see you, of course. I wanted to make sure you didn't tell…'

'Didn't tell Amy?' Charlotte's voice broke on a sob. 'Of course. I was stupid to think you must want to see me.'

'I did.' Joss could hear him making an effort to placate her and he could imagine the man putting a hand out to touch the woman as she reached his side. They were so close…

He could just reach out and tweak the curtains…

The curtains around the beds gave an illusion of privacy. Behind them the two could imagine they were alone. As they did. Maybe Malcolm didn't know he was here, and Charlotte believed that he was asleep.

'I wanted you so much,' she was saying.

'So I came.'

'You almost killed yourself.'

'Yeah, I was a fool. But I wanted to see our daughter.'

'Not a fool. Oh, Malcolm…'

Yeah, he's a fool, Joss felt like saying, but he showed great forbearance and didn't. Sheesh, the weather was easing! The ferry could be up and running by morning. He'd needed to see his daughter, so he'd risked her being fatherless?

He'd risked Joss being lifeless!

And… *Malcolm was the baby's father?*

But something else was bothering Malcolm. 'You didn't tell Amy?' The guy was in deep pain, Joss thought, listening to his voice. He should pull back the curtain and check his obs and give him pain relief.

Not yet.

'I didn't tell Amy,' she repeated dully. 'I wanted to. That was why I came here in the first place. I was sitting outside her house, waiting for her to come home. I knew, you see. I asked at the post office and they said she knocked off at two and came home for a couple of hours. I'd come too early so I had to wait, because I wasn't brave enough to come here. Only then I went into labour and panicked and tried to drive home. And I crashed. Then…when I was here and Amy was so nice… I couldn't tell her. I tried to but I couldn't. I'd thought…if I could only get her alone, I could explain.'

'Explain what?'

'That we're in love,' Charlotte whispered. 'That I was carrying your baby. That we want to marry.'

'But we don't want to marry. We can't. Not yet.' It was an urgent demand. Charlotte must have completely forgotten that there was someone in this bed—or else she didn't care—and Malcolm surely hadn't realised.

'Of course we want to marry. You have a daughter. Surely

you want to acknowledge her. And you don't love Amy.' She was verging on hysterics.

'Charlotte, remember our plans. I'm engaged to Amy and it'd be stupid to break it off. I'm all she has.'

'But you love me.'

'I can't break off the engagement with Amy. You must see... That's why I came the way I did. I thought no one would be at the harbour mouth in this weather. I'd park the boat by the old moorings and come in when Amy wasn't around. Sunday afternoon there's always so many old folk visiting I wouldn't be noticed. I could avoid the staff and just ask one of the oldies where you were. I had to stop you from being stupid.'

'Stupid—to tell her we're in love?'

'Charlotte, no.' The intensity was too much for Malcolm, Joss thought. He could hear the desperation in the man's voice. He should get up and stop this—tell Charlotte that Malcolm was in no state for visitors.

He did no such thing. Not yet. He waited.

'It's the money,' Charlotte said flatly, and Joss heard Malcolm draw in his breath. The money. Of course. 'You still think she'll marry you and then you'll get a share of all the money she inherits. That's why you panicked and rode that damned speedboat into the rocks. You didn't trust me to be quiet. When you rang last night and I was so upset... I might have known you'd do something stupid.'

'You weren't being logical last night,' he told her wearily. 'You weren't making sense. Charlotte, this is all about our future. Our baby's future. Amy's worth a fortune and if I marry her, if I support her for the time she's trapped in Iluka... Charlotte, it'll set us up for life. Even if I only get my hands on ten per cent of what she's worth, it'll be enough. It's only at weekends. You know she can't leave Iluka. During the week we can be together, like we always have been.'

'And our baby?'

It was too much. Malcolm gave a grunt of sheer exhaustion. 'Charlotte, I can't think. Not now... Please.'

It was time for the physician to call, Joss decided. He might be riveted to this conversation but he didn't want Malcolm to collapse.

The sciatic nerve was a hell of a nerve to insult. Malcolm would be in pain for months, and Joss thought it couldn't happen to a nicer person. He took a deep breath, rose and twitched back the curtain.

They stared at him in the dim light. He must look quite a sight, he thought. Surgeon in hospital gown, having slept off the effects of coming close to drowning.

They didn't look too flash themselves. They might be as old as he was but they looked for all the world like two silly kids in trouble.

Malcolm closed his eyes—he didn't know who Joss was and his body language said that he didn't much care. Joss gave him a searching look and rang the bell. OK, the man had treated Amy like dirt but he needed morphine.

'I'll get you something to ease the pain,' he told Malcolm, and then he looked at Charlotte. Charlotte knew who he was, and he could tell by her dawning horror that she'd figured he'd heard everything that had happened.

His argument wasn't with Charlotte. She was as much a victim here as Amy was. Maybe more.

'You need to go back to bed,' he told her gently. And then, as Amy appeared at the door and looked in bewilderment from Joss to Charlotte to Malcolm and finally back to Joss, he said, 'Amy, here's Charlotte ready to go back to bed. Can you bring me ten milligrams of morphine for Malcolm? Then maybe you could go and tuck Charlotte in. She has something to tell you.'

Then, as Malcolm jerked into awareness and started to speak, he held up his hand.

'Leave it,' he told Malcolm. 'You've done enough damage

as it is. I risked my life saving you and now I'm not sure why. For now, Charlotte has a choice. She tells Amy what I've just overheard—or I do it for her.'

The helicopter arrived an hour later to collect Malcolm. It landed on a newly gravelled patch at the back of the golf course, the rain had miraculously stopped, the wind had eased back to moderate and the landing was easy.

Iluka was back in touch with civilisation.

'You can go, too,' Amy told Joss. It was a subdued Amy who'd returned from seeing Charlotte to hand him a pile of cleaned and dried clothes. She'd said nothing—just shaken her head in mute misery at his enquiry. Now she returned to his bedroom to find him fully dressed and looking down at a sleeping Malcolm. 'If you want to go back to Sydney you can go with him.'

If he wanted to go...

He gazed across the bed at Amy and he thought, Why the hell would he want to go to Sydney?

Why not?

'Um...my dog's here. I can't leave Bertram.'

'We can take care of Bertram until you have time to come back and collect him. If you like, I'll have someone drive out and collect your belongings from White-Breakers.' She glanced at her watch. 'Jeff's bringing the helicopter team here now to prepare Malcolm for the flight. They're paramedics, so you're not needed on the flight, but if you want to go...' She took a deep breath. 'If you want to go, then decide now.'

He thought about it for another two seconds. 'No.'

'No?'

'Let Charlotte take my place.'

'Charlotte wants to stay here.'

'Does she?'

'She's one mixed-up lady,' Amy whispered. 'Just like me.'

'Do you feel like kicking this louse?' he asked curiously, and she thought about it.

'No,' she said after a long time. 'For one thing, he's already kicked himself harder than I ever could. For another...' She hesitated. 'He's not so bad.'

'He two-timed you.'

'Yes, but...'

'But what?'

'But maybe I would have gone mad without him.' She looked up at Joss and her eyes were bleak. 'You think that sounds soft. Maybe it is. But four years ago, when I knew I had to come back here, I felt I was living in a nightmare. Malcolm was my friend. He coped with all the paperwork—he made it possible for this place to be built—he was here for me.'

'He was here for Charlotte as well.'

'No, that came later.' She sighed. 'Charlotte is very...honest. She's explained everything to me. She met Malcolm a couple of years back and they started a friendship—which turned into a relationship. After all, what Malcolm had with me was a weekend once a fortnight.'

'And the promise of a fortune.'

'Maybe.' She was watching Malcolm's face. He was deeply asleep, his chest rising and falling in a regular rhythm, his body sleeping off the battering shock it had received. 'Charlotte said that wasn't the only reason he wanted to keep the engagement going. Why he wanted to marry me. She said he was worried about me.'

'And you believe that?'

'Maybe I do.' She met his look, and her eyes were challenging. 'Maybe I need to.'

'Why?'

'Because he was all I had.' She swallowed. 'He was a future. A husband. Babies. A semblance of normality.'

'You're not thinking of still going through with it?' he demanded, and she shook her head.

'Of course not. Charlotte's had his baby. Regardless of what Malcolm wants, as far as I'm concerned our relationship is over.'

She tugged at the engagement ring on her third finger until it came off. Then she stood staring down at the diamond glistening in her palm. 'The helicopter's here,' she said bleakly. 'You can go. You can all go.'

'Do you love him?' Joss asked, watching her bleak face.

'I...'

'Amy?'

'Leave it,' she whispered and turned and walked out the door.

Should he go to Sydney?

Joss rang Jeff who said, yes, the chopper was here, the machine could fit four passengers and they were prepared to take him as well as Malcolm. He was bringing the van to the hospital now to collect anyone who wanted to go.

Could he be ready himself?

No.

Malcolm was as ready as he ever would be. Joss wrote up a patient history ready for handover and then walked out to the living room.

Lionel was there, cutting a vast ream of yellow fabric into kite pieces. He'd lost his favourite kite and another one had to be made pronto to take its place. Heaven forbid that there ever be spare space in the living room!

'More kites?'

'There are never enough kites,' Lionel told him, and Joss nodded in full agreement. No. There were never enough kites. He looked around at the jumble of crazy constructions that Amy put up with and he wondered how many nursing-home managers would have allowed it.

There were never enough kites.

There was never enough...joy?

'You should sell them,' Joss said, more for something to say than anything else. 'You make great kites. You could make some money from them.'

'Not here I couldn't,' Lionel said morosely. 'When I retired I thought I'd set up a little shop here and sell them to kids coming to the beach. That's a joke. Even if kids came—which they don't—the only place I could sell them now is from the nursing home. Who comes to a nursing home looking for a kite?'

'Why could you sell them from a nursing home and nowhere else?' Joss said slowly, thinking it through. Lionel was a bit confused. Was this just another example of his confusion? 'Why not out of your garage?'

But Lionel wasn't confused about this. 'There are caveats on every other damned place,' he said. 'There's one quarter-acre block zoned for commercial use for the post office and general store and that's it. The rest of the district is zoned purely residential to perpetuity and use for commercial purposes is banned. Except this place. But I can't see me sticking up "Kites for Sale" above the nursing-home sign. Can you?'

'I guess not,' Joss said, but his brain was beginning to tick over.

An idea was stirring at the back of his mind. It probably wouldn't have a hope of working. There probably wasn't a loophole.

But if he was right...well, why not?

Did she still love Malcolm? That was the last unanswered question.

The helicopter team arrived and together they organised Malcolm for the long flight to Sydney. Joss helped immobilise his leg, administered more painkiller and sedative to help him with the flight and then stood back as Malcolm said his farewell to Amy. Charlotte was nowhere to be seen.

'I'm sorry, Amy,' Malcolm told her as they lifted his stretcher into the police van. He took her hand and she submitted to his urgent grip. 'Listen, Charlotte and I...' He was speaking urgently. 'I don't...'

'You don't have to tell me that what's between us is over.'

She smiled down at him and there was the trace of affection in her voice. 'You needn't bother. I know. It *is* over.'

'Charlotte wants to stay here.'

She was deliberately misunderstanding what he was trying to say. 'That's OK. We'll look after her for you.'

The conversation wasn't going the way Malcolm had planned but his head was too fuzzy to do anything about it.

'Amy...'

'I'll give your engagement ring to your father,' she told him. 'I'd give it to you now but it may get lost. Or would you like me to give it straight to Charlotte?'

'No! Amy!'

But she was shaking her head and she even had a rueful smile on her face. 'Maybe you're right. That would be bad taste. Almost as bad taste as fathering a child while you're engaged to someone else.' She hesitated and then stooped and kissed him lightly on the forehead.

'Goodbye, Malcolm,' she said and stood back to let him go.

She was...crying?

Joss turned to find there were tears welling in Amy's eyes.

Damn the man. He was so angry he felt like following the van, stopping it and dislocating the other hip.

Had he been mistaken in telling her about Malcolm's infidelity? Or in forcing Charlotte to tell her?

He thought about it. Maybe Malcolm could have convinced Charlotte to keep quiet. Maybe Amy would still have married him, had a couple of kids, been happy with her weekend husband until her six years were done.

What else was there for her?

Anything, he thought angrily. There had to be a life for this woman—a life that she wanted rather than the one dictated by the despotic old fool, her stepfather.

He scowled at the retreating back of the police van and then looked up to find Amy watching him.

'Why didn't you go when you had the chance?' she asked. 'You could have escaped.'

Was that what he wanted? To escape? He thought about it and looked at her pale face and thought about it some more.

'I talked to Jeff,' he told her at last. 'He reckons if the rain doesn't start again they'll have a ferry lined up by tomorrow. Bertram and I can drive out of here under our own steam.'

Her face closed in pain—but he wasn't sure. Was it pain for him—or pain for Malcolm?

Maybe even she didn't know.

'Bully for you,' she said, and turned and walked into the nursing home without another word.

CHAPTER TEN

JOSS POPPED IN to check on Charlotte before he went home, and found her weeping into her pillows.

'He's just weak,' she sobbed. 'I didn't see it before. But he's a fool. Thinking I'd do something to ruin our future, dashing here in his stupid speedboat in this weather, thinking Amy wouldn't find out...' She took a deep breath. 'You know, I really did think he was doing this for Amy's sake. I thought he was committed, and it was too late for him to draw back. I was even sympathetic. But now... I just don't know any more. *And I loved that speedboat as much as he did!*'

Whew! It seemed Malcolm had blotted his copybook in more ways than one. If Malcolm wanted a long-term relationship with this lady, he had a few bridges to build, Joss decided. As it was, he'd gone from having a relationship with two women to being very close to having a relationship with neither.

Amy was looking as bleak as Charlotte.

They drove home in the dark together but there seemed little to say. There was a constraint between them that was growing worse all the time.

He should have kept his oar out of her affairs. She was looking like she'd lost her world.

What was it with the creep? What did Malcolm have that Joss didn't?

The thought brought him up sharply. For heaven's sake, was he jealous?

Jealous of a guy with two relationships?

No. He was jealous of a guy who'd had Amy's heart in the palm of his hand.

His leg hurt. All of him hurt. All of him ached, and it wasn't just physical. He ached for Amy. He ached for the impossibility of the whole damned set-up.

He ached.

Back at the house, Bertram greeted them with the joy of one who'd been abandoned for at least a month.

He needed a run.

'I'll take him to the beach,' Amy told him. 'You put yourself to bed. Your leg must hurt.'

It didn't hurt so much any more. Not if it meant not going to the beach with Amy.

This was his last night here. Tomorrow the ferry would be operating and he'd be out of here.

'I'll come.'

'Your leg...'

'My leg can drop off for all I care. I'll come.'

So they walked, slowly in deference to Joss's stitched leg. He'd have gone faster but she deliberately held back. She was wearing faded jeans and a big sloppy sweater. Some time during the day her braid had started to work free and she hadn't had time to rebraid it. She looked like part of the landscape, he thought. A sea witch. Lifting her face to the sea. Drinking it in.

She looked free.

She was anything but free.

The dog ran in crazy circles around them, the circles growing larger and larger as he revelled in this, his last night on the beach. Tomorrow Bertram would be back in his hospital apartment, Joss thought ruefully, limited to two long runs a day. After the freedom of the seashore it'd seem like a prison.

Sydney would seem like a prison.

He put a hand down and suddenly Amy's hand was in his. It was almost an unconscious gesture on his part—to take her hand—but when he'd done it, it felt good.

It felt great!

She felt like his woman.

She loved Malcolm?

'He's a rat,' he growled, and he felt rather than saw her surprise.

'I know.'

'You won't take him back.'

'No. I won't take him back.' She was speaking as if from a distance—as if speaking to herself. 'I never should have got engaged to him in the first place.'

'Why not?'

'Because I didn't love him.'

There. The thing had been said. It was out in the open, to be faced by the pair of them.

'But still you agreed to marry him,' he said cautiously and she nodded. She kicked a ball of sand before her and it shattered into a thousand grains and blew away on the wind. The weather was clearing by the moment. Joss was wearing her father's overcoat but he hardly needed it.

The moonlight was on their faces. The salt spray was gentle. It was their night.

'I just can't handle it,' she said tightly. 'I know I'm doing a great job here, I'm keeping all these people happy. Just…what about me? That was why I got engaged to Malcolm. So I could have a life—any life—apart from the nursing home.' She kicked another lump of sand but this time it didn't dislodge and she almost tripped. 'Damn,' she said, and he knew she wasn't speaking about the sand.

'Take me out to your rock,' he said on impulse, and she hesitated. 'Go on.' His hand was still in hers. 'It's my last night here.'

'It's my special place.'

'Share it with me.'

'You don't want…'

But he was propelling her forward. 'I want.'

'You'll get your feet wet.'

'Heroes don't mind wet feet,' he told her. 'Not when in pursuit of fair maidens.'

She stared at him for a long, long moment, and then, without a word, she turned and led him out across the rocks.

And when they reached it, he turned her and took her firmly into his arms.

There were so many things between them. There were so many obstacles. But for now, for this moment, they fell away as if they didn't exist.

The dangers, the pain and the confusion slipped away. Joss held Amy in his arms and once again the thought flooded his mind. This was his woman. Here was his home.

She smelled like the sea. His lips were on her hair and the sea spray was a fine mist, damp against his mouth. Her figure was a lovely curving softness against his chest. The fabric of her ancient sweater was as lovely as silk to him. He gloried in the softness against his hands as he felt the pliant contours of her body, and he felt his body surge in recognition of a longing he hardly recognised.

He'd wanted women before, he thought, wondering, but not like this.

She was his.

She had to be his. His need was so strong it was almost primeval, a surge of something as old as man itself. Here was his mate. Half of his whole. He held her tighter, savouring the moment, waiting for her face to turn up to him as he knew it must, for her lips to find his…

Waiting to claim her.

This was impossible. She was a captive in this place. She couldn't leave, and he couldn't stay.

But how could he leave her? All this time he'd been fighting against a commitment he didn't understand. He'd thought his father a fool for allowing himself to love, but love wasn't something you chose.

Love was here.

Love was now.

She was pulling back—just a little—just enough to see his face in the moonlight. What she saw seemed to satisfy her.

'Joss,' she said, and it was enough.

His mouth lowered to hers and he claimed her.

His woman.

And Amy...

This was an impossibility. This man... He had no place in her life. She was trapped here and tomorrow he'd be gone.

But tonight...

Tonight she held him close. She was twenty-eight years old, she'd been engaged to someone else for the last two years, it was six years before she could leave this place...

All of those things were as nothing on this night.

For tonight there was only Joss.

'I love you,' she whispered against his chest, so low that Joss could hardly hear against the sound of wind and waves. It didn't matter. She didn't want him to hear. It wasn't a declaration to him. It was a declaration to herself.

Tomorrow the loss and the loneliness would begin. Tonight there was Joss.

She lifted her face to his and she linked her hands behind his head and pulled him down to her.

'Joss,' she whispered, and after that she couldn't whisper a thing. For a very long time.

Afterwards, Joss could never remember how they made it to the house. Making love on the beach wasn't an option. Maybe in midsummer—but not when the sand was still soaked from two weeks of storms and the wind was still chill. No. He wanted this woman in the comfort of a bed.

Liar. If the bed wasn't on offer...

He wanted this woman any way he could have her. And he wanted her for ever.

She wasn't arguing. In that final moment as she placed her lips against his they both knew that they were surrendering themselves to each other. Completely. If this night was all they had, then so be it. Better one night than never. If this night was to last a lifetime then they'd take this night with joy.

They weren't protected. Joss had nothing and when he remembered he groaned, but Amy wasn't fussed at all.

'If you're happy to take the risk then so am I,' she murmured as they reached the bedroom door and paused. There was a brief moment of sanity to reassure Bertram—and lock him in the kitchen—and take stock of what they knew lay ahead. 'If I end up pregnant from this night I'd think it nothing but wonderful.' She smiled up at him. 'And you?'

He thought about that. *Nothing but wonderful...*

Amy carrying his child?

So much for his fear of commitment. The thought filled him with unadulterated joy.

'You're sure, my love?'

'I'm sure. I'd make a very good single mum.'

He had his own ideas about that. Single mum? Humph!

But now wasn't the time to declare his hand. Not until he was sure. If she thought she was headed for single parenthood, well and good. For now.

With a whoop of sheer loving triumph he swept her up into his arms so he was carrying her down the hall. He was laughing into her gorgeous dancing eyes and she was laughing back at him, loving him, wanting him...

'Then so be it,' he told her. 'So be it, my love. Let's see if we can make a baby. The way I feel tonight, we might even make quads!'

They were falling onto his bed, their clothes were disappearing. The moonlight was slanting across their bodies, as if in blessing...

Man and woman, becoming one.

Dawn came too soon. Or maybe it wasn't dawn. Something was ringing.

Joss stirred. Amy was cradled in his arms, her lovely hair was splayed out over his chest and she was cradled against him in love and in peace.

Who said married couples needed double beds? he thought sleepily. Single worked just fine.

'Um...it's the telephone.' Amy lifted her head. 'Why did we end up in your room when the phone's in my room?'

'The world's in the rest of the house. Here there's just us.'

Which was fine—but the telephone was ringing.

'Maybe it's urgent,' Joss said.

'I think we should forget the medical imperatives. Charles the First can give it a shot.'

Charles the First? Oh, right. The ancient doctor with dementia. 'Maybe.' But the ringing kept on. 'Maybe someone's dead.'

'There's not a lot we can do if they're dead,' she said practically. 'Call the undertaker—not us.'

'Amy...'

She sighed. 'Hey, I'm the conscientious one, not you.' She rubbed her face against his bare chest, and her hair felt like silk against his skin. The sensation was unbearably erotic. 'OK, oh, noble doctor. Go and answer the phone. I'll keep the bed warm.'

'Promise?'

She smiled down into his eyes, love and laughter fighting for supremacy. Love won. 'I promise.' But she was kissing him so deeply that he couldn't resist.

The phone stopped. Two minutes later it started again and Joss swore.

'It's nine o'clock on a Monday morning,' Amy told him, still laughing. 'The world has a right to intrude.'

'It's not nine o'clock.'

'That's what your watch says.'

'You're lying on my watch.'

'That's not all I'm lying on. Go and answer the phone.'

'Did I tell you I love you?'

She beamed. 'Yes. But tell me again if you like.'

'I love you.'

'There you go, then.' She kissed him lightly on the lips and pushed him away. 'That makes a hundred and eleven. But tell me again.'

'I love you.'

'A hundred and twelve. Go and answer the phone.'

It was Sue-Ellen from the nursing home.

'The ferry's operating. Emma's parents were the first over and they want to know if they can take their daughter home right away.'

Joss groaned. He really did need to check the child first.

'I'll be there as soon as I can,' he told her.

When he returned to his bedroom Amy was gone.

'Amy?'

'I'm in the shower.'

'You promised to keep the bed warm.'

'I lied. People do.'

He thought about that as he hauled open the bathroom door to find her under a cloud of steam.

'I don't,' he told her.

'Yeah, right.'

There was only one way to handle insubordination like that. Joss hauled the shower screen wide and swept Amy up into his arms. They stood naked as the water poured over them and he kissed her so hard she lost her breath and had to pummel him away with her fists. Breathless and laughing, she leaned back in his arms and looked up at him with love.

'If you need to see Emma before she's discharged, we need to go.'

Damnably they did.

'Joss...'

'Mmm?'

'Thank you for last night.'

'It's the first of—'

'No.' The laughter died then. 'Joss, it's not the first of anything. It's a one-off. Today you'll get into your stepmother's amazing pink Volkswagen and you'll drive onto the ferry and out of my life.'

'No.'

'Yes.' She struggled to be free and reluctantly he loosed her. Not so much as you'd notice, though. She was still linked within the circle of his arms.

'I've had a long-term engagement,' she told him. 'I don't want another.'

'But—'

'No.' She was holding him close but her voice was urgent. 'Joss, you know I can't leave here for six years. This place would die. So many people would lose so much. I can't hurt them and you wouldn't want me to.'

He thought about that. In truth, he'd been thinking of little else. Except for how wonderful this woman was.

How he needed to keep her.

'You can't stay here,' she told him.

He thought about that.

'Joss?'

'Mmm?'

'You need to return to Sydney.'

He did. Damnably, he did. There was so much to do.

'Remember me,' she told him. 'But not...not with faithfulness. I'm not waiting for you and you're not waiting for me. We're free.'

Free.

Once it had seemed the only way to be. Now, as he kissed her one last long time, it seemed a fate worse than any he could think of.

Free?

Where was the joy in that?

They made their way back to the nursing home in almost as deep a silence as the way they'd driven home the previous night.

So much had changed—and yet so little. They reached the nursing home and they were surrounded by need.

Emma's parents were waiting to see him, desperate to know her poisoning hadn't caused long-term damage. Charlotte's father had appeared, wanting to blast someone for his daughter's unhappiness, Rhonda Coutts's daughter had come to make sure her mother was being well cared for and was recovering. And more...

There must have been a longer queue on the far side of the river waiting to come to Iluka than the queue on the Iluka side waiting to get out, Joss decided. He fielded one query after another, always conscious that Amy was working close by. Amy was here.

Amy would always be here.

'Now the ferry's operating, Daisy's happy for you to take her car back to Sydney,' his father told him, and he had to raise a smile to thank her. Driving a pink Volkswagen would get him a few odd looks but those looks were the least of his problems. 'That is,' his father added, looking sideways at his son, 'if you still want to go.'

He didn't, but it was never going to get easier. Another night like last night and it'd be impossible.

His life was waiting in Sydney. Or...the chance of a new life?

'He's going.' Unnoticed, Amy had come up behind them.

She smiled at David, who'd driven in to the nursing home spe-cifically to find his son. 'He's being kicked out of his lodgings, so he must.'

That was news to Joss. 'I'm being kicked out?'

'Yes.' Her face was strained and pale but somehow she sum-moned a smile. 'It's far too crowded with two people, one dog and only ten bedrooms. Someone has to go. I drew straws and Joss is it.'

'Will you keep Bertram?' Joss demanded suddenly. He couldn't bear to think of her in that mausoleum alone. But she shook her head.

'Of course not. He's your dog.'

'I'll buy you a pup.'

'Thank you, but no.'

And into his head came a faintly remembered line. 'I want no more of you...' Where had that come from? Schoolboy Shake-speare? Wherever, it was apt.

It was time to go. He couldn't commit himself to this woman. At least...not yet.

He still had almost a week of leave left. He could stop at Bowra and then...

'You look like you're aching to get back to Sydney already,' David said, watching Joss's face. He smiled at Amy and ex-plained. 'Joss always gets this far-away look when he's making plans, and he's making plans now. What's on back in Sydney?'

'I'm not sure,' Joss said slowly. 'I won't know until I get there.'

There was one more heartbreaking moment as Joss stood in front of the little Volkswagen ready to leave. Bertram was stick-ing his head out the window and wagging his tail in anticipa-tion, waiting for Joss to say goodbye.

This was no aching farewell of two star-crossed lovers. Star-crossed lovers didn't get a look-in at Iluka, where everyone's life was everyone's business.

David and Daisy were there, plus almost every nursing-home

patient and close to every Iluka resident as well. In these few short days Joss had won Iluka's heart.

As they'd won his heart. He could see why Amy couldn't leave.

'Come back soon,' they called, and he looked at Amy's ashen face and thought not.

Not until some of those plans came to fruition.

CHAPTER ELEVEN

JOSS SPENT THE first night in Bowra. First there was a long appointment with Henry, Malcolm's father. To his relief Henry was no Malcolm. The old lawyer was intelligent and interested, and once he learned what Joss intended he couldn't do enough to help.

'God knows, that woman has suffered enough,' the old man told him. 'When I think of how my stupid son has treated her... And now there's Charlotte, of all women. I know Charlotte— she's the daughter of friends of mine. How the hell he managed to keep their relationship secret...

'By the way, you needn't worry about Charlotte,' the old man added grimly. 'I'll see to it that Malcolm marries the girl if that's what she wants. And if she decides not to—and who could blame her? Well, Malcolm will provide for her anyway. He'll do it if I personally have to cut off his inheritance to see it done.'

'I think we've had enough of inheritances,' Joss told him, and the old man agreed.

'Well, let's sit down and see what can be done about this one. This idea of yours... I never thought— It'll take courage.'

'More than courage,' Joss told him. 'But do you think it can be done?'

* * *

Then there was a meeting with Doris, the Bowra doctor, who greeted him at first with suspicion and in the end with excitement.

'If you can pull it off…'

Another person wishing him joy.

His father was working on the Iluka council members, and as Joss left Bowra and headed for Sydney he rang David on his cellphone, pulling over to the side of the road to take the call.

'Here are the figures you asked for,' his father told him. 'Hell, Joss, it looks good. It looks great.'

'And the bridge?'

'We reckon we can do it.'

Now there was only the medical side to contend with, Joss thought as he steered the Volkswagen back onto the road. And the bank.

And the government authorities.

Only.

It was a month before Joss returned. He'd hoped it would be sooner but his plans had been extensive. No half-measures would do and he wanted to be sure.

Now he was as sure as he could be. The old lawyer in Bowra was chuckling to himself in huge delight. Amy's stepfather would be turning in his grave, he decreed, and he couldn't think of a better fate for the man.

Joss's father had taken the train to Sydney and was following behind in the pink Volkswagen. Joss was driving something better.

The rebuilding of the bridge hadn't been started yet—they still needed to use the ferry—but once the work started Amy would guess what the plan was and he wanted to be the one who did the telling. He was as sure as he could be that they could pull this thing off. It was time she was told.

So Joss put his brand-new Range Rover—with a strange new sign on the driver's door—on the ferry, and then drove it around the cliffs where he'd crashed a month before and pulled up outside the Iluka nursing home. Bertram was out of the car the moment he opened the door, flying in to find all the friends he'd made on their last visit.

Joss followed.

Amy was in her office. She heard the twittering from the living room, she heard the mah-jong set clatter as it hit the floor, and then the big red dog burst into her office. He came bounding up to greet her, his paws landed on her shoulders and she darned near fell over.

Bertram!

David will have brought him back from Sydney, she told herself, fighting down the sudden surge of stupid hope. David and Daisy had told her they were going to Sydney to collect the Volkswagen. What could be more sensible than them bringing the dog back home for a visit?

Joss wouldn't be here.

She glanced out the window to see a gleaming new Range Rover parked at the entrance. It had a sign on the door. ILUKA HEALTH RESORT.

It didn't make sense.

But before she could fully take it in, Joss was standing in the doorway. He had an absurd expression of hope on his face, like he was Bertram and he wasn't sure whether he'd be kicked or hugged.

'Joss…'

Her voice faltered. She'd made such resolutions. He'd come back to visit his father occasionally, she'd told herself, and she had to greet him as a friend. Nothing more.

But he was still looking at her, his expression was just the same and it was too much. She was across the room and hugging him, kissing and being kissed, welcoming him with all the love in her heart. 'Oh, Joss.'

'Amy.' He was beaming and beaming, putting her away from him so he could take her all in. 'You haven't changed a bit.'

'You've only been away for a month.'

'I thought you might be pregnant.' There was a gasp behind them and Joss's beam widened. 'Hi, Kitty.'

'H-Hi.' The secretary rose on feet that were decidedly unsteady. She was choking on laughter. 'Pregnant, huh?'

'I am not,' Amy told him indignantly. 'After one night—what do you think you are?'

'You reckon it'll take more than a night? What a good thing I'm back.'

'Joss...'

'I'll leave you to it, shall I?' Kitty managed, and sidled out of the door. She very carefully didn't close the door behind her.

'Amy.' Joss kissed her again and from outside the door there was a collective sigh. Iluka's residents *en masse*.

'Um...' Somehow she pushed him away.

'Um?' He was smiling down at her, with the smile that had the capacity to make her heart do handsprings all on its own. 'Is that all you can think of to say?'

But she was recovering, just. Friends. She had to greet him as a friend. What she was feeling was the way of insanity.

'Joss, I can't...'

'You can't what?'

'Love you.' There. The thing was said. She waited for him to take it on board and step back.

He did no such thing.

'You can't love me?'

'No.'

'But the future I've planned is founded on just that.'

'What?'

'The fact that you love me.' He looked deeply concerned. 'Are you sure you can't? If you try very hard?'

'Joss...' She was torn between tears and laughter. It was so good to see him again. It was wonderful.

'Maybe you can just pretend,' he told her. 'You see, I don't think I can stay here as Medical Director of Iluka Health Services if I don't have a wife to support me. A man of such importance needs a wife.' He was grinning at her like a fool. 'All those opening ceremonies, all that ribbon-cutting—a man needs a wife, if only to hold his handbag.'

'You,' she said slowly, 'are being ridiculous.'

'Nope. I'm proposing.' He delved into a back pocket and produced a tiny crimson box. He flipped the lid and there lay the most beautiful ring she'd ever seen. A band of gold held a magnificent central diamond, twinkling and sparkling in the morning sun coming in from the window by the sea, and a host of tiny sapphires surrounding it.

'Oh, Joss.' It took her breath away.

'Do you like it?'

'It's...it's beautiful,' she told him, and he grinned.

'Yep. And it's bigger than Malcolm's.'

She looked up at him then and gasped in indignation. 'Of all the—'

'Wonderful men?'

'Conceited, arrogant—'

'Wonderful men,' he repeated, and lifted the ring from the box. 'Can I put it on your finger?'

But she hung back. 'Joss, you must see that I can't.'

'No.' His smile faded and he took her arms in his and held them. His eyes were on hers, and what was in his eyes made her catch her breath. Love and care and trust.

Love...

'Amy, I've organised us a life. If you'll listen.'

She thought about it. She'd give him the benefit of the doubt, she thought. She'd indulge herself as well as him. Pretend for a few short minutes that they had a future.

But Joss had released her. He crossed to the door and flipped it open and there were no fewer than fifteen faces and one dog crammed into the doorway. Grinning, he took a folder from his father and closed the door—but not completely. The fifteen noses would have been squashed. Then he marched over to the desk.

'This,' he said, unfolding a huge blueprint onto a desk, 'is the plan for our future.'

Amy stared at him. Then she stared at the plan.

And gasped.

It was a map of the bluff—the tract of land that held the nursing home. The nursing home took up about five per cent of the available land. But now...

The plan included the nursing home but much more. There was a hospital, about twice the size of the nursing home. There were a score of houses dotting a park-like setting and overlooking the sea. There was a row of shops—more than a dozen with places earmarked for more—plans for a cinema, an indoor heated pool, a remedial health centre, doctors' surgeries. A hotel named 'Iluka Coastal Life'. There was even a school! A school labelled 'Educational Facility for Children of Resort Staff'.

'What is this?' she gasped, and he beamed.

'The whole thing's the Iluka Health Resort,' he told her. 'What else?'

'I don't...'

'You don't understand?' He lifted the plans and folded them away, then took her firmly in his arms again. 'Amy, your stepfather put caveats on all this land—except the bluff. The caveat on the bluff simply says that it's to be used as a nursing home. But he specifically states that the nursing home is to be built as a resort. Now, my lawyer and I...'

'Your lawyer?'

'Henry,' he told him. 'Malcolm's father. We spent a bit of time looking at resorts on the internet, and nearly every resort we found had shops. And swimming pools. And lots of commercial extras. The big ones even had medical facilities.

We looked a bit further and we found resorts like this one will be. A health resort with an acute-care hospital and all the ancillary things. Pharmacies, physiotherapists...you name it, we can have it here. Your stepfather left enough money to build the nursing home itself, but as it is it's not a real resort. So we approached the bank.'

'You approached the bank.' Amy was almost speechless.

Joss beamed. 'Yep. I even wore a tie, and Henry came, too. They were really nice to us. Especially when Henry outlined the financial foundations this place is built on. You have a mansion worth millions and a great nursing home and incredibly valuable land—and you own the lot.'

'But—'

He was brooking no interruptions. 'You know, in six years you stand to be an obscenely wealthy woman. This place is worth a fortune, and it'll be worth much, much more if you develop it. And with what's here already—the climate, the place—Iluka is the best place in the world to recuperate in. We'll attract clientele from around the globe.'

'But I can't afford—'

'Yes, you can,' he told her. He was holding her then, cradling her in his arms and enjoying her confusion. Or enjoying just holding her. Life had been cruel to this woman for far too long. This was his gift.

As Amy was his own sweet gift.

'We've done our homework and the bank sees this as a really viable investment,' he told her. 'It won't all be done at once, but as every stage works out we'll go on to the next. We have provision for a wonderful little town, whose main industry will be a state-of-the-art health resort. Its centre will be the hospital. This place is a gold mine, and the finance people agree. The bank will do very nicely out of it.'

'I don't understand.' She was so confused she was almost speechless, and his enjoyment grew. This felt...wonderful!

'We'll attract medical people from everywhere,' he told her.

'In fact, we already have. This district is screaming for decent medical facilities. When the council builds a new four-lane floodproof bridge and improves the road to match...'

'A bridge?'

'The council's agreed to build a bridge, and they've already negotiated government assistance. They see—like me—that this is a goer. And it is! Amy, I've already sounded out four doctors who have been aching to find somewhere like this to settle. So far there's two physicians, an anaesthetist, a gynaecologist—and me. We have everyone behind us. The government authorities are more than eager to have a major medical centre established in this area but until now they haven't had anywhere that would attract doctors. Doris in Bowra is so overworked she's near to collapse and she almost fell on my neck when I ran this plan past her. So...' He smiled and held her back at arm's length. 'How does that sound? For a beginning?'

'I...' She stopped, unable to go on. 'It sounds unbelievable.'

'It's not.' Joss's eyes were lit with excitement, aching to share his wonderful dreams with her. 'It's entirely believable. And workable. As part of the resort we'll build smaller cottages to house all the new workers, plus specialist houses for people like Marigold and Lionel who need help but want to stay in their own homes. We'll build a huge workshop for activities—we've even designed a shop-front for it so that Lionel can sell his kites and all those matinée jackets can find a home. Anything that's part of the resort can be as commercial as we like. By the way, the place will be big enough to need part-timers—volunteers—so people like Marie and Thelma will be able to do as much or as little as they like. Oh, and Malcolm...'

'Malcolm?' Amy was no longer breathing. She didn't need to. Who needed to breathe with this joy?

'I've spent some time with Malcolm in Sydney,' he told her. 'He's recovering but he's one very sorry boy.'

'As he should be.'

'Charlotte's been to see him, too, and laid his future on the line. If he wants to marry her then he comes to live here because Iluka's full of people who care. That's what she said. And he's desperately worried about how you'll take it, but…'

'But?'

'Well, the man is a decent accountant, even if he is a dope where relationships and boats are concerned. In fact,' Joss said grudgingly, 'despite his dopiness where boats are concerned, he's really quite clever. He worked out all the financial stuff. We do need a competent accountant, and he's incredibly excited about the project. So if you think you can bear seeing him again…'

'Why could I not bear to see him?' She was breathing again, but the joy within was threatening to overwhelm her. 'Why on earth not?'

'He betrayed you.'

'He betrayed Charlotte and she loves him. If she can forgive him, who am I to be judgemental?'

'You don't still love him—just a little bit?' He was looking anxious. That was crazy, Amy thought jubilantly. Crazy.

'How on earth can I love Malcolm—when I love you?'

'You love me?'

'I'd better,' she said. 'If you're going to be Medical Director and cut ribbons then I don't see that I've got a choice but to stick around.'

'You're going to be Director-In-Chief, and you can cut ribbons, too.'

'I thought I got to hold the handbags.'

'I'll leave my handbag at home,' he said magnanimously. 'If that's what it takes.'

'Gee, thanks.'

'But it could work.' He was still anxious, she thought. He was gazing at her with all the hope in the world. Like Bertram asking for someone to give him a ball.

No.

Not like Bertram.

Like Joss, asking her to give him a future.

She closed her eyes, and when she opened them he was still looking at her with hope.

'Amy?'

'Mmm?'

'Will you marry me?'

There was a long indrawn collection of breath and Amy glanced toward the doorway. How many heads could fit around one door?

'Can I have a puppy?' she asked.

'Ten.'

'Can I have a baby?'

'Ten.'

And she was laughing, joy and love and wonder all struggling for supremacy.

Love won. It always did.

'Of course I'll marry you,' she told him as he gathered her into his arms and held her close. 'Of course I'll marry you. Oh, my love... Now and for ever.'

The entire population of the Iluka nursing home broke into applause—and Amy and Joss didn't even notice.

Iluka was as it should be.

Almost as soon as the new bridge was built people started drifting toward Iluka. There were things going on here. Jobs were being advertised. Construction was starting on the new hospital.

People came and saw and fell in love.

The day had been sun-soaked and beautiful. Families were packing up on the beaches. The ice-cream van had closed for the day. There were elderly couples walking on the beach, catching the last of the sun's rays.

It was the end of another glorious day in paradise, as a cluster of Iluka's long-term residents stood on the sand to watch Joss Braden and Amy Freye exchange their vows.

'Come prepared for wet feet,' the wedding invitation had

stated, because Joss and Amy knew where they wanted to be married. So this motley assortment of wedding guests hoisted their skirts and rolled up their trousers. Their bare toes were soaking in the shallows.

Amy and Joss stood on their rock above the waves, and the last of the sun fell on their faces as they faced each other with love. And certainty.

And joy.

'Do you take this woman…?'

'I do.'

'And you, Amy. Do you take this man…?'

'I do.'

There was such love here. Who could not wish this couple all the joy in the world?

In the last few months they'd transformed Iluka into the paradise it had always promised to be. There were a few disgruntled millionaires, but even they had been known to wander down when no one was watching and buy an ice cream from Mr Whippy. Their children played with Lionel's kites on the beach.

One of Lionel's kites was flying now.

No. Not one. Two of Lionel's kites. Huge box kites, being manoeuvred by children on the beach. They must have been primed by Lionel, because Lionel himself was knee deep in water, holding hands with Marigold, and beaming and beaming.

Everyone was there.

Daisy and David. Charlotte and Malcolm and tiny Ilona—Charlotte holding tight to Malcolm with a proprietorial air that said Malcolm had better not put another foot wrong if he knew what was good for him.

The look on his face said he knew very well what was good for him and he'd found it right here.

Bertram was here, though he wasn't venturing out into the water. He had enough to contend with—a brand-new springer spaniel puppy was trying to chase his tail and the dogs were spinning in circles of delight in the sand.

Who else? So many. Mary, Sue-Ellen, Marie, Thelma, old Robbie who'd been installed as head gardener—all the people they loved were here. It was just perfect.

The ceremony was over.

'I now pronounce you man and wife.' The celebrant beamed as Joss lifted Amy into his arms and kissed her.

'My wife,' he whispered. 'My love.' The whole world seemed to hold its breath as their kiss sealed their vows.

Above their heads the kites intertwined—only now there were three. Three box kites spun against the sunset, each painted crimson with huge white lettering. They'd been painted in an act of love from all the residents of Iluka Nursing Home.

One spelled Joss.

The second spelled Amy.

The final kite spelled FOR EVER.

* * * * *

The Surgeon's Second Chance

Meredith Webber

Dear Reader,

Although I usually use fictitious places in my books, I always have some definite town or city in mind as I write. Then all I have to do is give the place a different name. Summerland in this story is my home city of the Gold Coast, a beach resort in south-east Queensland, which attracts visitors from around the world. But it is the Gold Coast of about twenty-five years ago, when the city was a string of small beachside suburbs, with new development pushing west toward the mountains. Surfers Paradise was *the* place to visit, and tourists flocked there.

Using a place where I've lived for nearly thirty years as the setting for my story made it easy to write, while the characters, Harry and Stephanie, seemed like people I've always known.

I hope you enjoy getting to know them and, although you won't get much of an idea of the fabulous Gold Coast from the setting of this book, why don't you come visit it sometime?

Meredith Webber

CHAPTER ONE

WITH AN UMBRELLA that was proving useless against the deluge from the heavens, Harry picked his way through the mud, slush and landscaping debris in front of the new hospital building, finally skidding to a halt in the sheltered entrance.

The wide glass doors slid efficiently open, and he entered the foyer, stepping carefully on mats spread over the thick plastic protecting the new carpet. Plastic pathways led in various directions, but he'd been told where to go and took the one leading to the left, which fetched up at a door marked CHIEF ADMINISTRATOR'S OFFICE.

The man who bade him enter wasn't the new chief administrator but the real power behind the hospital—the man who'd built and owned it, Bob Quayle.

'Harry! Good to see you, my boy!'

Bob, smooth, sleek and silver-haired, rose from behind the desk, and came around it, hand outstretched, to shake Harry's, then throw a friendly arm around his shoulders.

'So, you've finally returned to the best country in the world, and rumour has it you'll soon be the most sought-after plastic surgeon in Queensland.'

'I don't know where you heard that rumour, Bob.' Harry deflected the praise with ease. 'Starting up a practice takes time. I have to meet and gain the confidence of the local GPs for referrals, and to do whatever public hospital work I can get, so my name becomes known in the local profession.'

'Ah, but once people know you've exclusive rights to practise in the newest, most up-to-date private hospital in the whole south-east region, you'll have referrals flocking in,' Bob assured him. 'Summerland's become more than a holiday destination these days, it's one of the fastest-growing cities in the state. And with more and more wealthy people retiring to the new secured estates along the ocean front, you'll have a continual flow of potential customers.'

Harry thought of explaining, again, to Bob that elective cosmetic surgery was only a very small part of his work, but, knowing the older man wouldn't listen, he swallowed the protest.

'The thing is,' Bob continued, 'as you saw when you came in, the rain has set us back a few weeks.'

He hesitated, then said, 'It will be a month before anyone can start work in the new specialists' suites, and probably some weeks after that before the hospital becomes fully operational.'

Harry wasn't surprised by this news. He'd guessed it was why Bob had asked to see him.

'That's OK with me,' he assured the older man. 'I've only been back in the country a couple of days and I need to find a flat, unpack, then organise furniture, equipment and staff for the rooms. A month's delay won't bother me at all.'

'Well, maybe I can help you with the flat,' Bob said expansively. 'I've a couple of apartments I keep for visiting friends and relations—all furnished, of course. Why don't you take one of them for, say, three months? That'd give you time to get to know the place a bit better and decide where you might eventually like to live.'

Harry studied his benefactor. Although he didn't know Bob Quayle the businessman all that well, instinct told him this man didn't give much away.

But accepting the offer would save him looking for a place—

and finding furniture—and he couldn't think of any really impossible strings Bob might attach to the offer.

'Sounds good. I'd be happy to pay rent,' he said, but Bob waved his offer away.

'Nonsense! I think of you as family—you know that!' he said, his voice suddenly gruff.

Does he? Harry wondered, thinking of the man's real family—his son, Martin, who'd been one of Harry's two best friends at university. He and Martin and Steph—a tightly bound threesome from the time they'd met in a lecture theatre on the first day of their medical course, when their surnames had linked them into a study group...

'Besides, you could do me a favour at the same time.'

Bob paused and looked directly at Harry.

'One good turn deserves another and all that. I don't mean the flat, that's nothing, but the bed you negotiated as part of your tenancy at the hospital. I'm still not sure how you talked me into that.'

Harry shifted uneasily. When he'd first asked Bob about the possibility of the free use of a theatre and an occasional free bed in the new hospital, Bob had seen the potential of the good publicity special charity cases could generate, but it had still been a struggle to convince him it was worth agreeing.

Was this payback time?

'The apartment I have in mind for you is on the twelfth floor of Dolphin Towers,' Bob continued smoothly—certain he'd got his message across. 'It's one of the first buildings I built in Summerland, on the main road in the centre of the tourist strip. There are shops and offices on the first three levels, and a twenty-four-hour medical clinic, catering mainly to tourists, on the ground floor.'

He paused and his keen grey eyes studied Harry for a minute.

'It's the clinic where you could do me a favour. It ran into a bit of financial trouble recently, and I ended up buying out the owner. My accountants assure me it should be a viable concern, but though they're clued-up about hospitals now, they know nothing about how medical practices run. I wondered, as you'll be without rooms to practise from for a month, if you'd mind taking a look at the clinic for me. Maybe spend a couple of days there so you get a feel for the place and see how it works—staff rosters, patient flow-through, things like that. I'd pay you, of course, and throw in the apartment.'

Ah! Harry thought as the words confirmed his instinct that Bob Quayle gave little away.

But with a furnished flat provided while he settled into the holiday city, he *would* have time on his hands...

'I'd like to help out, Bob,' he said, 'but it's years since I've done any general practice, and—'

'But I don't want you doing medical work,' Bob broke in before Harry had properly organised his thoughts. 'Just take a look at how it's operating. There's a part-time office manager you can talk to, and a desk in her office you could use. You're a clever man, you can't deny that. And you did work shifts in twenty-four-hour clinics when you first graduated and were saving money to go overseas. You should be able to see where things are going wrong. Discreetly, of course. It's not public knowledge I'm the new owner, and I'd like to keep it that way. Especially with the staff.'

Harry ran the conversation over in his head, and though a niggling feeling of suspicion lingered deep in his subconscious—maybe because Martin had always talked about his father's devious streak—he could see no harm in granting the older man's wish.

'I guess I can take a look at things,' he said, 'though I can't promise you I'll find anything. Have you any ideas about its future yourself? Do you want to get into running medical practices as a sideline to private hospitals?'

Bob shook his head.

'To tell you the truth, it's a complication I don't need. But it's hard to lay off staff these days, with all the problems of workplace agreements and contracts. I guess if I can prove it's not viable, it would give me a reason to close it.'

Harry nodded. That sounded much more like the canny—probably greedy—businessman he guessed Bob to be. The space could probably be used for something that would bring Bob in a lot more money.

They talked a little longer—about the past, Harry's friendship with Martin, and about Doreen, Bob's wife, who'd suffered ill health since Martin's death. Then Bob gave him the phone number of his business manager, who would show Harry the apartment and the clinic, and generally help him get settled in.

As Harry squelched back through the mire at the front of the hospital, he wondered about the people who hadn't been mentioned in the conversation—about Steph and her daughter, Fanny.

Martin's daughter Fanny.

Stephanie Prince tucked her daughter into bed, and bent to kiss her on the forehead.

'Tell me the story of Daddy falling off the horse when you all went out to Uncle Harry's farm,' Fanny demanded.

Steph smiled at the little girl, and gently touched her cheek. Was it because Fanny had never known her father that stories of his deeds and exploits were far more interesting to her than fairy-tales?

'It was a long time ago,' she began, 'not long after Daddy, Uncle Harry and I first met.'

She'd told it so often the words came out automatically, while in her head she was remembering those days. She, Harry and Martin—brought together by the accident of surnames—Prince, Pritchard and Quayle. But against all odds, Martin, the spoilt darling of a wealthy family, she herself, the girl from the wrong side of the tracks, and Harry, who claimed he came from so far west there were no tracks, had become friends, and then an inseparable threesome.

In the later years of their medical course, clinical rotations had often separated them for months, and during their intern year they'd seen even less of each other. But the bond had always been there.

Until—

She shook off the shadows of the past, and concentrated on the story.

'So Daddy's sitting on this horse, and pretending he knows all about riding, when Uncle Harry flicked his fingers to his dog, and the dog barked right behind the horse's hooves. The horse reared up and Daddy, who'd got such a fright he'd let go of the reins, slid off the saddle and right back down over the horse's rump and tail and, bump, landed on his backside on the ground.'

Fanny, who at four thought backsides irrepressibly funny, laughed and laughed, and Steph, who'd been finding life far from funny lately, felt her heart swell with love for this darling daughter who was all that remained to her of that other, carefree, happy existence.

Except her surname, of course, which she'd determinedly kept for professional reasons back when she'd married Martin, and since his death had used solely for personal reasons...

'Now, off to sleep, Fanny mine,' she said, smoothing back the blonde curls from the small, flushed face. 'I'll see you in the morning.'

Fanny gave her a final hug, then, clutching the ragged bear who was her favoured bed-mate at the moment, turned over and closed her eyes.

She *is* secure, Stephanie reassured herself as she left the room. An insecure child wouldn't go off to sleep so happily.

But worry had been her constant companion lately, so the reassurance didn't do much to banish her guilt that in another hour she'd leave her sleeping child and go to work.

'You would hear her if she woke in the night, wouldn't you?' she asked, directing her question at the young girl who sat, head bowed over a book, in her living room.

Tracy looked up and grinned at her.

'Do you know, you ask me that every night?' she teased. 'And every night I tell you I would hear her. In fact, a week or so ago, she lost Adeline—you know, that incredibly ugly doll those grandparents gave her—out of bed and yelled for me to come and find her. She went straight back to sleep afterwards.'

Steph nodded, knowing Tracy was telling the truth but finding little comfort.

'Look,' Tracy said, with all the confidence of eighteen years, 'your mother was a single parent and you turned out all right.'

'But my mother didn't go out to work. She worked from home. I should have been something I could do from home.'

Tracy sighed and Steph recovered a remnant of her sense of humour.

'I know,' she said, 'I'm obsessing. I'm sorry. Especially as it makes it seem as if I don't trust you.'

She reached over the back of the couch and gave her cousin a warm hug.

'You're the best thing that could possibly have happened to Fanny and me,' she said. 'I think it's just that I've worried for so long that now things seem to be working out, I keep waiting for something bad to happen.'

The foreboding hovered on the fringe of her conscious mind as she prepared for work, showering then shaking her super-short hair into place and pulling on jeans and a T-shirt, comfortable garb to wear under a white coat.

A final peep at Fanny, sound asleep, then she was off.

'See you in the morning,' she called to Tracy as she opened the back door, looked out at the flooding rain and sighed. Even with an umbrella, she'd be soaked by the time she reached the car. And then the aging vehicle, which hated wet weather, would probably refuse to start.

'One day!' she muttered to herself, looking up at the heavens where the planets ruling her life were surely permanently misaligned. 'One day my luck has to change!'

It did, in so far as the car started the first time, but when she reached the underground car park, the parking spaces designated for clinic staff were all full and she had to drive down into the bowels of the earth to find a vacant spot.

'You're late!' Rebecca, the clinic receptionist on night duty greeted her, and Steph glanced automatically at her watch.

Rebecca laughed.

'Honestly, Steph, you fall for that every time. But you are five minutes past your usual arrival time—only ten minutes early instead of fifteen.'

'Someone's pinched the parking spaces again,' Stephanie told her. 'I wish the guy who's supposed to clamp illegally parked cars would just once clamp the cars in those spaces.'

'Well, one's mine,' Rebecca said, 'and Peter's still here so his car is probably there, and Joanne's, and maybe the new bloke. That'd make four.'

'The new bloke? What new bloke? Don't tell me we're getting a second doctor for midweek night duty? Miracles do happen!'

'Yeah?' Rebecca's tone echoed her disbelief. 'I don't know that he's a doctor, just that Muriel left a message saying some new bloke's coming to check out the place. Succinct and informative as ever, our Muriel.'

Stephanie chuckled. She'd never met Muriel, the late-shift day receptionist at the clinic, but was aware she and Rebecca had a running battle over messages, charts, information-sharing and probably the number of spoons in the tearoom.

'But if he was here, you'd have seen him,' she pointed out.

Rebecca shrugged.

'Not necessarily. He could be hiding in the administrator's room. No one's been in there at night since the clinic changed hands—and Flo's only been working part time for months.'

Steph nodded. Flo had been the full-time office manager, and had often worked in the evenings so she could keep an eye on things on the night shift, but her hours had been drastically reduced since the new owners had taken over.

'We could sneak the door open and have a look,' Steph suggested, but at that moment the front door opened and three young Japanese—two women and a man—came in, brushing rain off their jackets and looking around for somewhere to put their umbrellas.

Rebecca hurried out from behind the desk, showing them the makeshift holder she'd fashioned from a waste-paper basket.

Speaking in fluent, if Aussie-accented Japanese, she welcomed them and led them across to the desk. Were they all ill, or only one?

She pushed a form, printed in Japanese as well as English, across the desk, and the young man began to fill it in, at the same time explaining he was a tour guide and it was one of the women who was ill.

Rebecca introduced Stephanie, who led the sick young woman to a consulting room. As the area attracted predominantly Japanese tourists, all the staff in the clinic spoke at least a smattering of the language. Her own command of it was proficient, although medical terms defeated her.

Tonight, however, the tour guide, who'd followed the patient into the consulting room, could speak English, and it was he who explained that the holiday maker had a sore throat.

Stephanie began her examination by taking the young woman's pulse, feeling the fast beat and heated skin immediately. Explaining each move in Japanese while she worked, she then took her blood pressure—higher than it should have been for a young woman—and finally examined her throat.

The tonsils and pharynx were an angry red, with whitish blotches on the tonsils.

'We call it in English a strep throat,' Stephanie explained. 'A streptococcal infection. I can give you an injection of penicillin to start fighting it, then follow up with tablets to take. Have you had penicillin before?'

The young woman nodded.

'Did you have any allergic reaction?'

A definitive shake of her head.

'Have you any other allergies you know of?'

Again the head shake.

Stephanie rang for Joanne, the nurse on night duty, and, when she came, told her what she needed. As Joanne departed, Stephanie turned her attention back to her patient, concerned that the young woman, who was now shaking with feverish chills, would have to go back out into the inclement weather.

And possibly continue a gruelling 'holiday' schedule.

'Where are you staying?' she asked.

'Just down the road at the Whale Beach Resort,' the guide replied.

It *was* just down the road—perhaps only five hundred metres—but in the rain...

'I think you should get a taxi back there,' she told the man, speaking Japanese so the patient would also understand. 'And—' She checked the completed patient form '... Reiki should spend at least tomorrow in bed.'

'But tomorrow we go to see the dolphins!' It was Reiki who protested, and Stephanie knew it was useless to argue. The young woman had probably been feeling sick for days, but was soldiering on because she'd paid good money for her holiday and wanted to make the most of it.

However, the doctor in Stephanie had to make the effort.

'You should stay in bed,' she repeated. 'If you don't, you could become even sicker.'

Reiki's obsidian-dark eyes filled with tears, as if the thought of feeling worse was truly horrifying.

Maybe she'd listen to the advice.

Joanne returned and, after asking the guide to leave the room, Stephanie gave the intra-muscular injection of benzathine penicillin G into Reiki's buttock.

'Stay in bed,' she warned again, as she showed the young woman out.

'Bet she doesn't,' Rebecca said, when the three had departed.

But more patients had drifted in so, although Stephanie agreed, she didn't have time to chat.

Jet lag struck at midnight, but for a couple of hours Harry refused to give in to it.

'Damn it all, I took my melatonin, I was flying west to east. This isn't supposed to happen!'

He was striding back and forth in front of the wide windows of the apartment so kindly loaned to him by Bob Quayle. Outside, the rain still lashed down, blurring the streetlights and hiding from view the ocean he knew was only a block from where he stood.

'Maybe it doesn't happen when you're flying east-west, not west-east!' he muttered as he made his way to the kitchen and opened the refrigerator door, bending over to eye the edibles Pete Jennings, Bob's business manager, had organised for him.

No, it wasn't food he needed, but sleep.

He strode back to the living room and slumped into an armchair, wondering if it might be more conducive to sleep than the bed.

But nothing worked, except his brain, which was alive and alert and looking for some action.

Action!

Ha! Maybe that was the answer.

In return for the largesse of the apartment, he'd told Bob he'd take a look at the twenty-four-hour clinic somewhere downstairs in this very building. Twenty-four hours meant open all the time. It should be open and operating right now.

He leapt out of the chair, strode through to the bedroom, pulled on trousers and a long-sleeved shirt that could have done with an iron, but at two in the morning he didn't care, and headed down to ground level to find the ailing medical centre.

Steph was battling with Tom Butler, a regular patient with a bipolar condition. She'd seen Tom a few times when he was in his depressive phase of the illness—feeling suicidal and needing someone to assure him he was wanted on the earth—but tonight he was the opposite, flying high, not on drugs but on the curious chemical imbalance in his system that caused his mood swings.

'So I thought I'd come and show you how well I am,' he said, grabbing Steph and swinging her off the ground, then dancing around the waiting room with her in his arms.

'Put me down!' she shrieked, while Rebecca pressed the hidden alarm bell to summon a security man—just in case.

Steph heard the asthmatic wheeze the doors made as they opened, and tried to see if help—in the form of the security man—had arrived, but it wasn't until Tom completed his arc that she saw the newcomer. Tall and angular, his midnight-dark hair tousled and untidy, his so-familiar face a study in disbelief.

'Harry?'

Harry heard his name, and stared in total bewilderment at the woman dangling in the arms of a dancing maniac. The beautiful dark red hair was cut so close to her head she might have been shorn, while her face was too thin—all flat planes and angles and huge, huge eyes—but it was still Steph.

'Steph?'

He heard his voice say her name—heard the incredulous shock in it.

'Put me down!' she was saying to the man who held her. 'Now, Tom!'

The man not only ignored her but whirled her around once again, while, behind Harry, the doors slid open again and a very large security guard entered.

'Put me down, Tom,' Steph repeated, more sternly this time.

The dancing man—Tom—did just that, dropping his burden so Steph crashed to the floor. Instinct sent Harry towards her, rushing to her aid, his hand outstretched to help her to her feet.

She looked up at him, and flinched—the movement so apparent he drew back, muscles stiffening with shock, his heart wincing, his mind numb with regret.

Then she scrambled to her feet, thrust her hands on her hips and glared at him.

'If you're not here as a patient then get out right now, Harry Pritchard,' she said, but her voice was shaking and her smoky grey eyes were bright with unshed tears.

Harry felt the wince become a clenching kind of pain. He opened his mouth to explain, but she'd moved away, motioning to the man who'd dropped her, sending him ahead of her into what was probably a consulting room.

'Are you a patient?'

For the first time he noticed another woman, this one behind a desk in the far corner of the waiting room, her arms folded as she awaited an answer from him.

'No, I'm to be working here,' he said, turning towards the security man to include him in the conversation. 'My name's Harry Pritchard. The new owner has asked me to take a look at the way things are run. His business manager was supposed to let you know.'

The woman behind the desk—Rebecca Harris if the name plaque was correct—studied him for a moment.

'We heard a bloke was coming,' she said, shrugging as if his arrival was a matter of supreme indifference to her. 'But we hardly expected you to start work in the early hours of the morning.'

'That was obvious!' Harry snapped, as a vivid picture of Steph in the man's arms flashed across his mind. 'Do those kind of shenanigans go on all the time? Do you all mix business with pleasure?'

Rebecca—if she was Rebecca, introductions had been by-passed—looked at him as if he was mad.

'Mix business with pleasure?' she repeated. She shook her head. 'I have no idea what you're talking about.'

'I'm talking about that man dancing around the waiting room with that woman in his arms,' Harry said, growing angrier—mainly with Steph—by the moment.

'But she didn't want to be in his arms,' Rebecca told him, still frowning dubiously at him. 'That's Tom. He's a patient. Bipolar, and apparently in a manic phase. Dr Prince came out to call him—he was the next patient—and he grabbed her. I called Security—that's what Ned's doing here.'

She nodded towards the large man who was still standing like a misplaced monolith just inside the front door.

'Oh!' Harry said, then struggled to find something else to add. 'I'm actually jet-lagged. I woke up and couldn't get back to sleep.'

They weren't the best couple of sentences to have found—pertaining as they did to a much earlier bit of the conversation. But as the woman showed no signs of rescuing him from this conversational morass, he plunged valiantly on.

'That's why I'm here at this hour.'

'You can go, Ned,' she said, looking past him to the security man, who touched his uniform cap and departed. 'As for you...' She turned back to Harry. 'I don't know what you're supposed to be doing, but I'd advise you to do it during the daytime in future. From the sound of things, you know Dr Prince, and if she's not happy having you here when she's on duty, then neither am I.'

Harry watched her draw herself up to her full five feet six and puff out her chest as birds did when they wanted to make themselves look bigger, and fiercer—and he had to smile.

'Actually,' he said, hoping his voice sounded properly apologetic, 'Dr Prince has no say over when I'm here and when I'm not. But I will try not to antagonise her.'

Lie! Of course he'd antagonise her. He didn't even have to try. There was so much unfinished business between them it was inevitable.

CHAPTER TWO

SOMEHOW, STEPHANIE MANAGED to calm Tom down enough for him to answer questions about his medication.

'But I don't need it when I'm well,' he told her. She forced herself to concentrate on the patient, explaining slowly and carefully that it was just as important when he was feeling well as when he was depressed.

'It keeps the chemicals in your body balanced,' she told him— for possibly the twentieth time since he'd first become her patient.

'But I'm better now,' he argued, though in the end he agreed to take the tablets—but only because she'd asked him to.

The phone buzzed, and she turned to Tom.

'Rebecca only interrupts if it's something urgent,' she said to him, hoping he'd take the hint.

But, being Tom, he didn't.

'I'm as urgent as anyone,' he said, his jaw setting belligerently.

'Of course you are—and more important because you're a regular—but this could be a child in serious trouble, Tom. I have to go.'

She stood up and walked towards the door, praying he'd follow because there was no way she could leave him in a consulting room on his own.

He did follow, but as he reached the door he grabbed her again.

'Ah, my favourite doctor,' he cried, lifting her from behind this time so she was able to kick back with her heel, hitting him in the knee.

Bang. Down she went again, while Tom clutched his knee and scowled.

'You didn't have to do that!' he grumbled at her, but as he turned, as if to touch her again, Harry appeared, seizing Tom by the elbow and steering him towards the reception desk.

'There's a woman in the second consulting room, coughing badly and slightly cyanotic around the lips.'

Joanne had appeared and now helped Steph to her feet, then drew her towards the second door.

'I've put an oxygen mask on her.'

She thrust a new patient form into Stephanie's hand, then opened the door and followed Steph into the room.

The woman was sitting on the examination couch, clutching the oxygen mask in one hand while she coughed and wheezed and gasped for breath. Steph could smell the mix of cigarette smoke and alcohol fumes from the door, but to give the woman her due, she might not have been smoking. A person's hair and clothing could absorb the smell just being in some of the night-clubs where smoking was still allowed.

'Put the mask back over your nose and mouth and breathe deeply,' she said when the spasm of coughing stopped. 'And don't try to answer—just nod or shake your head.'

The woman nodded to indicated she understood.

'I'm going to listen to your chest. Have you had this kind of attack before?'

Another nod.

'Has it been diagnosed?'

Again the agreement.

'Bronchitis?'

Nod.

'Chronic?'

Nod.

'Do you use a puffer of any kind?'

The woman shook her head.

'Take any preventative drugs regularly?'

Another head shake.

Stephanie finished her examination and straightened up, looking directly into the eyes of the woman who was now breathing more easily.

'Do you smoke?'

The woman nodded, and her eyes shifted, suggesting she'd been told—probably more than once—she should give it up for the sake of her health.

'And it's worth it even though you have to put up with attacks like this?' Steph asked.

The woman shook her head.

'I'll give you antibiotics now to help you through this attack, but the problem is,' Steph continued, 'if you keep on having these crises it will eventually affect your heart. I can't see any sign of it yet, but there's a condition called cor pulmonale where, because of the extra work it's called on to do, the section of the heart that deals with blood flow to your lungs becomes enlarged. This is serious stuff, so it's up to you to decide if you want to risk it.'

She waited a moment for this to sink in.

'Your own GP has probably told you all the things you need to do to get rid of the bronchitis, but I'll repeat them. First is give up smoking—there are really good medications available to help with that these days. Then you need to increase your exercise—walking is the best, starting slowly then building up until you're comfortable walking briskly for at least twenty minutes every day.'

She went on to ask the woman about allergies, and prescribed ampicillin and a bronchodilator, which would help prevent bad attacks if used when wheezing first started.

'But it's mainly a matter of avoiding irritants until your lungs are in better shape,' she added. 'As well as cigarette smoke, things like hair spray, aerosol insect sprays, even occupational chemicals can all affect damaged lungs.'

The woman—Beth Graham, Steph had finally deciphered the writing on the patient form—now removed the mask.

'That's all very easy for you to say,' Beth snapped, 'but it's impossible to do. I'm a barmaid. I work in cigarette smoke all the time—and I've tried all the patches and tablets ever invented in an effort to stop smoking. Then I think, Why bother when I have to breathe in other people's smoke in my job? As for chemical irritants, you should smell the stuff we use to clean out the beer pipes and the area behind the bar when we close up for the night. I love doctors who say do this and do that, and never think about whether it's possible or not.'

'I'm sorry,' Steph said. 'We do tend to preach.'

She studied Beth's tired face, then checked the form again. At thirty-five, Beth was only five years older than Steph herself.

'There's no other job? Or maybe a day shift so you're not out in the night air—and don't have to do the cleaning?'

Beth shook her head.

'I've three kids—the oldest is fifteen, so I can leave her in charge at night, but the baby's only six and I want to be home for her when she goes to school and comes home. Earlier shifts just don't work.'

Steph raised her hands out from her sides.

'Tell me about it!' she said. 'I'm not exactly crazy about working nights myself, but I've a four-year-old and I feel the same way about being home for her.'

They talked a little longer, Steph trying to think of alternative occupations for a woman who preferred to work at night.

'I've tried a few others,' Beth said. 'Drove a limo for a while, but nothing pays as well as night-shift bar work and with Desiree, my eldest, now wanting all the things teenagers want, I need the money.'

'But it shouldn't be at the expense of your health,' Stephanie said. 'Have you considered retraining? Doing a course that might get you into something you can do at home?'

Beth nodded, then shrugged.

'And who keeps us while I do the course? That's what it always comes back to, doesn't it?'

She picked up the scripts and Steph walked with her to the door, then, as Beth departed, Steph continued on to the reception desk.

'We could form a club of women who work nights so they can be home for their kids during the day. That was another one.'

'Well, I'm only doing it for another year at the most,' Rebecca said. 'Once Dyson's in high school, I reckon it's going to be more important for me to be home nights than days. It'll mean a pay cut, but you just wait—I'm going to get a receptionist job in a real doctors' surgery, where you get to know the patients and have regulars bringing in bottles of jam and crocheted facecloths.'

Stephanie laughed.

'We have our regulars,' she reminded Rebecca. 'Look at Tom!'

'And a couple of drunken derelicts, and a group of homeless kids,' Rebecca snorted. 'Some regulars!'

Harry, sitting in the administrator's office flicking through files in a drawer on the left hand side of the desk, heard them talking. The administrator's office must have been an afterthought, built by putting a thin partition across part of the reception area, so the sound carried easily.

The conversation was revealing enough in its way, but in other ways he was more confused than ever.

Seeing Steph again was the primary source of confusion, but beyond that so many things didn't even begin to add up, he wasn't sure where to start sorting them out.

Did Bob Quayle know Steph was working at the clinic—and, if so, why hadn't he mentioned it?

And why was Steph talking as if she *had* to work, and juggle work and child-care? Even if Martin had left no money when he'd died, surely the Quayles could afford to provide financial support for their only grandchild?

The two women were still talking—about children now. Rebecca was complaining about the language kids picked up at school.

'You know the bloke I said was coming in?' she added, switching conversation with the rapidity only a woman could manage. 'Well, that's him—the chap you know. The one you called Harry. He's the bloke Muriel mentioned in her note.'

Harry tried to imagine Steph's reaction and failed, but now they were talking about him, he'd better make his continued presence known, in case they didn't realise how thin the wall between them was.

'Harry's the bloke?' he heard Steph say as he rose from behind the desk. 'What do you mean?'

'He's here to see how the clinic runs.' Rebecca expanded on her explanation.

'At three in the morning? You've got to be kidding!'

'Jet lag!' Rebecca explained, as Harry opened the door and stepped out.

'Good morning, Steph,' he said, hoping he sounded more confident than he felt. 'How's everything with you?'

She gave him a look that would have made a lesser man turn tail and run, but he'd been on the receiving end of Steph's black looks before, and was able to ignore it. But he couldn't ignore the alarm he felt, seeing her so pale and tired looking, and far too thin—yet, strangely, more beautiful than she'd ever been.

'What, exactly, are you doing here?' she demanded, ignoring his question and going on the attack instead.

'Checking out the place for the new owner.' Now Bob Quayle's request to keep his identity a secret seemed odder than ever. But wouldn't Steph know her father-in-law was the new owner? 'Apparently the clinic was in financial difficulties when the current owners bought it and the directors of the company would like to know why.' Damn the woman—he was becoming more and more confused.

Her eyes narrowed with suspicion.

'Oh, yes! I can just see the headlines!' she sniped. '"Eminent cosmetic surgeon takes on investigation into dead-broke, run-down medical centre".' She used her long slim fingers to provide the quotation marks. 'You've certainly got the qualifications! Not!'

'It's a favour for a friend,' Harry said, remaining calm though the urge to shake her was becoming stronger by the second. 'And you know I've worked in places like this before.'

He was explaining too much, he realised, so he added a curt, 'Not that it's any of your business,' just to put her in her place.

But Steph had never known her place—which, in days gone by, Harry had felt had been in his bed rather than Martin's—and she stepped towards him, suspicion now radiating from her in almost visible waves.

'What friend?' she demanded, but before he could reply—or duck a reply—the doors opened again and three obviously inebriated youths came in, two of them supporting the third who was bleeding profusely from a head wound.

'He fell over,' one explained, as the threesome lurched and staggered closer to the desk.

Steph responded first, stepping forward and taking hold of the injured man, telling Rebecca to get details and call Joanne to the treatment room.

The first thing I tell Bob Quayle, Harry thought as he swept around the desk in time to support the other side of the injured youth, is that women shouldn't be working night shifts in a place like this.

'It's ridiculous!' he growled, only realising he'd spoken aloud when Steph turned and raised an eyebrow in his direction.

'There being only women here.' He put his thoughts into words, while he steered their patient towards a table set up in the middle of the room. 'Look at you—so thin a decent puff of wind would blow you over! How are you expected to manage drunks like this?'

The youth had lurched across the table and was going a peculiar green shade, but Steph had clearly been here before because she grabbed a basin and held it while the youngster threw up a great deal of the evening's alcohol intake.

The nurse, slightly better built than Steph but still no Amazon, now appeared and bustled about, emptying the dish, cleaning up the man's face with a towel, producing a tray with antiseptic solution on it so Steph, who now had her patient sitting on the table, could clean the head wound.

Fuming inwardly at the absurdity of the situation, Harry remained on the far side, one hand resting on the patient's arm in case restraint was necessary.

Steph was talking, asking the lad his name—Jerry—and what they'd been celebrating to be out so late on a week-night.

Jerry launched into a somewhat disjointed explanation that was still logical enough to assure Harry—and no doubt Steph as well—that he wasn't suffering concussion as a result of the head wound.

'How did it happen, do you remember?' Steph asked.

'Fell off the railing,' Jerry told her.

'Railing?'

Jerry grinned.

'The one around the fountain in the mall. We were going to take a swim and Todd said first we'd better walk around the railing to see if we were sober enough.'

'Of course,' Steph said, as if such outrageous behaviour was perfectly logical to her. Then she glanced at Harry and grinned. 'It's a good test but not everyone passes it.'

And Harry remembered.

They'd been in first year Med—or maybe it had been second—a long time ago anyway. Holidaying at Martin's family home after the exams, celebrating the end of semester, and Martin saying they had to walk around the railing to prove sobriety before they could swim in the fountain.

Steph had been the only one who'd made it all the way round...

Steph, with her long, lean limbs and lissom grace...

She was suturing the cut and talking soothingly to Jerry as she stitched, establishing he was a local, not a tourist, explaining he should see his own GP in a week to have the stitches removed.

'I'd rather come here for you to do it,' Jerry said, making a grab for Steph's hand.

'I know you would,' she agreed pleasantly, while easily avoiding his grasping hand. 'But I might not be on duty and you'd get a big, rough, bearded first-year doctor who'd rip them out without caring whether it hurts or not. Best go to your own GP.'

She cut a waterproof dressing and put it over the top.

'Don't take that off,' she warned, then she helped him off the table.

He went pale again, and the nurse produced the basin, but the lad steadied, and even had the grace to apologise for throwing up earlier.

'That's OK,' Steph told him. 'But you go straight home now.'

He nodded, felt the injured place on his head with careful fingers, then let Steph lead him to the door. Though Harry wanted to follow, he restrained himself and instead introduced himself to the nurse.

'Are you always on night duty?' he asked, conscious of the fact he was supposed to be doing a job.

Joanne shook her head.

'Twice a week,' she explained. 'That's all I need to do because the pay is higher for night duty and I make as much on two nights as I would on three and a half day shifts. I'm a student and when it's not busy I study. Steph's very good—she only calls me in if she needs something.'

I'm sure she does, Harry thought—thinking of everyone but herself.

He talked to Joanne for a while longer, discovering she was studying for a higher degree in nursing and hoping to go into teaching eventually.

'Teaching has better hours for when I have a family,' she explained, and Harry shook his head, seeing once again the problem of shuffling work and family.

He walked out of the treatment room, still thinking about it—though his thinking ability was declining as his jet-lag phase switched from full alert to heavy-eyed exhaustion.

He'd have to think about it later.

Think about Bob Quayle and the job later as well.

But not Steph—he'd talk to her now.

She was nowhere in sight, and behind the reception desk Rebecca was chatting to an alert-looking woman in a vivid red suit. She was of medium height, and very pretty, with sleek blonde hair pulled back into a neat pleat at the back of her head.

'This is Linda—she's the early-shift receptionist this week,' Rebecca said, waving him towards the desk. 'She'll introduce you to the other day staff. That's if you're still in hyperactive mode and want to stay.'

She turned to Linda.

'He's Harry Pritchard—working for the new owners—checking to see we all do our jobs and don't pinch money from the till.'

'Some hope of that,' Linda said, 'when most of our patients are on Medicare.'

But she smiled at Harry and gave him an assessing look—then another, much warmer smile as she added, 'But if I can help you in any way, just let me know.'

Harry smiled politely and excused himself. She'd put too much emphasis on the 'any' for him to miss the meaning, but he wasn't interested in pretty blondes—not right now.

Right now—as the night shift had apparently ended—he wanted to catch a certain redhead before she left work, and demand answers to at least some of the questions jostling for attention in his head.

He'd explored the place earlier and found the tearoom, which appeared to double as a staff cloakroom, but though Joanne was there, chatting to a young man about the night they'd had, there was no sign of Steph.

'She's gone,' Rebecca told him, when he emerged and was looking down the corridor towards the back entrance to the clinic.

'I beg your pardon?' Harry snapped, sure he hadn't been so obvious in his quest.

'Steph! She's gone. She likes to get home before Fanny wakes up and her old car's so unreliable she shoots out the moment the relieving doctor arrives. That way, if it doesn't start, she can walk home and still be there for Fanny.'

Disappointment blurred with anger that she'd taken off without so much as a good-bye—but, then, she'd hardly been welcoming, had she?

Harry nodded curtly to Rebecca and strode back to the administration office. He'd flicked idly through the main bank of filing cabinets in the early hours of the morning, now he'd take a closer look. Personnel files would have employees' addresses. Though he'd always assumed she still lived with the Quayles—he'd been sending Fanny's presents to that address.

But if she lived with Bob and Doreen, then she'd know Bob owned the clinic. Wouldn't she?

Damn her, dashing off like that—he really needed to talk to her.

Forget it! common sense said. You're far too tired to think, let alone carry on a sensible conversation—especially with a woman who hates your guts.

But as he made his way back up to the apartment—Bob Quayle's apartment—his mind continued to question what he'd seen and heard and learnt.

Nothing made sense—least of all Bob Quayle asking him to check out the clinic.

And not mentioning Steph worked there...

Not mentioning Steph at all!

* * *

It was still raining—it already seemed like forty days and forty nights—as Steph drove home. The not unpleasant weariness she usually felt after a night on duty had deserted her and in its place a high-strung tension sang and shimmied along her nerves.

For a start, there was Harry.

No, Harry wasn't so much a start as a huge, gigantic, enormous and probably insurmountable obstacle the misaligned planets had dropped into her life. Like a meteorite so dense she could see no way through or around or over it.

A meteorite with a distinct whiff of fish.

She wasn't naïve enough to believe Harry had just happened into her workplace. Fate wasn't that cute.

And a cosmetic surgeon appointed to check the running of a twenty-four-hour clinic? The fish smell was becoming stronger.

She drove slowly through the deserted streets—not even the most dedicated of joggers were out this morning—while her mind tossed up possible explanations.

Harry's second cousin's wife had bought the business and he was doing her a favour?

He was here for a quick visit and this filled in the time?

His parents had left their property in the west and retired to Summerland? Maybe *they* had bought the clinic as an investment, and he was checking it out for them? Ah, now that was feasible, wasn't it?

If you believed in fairy stories…

She pulled into her drive, thoughts of Harry set aside for a moment as she did the mental arithmetic she usually did on mornings like this. If she bought absolutely nothing but essentials for the next six months, she'd have enough money saved to build the garage she badly needed for the car—then, three months after that, enough for a covered walkway from the garage to the house.

Nine months—that wasn't long. Like being pregnant. That had passed.

Bad comparison.

She slumped forward in the seat and rested her head on the steering-wheel. She considered thumping it there once or twice to empty out the thoughts she didn't want to have, then, realising Fanny could be waking any minute, she straightened up, found her umbrella, eased open the car door and made the dash across her muddy back yard to the door.

Her house was warm, and silent in the comforting way that told her all within were sleeping soundly. She checked Fanny anyway, smiling to herself as she looked at the little body splayed across the bed, rosy cheeked from sleep, gold curls tousled around her small head.

Making her way back to the kitchen, Steph poked her head around Tracy's door as well, flinching at the mess then remembering she'd been a messy teenager herself. There'd been so much to see, and do, and learn, there'd never been time to put things away.

Satisfied all was well in this, the most important corner of her small world, Steph put on the kettle, popped bread into the toaster and wondered how long it would be before her budget would stretch to a home-delivered daily paper.

'It would have been wet this morning, anyway,' she comforted herself, turning on the radio instead, so at least she'd learn something of what was happening in the world from the morning news.

Fanny erupted into the kitchen as Steph finished her toast.

'I forgot,' she told her mother, casting herself into Steph's arms for a good-morning kiss and hug. 'Today we have to take our favourite toy to kindy for a toys' teaparty.'

'Well, that's OK,' Steph said, smoothing hair back from her daughter's forehead. 'You've plenty to choose from.'

'But that's the problem,' Fanny said with a dramatic sigh.

Steph smiled to herself, knowing she used the same phrase to Tracy all the time—usually when discussing either their individual timetables or budgeting considerations.

'What's the problem?' she asked the little drama queen now snuggled on her lap.

'I don't know what's my favourite.'

Another huge sigh.

'You're taking Bear to bed these days, maybe you could take him.'

'But then Adeline will get cross,' Fanny told her.

Steph, knowing this conversation could go on for two days, opted out.

'Well, you run back to your bedroom and have a look at all of them while I fix your breakfast. You can get dressed while you're thinking and call me when you're ready for me to do your hair.'

Fanny accepted this suggestion with good grace, and in the end decided Bear should share the kindy treat.

Steph tied a red ribbon around his neck, finishing it with a big bow so he looked properly festive, then, with Fanny and the bear both wrapped in her raincoat, she carried the pair out to the car and drove down the road to the kindergarten.

'Don't forget Tracy's picking you up this afternoon,' she reminded her daughter.

'Because it's Friday!' Fanny said, showing off her knowledge of their routine.

Steph kissed her goodbye, checked that the kindergarten staff knew Tracy would collect Fanny, then departed. If she went straight home, she could get in five hours' straight sleep.

If she didn't let thoughts of Harry's unexpected re-emergence in her life intrude, she *might* get five hours' straight sleep.

But how could she not think about it…?

Not think about Harry with his dark, all-seeing eyes, and his long, lanky bushman's body…

She must have slept eventually, for she woke at one, unrefreshed—in fact, so fuzzy and disoriented she knew she needed a whole lot more.

She could doze for another hour, or do a quick house-clean and wash. With the wet weather, everything felt damp.

Opting for housework, she clambered out of bed, made herself a cup of tea and a sandwich, then put on a wash and whipped through the housework. When she had a garage she could hang washing in it when it rained, she reminded herself as she spread the wet clothes over drying frames on the front veranda.

Or maybe, after the garage but before the covered walkway, she could buy a dryer.

'Dream on, Prince!' she muttered to herself, late now and needing to hurry to get to the local medical centre by three.

Fifteen women, in various stages of pregnancy, greeted her enthusiastically. Although the public hospital offered antenatal classes for pregnant women, it was a long way to travel for a half-hour session, so Steph, in conjunction with a local medical practice, did an hour a week, combining their regular health checks with information on nutrition and the process of childbirth, followed by breathing and exercise classes. It was a nice little supplement to her income and she enjoyed the interaction with the women, sharing their excitement as they approached the birth.

But this afternoon the usual joy was missing, and she made her way home afterwards, eager to see Fanny, but unable to blot from her mind thoughts of Harry Pritchard and his sudden reappearance in her life.

'Forget him,' she told herself, as she swung into the drive, nearly hitting the car already parked there.

She frowned at the intruder, a dark green sedan, its shape suggesting it was a fairly recent model.

Had one of the kindy mothers given Tracy and Fanny a lift home, and been invited in for coffee?

Or perhaps someone had driven Tracy home from lectures then stayed on so she could collect Fanny in a car, rather than walking her home through the rain.

Steph considered these and other options, then wondered

why she didn't just get out of her car and go inside—find out who the stranger was.

Because it meant dashing through the rain and she was sick and tired of being wet.

And if whoever owned the car wanted to leave before her—which was likely as she didn't leave until after eight—she'd have to dash out again and shift her car.

With grudging reluctance, she started her car again, backed out and parked beside the kerb opposite her front gate. Slightly further to dash, but what the hell. Being wet was minor compared to other problems she had right now.

One of which was sitting on her front veranda, almost hidden among the drying racks and draped laundry.

'What are you doing here?' Steph demanded, staring in disbelief at the man who'd sabotaged her thoughts, ruined her sleep and had now invaded her home.

'Your babysitter told me she wasn't allowed to invite strangers in without your permission,' he said, rising to his feet so he towered over her in the limited space left by the washing. 'And though Fanny acknowledged she had an Uncle Harry, she produced so ancient a photo of me, no one could see the resemblance.'

He gave a small, apologetic smile—an expression so familiar Steph felt her heart cramp with pain.

'We compromised by me staying on the veranda—because of the rain—until you came home and introduced us.'

Another smile—another cramp.

'Fanny does seem quite anxious to meet me,' he said, sliding in under her defences.

Steph stared at him in disbelief.

'Why are you doing this? Why are you here? What's going on, Harry?'

Her voice was so full of pain and anxiety, Harry found himself wincing again. What had happened to make her so tense and suspicious?

OK, so they hadn't parted friends—in fact, she'd vowed to never speak to him again—but she'd always sent thank-you notes for the gifts he'd sent to Fanny, and Steph had never been one to hold a grudge.

He shook his head, realising he had no idea how to answer her—and no inkling of the answers to his own mental queries.

Fanny broke the deadlock. The beautiful child, with eyes so like Martin's Harry found himself staring at her, appeared in the doorway, the old photo still held in one hand.

'This man says he's Uncle Harry!' she said to her mother, casting a stern look in Harry's direction as she spoke.

Harry saw Steph hesitate. He'd heard enough of Fanny's conversation with the babysitter to know Steph had spoken kindly of him to her little daughter. Now she was stuck in a dilemma of her own making—did she throw him out then explain to Fanny why she'd lost her godfather, or invite him in and pretend he was the friend Fanny thought him?

'He is Uncle Harry,' Steph said, kneeling beside the little girl and giving her a kiss and a quick hug. 'He's just got older so he doesn't look quite the same as he does in your photo, but if you look at his eyes in the photo and then at his real eyes, you'll see they're the same. And his smile...'

She looked up at Harry, her own eyes as cool as ice water.

'Smile, Uncle Harry,' she ordered—voice even cooler than the eyes. 'See,' she added, turning back to Fanny. 'It's kind of like the same smile.'

It was nothing like the same smile, and Harry knew it. He knew the photo Fanny held for comparison, because he had an identical one himself. It had been taken when he'd first realised he loved Steph—loved her as more than a friend—and that love had shone in the smile.

Even though she hadn't seen it.

CHAPTER THREE

ONCE ASSURED THIS was her Uncle Harry in the flesh, Fanny took over, inviting him in, taking him into her room to become reacquainted with all the toys he'd sent her over the years, chattering on as if she'd known him for ever.

Which, in a way, she had, Steph realised.

Tracy, too, was obviously impressed by the visitor, apologising for her earlier doubts, offering tea or coffee. If Steph hadn't been so disturbed by his presence in her house, she'd have laughed at the way the pair of them vied for his attention.

It was almost inevitable that Fanny would invite him to stay for dinner, Steph realised later as she added a tin of tomatoes to the mince she was making up into shepherd's pie for their meal.

Though not as inevitable that he'd say yes!

What was he doing here?

Why had Harry come back?

She sneaked looks at him when she thought he was well occupied with Fanny's chatter—saw the slight lines nearly five years had left in his face. Caught glimpses of his brown eyes, glowing with good humour and kindness as he talked to her daughter.

Did he feel a bond with Fanny because he'd seen her born—because he'd held Steph's hand right through the delivery? Taken Martin's place because Martin—no, she wasn't going to follow that particular strand of memory...

Somehow she got through the meal, but when Harry offered to wash up, she knew she couldn't share the kitchen with him a minute longer.

'Good,' she said. 'Tracy and Fanny can help you and I'll have my shower. I wouldn't mind getting to work early tonight, I've some paperwork to do.'

She whipped away, showered, then, wrapped in a towel, dashed across the hall to her bedroom. Where she surveyed the contents of her wardrobe and sighed.

Jeans and a T-shirt. It's what you always wear to work, she reminded herself, but tonight she wished she had a new T-shirt or one pair of slightly less faded jeans. Tonight she'd have liked to look—well, attractive...

For Harry?

Or because he's a man?

She tried to tell herself it was because he was a man and it was normal for the female of the species to preen for men, but she didn't believe it for a moment. She wanted to look good for Harry, because Harry had always told her she was beautiful.

Though usually the assurances had come when she'd broken up with a boyfriend and had been in need of a confidence boost! Back in the early years of their friendship, they'd shared the highs and lows of their relationships with the opposite sex. Harry and Martin vetting the boys she went out with; she introducing them to girls she knew, giving them advice—from her admittedly limited experience—on how to win a woman...

She peered dolefully into the mirror.

Beautiful?

Bah! As if it matters what you look like, or what Harry used to tell you. What should be occupying your mind is what he's doing here, and whether whatever it is will impact on the hard-won security of your little family.

She pulled on her oldest pair of jeans and a T-shirt that had a mouse with boxing gloves shaping up to an elephant—a gift from Tracy—then sallied forth, ready to do battle to protect her home and daughter from whatever new threat might be hovering above their heads.

'Love the shirt!' Harry said, when his eyes had raked over her and showed more disapproval than admiration.

'Whatever I wear is covered by a coat anyway,' she told him, shrugging off his reactions and turning her attention to Fanny.

'Bedtime for you, kid,' she said, but the excitement of meeting Uncle Harry in the flesh had gone to Fanny's head and, in a rare display of contrariness, she argued.

'What if I read you a story when you're in bed?' Harry offered, and, as Fanny's tantrum turned to smiles, Steph felt her insides knot with a mix of anger and something that could only be jealousy.

Determined not to let it show, she forced a smile, then took Fanny's hand and led her off.

But hiding her emotions only made things worse, for they seethed and bubbled inside her, so when it was finally time to leave for work, she was so uptight she flooded the car engine and then couldn't get the wretched vehicle started.

The passenger door opened and Harry poked his head in.

'Come on, I'll drive you,' he said.

'Don't bother, I can get a cab!' she snapped.

'You're still as stubborn as a mule, Stephanie Prince!' Harry said. 'But you were never stupid. How easy do you think it will be to get a cab in this weather on a Friday night? Besides, we need to talk.'

'No, we don't,' Steph told him, but he was right about the cab situation. Cursing under her breath, she gathered up her handbag and found her umbrella, then clambered out into the rain.

Again!

'Nice car!' she muttered as she strapped her damp body into the passenger seat, and sniffed the newness appreciatively.

'It's a hire car. I've only been back a week—less, really.'

She glanced across at him, backing expertly out of her drive, and wondered at how things had gone so wrong that she and Harry were reduced to such an inane conversation.

'What are you doing here?' she asked again—though this time she was going to get an answer.

He turned and grinned at her and she felt a tide of emotion swamp over her, so deep and forceful she must surely drown.

'In the car?' he teased. 'Driving you to work. In Summerland? I've come to work here—to open a specialist clinic.'

'Well, you've come to the right place,' Steph retorted, upset because the thought of Harry being permanently in the place she now called home had thrown her into more turmoil. 'Plenty of wealthy, aging women wanting to look younger.'

The glance Harry cast her way this time had no amusement in it at all.

'You used not to be bitchy, Steph,' he said in a voice cooler than the rain beyond the windows. 'It was one of the things that made you special.'

'Special enough to be Martin's wife, but only one of his many women,' she snapped. 'Well, that Stephanie's gone, Harry. I've had enough bad things happen to me lately to justify me being the bitchiest woman in the world for the rest of my life.'

Harry tried to speak, but the thought of what Steph must have gone through stopped his breath. And she'd said 'lately'. Bad things were still happening? Or had happened recently?

Since the terrible night when she'd given birth to Fanny, and Martin had been killed, racing to get to the hospital? Late because no one had been able to contact him. Late because he'd been away, not at the conference he'd used as an excuse but on a stolen weekend with another woman...

'OK,' he said at last, 'I guess that's up to you.'

Harry glanced at her again, but she was staring out the window, studying the rain as if someone might later question her about its force or wetness. But the shape of her head, visible beneath the short-cropped hair, was beautiful, and he had to grip the steering-wheel more tightly to stop his hand reaching out and his fingers feeling those newly revealed bones.

'You can drop me in front of the clinic,' she said, turning away from the window, but only to stare out through the wind-screen—determined not to look at him.

'No, I'll take you through into the car park,' he said. 'I need to park the car. I'm coming to work with you.'

That got her! Steph's head swivelled so fast it was a wonder she didn't rick her neck.

'You're what?'

'Coming to work with you,' he repeated, and made no effort not to sound smug. 'Friday night—two doctors on duty. I've been asked to see how the place runs, so how better to achieve that than by working there?'

'You can't do this to me!' she stormed, her hands curled into such tight fists he knew it was only with difficulty she refrained from pummelling him.

He pulled into one of the doctors' spaces behind the clinic and turned to her.

'Do what, Steph?' he asked quietly.

'Come back into my life like this. Haunt me this way. Why, Harry? Why?'

She was so distressed he reached out and rested the back of his fingers, oh, so lightly against her cheek.

'I would never do anything to hurt you, Steph, you must know that. And as for haunting you—I didn't know you were working in the clinic. Yes, I'd have contacted you, probably tomorrow or the next day. I wanted to see Fanny. Wanted to see you...'

There—he'd said it. But whatever reaction he'd expected it certainly wasn't to hear Steph laugh.

True, there was an edge of hysteria to the laughter, but she was still laughing.

'I don't believe it,' she said, shaking her head, then turning to him so he saw the wetness of tears glistening on her sculpted cheek-bones. 'First, however many years ago it was, fate put us together because of our surnames. Now you're telling me it brought you here—in a city of thirty thousand people—to the very place I work?'

He wasn't sure from her tone whether she was pleased or displeased with the machinations of fate, but Harry suspected it wasn't fate at all, but Bob Quayle who'd brought them back together. And the suspicion rested uneasily on his shoulders.

Once before, he'd kept a secret from Steph—the secret of Martin's continual and continuing infidelity—and it had cost him her friendship. Now he had another secret to keep. Martin's father's secret.

Steph opened the car door and stepped out. She knew Harry must think she was mad, but the tension inside her had been winding tighter and tighter, and when he'd said he'd wanted to see her, something had ripped open.

Harry had wanted to see her...

If he only knew how often she'd felt the same way—how often she'd longed to see him, talk to him, feel the security of his friendship.

His love...

She walked into the clinic, knowing he was following, so aware of him her entire back prickled as if she'd come out in a rash.

And things only got worse.

Friday night began, as it usually did, quietly enough, but at about ten-thirty a woman came in, accompanied by her husband and another couple with whom they'd been at dinner. All four had enjoyed pre-dinner drinks, wine with dinner and a liqueur to finish the evening. While not boisterously intoxicated, they were still relaxed enough to be uninhibitedly noisy.

'It just happened,' the husband said, pointing to his wife's face. 'We all saw it kind of drooping and now she can't feel anything.'

The others joined in with descriptions of the woman's problem, while the actual patient looked far from worried, blaming it on the red wine which she normally didn't drink.

With difficulty, Steph detached her from the group and took her into a consulting room.

'I'm just going to touch you in various places to see what feeling you've got,' she told the woman, using first her fingers, then the end of a pair of sharp forceps to find the extent of the loss of feeling in the woman's face.

'It looks like Bell's palsy, a paralysis of the facial nerve.' She unrolled a chart on the wall, and pointed to the nerve. 'It can be caused by injury of some kind, or an infection, or maybe compression of the nerve inside the brain.'

'Like a tumour?'

'It's a possibility that you'll have to rule out,' Steph told her, 'but quite often it just happens and we put it down to some infection you were probably unaware of having.'

'Will it go away?' the woman asked, pressing desperate fingers to the numb side of her face.

'It might,' Steph told her. 'It's hard to predict. It can be transient or permanent, it can affect both sides of the face or, as in your case, only one. The main problem is with your eye.'

She held up a small mirror so the woman could see the obvious droop of one side of her mouth and one eyelid.

'Try blinking,' she suggested, and was relieved when the eyelid moved, if only slightly.

'Blinking spreads a sheet of moisture across your eyes, protecting them from drying out. I'll give you some liquid that simulates tears, and I want you to use it regularly—at least until you've seen your own GP and made arrangements to see a specialist to have possible causes ruled out.'

'But what about my mouth—and my eyelid? What if it doesn't go away? I don't want it to stay that way.'

'I know there are surgical procedures that can help,' she said, then realised she had someone on the spot who could explain these far better than she could. She lifted her phone and spoke to Rebecca, who put her through to Harry.

'My patient is just leaving,' he said, when Steph explained, briefly, what she wanted. 'I'll pop in as soon as I've seen him out.' He was as good as his word, appearing within minutes, then examining the woman's face and explaining what could be done should the condition prove permanent.

'So it wouldn't be noticeable at all?' she asked, and Steph saw the slight puckering of a frown as Harry considered his reply.

It was a silly thing to go all limp-boned about, but it was so familiar—so Harry somehow—worrying how to say something so it caused the least pain.

'We can't work miracles,' he told the woman, 'and if the condition is permanent we can't make the muscles work again, but there is a lot we can do, cosmetically, to fix the slackness.'

He smiled encouragingly and the woman nodded. And though Harry hadn't given her any really good news, she seemed a lot happier.

Amazing what a smile will do, Steph thought, especially one of Harry's smiles.

The thought pulled her up—maybe she *had* become bitchy!

Harry departed and she walked the patient out, realising, as she saw the waiting room, that the usual Friday night mayhem was developing nicely. If Harry Pritchard wanted some action, he'd certainly get some tonight.

By two, the rush had died down. Two teenage girls who'd become ill drinking cocktails had been packed into a cab and sent home; three youths who'd been kicked out of a nightclub then started a fight with a twenty-stone bouncer had been despatched to A and E at the general hospital for X-rays; and a woman who had a child with croup had been comforted with cups of tea while a humidifier had eased the little boy's terrible barking cough.

With a temporary lull in the patient flow, Steph headed for the tearoom. When she'd first begun work at the clinic, a refrigerator in the room had been stocked with packets of sandwiches, and the staff had been free to help themselves to a snack. But these days—she guessed since the new owner took over—the sandwiches had disappeared and she usually brought her own snack.

But tonight, with Harry in the house, she'd forgotten.

She was searching through the cupboards, hoping to find a leftover biscuit, when the delicious smell of fresh coffee alerted her to another presence in the room.

'Ready for a snack?'

Harry was standing just inside the doorway, a box with four coffees held in one hand and a white plastic bag dangling from his fingers.

'I spent long enough in the US to learn the benefits of doughnuts as a quick carbohydrate boost,' he said, setting the coffee on the table and opening the plastic bag to reveal a box of garishly decorated doughnuts.

He must have seen Steph's dubious look, for he added, 'Actually, it was the only place open in this complex that sold both coffee and food. I figured the closer I was to the clinic the hotter the coffee would be. Help yourself—I'll take two cups out to reception. Rebecca and tonight's nurse—Peter, I think is his name—are playing some on-going card game.'

Steph selected one of the remaining cups of coffee, added a couple of straws of sugar which Harry had brought along and stirred it, then studied the doughnuts he'd left behind.

The least lurid was one with jam and cream so she picked it up, eased a little of the filling into the bin, then bit in.

It was absolutely delicious, the sweetness flooding her mouth.

'Ooh!' She all but whimpered out her delight, then looked at the remaining bite of the doughnut.

It couldn't possibly have been that good. She must have been starving to have even considered eating it. She popped the last piece into her mouth and was revelling in its sugary sweetness when Harry returned.

'Good?' he said, smiling at her then reaching forward and

touching her cheek with his forefinger. As she leaned back—too late to avoid that gentle caress—he held out the finger to show her the dollop of cream he'd rescued from her cheek.

'Oh!'

But as he licked the cream from his finger an internal 'oh' happened—an 'oh' as if someone had touched an old, forgotten bruise deep inside her and she wasn't certain if what she felt was pain or pleasure.

'Have another,' Harry said, pushing the box towards her so casually she knew she shouldn't have been affected by him licking her cream off his finger. It meant nothing.

'Did you like America?'

It was a desperation question—an attempt on Steph's part to regain a little bit of stability in a life that had tilted off its axis since Harry's arrival in the clinic the previous night.

'Loved it,' he said. 'It's so big and beautiful, a bit brash in some ways, but so varied it's like travelling through a lot of different countries.'

He spoke of Boston, where he'd spent most time, and the mountains in Colorado where he'd walked in the summer break. Spoke of friends, the lack of names suggesting they might be women, but of course Harry would have had women friends.

And lovers...

Hadn't he always?

'And Europe? You went back there after your stay in the States.'

She saw the shadows cross his face.

'Yes, I went back there,' he said, then, as the bell rang to tell them a patient had arrived, he changed the subject with an almost abrupt, 'I'll go. You take a decent break. Have another doughnut.'

It didn't take a genius to know he'd been pleased by the interruption, which made Steph wonder what had happened to Harry in Europe. A disastrous love affair?

It hurt the bruised part inside Steph to think of Harry hurting, especially as she'd hurt him once herself.

Hurt him more than once...

Another ring summoned her back to work and she drained her coffee, then chose a doughnut with chocolate icing, taking a quick bite of it to keep her going until the next break.

It was the last bite of the night. She was seeing out the patient she'd been summoned for—a twenty-year-old with an acute asthma attack who'd been put on a nebuliser until the attack eased—when the screech of tearing metal brought all the staff to the door of the clinic. Almost immediately outside, a car had mounted the kerb, dislodging a parking meter then slamming into the window of the opal shop next door.

'Don't go rushing out there!' Harry said, grabbing Steph's arm as she was running towards the car. 'It could be a ram raid. They could be armed.'

'They could also be injured.' Steph wrenched her arm free and continued on her way.

Peter was already at the car, trying to open the passenger side door while the opal shop alarms were making so much noise it was a wonder they weren't all deafened.

Perhaps realising no one was about to leap from the car and grab jewellery from the shop window, Harry had followed Steph to the driver's side, but the engine had concertinaed the car's interior and it was impossible to open the door.

Peter had his side open and was kneeling beside the unconscious woman passenger, while Rebecca appeared in the clinic doorway to let them know she'd phoned for an ambulance.

'There's no obvious bleeding but I guess we shouldn't move her.' Peter made way for Harry, and at that moment the police arrived, their flashing red lights turning the street into a macabre movie set.

Two tow trucks beat the ambulance to the scene, but not by much, and with so many people now milling around, Steph sent Peter back to the clinic but remained close by in case she was needed.

With infinite care, the paramedics from the ambulance first braced the woman's neck and back, then lifted her onto a waiting trolley. Her airway and breathing were checked, then her body scanned for any external bleeding before her blood pressure was taken and fluid lines were inserted.

Meanwhile, the police were assisting another attendant who was using cutting tools to free the driver. Harry stood behind them, watching carefully, and Steph could see that the man must have been thrown forward into the windscreen by the impact, for his face was a mask of blood.

'No damned seat belt—when will people learn?'

Harry had left the experts to their job and joined her on the sidelines.

'If his face hit the windscreen, his chest hit the steering-wheel with equal force. He could have internal bleeding, lung damage, even a ruptured aorta.'

Harry looked so fierce for a moment Steph thought he might say 'Serve him right', but all he did was nod acknowledgement of her recital of the injuries A and E doctors would check first.

Although the action had seemed to be taking place in slow motion, it was only fifteen minutes later that the ambulance with its two comatose patients departed. The police photographed the scene, more flashes of bright light, then a tow truck hooked up to the back of the vehicle and, unable to lift it beneath the shop awnings, towed it off the footpath. As it bumped over the kerb, the back door, released as the car body stretched under tow, flew open and Steph saw the crumpled figure on the floor behind the seats, the long blonde hair pink in the turning light, but so familiar a scream of utter despair erupted from her throat.

All motion ceased, then she was flying towards the car, Harry's footsteps thudding behind her.

'It's not Fanny,' he said, reaching out and grabbing her shoulders, while a policeman moved in front of her to peer into the car.

It *wasn't* Fanny, but the little girl was dead, though she and Harry refused to acknowledge it, performing CPR on the small body until another ambulance arrived.

As it drove away, Harry put his arm around Steph's shoulders and led her back into the clinic.

'We should have looked,' she whispered brokenly. 'If we'd seen her earlier we might have been able to save her.'

'We wouldn't have seen her,' he reminded her. 'The front seat was jammed right back there. She was thrown forward by the impact and I think her neck was probably broken when she hit the seat. Poor wee mite—killed by the carelessness of parents who didn't strap her in.'

Inside the clinic, the various members of the day staff had arrived and were all now clustered in the waiting room, hearing about the early morning excitement.

Harry steered Steph past them, into the tearoom, where her half-eaten doughnut mocked her from the table.

'Get your bag, I'm taking you home,' he said, and she nodded, her mind and body so numb she was pleased to have someone else making decisions for her.

But her limbs had forgotten how to move, and she stood there, her body tight with remembered fear, until Harry took her in his arms, tucked her in close to his warmth, massaging life back into the muscles of her neck and shoulders, softening the tension that had paralysed her.

Her body relaxed—and with the relaxation came tentative flutters of awareness, like the tiny tendrils of a delicate new vine reaching out in search of support.

And finding support in Harry's strong but loose-limbed body. Surely not...

'OK?' Harry murmured, and she was so startled by his voice she lifted her head from where it had nestled itself on his shoulder and looked into his concerned brown eyes.

'I think so,' she managed to say, though the words stumbled

from her lips and she knew she must be frowning as she tried to make sense of her reaction to being held by Harry.

'Maybe this will help,' he murmured, his gaze holding hers as he bent his head a little closer and kissed her firmly on the lips.

Steph was stunned by both the kiss and the effect it had on her, so much so that she couldn't respond immediately. Then, by the time she'd realised how pleasant being kissed by Harry was, and was considering kissing him back, it was too late. He'd not only lifted his head, but he'd stepped away from her, and her body no longer had his support or warmth.

'Come on, I'll take you home,' he said, his voice so devoid of emotion she knew he hadn't felt a darned thing—either from holding her in his arms, or from the kiss.

He escorted her, close but not touching, out to his car, but instead of turning towards her place, Harry drove in a different direction. She wanted to ask why, but she was still shaken by the accident, not to mention the tendrils and the kiss, and didn't want to make a fool of herself by stumbling over the question.

'I drove down here the other morning, and noticed Albert's is still in business,' he said, calmly explaining what she needed to know. 'You're in no fit state to face Fanny if she wakes early. We'll stop there, have a big greasy breakfast and talk about it. You know it's the only way to get the images out of your head.'

Steph knew he was right, even though images of the accident were no longer in the forefront of her mind. But she didn't want someone else—even Harry—being responsible for her well-being. It was the kind of thing she might come to rely on, and once that happened, hurt followed.

'I'll probably throw up after a big greasy breakfast,' she told him, attempting to negate the 'being looked after' feeling.

'I'll take the risk,' Harry said. 'I'd go so far as to hold your head if you like.'

'Yuck!' Steph retorted, but she had to admit that even an asinine conversation like this had diminished the effect of the kiss—which had, itself, lessened the impact of the accident.

Of course, walking into Albert's brought on a whole new set of problems. She, Martin and Harry had often breakfasted there, usually when they'd been staying at the Quayles' for study week, and a night of study had been rewarded with breakfast at Albert's.

But they'd eaten there at other times—at the end of a night of celebration, often with the people they'd been seeing at the time—and because Albert's hadn't changed at all, the memories came crowding back.

'Bad choice?' Harry asked, picking up on her ambivalence.

'No,' she said firmly. 'Admittedly I haven't been here for years, but we had good times here, Harry, and I'm entitled to remember those.'

Albert himself was nowhere in sight, and the young man behind the long counter was a stranger. So, with his arm once again around her shoulder, Harry led Steph to a booth at one side of the café, waited until she'd slid into the seat, then crossed the room to order two breakfast specials.

By concentrating on the mundane he could—almost—forget the kiss. How could he have been so stupid as to kiss her when she was so prickly and antagonistic towards him? It had been odds on she'd respond the way she had.

With no response at all!

Hell, slapping his face would have been better—at least it would have shown she felt something!

He took the pot of coffee the young man offered, and two mugs, and returned to the table, back in his role of supportive friend, even if it was a friend she treated with suspicion.

'You're off duty till Monday, so will you risk another coffee?'

He waved the pot in Steph's direction and she nodded.

'I think I need it. I'm sorry I made such a spectacle of myself,' she said, pouring sugar into the mug, speaking of the accident not the kiss—she hoped he hadn't picked up on her reaction to the kiss. 'But I thought of Fanny.'

Harry covered her hand with his.

'Of course you did, and you didn't make a spectacle of your-self. You reacted as any parent would. I had a terrible wrench-ing feeling myself when I saw her.'

Steph smiled at him, because she believed him, and her hand felt good in his, and it was so nice to be with Harry again—to have a friend when she really needed one.

But beneath this very thin veneer of comfort lurked so many black holes of doubt she knew it wasn't wise to relax.

Perhaps she could risk it for a short time—just while they had breakfast together...

Not when you reacted to him the way you did back there! Talk about lurking danger...

Harry watched her thoughts reflected in her eyes and knew she was debating how far she could allow this truce to continue. He longed to reassure her—to tell her he would never let her down. But memories of what she'd seen as the ultimate betrayal of their friendship had been reawakened by the invidious posi-tion in which he now found himself.

And once again it was a member of the Quayle family tying him in knots.

He was about to make a declaration—'I won't let you down again' were the exact words he had in mind—when the youth from behind the counter arrived with their meals. Crisp bacon curled around fat sausages, eggs nestled on thick slices of toast, and grilled tomato slices added decorative colour to the plates.

'Oh, I hadn't realised how hungry I was,' Steph exclaimed, looking up at him with genuine delight shining in her eyes, so he wondered if he'd imagined the doubts earlier.

He watched her attack the food with such gusto he found himself smiling, for this was the Steph he'd first known—the girl to whom everything in life was fun, exciting or a challenge to be met and overcome.

To find that girl still existed within the too-thin, tired-look-ing woman was immensely encouraging, and with a sense of wonder, mixed with a leavening of almost fearful despair, he realised he still loved her.

Shocked almost numb by this revelation, he picked up his knife and fork and tried to concentrate on his meal. Something must have worked, for as Steph's fork flashed across the table to stab at one of his pieces of bacon, he automatically pinned it to the plate with his knife.

'Ask nicely,' he said, looking up and seeing a glimpse of laughter in her eyes, soon washed away by a sadness so deep it caught at his guts and cramped his lungs.

'We can't go back to those days, can we, Harry?' she said softly, then she pushed her plate away and picked up her coffee, cupping her hands around it as if she needed its warmth and studying him over the rim.

'No, Steph,' he said, carefully placing the bacon on a piece of toast before passing it across to her. 'But there's no reason why the days ahead can't be just as good—or even better.'

She took the toast, studied him for a moment, then said, 'Isn't there?'

He had no answer, but he knew she was ready to go—no doubt anxious to see Fanny and reassure herself her daughter was all right.

He ate a little more while she toyed with the toast and bacon, finally taking a bite before putting it back on the plate as if it were somehow tainted.

'Come on, I'll take you home,' he said, when it was obvious she'd finished eating and he'd realised the fat overload was making him feel ill.

They drove to her house in silence, surprised to find the rain had suddenly eased. By the time he pulled up outside her front gate, a shaft of sunlight had broken through the clouds, illuminating the cottage and its straggly, waterlogged garden.

Harry waited, willing Steph to invite him in, but at the same time knowing the less he saw of her the better—at least until he'd sorted out what was happening with Bob Quayle and found out a little more about why Steph was living as she was.

'Thanks, Harry, for being there for me this morning,' she said, resting her hand on his arm. 'I really appreciated it.'

So there was no invitation for him to resist, but the hand on his arm presented a new temptation. He closed his own around it, then remembered there were too many things he didn't know, so he bit back the 'Anytime!' he'd been going to say. He'd talk to Bob Quayle first, find out what was going on, then come to Steph with no secrets between them.

'Give my love to Fanny and tell her I'll see her soon,' he said. He leant across and kissed Steph on the cheek, feeling the coolness of her skin, smelling coffee and bacon and the faint essence of woman beneath them.

CHAPTER FOUR

BY THE TIME HARRY WOKE, it was midafternoon, and Bob Quayle wasn't at home or answering his mobile. Restless and ill at ease because what he wanted to do was visit Steph—something he also didn't want to do until he'd spoken to Bob—he walked down to the beach, then back through the tourist shops to the apartment block.

As he reached the doors of the clinic, he realised that another answer to his dilemma would be to get Bob's job done as quickly as possible then get out of the place. Once he was no longer connected with the clinic he'd lose the feeling that he was spying on Steph and could start again with her.

At least as a friend, though the nagging ache in his body whenever he thought of her kept reminding him he wanted more.

He walked in to the clinic, introducing himself to staff he hadn't seen before, then made for the administration office, where he pulled out the files he needed—staff rosters, staff wages, patient and procedure numbers, and the figures submitted to the government for Medicare payments. He wasn't an accountant, but he'd looked into the finances and staffing of a lot of practices, both general and specialist, in order to learn about setting up his own. The basic accounting tactic was to look at incomings and outgoings and see how they balanced.

And the books were all here.

There was a second desk in the room, which he knew belonged to a part-time practice manager, but twenty-four-hour clinics he'd known in the past had had full-time managers. Maybe that was part of the problem. The manager—whom he had yet to meet—was overworked.

Looking at the staff-patient ratio, the place certainly wasn't overstaffed so that didn't explain any shortfall in the income. And if the problem wasn't in the income, it had to be in outgoings.

He tracked through the ledgers available to him, and finally found the answer. About twelve months earlier there'd been a big hike in the rent. The books didn't tell him why, just that the rent had almost doubled. Going back, it appeared it had been some years since there'd been a rent rise, so maybe the previous owners had negotiated a long-term contract which had finally expired, allowing the building owner—Bob Quayle under a company name—to charge more for the space.

It was more per square metre than specialists like himself would be paying for their suites at the hospital, but he had no idea of the cost of space in the tourist centre of Summerland, so Harry couldn't tell if the rise was fair or not. But it had happened and had certainly contributed to the decreased profitability of the clinic.

Though if the place stopped bulk-billing the government for patients on Medicare and instead charged patients a normal fee, it would not only make more money but it would pay less interest on its overdraft facility which was currently needed to meet the rent when government funds from bulk-billing hadn't come through. By charging normal fees, it would soon find itself back in the black, and from all Harry had seen, this clinic—or *a* clinic—was needed in the area.

He stretched his cramped, tired limbs, then, mainly because he felt so uncomfortable, checked his watch. It was after midnight and, as far as he could remember, he'd had nothing to eat since the breakfast special.

But far more disturbing than missing a couple of meals was the fact that any number of Bob Quayle's minions, by going through the books as he had, could have seen the problem with the clinic's cash flow. Was he so tight-fisted he wouldn't pay someone to do that? So mean he'd asked Harry to do it as a favour?

Harry wouldn't have minded accepting this explanation, but a feeling of unease told him that was too easy an answer. He said goodbye to the night staff now on duty and went up to the apartment, determined to phone Bob Quayle first thing in the morning.

Bob, sounding excessively pleased to hear from him, invited him to lunch, thus spoiling Harry's plan to visit Steph and Fanny. But the sooner he got his business with Bob over and done with, the sooner he could approach Steph with a clear conscience and no secrets.

Oh, yeah!

The first thing Bob told him, after welcoming him back to the house where he'd holidayed so often, was that Steph and Fanny were expected that afternoon.

'It's our access visit,' the older man said, and there was no mistaking the bitterness in his voice. 'Ordered by the courts and supervised by Stephanie herself, would you believe?'

Harry felt his intestines crunch together, as if reacting to a blow they'd been expecting, but though some of his suspicions were being confirmed, he still didn't know why this apparent animosity existed.

'I've already seen Steph. She's working at the clinic. You must have known that.'

If Harry had expected Bob to look embarrassed, he was disappointed, though, considering it, Bob had probably lost the ability to be embarrassed very early on—one didn't build an empire the size of his without treading on toes along the way.

'Yes, I'd heard she was,' Bob said, as if the matter was one of supreme indifference to him. 'With some teenager left to mind Fanny. The girl could be on drugs, or having unsuitable young men over at the house. It's a most unsatisfactory arrangement.'

Harry said nothing, though the urge to defend Tracy—who'd seemed on brief acquaintance to be an exceptional young woman—was strong. Instead, he asked after Doreen and was eventually led out to the poolside patio, where Doreen lay on a lounger, tanning her fashionably thin body.

Harry greeted her fondly, remembering how kind she'd been to him when he'd been a student and far from his own family. They talked easily, about the old days, and Martin, and the fun they'd had, but as they ate a delicious lunch, served out near the pool by a middle-aged woman who was obviously a house-keeper, Harry's unease began to escalate.

His mind listed his problems quite succinctly.

First on the list—Steph and Fanny were coming.

Second—there was obviously some ill feeling between Steph and the Quayles.

And whose side would he appear to be on, when Steph arrived to find him drinking fine wine and eating a sumptuous dessert with people she might well regard as the enemy?

'I really should go,' he said, pushing the rest of the dessert away and setting down his glass of wine. 'Didn't get much sleep last night.'

'No, please, stay.'

Doreen rested her beringed hand on his arm, while Bob, murmuring something about phone calls, excused himself and vanished into the house.

'Please, Harry. It's been so difficult for us, so very hard, to lose our beloved Martin first, then to be separated from our only grandchild. I don't know what Bob has told you, but we did hope, he and I, that you might be able to talk to Stephanie for us.'

Did that explain Bob asking him to look into the clinic? Maybe.

But talk to Steph on their behalf?

Yeah, right! Any minute now she's going to get here, fire killer looks in my direction the very moment she sets eyes on me, and never speak to me again.

How the hell did he get into this situation?

More to the point, how the hell could he get out of it?

Doreen was still speaking, and he tried to follow the conversation, but he suspected either his brain had stopped working or she'd overdone the wine, because not much was making sense.

'Natural she'd be upset over Martin's death, but she could hardly blame us for that. But bitter! And unjust. Unnecessarily so. We'd suffered just as great a loss as she had, worse, in fact, for the loss of a child must surely be the worst pain in the world.'

'Yes, of course,' Harry said, wondering if this conversation was leading anywhere, and how he could terminate it.

'She blames him, as if it was his fault he was killed,' Doreen continued. 'Now she won't even speak his name if she can avoid it, but it wasn't his fault he was killed. If anything, it was hers, having the baby a fortnight early.'

Harry stared at the older woman, wondering if she could really believe what she was saying. And had she told Steph it was her fault? Or made this opinion clear to her?

No wonder there was animosity between the two parties!

'Here's our little doll—our darling.'

Bob's voice, presumably announcing Fanny's arrival, cut off any hope of escape for Harry and, just as he'd expected, the fury in Steph's eyes as she took in the conviviality of the lunch table cut through him like a sabre thrust.

Fanny, however, was delighted to see him, though she had enough sense to greet her grandmother with a polite kiss, before flinging herself with great delight at Harry.

'Are you going to have a swim with me and Grandad?' she asked. 'Mum thought it would be too cold, but I knew Grandad would want a swim, so I brought my bathers.'

Fanny ran back to her mother, who stood like a pillar of stone on the edge of the patio.

'I really must be going,' Harry said, though he knew the damage had already been done as far as Steph was concerned.

Bob looked from him to his daughter-in-law, then back to Harry, but his face revealed nothing.

'I'll talk to you tomorrow,' Bob said. 'And now the rain seems to be finished, you might want to pop in at the hospital and talk to the decorators about the soft furnishings—curtains and such—you want in your suite of rooms.'

Harry felt, rather than saw, Steph's reaction—the air between them solid with distrust—and when he turned to say goodbye, the look she sent him, through slitted eyes, could only be described as venomous.

Steph nodded politely in response to Harry's goodbye, but regret ached within her when she saw Fanny's reaction to his departure. Harry was promising he'd see her again soon, but Steph knew it was impossible, and her little daughter was going to lose her Uncle Harry before she'd properly had a chance to get to know him.

But once again she'd been lured into trusting Harry—or almost trusting Harry—only to find him ensconced in the enemy camp.

She moved across the patio, settling into a chair not far from Doreen, a chair, she now realised, which was still warm from Harry's body. Fanny delved into the big bag, producing her bathers, and, knowing the routine, dashed into the little shower pavilion on the far side of the pool to get changed.

Bob was also ready for his swim by the time he returned from seeing Harry out, and Steph watched as the big man and the little girl swam and frolicked in the pool.

'She could swim every day if you lived here,' Doreen pointed out, repeating the words she said every Sunday afternoon.

'Yes,' Steph said, because agreeing usually stopped the conversation.

'Now your mother's remarried she doesn't need you,' Doreen added. As this was a new tack, Steph hesitated before replying, but she could see no hidden traps beneath the statement. 'She's travelling overseas for two years, isn't she?'

'She didn't ever need me as much as I needed her,' Steph said, ignoring the remark about her mother's travel. 'Especially when Fanny was a baby.'

'You could have lived here. You should have lived here! This should be Fanny's home.'

Doreen's voice became shrill and Steph sighed.

'Let's not get into this conversation again,' she pleaded, wondering for the umpteenth time why she hadn't ever come right out and told the Quayles exactly why she'd refused to live with them.

But it would have destroyed their image of Martin and tarnished his memory in their eyes, and they'd done nothing to deserve that.

Nothing more than loving him too much—and giving him too much.

'She could be such a wonderful swimmer,' Doreen said, and Steph closed her eyes and prayed for patience as the same conversation began all over again.

By Monday evening when Steph left for work, she was tired, uptight and very apprehensive.

'If Harry Pritchard turns up,' she told Rebecca, 'I do not, under any circumstances, want to see him.'

Rebecca looked so startled Steph replayed the words in her head, then realised it must have been her tone as much as the content which had taken Rebecca aback.

'OK,' Rebecca agreed, but the warning proved unnecessary as Harry didn't appear.

Steph didn't know whether to be relieved or angry. She told herself she didn't want to see him—ever again—but she would have liked the opportunity to vent a little spleen by telling him exactly what she thought of him.

Within the clinic, rumours abounded. The clinic had been

sold again—it was closing—no more bulk-billing. So many stories, but nothing changed until the following Friday when, along with a slip detailing what pay had been transferred to her bank account, was a dismissal notice. Alerted by the disgruntled day staff, the night shift had gathered in the tearoom, where they'd all fingered the little envelopes before opening them.

According to the notice, the clinic was no longer a viable concern and the owners had been forced to cease operations.

As from this Sunday! She was to work out the night, and weekend staff would operate, but the Sunday night shift would be the last. The clinic would not be open Monday.

Steph stared at the words, sure there must be some mistake, but loud wailing from Rebecca suggested she'd received the same information.

'It's ridiculous,' Colin, the second doctor on night shift that night, said, staring at his own piece of paper. 'You can't just shut the doors of a place like this. Look at the patients we see, the people who need attention immediately. Where are they supposed to go? Another ten kilometres to the public hospital where they might wait six hours before being treated?'

'You're a far nicer person than I am,' Steph told him. 'I've been wondering where I'll get another job, not where the patients will have to go.'

'I guess I'll go back to the agency,' Colin said. 'They can usually get me night work in A and E at the General.'

He smiled encouragingly at Steph.

'They'd probably take you on as well,' he said, but she shook her head.

'The shifts are all wrong,' she told him. 'I'd either be starting late afternoon, when I'd prefer to be with Fanny, or finishing late in the morning, so I couldn't be home for her when she wakes up. That's why this job was ideal.'

'It's that bloke that did it!' Rebecca muttered, turning to Steph. 'Your friend Harry.'

'No!'

The protest was automatic, but a swirling nausea in her stomach belied her denial. Harry *had* been here to look at how the clinic was working—but why was it any of his business? Who had asked him to do this?

Who were the new owners?

With her stomach churning even harder, she remembered walking into the Quayles' mansion on Sunday and seeing Harry sitting there.

Had the Quayles' vendetta against her reached the stage where Bob would buy the clinic and close it down in order to put her out of a job?

And so force her to take up their offer to house and keep both her and Fanny?

She worked through the night, and by morning knew exactly where to lay the blame for her current unemployment situation. Bob had said something about Harry taking up a suite of rooms in his new hospital. Maybe the hospital would have a phone number for him.

But as she said a tearful farewell to Rebecca, promising to keep in touch, a chance remark saved her the phone call.

'We should go straight upstairs and tell that Harry Pritchard what we think of him,' Rebecca said.

'Upstairs?' Steph echoed. 'Upstairs in this building? Harry's staying in this building?'

'Didn't you know?' Rebecca said. 'No, I guess you wouldn't, but that first night he came in, when he was jet-lagged, he said he'd come down and I asked him where he was staying. Unit seventy-four on the twelfth floor—heaven knows why I remember it!'

It all began to make sense. Bob had built Dolphin Towers and, according to Martin, his father had always kept a couple of apartments in the buildings he built. Bob had bribed Harry to spy on her workplace with the offer of free accommodation.

'You go on home,' she said to Rebecca. 'Leave me to deal with Harry Pritchard!'

Shaking with fury, she made her way into the foyer where lifts served the residential tower. She jabbed her finger on the 'up' button, and wasn't the least bit mollified when the doors swept open immediately. She stabbed at the button marked twelve, and as the metal cube slid silently upward she told herself to calm down—to think through this confrontation.

But a red mist of anger prevented any sensible thinking, and she strode out of the lift on the twelfth floor, looked around and spied number seventy-four. It *would* be the one with the views to the beach and out across the wide Pacific Ocean! Bob would keep the best for himself.

Another button to press but, rather than jab at this one, she put her forefinger on it and held it there.

'I'm coming, I'm coming.' She could hear Harry's exasperation through the door, but didn't move her finger so the chiming bell sound continued to jangle within the apartment.

Finally, he wrenched open the door, and Steph's fury froze momentarily, her heart kicking up a notch or two of pace as she came face to face with Harry's broad, bare chest. Her gaze slid lower. Fortunately, from the waist down, he was clad in an ultra-conservative, blue striped pair of pyjama bottoms.

'Steph?'

His surprise—or mock surprise—reminded her of her mission, and she jabbed her finger out again, this time into the middle of the bare chest. She'd teach it to give her palpitations.

'You slime-ball, Harry Pritchard! You cheat! You traitor! I can't believe you've done this to me again. To think I let you see my daughter—that I told her only nice things about you so she thinks you're wonderful, and then you come back to Australia and muck up my life once more.'

Harry had stepped back, possibly because of the jabbing, but he wasn't getting away that easily. Steph followed him and continued to emphasise her points with forefinger on the slight indentation of his sternum.

'Well, let me tell you, it won't happen. The Quayles won't

win, and do you know why? Because you're going to make up for this. You're going to find me another job—right now—and if it means I have to come to work for you in your swanky new suite of rooms in Bob Quayle's hospital, then so be it. But even if I'm only vacuuming the carpet, I work the hours I want and you pay me as a doctor. OK?'

She was surprised to hear this declaration, as she certainly hadn't thought it through to that extent, but if she was surprised, Harry was far beyond that emotion. Beyond stunned as well, she guessed.

Which made it a good time to press the advantage.

'Agreed?' she demanded, then, worried she might be late home for Fanny, she glanced at her watch.

Could it only have been five minutes since she'd left the clinic?

'Let's have a cup of coffee and talk like real people, not actors in a daytime soap,' Harry suggested. 'The kitchen's this way.'

He walked away and she had the choice of following—which was the only way she could push through to his agreement to her demands—or not following, which would get her precisely nowhere.

But she didn't like the fact he was now the one giving orders any more than she liked having to obey.

She went as far as the bench dividing the dining room from the kitchen and stopped there, looking out through uncurtained windows to the still dark expanse of ocean and the brightness of the eastern sky where the sun would soon rise.

Harry ignored her, keeping his back—broad but tapering down to where the pyjamas hung on his hips—to her as he delved into cupboards, producing mugs and instant coffee, filling the electric kettle and turning it on. Then the coffee was made, and he pushed a mug towards her.

'Still black with sugar?' he said, placing a teaspoon and sugar bowl beside the mug.

She didn't bother answering, merely waiting until he brought his own cup across to the bench and settled on a stool opposite her.

'Now, start at the beginning,' he suggested, looking sternly at her. 'Not the slime-ball part but before that. What's happened that you need a job?'

'The clinic's closed as from Sunday.' She shot the words at him, adding, 'As if you didn't know,' with reheated rage.

He didn't take advantage of her short pause, so she leapt back into the attack.

'Just what did you tell Bob Quayle? I presume it was Bob who'd bought the place. Bob, the new owner, identity kept secret, who wanted you to do his dirty work. Only he—'

'Steph.' Harry's quiet voice interrupted her tirade, but he reached out to take her hand at the same time, and it was more the touch of his fingers on hers that made her pause.

She snatched her hand away, but not soon enough apparently, because the sense of warmth his fingers generated lingered on her skin.

'Tell me what's happened. Why you're so paranoid about the Quayles. Why you feel only Bob would shut down the clinic. Why you think he'd deliberately put you out of work.'

Harry's voice was gentle but, as ever with Harry, there was steel beneath the velvet.

She met his steel with a sword thrust of her own.

'Are you saying Bob isn't the new owner? That you weren't working for him?'

'No, I'm not saying that at all,' Harry told her. 'Bob did buy the clinic, and he did ask me to look at it—'

'And you told him it should be shut down.'

'I didn't tell him it should be shut down. In fact, I told him the opposite—that the clinic could be a lucrative investment if it stopped bulk-billing.'

'Well, according to the dismissal slips we all received in our pay packets, an independent advisor had pointed out the clinic was no longer viable and monetary considerations were, regretfully, forcing the owners to cease operations. You're saying you're not that independent advisor?'

'I'm saying I didn't tell him to close down,' Harry repeated, hoping he sounded more in control than he felt.

For a start, Steph had never been irrational, yet there had been something definitely irrational—close to paranoid—about her vilification of Bob Quayle's behaviour.

But he couldn't let Steph's paranoia get to him. True, there were strange currents flowing here, and apparently the clinic *had* been shut down against his recommendations, but for Steph to be imagining a vendetta against her...

'What's happened between you and the Quayles?' he asked again, and saw her reaction in a sudden stiffening of her body, followed by tremors obvious from his side of the bench.

'Steph!'

He had to go to her, to hold her, but she twisted out of his grasp and walked away, ignoring the coffee, making for the wall of glass on the far side of the living room, where she stood, head bowed and shoulders hunched, her arms wrapped protectively against her body—silhouetted against the magic colours of the rising sun yet oblivious to its beauty.

She stood so still she could have been a statue, long limbs and classic profile carved from the finest marble. The artist would have called it 'Pain' or perhaps 'Despair'.

Harry followed, but didn't venture too near and though his arms longed to draw her close, and his heart wanted desperately to comfort her, he knew she'd retreated so far from him he might never get close again.

A matching despair settled like a yoke around his shoulders, but he had to ignore it for the moment.

'Tell me what's happened?'

That won a huff of mocking laughter.

'Where do I start?' she said. 'And why should I, when you obviously won't believe a word I say, even though you've now seen Bob in action? The basic facts are that Bob Quayle doesn't like to lose. What he wants, what he's always wanted, is for Fanny and me to live with him and Doreen, and he'll go to any lengths, including rendering me unemployed, to do it.'

She turned now, straightening her shoulders and looking directly into his eyes, although, with the strengthening sunlight behind her, her face was shadowed.

'He'd actually prefer Fanny without me—they both would—and that's always the second string to his bow. The moment he gets even a whiff of something that might prove I'm an unfit mother, he'll have a custody case in court so quickly we'll all skid along the pavement.'

She paused but only to take in air for the next attack.

'Do you know, he had the hide to have Tracy investigated? My little cousin, just down from the country, followed about by a couple of thugs Bob had hired to check her out? They were too stupid to keep out of sight, and she was terrified, thinking she was being stalked, but when we called the police and Bob explained, it was all laughed off as a big joke.'

'Steph, I hear what you're saying, but is it all so bad? If you look at it from Bob's point of view, would living with them in luxury be so awful? And was it wrong of him to want to know who's caring for his grandchild when you're not there?'

'He could have asked me about Tracy,' Steph snapped, answering the last question first. 'As for living with them, can you really ask me that, Harry? Can you consider, coolly and rationally, the kind of person Martin was at his core, and deny it was his upbringing that made him that way?'

She shrugged her shoulders.

'We both loved Martin, Harry. He was clever, and fun to be with, and kind and generous, but underneath that Martin was the other Martin, the one who'd grown up with every wish granted, with the money to buy whatever he needed, and the notion that just wanting something was enough to justify having it. Or taking it! The psychologists even have a name for it—

entitlement. A person truly believes he or she is entitled to have whatever they want.'

She half turned, so her face was now in profile against the colours of the morning sky, and Harry felt an inner wince again when he read the sadness in her stance.

'Did it never occur to you,' she said softly, 'that it wasn't until you started showing an interest in me—seeing me as a woman instead of a friend—that Martin made his move? He swept me off my feet with all the considerable charm and wealth, and, now I see it, expertise at his disposal. And I went along—fell in love with love, the way he offered it—and believed every lie he told me.'

Her shoulders squirmed, as if shedding the skin of the past, and she looked directly at Harry.

'I will not have my daughter grow up like Martin!' she said, challenge in every syllable of every word.

Then she walked towards the door, turning as she opened it.

'I'll be in touch about the job,' she told him, then disappeared from sight.

He was too stunned to follow—too blown away by all she'd said, particularly her reading of Martin's sudden pursuit of her.

But even if she was right, he decided much later, it didn't mean she was also right about the Quayles. He could see they'd want the best for their granddaughter, so, to a certain extent, he could even understand them wanting people who minded Fanny checked out. But to deliberately take away Steph's job?

She was getting into the realms of fantasy.

Wasn't she?

The questions spun around and around in his head until, by late afternoon, he knew he had to see her—to find out if her fears had any basis in fact.

Apart from Bob closing the clinic, of course.

But he'd have had his reasons for that...

Fanny was playing in the front yard when he pulled up outside, and she greeted him with such delight he swung the little girl into his arms and tossed her into the air.

'That could send her brain bumping against her skull.'

Steph stood at the top of the steps that led up to the veranda, her arms folded, not defensively in the way that said she was defending herself, more defending her home—her family.

'I won't do it again,' Harry promised, settling Fanny on his shoulders. 'Ouch, not too tight!' he added, as the small hands gripped his hair.

'Oh, poor Uncle Harry!'

The child was instantly contrite, smoothing her fingers down his face.

'Can we talk?' Harry asked, as Fanny called to Tracy to come and see how high she was.

'Only if it's about a job.' Steph was obdurate.

Harry felt the frown gathering on his forehead. He was frowning inside as well.

'That's another thing,' he growled. 'The job situation. Not about getting you a job—I'll do what I can to help—but it's ridiculous for you to even consider doing a job you're overtrained for.'

'People do it all the time,' Steph told him, leaning one shoulder against the wall but not uncrossing her arms.

'I know, I know.' He waved aside the objection—and that subject. 'It's the other job I'm talking about. Your GP work. You were always going to specialise—do surgery. You'd even been offered a place on the surgical programme. What happened?'

He could feel her disbelief radiating in waves towards him.

'What happened to being a surgical registrar and working twelve or fourteen hours a day with a new baby? Can't you guess?'

He could, of course, but Fanny was nearly five now.

'But later—you'd already deferred. The Prof would have let you defer again.'

He wanted to add, 'And if you'd been living with the Quayles, it would have been easy,' but discretion was definitely the better part of valour at the moment.

Tracy had appeared, and he lifted Fanny off his shoulders, kissed her cheek, then watched her chase her friend across the yard.

When Steph didn't reply, he turned towards her and saw she, too, was watching Fanny. But the look on her face held little joy—in fact, it was heart-wrenchingly sad.

CHAPTER FIVE

'YOU'D BETTER COME IN,' Steph said, turning back to face Harry, the invitation so reluctantly issued he didn't want to accept it.

Part of him didn't want to accept. The other part was willing to accept any scraps of time Steph might throw his way. *That* part was desperate to see more of her.

He followed her through to the kitchen, where it was her turn to fill a kettle, pull mugs from a cupboard, make coffee. Only hers was filtered, not instant, made in the plunger he'd given her for her twenty-first birthday.

Martin had given her a car.

Which she'd promptly given back.

Growing up in a single-parent household, she'd learnt to fend for herself—and to pay for what she needed. Her fiercely independent spirit must be part of her war with the Quayles.

'So, tell me,' she said, when she'd poured them each a coffee and pushed his across the table to him. She didn't sit, but leant against the kitchen cupboards, arms not folded, though her attitude was still as defensive as it had been earlier. 'What staff will you be employing? Is it already a done deal? Have you signed people up? Will you be able to find a place for me?'

'Steph!' The protest blurted from his lips. 'You can't be serious about this job. I know you were upset this morning, but don't tell me there's such a surplus of trained doctors at the moment that you couldn't register with an agency and have a job to start on Monday.'

'Not a job that allows me the time I want to spend with Fanny,' she retorted. 'I've been there and done that, Harry. Agencies don't actually care about people—they care about the number of vacancies they can fill. That's how they make their money. Oh, they're charming enough at the initial interview—of course, Dr Prince, we understand completely—and I start off working nine to two-thirty, or night shift nine to five, then next minute the schedules change—they're always very sorry—and I'm paying for extra hours for Fanny to stay late at kindy, which she hates, and I hate, and the Quayles jot down as yet another black mark against me.'

Harry sipped his coffee.

'But I don't see how I can help,' he said. 'I'm setting up in practice—I'll be touting for business. I thought to begin with all I'd need would be a receptionist who can double as a nurse if I need one. I've registered to be on call for the General as from Monday and I'll be happy to do whatever hours they give me, but as for staff...' he tried to lighten the atmosphere with a smile '... I'm hoping the cleaners come as part of the deal with the hospital.'

But if he thought Steph would be deterred by a smile, he was wrong.

'And have you employed this nurse-receptionist?' she demanded. 'Signed her or him up?'

Harry shook his head.

'Not exactly,' he admitted. 'I've spoken to an agency—they're sending people for interviews on Monday. I can't see patients in the suite for another three weeks so there's been no urgency.'

'Until I was made redundant,' Steph said crisply. 'You'd better cancel the interviews.'

He stared at her, unable to believe she could play so tough.

'Steph—' he began, but she held up her hand to silence his protest.

'No, it's absolutely perfect,' she said. 'You're just starting off, so won't have many patients. I can work nine to two-thirty, take my lunch-hour then, and pop out to collect Fanny, bring her back with me to your rooms and she can play there until I finish.'

She grinned at him and he felt an answering smile somewhere in the region of his heart, although his head was warning him things were only getting worse.

'Best of all,' she said, confirming the warning, 'it'll drive Bob absolutely nuts to think he turfed me out of one job, and there I am, working in his precious new hospital!'

'Steph, they're Fanny's grandparents. Does it have to be so— so warlike between you?'

'Yes, it does,' she said decisively. 'And if that bothers you, too bad. You chose your side back when you decided not to tell me about Martin's infidelities, and you obviously haven't changed sides since. But as well as being their granddaughter, she's also your god-daughter, and if you want what's best for her, you'd better agree to employing me—at least while I look around for something with the right hours.'

Steph hoped she sounded more confident and determined than she felt. Inside, she was a wobbling mass of insecurity, made worse by knowing she was hurting Harry, talking the way she was. But Harry had hurt her, and though she was doing this for her daughter, not out of vengeance, a little bit of vengeful sweetness flavoured her decision.

Until she looked into his face and read the pain in his dark eyes.

'Harry, it's not just me!' she said, instantly regretful and pleading for his understanding. 'You said yourself you'd advised Bob to keep the clinic, yet he's closed it—it's a pattern that's gone on since Fanny's birth.'

But it was too late. He was on his feet, and moving towards the front door.

'No doubt you know where the hospital is—you can start at nine on Monday. You'll have to organise furniture, computers, a patient filing system, appointment records, the lot. I assume you can do it?'

'You'd better believe I can!' Steph muttered to herself, already planning on phoning Rebecca to talk about exactly what she'd need. She'd worked in Reception in medical offices to earn money during her student years, and was sure it would all come back to her. But furnishing an office?

He didn't wait for her reply, but he did stop in the front yard to play with Fanny for a while, before kissing her goodbye and promising to see her soon.

Steph felt as if she was being split in half. For a start, Fanny would benefit from the involvement of Harry in her life. In spite of whatever was going on with him and the Quayles, he would be a good male influence in her life. But if she trusted him in the way she'd once trusted the Quayles, was she risking losing her child again?

'It's ridiculous,' Harry muttered for the twentieth time that morning. It was the following Wednesday, and the strain of having Steph behaving as if she really was a receptionist was grating on his nerves. 'A trained doctor ordering office supplies.'

'Get used to it!' Steph snapped at him. 'And bear in mind you're paying me as a doctor, not a receptionist.'

'You must realise I can't afford it,' he grumbled. 'You know the cost of setting up a practice.'

'So borrow more money,' Steph told him, determined to make him pay for his involvement in the loss of her previous job. Then she relented. 'It won't be for ever. I've contacted the agency and let them know what I want. You might be rid of me by Friday, but in the meantime Fanny has to eat and I've a mortgage to pay.'

Harry was caught in a bind. Getting rid of her by Friday should have made him delirious with joy as it was obvious that having her around was going to be so distracting he doubted he'd ever get any work done. But not having her around might be worse.

Would be worse, part of him confirmed.

The phone, on the floor by the wall until the furniture arrived, rang and she dropped down, cross-legged, to answer it.

'Dr Pritchard's rooms.'

Harry studied her while she listened to the caller, pulling a notepad towards her and jotting down words or figures. She might only be acting as a receptionist but whatever Steph tackled she did well, focussing on the task or position with such intensity she was, at times, unaware of what went on around her.

Which had made it easy for Martin to cheat on her.

She'd dropped the phone back into its cradle and was scribbling on the notepad.

'That was Medi-Rentals. From a tax perspective you'd have more immediate deductions renting, but if you borrow money to buy the equipment you need, the interest is also tax deductible and you end up owning the stuff.'

She hesitated, frowned at him, then added, 'Though, with specialist medical equipment, that's not always good because it needs upgrading regularly, so it could be a false economy. I'll do a few sums and set them out on a sheet of paper so you can compare and decide.'

Harry stared at her. This was not what he'd expected when Steph had blackmailed her way into his office. Though he realised now it was no more than another example of her intensity and focus. He wanted to say something—to tell her he appreciated the effort she was putting in—but the phone rang again, and this time when she answered it her face grew grave and she passed it up to him.

'It's a child with facial injuries—a fractured eye socket from a fall off a bike. Possible depressed fracture of the maxilla as well.'

Steph touched the bone that swept around the nose and held the upper teeth in place, imagining the outcomes for the child if he or she wasn't operated on. She was thinking of how she'd react to Fanny being injured when Harry replaced the receiver and asked his question, so at first it made no sense.

'Did you ask if I would assist? In the operation? You can't just take anyone you like to assist in an operation at the General. It's a public hospital.'

'The patient's been admitted to Summerland Private,' Harry explained. 'That's the first hospital Bob Quayle built—the one close to the beach—isn't it?'

Steph nodded, more intent on Harry's offer than on where the hospital was—although now she did consider the hospital, she felt a shudder of distaste run through her. But Harry's offer was too good to refuse, though in all conscience she had to point out a few things.

'I haven't done any surgery since my first year as a resident,' she told him.

'Maybe not,' he said easily. 'But you've been stitching people up in the clinic, and I've no doubt you can still hold a clamp on a blood vessel.'

He'd been shrugging into his jacket as he spoke.

'Come on. The sooner we start, the easier it is to put the pieces back together and the less likelihood there'll be of infection.'

Slightly dazed, but essentially excited, by this turn of events, Steph followed him out the door, turning to lock it behind her.

'Why did they phone you?' she asked, when they were in the car.

Harry smiled at her.

'You make it sound as if I'd be your last choice,' he teased. 'Actually, the A and E doctor at Summerland Private who first saw the boy worked with me in Paris for a while and knew I'd done a lot of reconstruction work with children. I was talking to him last week.'

In Paris? It seemed odd to Steph, but the closer they drove to the hospital, the more uneasy she felt, and she was so focussed on *not* thinking about the last time she'd been there, she missed the opportunity to ask for more information about Paris.

'Have you been back since?'

Harry had either caught her apprehension, or was mind-reading. He certainly wasn't thinking about Paris!

'No!'

He glanced her way, but said nothing, negotiating the turn into the hospital grounds and pulling up in one of the spaces reserved for specialists. But when he'd turned off the engine, he reached out and took hold of her hand.

'This place had nothing to do with what happened, and if you think of it as where Fanny was born—that's surely a happy thought—rather than where you learnt of Martin's death, it might be easier.'

Steph leaned across and kissed him on the cheek.

'We're still not friends,' she warned. 'You're too firmly in the enemy camp. But thanks for that, Harry. Having Fanny is definitely worth everything that's happened.'

Once inside the hospital, she had no time to think of the past. They were escorted into a small operating theatre usually used for day surgery.

'The two main theatres are being used, but this theatre has been fitted up for cosmetic surgery so will have everything you need. We've called an experienced theatre nurse back on duty and we've an anaesthetist standing by.'

All this information was directed to Harry, though from time to time the woman delivering it—one of the theatre administrative staff, Steph guessed—cast sideways glances at Steph, who, as usual, was in jeans and a T-shirt. Today's proclaimed her to be the sexiest woman in the world—with a huge Not written on the back.

If this job lasted until Harry started seeing patients, she might have to upgrade her wardrobe—or at least censor the T-shirts.

'This is Dr Prince—she'll be assisting,' Harry was saying, and Steph put out her hand and introduced herself by name to the woman, who was obviously too startled by Harry's revelation to offer her own name.

In the small dressing area adjoining the theatre, more introductions followed—to the anaesthetist and two theatre nurses, all of whose names passed completely over Steph's head as she pulled on theatre garb and wondered if she'd remember any of the surgery she'd once done.

The little boy, heavily sedated and accompanied by his mother, was wheeled into the theatre anteroom, where the nurses took over, positioning the trolley beside the operating table, then gently sliding him across.

Monitor leads were already in place on his chest, and a shunt was taped to the back of his small hand. He didn't look much older than Fanny, and Steph couldn't help thinking how she'd feel if it was her child.

Then Harry slid the X-rays into the light-boxes on the wall, and she stopped thinking of the small person and concentrated on what they had to do.

'We'll cut the skin here, near the hairline, and peel it back. Steph, your job will be to keep it irrigated. Because he's so young and his bones are still growing, they should heal well, but we need to make sure they're aligned properly and check for nerve or blood-vessel involvement.'

Steph nodded, knowing a nerve pinched between two pieces of bone would soon die and the child would end up palsied, like her patient of the previous week. Had it only been last week that Harry had reappeared in her life?

She glanced at him, but he was focussed on the child, and she joined him, keeping out of his way but close enough to be useful.

'If you're not putting in pins to hold the bones together, how do you stop a child his age from damaging his face again before the bones have calcified over the break?'

'We can use a mask. I don't know if they're available here, but overseas I've seen masks made like Spiderman and Batman, even Superman. For little girls there are fairy masks. So rather than bandage the whole face so he looks like the mummy from hell, we can pad the damaged area then use a mask.'

He glanced towards the theatre sister.

'Do you know if they're available here?'

She shook her head.

'Perhaps we can make one,' Steph suggested. 'Plaster might be too heavy, but fibreglass could be used—from the rolls used for plastering breaks now.'

'Maybe we could,' Harry agreed. 'We'll bandage him to start off with, and enquire about masks later on.'

He was cutting as he spoke, separating the skin from connective tissue underneath so he could peel away the upper layer and get at the damaged bones beneath it.

Steph, working close beside him, felt transported back in time to when they'd first qualified and worked surgical rotations together, Harry's eyes meeting hers over the top of his mask. Harry's eyes telling her things his lips hadn't said.

Then Martin had decided he loved her, and had swept her off her feet...

Concentrate! she told herself.

It became easier as Harry began to manipulate the child's fragile bones back into their rightful positions. But the maxilla proved a problem. It was cracked through just below the child's nose, and would need to be plated in order to save his teeth. But though a plate could remain in place for ever in an adult, with a child it would have to be removed later to allow for growth.

'If his new teeth had been right through, I could have wired them to hold the bone in place.'

Harry's voice echoed his frustration. Steph understood he'd been hoping to save the child another operation later.

'No, we'll have to plate it.'

The circulating nurse was sent to find a selection of small plates and screws, while Harry removed some chips of bone.

'How did it happen?' Steph asked the anaesthetist, who'd seen the child earlier.

'Riding his bike, hit a kerb and flew over the handle-bars into a brick wall. He was wearing a helmet but his face took most of the impact.'

Steph shivered, thinking how easily accidents could happen, then Harry's arm brushed against hers, and though there were several layers of covering between them, she still felt comforted.

You can't trust him, she reminded herself as she helped him set the plate he'd selected into position, then prepared the skin for closing. But as she watched him place the final tiny staples to close the outer layer of skin, wanting to do it himself to make sure it was perfect, she remembered the Harry she'd operated with before, and the way she'd begun to feel about him—before Martin had stepped between them.

'Done!' Harry said, stepping back and peeling off his gloves with an air of great satisfaction.

The child's face had been protected by layers of wadding, then bandaged to provide more protection. Seeing the mummified look, Steph understood why masks of any kind would be a kinder option for a child.

'You've done that before,' the anaesthetist said. 'That was as neat a job as I've seen in ages.'

'Practice makes perfect,' Harry said, shrugging off the compliment. But Steph caught the 'Unfortunately' he muttered, almost under his breath, and knew darkness shadowed the words. Again she wondered about reconstructive work on children. And Paris.

'I'm going to see the parents,' he said to Steph as they stripped off. 'Then there are a couple of people here I want to talk to. You can take the car back to the office—I'll phone when I'm done and you can come and get me.'

He tossed the car keys to her as he spoke, and she caught them automatically but, certain one of the people he wanted to talk to would be Bob Quayle who had an office here, she couldn't hold back a protest.

'I'm not your chauffeur!'

She threw the keys right back, hoping he'd miss the catch, but, of course, he didn't.

'No?' he said, eyebrows rising above treacly brown eyes. 'I

understood you'd offered to be anything I wanted you to be, Steph. Anything!'

The keys landed back at her feet and, before she could think of a reply, he'd walked out of the room.

Seething helped, but not much.

Calling him names wasn't much better.

And you did offer to do anything—as long as he paid doctor's wages, her conscience reminded her.

Anything?

This time she repeated it with the intonation Harry had used, and an inner tingle of excitement—the kind she hadn't felt for a long time—ran along nerve-paths she'd thought were dead for ever.

Hell! That was the last thing she needed. Harry Pritchard is inextricably linked with the Quayles, she lectured herself. You've blackmailed him into employing you for the moment, and you might—repeat *might*—reach some kind of understanding with him so Fanny can see him regularly, but lusting after him—and that's all it could be—is definitely *not on*.

She drove back to the still-empty office and took out her bad temper on office suppliers who thought they might be able to overcharge her for their equipment.

'I would have thought your first priority would have been for a practice manager rather than a receptionist,' she told Harry when, obedient to his command, she'd driven back to Summerland Private to collect him. He'd taken the wheel for the drive back, which was a shame as it would have given her something to do with her hands other than wave them in the air, illustrating the extent of the job ahead of them.

'Have you considered bank accounts—patient trust accounts for people who want to pay something in advance? You're going to need at least one other signatory on those, unless you can handle being called out of an op to sign a rent cheque.'

'Overdramatising, Steph?' Harry sent a wry look her way.

'After all, regular payments like rent will be made by bank transfer.'

'And if there's no money in the operating account and you need some transferred?'

'Do it by phone or on the internet. Whoever I finally employ will know the access codes.'

Steph, who hadn't had enough money recently to worry about either internet banking or access codes, pondered this for a moment.

'You'll be putting a lot of trust in that person,' she pointed out. 'Are there safeguards you can put in place?'

Harry laughed.

'I doubt there'll be anything to worry about for the first few years,' he said. 'By the time I've covered overheads and interest, I imagine my receptionist will be earning more than me.'

'But cosmetic surgeons can earn huge amounts of money—and so much of what they do isn't time-consuming. Look at Botox. You could do half a dozen an hour and...'

She stopped, mainly because Harry had stopped—stopped the car! He'd pulled over to the kerb and had turned to face her, then he put his hands on her shoulders and turned her so she faced him.

'Steph, do you really know so little of me that you'd think I'm in this for the money? That I've set up to do nothing more than inject fillers into people's sagging faces, or poison into muscles that cause wrinkles? It's not even surgical work!'

Shame caused a momentary spasm in her heart, but she rallied.

'I thought I knew you once, Harry,' she reminded him, 'and maybe if you'd come back under different circumstances, we'd have got over what happened in the past. But since the day Fanny was born, Bob Quayle has been trying to get control of her life so, seeing your connection there, I can't help but be wary.'

'Oh, Steph,' he said softly, then he leaned forward and kissed her, oh, so gently on the lips.

She knew it meant nothing more than the previous kiss had meant. It had been a kiss of comfort, while this one was more a gesture of despair than love. But her physical self didn't realise that, and excitement buzzed down those recently re-alerted nerve tracks to the inner depths of her body, while the tiny tendrils grew to vines and choked her lungs.

She felt her own lips respond, parting to invite him in, to share the sweetness of the kiss, and for a moment he did, exploring her mouth with a tentative gentleness that teasingly promised passion yet held it back. Then he drew away, leaving coldness where the warmth of his mouth had been—more coldness in her heart.

Releasing her shoulders, Harry turned to stare out the window, then slapped his hand against the steering-wheel. Where had that kiss come from? He'd wanted to protest about her apparent distrust of Bob, but at the same time assure her he wouldn't ever do anything to hurt either her or Fanny. But he'd already, unwittingly, done that with the closure of the clinic.

Although he couldn't believe Bob had closed it to put Steph out of a job...

'What do you want me to do?' he asked, knowing she'd understand what he meant.

'Find rooms somewhere else, for a start.'

He shook his head.

'I can't do that, Steph. I've a particular reason for wanting to work from the new hospital.'

'Because Bob's bribed you with cheap rent? Promised you star billing among his collection of top specialists? Guaranteed you more operating hours than anyone else? Thrown in a free apartment?'

She was angry and he didn't really blame her, but until all the arrangements had been finalised he wasn't going to talk about the deal he'd done with Bob. Especially not to Steph who, from their long friendship, should have known that neither fame, nor fortune, nor star billing had any appeal to him.

Though the free accommodation had been a help...

He started the car and drove back to the new building, parking in one of the spaces reserved for his rooms. The feel of her lips—soft yet wanting—was burned into his brain, and the feel of her bones beneath her skin as he'd held her shoulders was imprinted on his hands.

'I went home and got a card table and a couple of folding chairs on the way back from the hospital earlier,' she told him as she opened the car door. 'I've put some comparisons—buying versus renting furniture and equipment—on the table. If you tell me what accounts you want, and what bank you prefer, I can get the forms you need to fill in on my way to collect Fanny. You'll have to take them back yourself as you have to show a heap of identity papers before you can open an account.'

She climbed out, leaving him sitting, slightly stunned, behind the wheel. He couldn't believe she could behave so—so ordinarily. As if the kiss hadn't happened.

As if she were nothing more than a real receptionist setting up his office for him.

And doing it efficiently, too, as far as he could make out.

He followed her into the rooms, then realised she'd unlocked the door. He had a key on the bunch with his car keys and she'd have used it earlier, but he hadn't given her one for her own use.

As if guessing his thoughts, she held up a small bunch of keys.

'Front door, drug cabinet and staff washroom,' she said, flipping them into the air then catching them again. 'I tracked down the hospital administrator and got them off him.'

She smiled and her eyes sparkled with devilment.

'And guess who was in with him at the time?'

Harry's startled expression must have given him away, for she smiled and nodded, as close to smug as he'd ever seen Steph.

'The man himself—Bob Quayle. But I didn't disgrace you, just tugged my forelock, asked for the keys, bowed and departed.'

'Steph!' The word that had been a plea earlier was now a

protest, but she'd turned away and was collecting a pile of what looked like brochures off the little table set up in the middle of the room.

'I'll get these out of your way. If you could look at the figures, and the different equipment the firm offers, and let me know which way to go, I can order it tomorrow and have it here by next Monday.'

She whisked away, presumably to collect Fanny, then returned almost immediately.

'You didn't say which bank.'

He named the bank where he kept his personal account, and saw Steph frown.

'Something else that doesn't meet with your approval?' he demanded, infuriated by her nonchalant behaviour.

'It's no skin off my nose, but it's well known their fees and charges are much higher than other banks'. However, they may offer more in other ways—perhaps in overdraft facilities. If you like, I'll get some information on what business accounts they offer and what the other big banks have that's comparable, then you can decide.'

She departed once again, leaving Harry feeling distinctly uneasy. She was determinedly antagonistic in some ways, suspicious of his involvement with the Quayles, yet she was doing far more than he'd have expected a receptionist to do—and thinking further ahead than he ever had when he'd decided to set up his own practice.

Steph drove carefully, hyped by the Miss Efficiency act she'd put on for Harry to hide her reaction to that kiss, but aware there was so much distraction going on inside her mind and body that she needed to concentrate.

Queen Street was the main business centre of Summerland, and all the major banks had branches within a hundred yards of each other. Checking she had time to do a quick dash down the road before collecting Fanny, she parked and set off, not waiting in the interminable queues but selecting from the assortment of

brochures set out for the public to take—brochures which ex-
tolled the wonderful benefits of each particular account.

Then to the kindergarten, where Fanny, involved in a game
with this week's best friends, was reluctant to leave.

'If I have to leave her here for work reasons, she complains,'
Steph said to Patsy, Fanny's group leader.

'Aren't women supposed to be contrary?' Patsy said. 'And
you have to admit, Fanny's all woman!'

All Martin, Steph sometimes thought. Capable of not only
charming birds out of trees, but charming the trees to do his—
or in Fanny's case, her—bidding as well.

'Are we going to Uncle Harry's place this afternoon?' Fanny
demanded, when she'd finally consented to leave.

The two previous afternoons, Tracy had been available to collect her from kindy and mind her until Steph had come home.

'We're going to the place where he'll be working, but there's
nothing much there yet. I brought some toys for you to play with
and some colouring in for you to do.'

'Will Uncle Harry be there?'

'Probably,' Steph admitted, though she fervently hoped he
wouldn't be. Perhaps he'd been called away, or he might have
gone to see the furniture she was thinking of getting. Although
Fanny was showing enthusiastic delight at the thought, Steph
knew that the less she saw of Harry, the easier her own life
would be.

But life wasn't meant to be easy, was it? Not only was Harry
in the suite but, to Fanny's double delight, so was her Grandad.

She greeted both men with joy, chattering on about her day,
while Steph, sensing the tension between the two men, wondered just what she'd interrupted.

The moment Fanny finished a story about a boy who'd called
her names, Steph took her hand and led her into the smaller
room destined to be a tearoom when the suite was furnished.

'Let Grandad talk to Harry now,' she said to Fanny. 'Here,

you do some colouring in while I do some work. We both have to sit on the floor.'

Fortunately, Fanny thought sitting on the floor was something of a lark, so she settled down, spilling pencils from her box, turning pages to find the picture she wanted to colour, while Steph picked up a notepad from the counter by the sink and dug the bank brochures out of her handbag. She'd do a comparison of the various accounts they offered, and let Harry decide.

But though she worked diligently through the information, her heart was racing with apprehension as she imagined what was now going on between Harry and Bob.

A little before five, as she was preparing to leave, packing away Fanny's pencils and discussing with her daughter what they'd have for dinner—'No, you had take-aways last week'— Harry walked in.

'I've taken a look at the figures and need to talk them over with you. The bank options as well, if that's what you've got there,' he said, nodding to where she'd set the bank brochures on the bench. 'I imagine you've still got Tracy living with you and she could take care of Fanny tonight. So how about I pick you up at eight and we have dinner together?'

He must have seen her lips moving to form a 'no', for he continued before she could voice a protest.

'You can take time off in lieu,' he said. 'Tomorrow, collect Fanny from kindy and go straight home. In fact, you could do that every day, and do any phoning or ordering that has to be done from your place. Keep an account of the phone calls. We'll need to set up a petty-cash fund, won't we?'

He smiled, which effectively ruined whatever excuse she might have come up with, because the smile lit up his dark eyes and made her skin feel warm, although she knew he was doing it to silence any argument, not warm her skin.

Fanny, who'd obviously followed at least the first part of the conversation, took Steph's hand and asked, 'Will you wear a dress?'

She then turned to Harry.

'Mummy's got a lot of dresses, but she doesn't ever wear them,' she confided. 'Though I wish she would because she looks so pretty in them.'

'I'm sure she does,' Harry responded gravely. 'Perhaps you could make sure she wears one tonight.'

Steph stopped feeling warm. Her temperature was notching now to hot, but from anger rather than any other silly emotion.

'I don't think being my boss means you can dictate what I wear,' she told him.

'No?' The eyebrows rose above the not-smiling-now brown eyes. 'I'd have thought it gave me exactly that right, and while I'll grant T-shirts and jeans are OK while we're still setting up, I think I'd prefer a uniform of some kind once I open. You'll be seeing to that, naturally.'

Shot down in flames, she still managed to rally.

'Not before tonight,' she retorted.

'Then wear a dress,' he said, making an order of the words, though a fraction of a second later he softened it with, 'Please, Steph?'

CHAPTER SIX

WEAR A DRESS?

Once again Steph stood in front of her wardrobe, and for the second time it was Harry Pritchard causing her indecision.

True, she had a lot of dresses—mostly bought when she'd been married to Martin. He'd loved to take her to the best boutiques and spend extravagant sums of money on her clothes.

So she fitted the image of Martin Quayle's wife!

And possibly to appease his conscience, though she hadn't known that at the time...

She flicked through them distastefully and came across a creamy silk shirt she'd always loved, but which Martin had labelled old-fashioned. And somewhere she had good black jeans—designer jeans admittedly, but at least she'd feel comfortable in them. She dug through the rack of clothes, and found them hiding under a jacket.

Unfortunately, Fanny came in as she was spreading this outfit on the bed.

'Uncle Harry said a dress!' Fanny said sternly.

'I know, sweetheart, but these are good, dressing-up jeans.'

'No!' The obdurate look, which Steph admitted came from her genes rather than Martin's, settled on Fanny's small features. 'It has to be a dress. I'll find one.'

Inevitably she chose a vivid emerald green ballgown which Steph had always hated.

'That's a dancing dress,' she told Fanny, 'not a going-out-to-dinner dress. Honestly, the jeans will do.'

But Fanny was searching again, finally coming up with a slim-fitting black jersey dress, which actually predated Steph's marriage to Martin, and, though old, was so simple in style it was dateless. She guessed Fanny had been attracted by the thin strip of jet and crystal beading around the deep V-neckline, but it was certainly an acceptable compromise.

'OK,' she told her daughter. 'But now you'll have to look in the bottom of the wardrobe to find some black shoes to go with it, then in the bottom drawer of my dressing-table for some black stockings or tights as well.'

Fanny was delighted, crawling into the bottom of the wardrobe and playing there for a while before producing the shoes, then crossing to the dressing-table where she pulled out all the stockings and a number of suspender belts Steph had forgotten she owned.

Getting dressed with Fanny's help took longer than a solo effort, but eventually she was ready.

She studied her unfamiliar self in the mirror, realising how thin she'd got since she'd last worn the dress when she saw the way it clung to her breasts and skimmed down over her hips, suggesting a shape, rather than hugging her figure.

And make-up—how long since she'd worn more than a touch of lip gloss?

The image in the mirror made her nervous and uncertain, but Harry was here already—and Fanny had left to greet him—so she couldn't put off her grand entrance for much longer.

Harry, crawling around the floor with Fanny on his back, sensed a movement and looked up, taking in long shapely legs encased in sheer black stockings, then a slip of a dress, a duller, denser black, making Steph's pale skin seem even paler in comparison, and the short red hair even redder.

'You're more beautiful than ever.'

He hadn't meant to say the words—after all, this was to be a business dinner—but they'd slipped out anyway.

'I'm not sure about compliments from a horse,' she said, a slight smile tilting her luminous lips.

Which was when Harry realised he was still on all fours, though his rider had dismounted and was now walking around her mother, nodding her approval of the dress.

He collected his senses, not easy as his eyes kept going back to the silky black legs, and stood up.

'Some dress,' he said, again forgetting it was a business dinner. 'Shall we go?'

He waited while she gave last-minute instructions to Tracy, turning to him to ask, 'Where are we going?'

'I asked the manager at Dolphin Towers. He recommended Travesty—he said it's fairly new and, though it has a funny name for a restaurant, the food's good.'

Steph crossed to the small phone table, pulled out a phone book and looked up the number of the restaurant, writing it down for Tracy. He had a feeling Steph was stalling, putting off the moment when the two of them would be together without the buffer of other people.

But that was ridiculous. She knew she was more than capable of holding her own with him—she'd proved that with the job situation.

'OK, let's go,' she said at last, picking up a minuscule handbag that couldn't possibly hold more than a handkerchief and her keys. She flashed a smile at him and added, 'You've got the brochures and the figures?'

He nodded, because he did have them in the car. He'd taken them home to study them, then, in the process of finding somewhere special to take Steph—preferably somewhere she wouldn't have been with Martin—he'd forgotten about them. But, even though she looked like pure pleasure, she wasn't going to let him forget this was business.

He said goodnight to Tracy, kissed Fanny and felt the delight of her soft plump arms around his neck, then escorted Steph out to the car, careful not to touch her in case the desire building inside him might escalate out of control if he felt the softness of her skin, or was close enough to smell the scent of her beneath the faint beguiling perfume she was wearing.

'I think I'll buy the office furniture and associated necessities,' he said, once settled behind the wheel and determined to damp down the flames with business talk. 'Bob was telling me there's a company willing to supply all the suites at a very good rate, then we can rent the medical equipment I'll need. That way we can upgrade as new inventions and innovations occur.'

Steph ignored the jab of pain the 'Bob was telling me' caused, and concentrated on the rest of the statement. The mix of 'I' and 'we'.

How seductive that 'we' sounded to her thwarted ambition of becoming a surgeon. True, she might not have gone into Harry's sub-specialty, but...

'That was a big sigh,' Harry said. 'Is it so hard to agree that buying furniture but hiring equipment might be the way to go?'

She had to smile.

'It was a sigh for something else—for what might have been, Harry.'

'Surgery?' he guessed, and his prescience caused a stiffening of her muscles and a prickling of the hair at the nape of her neck.

'Did you do a course on mind-reading while you were away?' she asked, desperate to keep the atmosphere light.

'No.' He glanced her way. 'But it was such a passion with you, I can't help wondering what happened. I know you mentioned Fanny, and understand you couldn't have done your registrar years with a tiny baby, but—'

'I didn't have to get pregnant right then?' she finished for him, hoping she'd learnt to keep the bitterness out of her voice. 'No. I didn't.'

Harry heard the blend of regret and pain and knew there was

no way she would regret having had her daughter. But if she hadn't wanted to get pregnant, what had gone wrong?

He thought back, reconstructing the past through new eyes since Steph had mentioned Martin's pursuit of her—and her contention that it had only been when Harry himself had become interested that Martin had swept her off her feet.

All Martin had ever wanted, as far as his medical career had been concerned, had been to qualify, gain some hospital experience in Brisbane, then return to Summerland to run the hospital his father had built for him. Martin had seen it as the start of an empire—and himself as the head of a national chain of private hospitals.

And Steph couldn't have done her specialty years in Summerland. Summerland General wasn't a teaching hospital.

'Weren't you on the Pill?' he demanded, when his thoughts had led him to an unpalatable possibility.

'I went off it for three months—it's what most of us doctors advise women to do from time to time.'

And Martin had been in charge of contraception, Harry guessed, though he didn't say it, merely reaching out to take Steph's hand and feeling the coldness of her fingers although the night, now the rain had stopped, was quite warm.

Steph slipped her hand out of Harry's, but his mind was occupied with thoughts of the man who'd been his best friend. Had finding out about Martin's infidelities affected Steph to such an extent she'd let bitterness colour her memories of the man? That could explain her animosity to the Quayles.

Or was she right? Harry had to admit Martin had been spoilt and used to getting his own way. But had he been devious enough to marry Steph purely because Harry had been falling in love with her? Sly enough to use a pregnancy to prevent her doing surgery? It had all happened so quickly—courtship, marriage, pregnancy—then, in a little over a year, Martin had died.

The problem was, the more Harry reconstructed Martin, the more he had to think about Bob, and being inextricably tied to

Bob meant he didn't want to be harbouring suspicions about the man.

'Wasn't that the place?'

Steph's sudden comment brought him out of his reverie. He pulled over, checked for traffic, then swung the car around in a U-turn, pulling up a couple of car spaces past the entrance.

'Thanks,' he said, climbing out and walking around the bonnet to open the door for her.

'Thank you,' she said, and when she kissed him lightly on the cheek, he knew it was for more than his politeness in opening the door. She'd called him a mind-reader, but had she sensed his thoughts? Were the old bonds between them still so strong they could follow each other's emotional shifts?

He rather hoped not, as some of his emotional shifts were practically X-rated.

He took her arm to walk into the restaurant, pleased she didn't draw away, though displeased by his own mental warning that holding her arm was as close as he was going to get.

She was as wary as a cat, and her mood changes as unpredictable as the weather, while suspicion about his involvement with the Quayles was probably providing her with more than adequate armour against any advance he might make.

The tables at Travesty were set apart, small groves of potted greenery providing privacy between them.

'This is lovely,' Steph said, her face lighting up with such honest delight Harry felt his chest cramp with the love he felt for her.

Then she looked at him—really looked—and added, 'You haven't brought the papers—the comparisons.'

Now his chest cramped with a different emotion. She might be relenting—slightly—in the war she'd declared on him earlier, but now she was reminding him this was business.

And that there was a big gap between a truce between them and acceptance back into her life as a friend.

As more than a friend?

Steph sat at the table they'd been allocated and watched Harry walk back out of the restaurant.

He looked fantastic, in a dark suit with a casual turtle-necked sweater beneath it, the dull maroon of the sweater complementing his olive skin and silky black hair.

As well as stirring that bit of her she'd thought dead for ever, he was intriguing her in other ways because though he was, in many ways, still Harry the friend she'd once have trusted with her life, he was an enigma as well.

Driving over here, he'd taken her hand, and she'd known he'd understood, without her having to say the words, what had happened between her and Martin that had put an end to her chance to specialise in surgery. He'd even seemed to understand how difficult it still was for her to reconcile the love she had for the child she'd borne from that unwanted pregnancy with the lingering bitterness of thwarted ambition.

Though he probably couldn't understand her resentment of Martin, who, she was now sure, had deliberately planned for it to happen.

But as Harry walked back in, pink plastic folders in hand, she pushed the past back to where it belonged and smiled, because the joy she felt at seeing him again—spending time with him—superseded even her suspicion of him.

He, however, couldn't be feeling the same joy, because he plunked the folders on the table, passed her a menu and said, 'Let's order then get down to business.'

And Steph, who'd been the one to remind him this was a business dinner, squelched the disappointment inside her and obediently studied the menu, her disappointment soon diminished by the sheer pleasure of deciding what to eat.

Harry had been determined to be as businesslike as she apparently wanted him to be, but when he saw her face light up as she pondered her choice, he forgot businesslike, wanting only to keep her looking as happy as she looked right now.

For ever.

'There are far too many choices,' she finally said, turning to him with her face still glowing with delight. 'What are you having?'

They debated the various options—fish or fowl, meat or vegetarian—finally deciding to share a seafood platter. Well, Harry decided, and though Steph nodded enthusiastically, she had another look at the menu and the glow faded from her face.

'No,' she said. 'It's the most expensive thing on the menu and you're already going into debt to set up your rooms. I know I told you to go into more debt to pay me, but I'll earn whatever you pay me, Harry. I'll do a good job for you. But this is different. Ordering the platter is sheer extravagance.'

He reached out and took her hand.

'I'm not actually broke,' he said apologetically. 'In fact, though I might have to borrow a little money to get set up, it won't be much. I've done quite well, and do have another source of income to back up my own savings, so one extravagant night out won't do any harm. And as you've already pointed out, if things look like they're going bad, I can do more rejuvenation work.'

She shrugged, as if ashamed she'd once put down his business, then frowned at him.

'What work do you mainly want to do? And what were you doing in Paris? Why would there be more children with facial injuries there than anywhere else in the world?'

He hesitated for a moment, then, knowing Steph would persist until she got a satisfactory answer, he told her.

'We, the general public, see the children—and adults, of course—who've lost limbs as a result of exploding land mines—anti-personnel mines they call them—on television all the time. And a lot of specialists and prosthetics manufacturers donate time and equipment to these people. But many of those injured have facial scars and deformities as well, where bits of shrapnel have flown up and gouged out not only flesh but bone as well.'

Her eyes widened, but urged him to go on.

'There's a clinic in Paris where children from the war-torn areas of Europe are brought. The specialists there use a technique of taking bone from another part of the child's body, usually the hip bone, shaping it, then grafting it into place to give definition back to the face.'

'Because kids can cope with a prosthetic arm or leg, but to carry a distorted face through life would be terribly destructive to their self-esteem?'

'Exactly,' Harry said, relishing the warmth of the hand she'd laid gently over his as he'd talked about the children.

'So, tell me more. Does the bone grow? That would be much better than plating or screwing bone together because there'd be no need to follow-up operations. Do you get rejection problems? What are the risks?'

Business was discarded—and any hope of a romantic evening also went west—as Steph demanded to know more and more about the work he'd done. Her excitement shimmered like an aura around her and he realised she'd probably been isolated from this kind of conversation for too long.

There'd been other doctors at the clinic where she'd worked, but only sharing duty with her one night a week, and from what he'd seen of Friday nights, there wouldn't have been much opportunity to talk shop.

So he fed her hunger for information, then fed her literally, peeling prawns and offering them to her, still talking, egged on by her keen interest.

'No! Eat yourself,' she finally protested. 'I'm going to tackle the sand-crab.'

She smiled across the table at him—a genuine, heart-felt smile.

'I must have sounded desperate,' she said, a little rueful now. 'But, Harry, it's just so long since I've sat and talked medicine with someone—and to hear about the things you've done...' She shrugged. 'I'd be lying if I said I wasn't envious.'

And Harry, who'd always thought of Steph as someone who

could have had it all—in fact, when she'd married Martin he'd assumed she *would* have it all—felt the grip of pain for what she'd lost.

'But you have got Fanny,' he reminded her, and was rewarded with a warm smile.

'Yes, I have got Fanny,' she said, and although the words shone with the love she felt for her daughter, beneath that sparkling polish he glimpsed patches of the dusty tarnish of regret.

They finished the meal, then did settle down to discuss business, both ordering coffee while Harry talked Steph into trying a slice of chocolate and macadamia torte as well.

'So, now that's sorted, how are you going to get known?' Steph asked him, licking a last piece of sweetness from her lips.

Harry was looking at her, but the blank expression on his face suggested he hadn't heard a word she'd said.

'You'll need referrals so you get patients. Your savings might pay for the rooms and furniture but for ongoing income you'll need paying customers,' she reminded him.

She saw the little frown appear and guessed he was dragging his mind back from wherever it had been.

'I know a couple of GPs in the area, and now doctors are allowed to advertise—to the extent they can announce they've opened an office—I thought I'd do that.'

Steph shook her head.

'Not enough!' she said firmly. 'You need to join the local branch of the medical association, and there's a specialists group here in Summerland as well. Then maybe a letter to all the GPs in the area, letting them know you're in town but, more importantly, telling them the kind of work you've done, the experience you've had, who you've worked under—things like that.'

He smiled at her and she felt a hot wave of blood colour her cheeks.

'Of course, you'd already thought of that,' she mumbled.

He reached out and took her hand, stilling the fingers that had been playing nervously with her discarded napkin.

'I had, but thank you anyway. Thank you for caring enough to be interested in whether I get patients or not.'

The warmth of his touch burned into her and the urge to turn her hand, grasp his fingers, and drag him across the table so she could kiss him properly was so unexpected she was left breathless—as breathless as she'd have been if the kiss had happened.

She had to get out of here—away from Harry—before more bizarre notions occurred to her.

'I should be getting home,' she said, removing her hand from temptation and pushing back her chair.

'Yes!' Harry stood up, and came around the table to hold her chair, then push it back under the table.

Contrarily disappointed that he didn't argue, she walked beside him towards the door, going on ahead when he paused to pay the bill but lingering on the path as the sweet scent of some hidden plant attracted her attention.

Drawn to it, she stepped off the path into the shadows, seeking among the rich banks of greenery for the white flowers of a star jasmine—for surely nothing else could be as subtly enticing.

'Hiding from me?'

Harry's voice barely broke the evening stillness, though the husky tones of his whisper caused agitation in her heart.

'Looking for the jasmine. I was going to pinch a bit of it. It grows from a cutting and if I planted it just below my front veranda I could enjoy that heavenly perfume every night.'

'Still a girl who loves the simple pleasures,' Harry murmured, coming closer and encircling her, but loosely, with his arms.

'Hardly a girl,' Steph managed, as Harry's nearness caused the breathlessness again.

'No, you're right,' he said, looking down into her face. 'You're a woman—and all woman, Steph.'

Then he kissed her, and this time she didn't have to tempt him, or even wonder what he was feeling, because this kiss was full of heat and hunger, and it burned deep down into her body, setting her aflame with so much desire a tiny moan escaped from way back in her throat, a moan of frustration that she couldn't press her body closer, feel his skin on hers, find the ultimate fulfilment that was part of being a woman.

A part she'd all but forgotten…

CHAPTER SEVEN

'COME HOME WITH ME?'

The request was whispered so softly it might have been the rustling of the night wind in the trees, but the seductive undertone, firing need along Steph's nerves, told her it was more than a passing breeze.

It had been so long...

Would it be so wrong?

This was Harry, whom she'd always loved...

He must have sensed her weakening for, with his arm around her shoulders and her body tucked protectively close to his, he led her back towards the car.

The excitement the kiss had generated grew, fizzing in her body like the bubbles in shaken champagne. Speech impossible, she sat, clutching one of Harry's hands while he drove, one-handed, back towards the centre of the tourist strip.

Still clinging to his hand, as if it was the only thing anchoring her to the real world, she stood beside him in the lift as it rose to his floor, then walked beside him into the apartment.

He must have been still unfamiliar with the placement of light switches, for he moved away from her, feeling along the wall, the only light in the room the red blinking of the message light on an answering machine.

For someone in the state she was in, it was a little bit of normality. So much so, Steph moved automatically towards it as she always did at home—when messages might occasionally change her work schedule from week-nights to weekends. As the lights came on, she pressed the button to play then, realising what she'd done—that it wasn't her machine—she turned, appalled, to Harry.

'I'm sorry—put it down to nerves,' she quavered, but her apology was lost as the booming voice of Bob Quayle echoed around the room.

'Have you spoken to her yet?' he demanded. 'It was part of our agreement, remember. Phone me when you get in.'

It was an unmistakeable order and an echo of Harry's earlier words—'I do have another source of income'—rattled in Steph's head.

She stared at Harry, unable to believe he'd betray her this way. Though Martin had betrayed her, and Harry had done nothing about that!

'I assume I'm the "her" he mentioned,' she said, wishing the jagged chips of ice in her voice would tear his skin and make him bleed.

'Yes, but it's not what you think. Steph?'

He came towards her, hands out held as if to grasp and hold her.

She stepped away.

'You don't know what I think, Harry,' she told him, evading his hands and moving towards the door. 'And perhaps it's just as well you don't.'

She was out of the apartment, pulling the door shut behind her, before he realised she was going, and as the lift was still on the twelfth floor, it took only an instant longer to enter it and press the button.

But the satisfaction she felt at the dismay on Harry's face as the doors slid closed was diminished as pain, deadened at first by the shock of Bob's words, now clamped her heart and lungs and made her clasp her arms around her stomach as if to protect her body from an even greater onslaught.

It was inevitable Harry would catch up with her. Taxis were never available when you needed one.

'At least let me drive you home,' he said, standing beside her on the footpath a few minutes later. 'You're being silly about this.'

She turned towards him.

'No, I was silly when I believed Martin loved me,' she said fiercely. 'And silly when I thought you and I could still be friends. Maybe even more than friends. Silly to think I could trust you—trust any man! But right now I'm being sensible. I'm going home in a cab, alone, and that's that, Harry Pritchard. But if you thought you could seduce me out of working for you, well, forget it. I'll be there tomorrow at nine, and the day after that, and the day after that. And seeing you've another source of income—' she let her scorn emphasise the words '—I might not even try to get another job.'

She would, of course, because working with Harry, particularly now when he must know how she felt about him, would be too torturous to handle. But he wasn't to know that.

Let him sweat!

A taxi pulled up in front of her, and as she'd been too busy telling him off to have signalled it, she realised he must have done it for her.

Ha! So, for all his protestations, he was glad to be rid of her.

He opened the door for her and she slid in, then remembered her manners.

'Thanks for a memorable evening,' she snapped, then she turned to give the cabbie her address.

To say the atmosphere was strained between them at work would have been the understatement of the century, but life was made slightly easier by Harry being out of the office most of the time.

Steph didn't try to keep track of his whereabouts, though

she did organise a pager for him so she could contact him if she needed to—or if he was offered some work at either of the local hospitals.

The computer and related software she'd ordered arrived, though the furniture hadn't, but she set up the computer on the card table and drafted a letter for him to send out to local GPs, leaving blanks for him to fill in his experience.

He'd returned the completed letter to the card table, coming in some time after she'd left work, and this became the pattern of their days—she leaving things for his perusal or signature, he returning them when she was absent.

Medical reps started calling, leaving glossy brochures on the drugs and equipment they were touting, often flirting with her, perhaps thinking she would influence her boss.

As if!

No alternative job materialised, so she was still there two weeks later. Furniture and furnishings had been delivered, and Steph began to take a proprietorial delight in the swish look of the suite of rooms, carefully setting the patient files, with their different coloured tabs, into slots in the open shelves, ruling up the appointment book, the day surgery book and the theatre appointments book.

She mastered the phone with its various options for transferring calls, arranged for direct cable access to the internet and had programmes for patient information, pathology reports and medical accounting installed on the computer.

'Have you heard when the hospital will open for business?' she asked Harry on one of the rare occasions their paths crossed. 'I've a number of patients already listed for appointments. I'm to call them back with a date and time as soon as you're ready to begin consultations. And I'll need to know what operations you can do as day surgery and which patients you'll need to hospitalise. Perhaps you could do a list...'

Harry stared at her. He couldn't fault her efficiency—she'd done far more than he'd ever have expected a receptionist to do—but now she was talking as if she'd be here for ever, and being near her, seeing her whenever he entered his own suite of rooms, was driving him to distraction. While frustration gnawed its way through his body, like a lion feasting on a dead beast.

The beast analogy fitted—it was exactly how she saw him.

He'd tried talking to her, and had been met with cold disdain as she refused to acknowledge the passionate embrace they'd shared—or how close they'd come to taking that passion further.

'From the number of enquiries and the people already waiting for confirmation of their appointments, I think you'll need two staff people sooner than you think, but probably an office junior, someone who can answer phones, write in appointments and handle filing would be better than a nurse.'

She continued talking as if the heat thrumming in the air between them didn't exist, but he knew she had to feel it—it was too strong for her not to.

'I was talking to the hospital administrator and he said they supply the nursing staff for both the day surgery theatres and the main theatre—apparently the cost is written into your rental agreement.'

Her lifted eyebrows told him just what shenanigans she imagined had gone into that arrangement, but he'd attempted, over a week ago, to explain about the phone call—and his private income. She'd refused to listen and he was damned if he was going to grovel to the woman.

Yet!

'Hire whoever you think you'll need—or the real receptionist will need. You're surely not planning to stay on once we open.'

'I haven't decided,' she said, but the wide grey eyes with their dark fringe of lashes didn't meet his and he didn't quite believe her.

Steph turned away because she'd never been able to hide anything from Harry. But, to a certain extent, she'd spoken the truth. She wasn't sure about her future.

What she was sure about was that she loved Harry. She ached

for him in a way she'd never felt before—with a depth of longing she hadn't realised could exist.

And it made her stupid—running her hands over letters he'd handled, touching his signature as if it could somehow connect her to him.

But Harry had betrayed her—as surely as Martin had done years earlier—aligning himself with Bob, all but seducing her so he could do Bob's bidding.

Though, she would admit honestly, when her interminable musings reached this point, she'd done a bit of the seducing herself. It hadn't all been Harry…

Another thing she was sure about was that she had to get away. Away from Harry. And from any chance of seeing Harry, and, wherever she went, she'd also need distraction—something to keep her mind occupied and fully focussed so thoughts and images of Harry didn't keep popping into her head.

As far as occupation was concerned, she was hoping the decision would be made for her.

That one operation, assisting Harry, had reminded her how much she'd enjoyed surgery and, seeking a good reason to escape a city she now considered too small for the two of them, she'd written to the board which chose likely candidates to take up surgical residency positions as the first step towards specialising, asking if she could be considered.

'You've done what?' Harry roared at her when, in order to bring up the possibility of Rebecca coming to work for him, she admitted she'd made this move.

They were in the tearoom, and she backed away from his anger, fetching up against the sink.

'Applied to be considered for a surgical residency. If the board agrees. I'll take the primary exams next year, and if I do well in those I'll be given a place on the programme.'

'But you'll have to go to Brisbane—or further north to another teaching hospital. And you'll need a general residency while you do your primaries. And you'll be either working or studying all the time—what about Fanny?'

They were in the small tearoom which seemed to become smaller by the minute as Harry loured and glowered and growled at her.

'I can live with Mum and Bill—that's her new husband. Bill was a widower, and he has a huge house with a self-contained flat where Fanny and I can stay. But Mum will be there to take care of her while I'm at work.'

'And what about your house here in Summerland?'

'I'll rent it out to pay the mortgage—Tracy has friends who'll move in with her.'

'Do you want to do surgery so badly you'd uproot Fanny and set yourself four years of really hard work when you'll barely get a chance to see her, let alone spend quality time with her?'

No, I don't, was the honest answer, but she couldn't tell him that.

'I'll make it work,' she said, tilting her chin and daring him to argue.

'Only if you run yourself ragged. And for what? A job that will continue to take you away from Fanny—a job where you can be called in at all hours of the day or night so you miss the important things in her life?'

His voice had softened, as if the anger had run out of him, and he stepped towards her.

'Isn't there something else—something less taxing—you can do? Aren't there other options you could consider?'

He didn't mention the Quayles but Steph could feel them hovering in the background of the conversation.

She could also feel the electricity they'd generated in the restaurant garden still vibrating like plucked guitar strings in the air between them.

'I don't think it's any of your business,' she said, as coolly as she could manage, given the heat searing through her body.

'No?'

The word hovered between them for less than a second, then Harry overtook it, one step bringing him close enough to grasp her shoulders and draw her firmly into his arms. And as his head, bending towards hers, blocked out the light, she knew that not only was he going to kiss her, but she was going to kiss him back.

And the consequences be damned. She'd sort them out later.

Hard, hot and urgent, his lips took command, mastering hers with such effortless ease she felt her boneless body slump against him.

She wound her arms around his neck, clinging to the anchoring strength of his solidity as she responded with all the pent-up emotion that had tormented her for the past few weeks.

His tongue flicked against her lips, seeking entrance to the warm cavern of her mouth. With a thrill of pleasure almost illicit in its power, she touched her tongue to his, tasted him, then let the invasion continue. Trembling now, she clung harder, while Harry led her nerves on an exhilarating dance, teasing first her mouth, then the soft, responsive spot behind her left ear, his moist tongue delving into the hollow at the base of her throat. And when she murmured her delight, silencing her with another assault on her lips.

One of his hands slid under her T-shirt, up towards her breasts, cupping the heavy, swelling mounds in turn, brushing at her nipples until she wanted to rip off her clothes—her bra—and feel those wandering fingers on her skin. Then that torment stopped, and the roving hand was at her waist, releasing the stud at her waist, sliding down the zip.

'I want to feel you—need to feel you, Steph,' he murmured, so huskily the words were like sandpaper on her skin. Then his mouth stopped any protest she might have made, and the clever surgeon's fingers slid beneath the elastic of her knickers, and she shivered in anticipation of his touch.

'Touch me!'

It was an order, and she knew she must obey before he'd do

the same to her and relieve the unbearable tension building in her body. With one arm still around his neck for support, she reached between their tight-pressed bodies, found evidence of how he felt and, with fingers shaking with uncertainty, slowly and carefully followed the outline of his arousal through the fine silky material of his trousers.

The phone rang but, far from jolting them out of their heated embrace, it seemed to accelerate the need for speed—to race to the inevitable conclusion. But Steph heard her own voice on the answering machine as it picked up the call, and the jolt she needed finally came.

She drew back, remembering the other answering machine and the message she'd never clarified.

'What did Bob ask you to ask me?'

The dazed look in Harry's dark eyes turned to puzzlement.

'Bob? Ask me to ask you? I haven't a clue. Dammit, Steph, we're about to make love and you drag Bob Quayle into the conversation!'

Steph stepped away, snapping closed the stud on her jeans, drawing up the zip.

'The other time we got this far—or nearly this far,' she reminded him, 'Bob had asked you to ask me something.'

Harry shook his head. Much more of this and he'd need a holiday in a quiet padded cell. He tried to think back, but his thought processes had been blocked by libidinous overload, and his brain was too busy bemoaning the cessation of pleasurable activities to remember past a couple of minutes ago.

'The answering-machine message,' Steph elaborated, but it still didn't help.

'Oh, forget it, then!' she stormed, spinning around and stamping belligerently away. She paused halfway out the door, and hope re-ignited in Harry's heart—and other parts of his anatomy. Only to die when she said, 'I've written out a list of the patients who want appointments and why they want to see you. You might go through it and work out if they're day surgery or theatre patients, then write down the time you'll need for the various operations. Then, as soon as I have your theatre times, I can slot them in as possible appointments and confirm after the consultation.'

Harry knew he was frowning—probably ferociously—but how the hell...?

'How the hell can you behave like this?' he demanded when he realised thinking about the question wasn't going to achieve much. 'Prepared to make love to me one minute, icily cold the next, then discussing patients as if nothing whatsoever had happened between us.'

'I can behave like this because I'm a professional!' she snapped. 'Anyway, nothing did happen between us, Harry Pritchard. And nothing will while you're Bob Quayle's messenger boy—even if you can't remember the messages.'

With the new mention of the hospital owner, something clicked in Harry's beleaguered brain.

'All Bob wanted me to ask you was if they could have Fanny for longer visits—maybe even overnight sometimes.'

He stepped towards Steph as he spoke, wanting desperately to get things right between them. 'Would that be too hard to allow? Couldn't you concede them that much?'

But far from getting things right, he'd made them worse. He knew that the instant colour flared in her cheeks and anger sparked from her silvery eyes like minute glinting arrows, sent to pierce his skin.

'The last time I allowed Fanny to stay overnight with the Quayles, they took her to Disneyland!'

The bitter words hit him harder than the angry arrows, but the message they conveyed must have lost something in transmission.

'Disneyland, USA?' he guessed, to Steph's back as she was packing up the papers on the reception desk with swift, angry movements.

'That's the place!'

The words were shot at him with the force and venom of a snake strike.

'But you can't go there on an overnight visit,' he protested, as the conversation made even less sense the longer it continued.

'Exactly!' Steph snapped, thrusting the straps of her capacious handbag across one shoulder and marching towards the door.

Harry made to follow, but the phone rang again. Perhaps it was just as well, as he really needed to get his brain back into function mode before he could follow up on Steph's accusations.

The phone call, from a woman who wanted information on laser treatment, reminded him of the questions Steph had asked—about patients and procedures and operating times. He pulled the list she'd left for him closer and studied it, seeing the number of requests for simple procedures as well as the appointments for people wanting complex surgery.

Laser treatments and simple procedures for preventing wrinkles or smoothing out those already present were more in the realm of a dermatologist, but he knew there wasn't one in Summerland. Specialist beauty clinics offered a range of these treatments, where trained technicians worked under the supervision of a specialist. He'd have to find out if such a place existed in the growing city, then check out the qualifications of its staff before recommending it.

He sighed. The amount of work in setting up the practice went far beyond anything he'd envisioned. In fact, without Steph, he wouldn't have got as far as he had.

Could he persuade her to stay? Find enough work to justify employing her? Not as a receptionist—she'd already refused to accept the professional wages she'd first insisted he pay her, taking only what a receptionist would earn. But for a lot of his surgical procedures he'd require an assistant, and she had sufficient surgical experience—and was good enough—to take that job.

Perhaps they could incorporate some beauty treatments into

the practice's work, treatments a qualified GP could do under supervision…

He shook his head in disbelief at the way his thoughts were turning, but when he considered the alternative—Steph shifting away from Summerland, not seeing her—the inner devastation he felt suggested he should look more closely at the idea.

Steph collected Fanny from kindy and drove home. The letter from the surgical board was in the mail box. With tactful kindness, it advised her their training programme was already full and the waiting-list of doctors wanting to join it so long it was unlikely she'd be accepted within the next few years.

'Damn!' she muttered, scrunching the piece of paper into a ball and hurling it at the front door.

'Bad word, Mummy!' Fanny chided, and, looking down at her daughter, Steph shook her head, acknowledging Harry had been right. Being accepted would mean four years of long hours, hard work and a heap of study. And success would bring even longer and more erratic hours, which wouldn't be fair on Fanny.

'I'll have to get a job!' she said. She didn't realise she'd spoken the gloomy thought aloud until Fanny said, 'But you've got a job with Uncle Harry. And it's a good job, because you don't have to work at night and be tired in the morning, and Uncle Harry likes us, so he'll let you come to my kindy when there's something special on.'

She paused, looking expectantly up at her mother.

'Maybe Uncle Harry could come too, some time. Like when we have a special day for fathers. Remember Grandad was going to come last year, then got busy?'

Steph looked down at the little girl who had her father's eyes, and the familiar cramp of almost painful love she felt for her daughter threatened to overwhelm her. She blinked back tears, and knelt to hug her.

'We could ask Uncle Harry,' she promised, knowing how much the child wanted a father-figure. 'But he might get busy, too. Uncle Harry's a surgeon, so he operates on patients. He couldn't leave a patient on an operating table while he dashes out to visit your kindy.'

'I suppose not,' Fanny agreed reluctantly. Then she shook her head, and with her usual determination, added, 'But I'll still ask him.'

The opportunity to ask him arrived far sooner than either Fanny or Steph expected, for Uncle Harry arrived in person, a little after six, with two plastic bags filled with take-away containers.

'I don't know if you all eat Chinese, but I thought I'd take the chance,' he said, putting his offerings on the table before swinging Fanny into his arms.

'I could have had dinner already prepared,' Steph told him, as her body battled with her mind—one part of her dancing with delight at Harry's presence, while the other raced suspiciously through possible motives for his appearance.

'In which case you could have put it in the fridge for tomorrow night.' Harry's good humour was undiminished by her cranky attitude. 'Shall we eat it while it's hot?'

He looked around.

'Where's Tracy?'

'She's at the library,' Fanny informed him, rolling her tongue around the unfamiliar word so a few too many 'r's sneaked into it.

'Studying with friends,' Steph said, then, as if the words had triggered her own memories, she looked up from where she was unloading the meal and frowned at Harry.

'We shared so much...were so close, the three of us...' she whispered, and he saw the sheen of tears in her eyes.

Harry felt his chest grow heavy with pain, and stepped towards her.

'Steph...'

He wasn't sure himself whether it was a word of comfort or a plea, but she backed away from him anyway, holding up a hand as if to ward him off.

Fanny broke the tension, taking his hand and leading him into the living room where she'd set out the pieces of a large jigsaw. Then, when the meal was finished, Fanny demanded his presence in the bathroom, 'Though I can wash myself,' she assured him.

A bedtime story, goodnights all round and finally Harry and Steph were alone. He apprehensive, and she, if he went on how she looked, wary and defensive.

'I don't want to talk about the Quayles,' she announced, settling into a big armchair and folding her arms.

Harry nodded.

'That's OK,' he said. 'It's not why I came.'

'No?'

Suspicion lengthened the word so it seemed to echo around the room.

'No!' he said firmly, then he realised he wasn't quite sure why he *had* come. Except that they'd parted badly and he hadn't wanted to have enmity festering between them.

And he didn't want her going to Brisbane, but he wouldn't mention that.

'I came because I've been thinking about your job situation. Not what you're doing now—though you've been wonderful. But a real job. I'll be needing a surgical assistant for a lot of operations. It's not full-time work, but it pays well, and you might pick up other assisting jobs from other surgeons.'

She studied him for a moment, as if trying to read some message behind the words, then said slowly, 'The medical practice where I do a session for pregnant women has offered me part-time work. If I could arrange hours with them that fit in with your operating schedules...'

Her voice was hushed, as if she didn't want to hope too hard that this might actually happen.

'I've been given a theatre Tuesdays and Thursdays, eight to

twelve—or later if I need it—for major surgery, all day Friday for day surgery,' he told her, hardly daring to hope himself.

'You wouldn't need me Fridays, then, or Mondays and Wednesdays, so I could safely ask for hours on those days.'

Harry nodded, then saw doubt cloud her eyes again.

'Are there strings attached to this? Is Bob involved? Was it his idea? A new way to bribe me?'

'Honestly, Steph, you're paranoid!' Frustration gave force to his explosive accusation. 'Can you hear yourself? First you have Bob rendering you unemployed by closing the clinic, now you suspect he's behind me offering you a job. It doesn't even make sense. In fact, I think I know why he closed down the clinic and it had nothing to do with rendering you unemployed.'

She looked across at him, frankly disbelieving.

'I went through the books—remember,' he told her, taking advantage of her silence to press the point. 'He owns the building and about a year ago he raised the rent—doubled it. I think he did it hoping the clinic would close. Think about it, Steph. He's building a hospital only three kilometres from the clinic and including a twenty-four-hour A and E service in the plans.'

She frowned at him.

'Twelve months ago? That was before I started working there. You think he didn't want the competition?'

'Exactly! But the clinic didn't close when he raised the rent, so he bought it, knowing he could close it himself. I was just a convenience, really. Someone who bobbed up at the right time whom he could send into the place so it looked as if he'd done the right thing by getting someone from the outside to make a recommendation.'

'I guess if I hadn't talked to you, no one in the clinic would have known your true recommendations,' she said, speaking slowly as if weighing each word.

'And knowing Bob, you must admit that killing off any competition to his new venture would fit with the way he works.'

Steph nodded.

'Yes, it does,' she admitted. 'But though my suspicions about the clinic might have been wrong, my distrust of the Quayles isn't. You haven't been where I've been the last few years, Harry. You haven't had trust stolen from you, not once but many times.'

A hint of tears now sparkled in her eyes, and his heart ached with the love he felt for her.

'Many times?' he echoed quietly, wanting to know more—to understand at least part of her antagonism towards the Quayles. 'Is Disneyland included in this catalogue of betrayal?'

'Disneyland!' Steph gave a wry gurgle of laughter. 'For a long time I couldn't even say the word without a red tide of rage rushing over me. But, yes, that's part of it.'

'So, tell me. Explain. Fanny went for an overnight visit and they took her to Disneyland?'

The incredulity he'd felt earlier coloured the words.

'What about a passport?'

Steph shrugged, then a little smile flickered around her lips.

'I guess, looking back at it, it's kind of funny,' she admitted. 'But, believe me, it's taken me two years to even smile about it.'

This time she sighed, then shrugged again, before settling herself more deeply into the armchair.

'You know Martin and I had been living with the Quayles here in Summerland for the last few months of my pregnancy. It was supposed to be a temporary arrangement, while he finished work in Brisbane, then we'd find a house of our own down here.'

Her voice was stripped of all emotion, and Harry guessed she'd come to terms with the fact that leaving her with his parents had made it easier for Martin to cheat on her.

'After he died, I couldn't go back there, so I went home to Brisbane—to Mum's place. Once a month I'd drive down here so the Quayles could see Fanny, and I'd get into an argument over not returning to live with them.'

She looked across the room at Harry.

'I couldn't do it, Harry. I just couldn't return to where I'd lived with Martin, or risk their spoiling Fanny the way they'd

spoiled him. But it didn't stop them asking—pleading, plotting.
When Fanny was about two and a half, they started a new cam-
paign. Could they see more of her? Could she stay overnight?
My mother had her company all the time, why should they see
so little of her? In the end I gave in, and she stayed a few times.'

She brushed a hand across her face, as if the memories were
cobwebs she couldn't escape.

'I used to worry she'd get sick and need me, so I stayed overnight here myself, in a cheap motel. Then one weekend I went
to collect her on the Sunday, and the housekeeper told me they'd
gone away. She handed me a laptop computer and a letter telling
me it was connected to the internet and all I had to do was log
on, and they'd send pictures and messages every day.'

Harry found the story so extraordinary he simply stared at
Steph.

'From Disneyland?'

'I realised that's where they were when I saw the pictures
they sent.'

'And the passport?'

'That was my own stupidity,' Steph admitted. 'Some time
before, they'd talked about settling Martin's estate.'

She gave a huff of cynical laughter.

'That was a joke! Martin, of course, had nothing, but had
conveniently left a will passing everything he didn't have to his
then unborn child. The Quayles saw that as his last wish, so told
me very early on they'd keep me, and give me an allowance, but
that Fanny would eventually inherit their wealth.'

She looked up at Harry, and he saw the hurt in her eyes.

'It was as if they thought I'd married Martin for his money,
or their money, and needed to make it clear I wouldn't get it.'

He stood up, wanting to go to her, to hold her and comfort
her, but she held up her hand to stop him.

'I got over it, of course, but at the time it hurt—not to mention making me so mad I could barely breathe—and it was then
they asked me to sign a lot of papers. It was my own fault for not

reading all of them, for signing without checking. The passport application was among them—I signed, giving permission for Fanny to be included on Doreen's passport.'

Harry shook his head. The story was too bizarre to not be true.

'This was two years ago?'

'About that,' Steph agreed. 'She was too young, of course, to even realise where she was, and at an age where people dressed up in costumes rather frightened her. Anyway, after they came back, I stopped visiting. Eventually, they took me to court, wanting full custody of Fanny, citing my work hours among the list of many reasons I wasn't coping with motherhood. They had a top-class lawyer and the battle was horrible, but the judge saw my side of things in the end, though they got permission for weekly visits. Mum had met Bill by then, and really needed a bit of space. Tracy got into the hospitality course at the uni college down here and was looking for somewhere to live, so I bought the house and shifted to Summerland to make the access visits easier. I kept thinking things would get better between us, but they don't. Doreen keeps nagging about us returning to live with them, and Bob—well, Bob's a man who's used to getting his own way.'

Harry shook his head. It seemed unbelievable, all except the last bit. Bob was definitely a man used to getting his own way.

And right now what he wanted was not only more access to his granddaughter—though that *had* been the reason for the message on the answering machine—but also for Fanny to cut the ribbon at the opening of the hospital—the Martin Quayle Memorial Hospital.

He'd only sprung that little bombshell on Harry late this afternoon. Followed, of course, by the inevitable request for Harry to sort it out with Steph!

CHAPTER EIGHT

'So, WHAT DO you think about the job?' Harry said, and Steph, who was still struggling out of the misery of the past, frowned at him.

'Assisting me at ops,' he added.

She knew her frown had deepened—maybe working with Harry she'd get free treatment for her frown lines.

'I'd love to do it,' she said, hoping her inner muddle of delight and apprehension wasn't apparent in her tone. 'But I wonder if I'm qualified—if I've the skills you'll need.'

Harry grinned at her.

'Didn't you qualify as an MBBS? Bachelor of Medicine and Bachelor of Surgery? I certainly did and we went through together.'

'Yes, but—'

'No buts,' he said, standing up and moving across to where she'd practically burrowed into the chair. 'Just think about it. You won't be required to do much in the beginning, and all your surgical skills will come back to you in no time.'

Steph peered suspiciously up at him.

'Why are you doing this? I don't want charity, you know.'

He sighed and shook his head, his dark eyes troubled as he studied her.

'Why do you think, Steph?' he growled. 'Because Bob asked

me to as part of some bigger plot? I can understand, because of what you've been through, that you've lost a lot of trust, but you can't continue to let the past colour all your thoughts. I'm asking you because I know you can do the job—and know that whatever you do, you do well.'

He hesitated, as if there was another reason, but maybe she'd just imagined that because now he'd turned away and was patting his pockets, no doubt searching for his car keys.

'I'll see you tomorrow,' he said, and though she knew she had to stand up and walk to the door—see him out properly—she was reluctant to leave the security of the armchair. 'I'll see myself out.'

That got her up, and she followed him to the door, the job forgotten as she studied his back—remembered how it had felt under her questing fingers, remembered the heat that had flared between them only hours earlier...

'Goodnight.'

He'd reached the front door and half turned to utter the politeness. Her body was heavy with longing, and her arm ached with a need to reach out and touch him.

But touching Harry brought nothing but trouble.

She clasped her hands behind her back and echoed his farewell.

'Goodnight.'

Then she stood in the doorway until the red glow of his taillights had vanished into the darkness.

The heaviness accompanied her to bed, damping down the excitement the job offer had generated. It made her toss and turn, unable to get comfortable—to remember how she usually lay to go to sleep.

'Damn you, Harry Pritchard,' she muttered in the darkness. 'I promised myself this would never happen again. That I'd never let a man sneak under my defences.'

And if she felt this level of frustration from just talking to him this evening, how would she cope if she continued to work with him?

But alongside the knowledge of her physical attraction to Harry came the doubts. There was something Harry hadn't told her, and she couldn't help thinking it was linked to Bob Quayle...

Guilt accompanied Harry back to the apartment. Steph certainly had reason to be distrustful of men—of him in particular, come to that. Yet, even knowing this, he still hadn't been entirely truthful with her—hadn't told her he'd offered her the job because he wanted her to stay in Summerland. Because he wanted her near him—wanted to be able to see her, touch her, eventually, perhaps, make love to her.

Adding to the unease was the fact he hadn't mentioned Bob's latest bombshell—mainly because he'd rather Steph considered the idea of working with him without any hang-ups over the name of the hospital. Once committed to the job, surely the name of the hospital would be irrelevant...

He went to bed, but not to sleep, lying on his back staring at the ceiling, wondering if he was being irrational in thinking things might eventually come right between himself and Steph.

Right to the extent they'd become lovers?

Hardly—the way things were at the moment. It was a case of one step forward and two steps back as far as any relationship between them was concerned.

Yet she'd responded to his kisses.

Had almost committed...

He hoped things would sort themselves out soon, because he wasn't going to be much use in an operating theatre if these sleepless nights continued!

Maybe once he'd talked about Bob's latest request, things would get back to normal.

'And just when were you going to tell me about the grand opening ceremony? And faithless Martin Quayle being immortalised in the name of a hospital?'

THE SURGEON'S SECOND CHANCE

310

Steph, with anger redder than her hair flaring out of her like a halo of flame, met him at the door of his suite of rooms the following morning.

Harry straightened his shoulders and let his own anger, honed by the sleepless night, rip.

'When you'd considered the job offer in a cool and rational manner, that's when. Look at you—if I'd told you about the name of the hospital, you'd have gone off into a rage and not even thought about the work or whether you'd enjoy it. And if you imagine I'm part of the plots against you, you're wrong. I only heard about the opening ceremony—and the name of the hospital—as I was leaving last night.'

'When Bob asked you to talk to me about it!'

She shot the words at him, almost stumbling over them in her fury.

'Exactly—because you're so damn irrational no one else seems to be able to get through to you. Heaven knows why Bob imagined I could.'

'Maybe because up to now you've jumped to do his bidding,' Steph said, aware she'd gone beyond bitchy to downright nasty, but so shaken by what she'd learnt that morning she was probably as irrational as Harry said she was. 'The mighty Bob's yes-man!'

She slammed away, taking refuge behind the reception desk, though it was no sanctuary as she could still see Harry, stiff with anger, frowning at her from the waiting room.

She could move behind the filing shelves but that might look as if she was hiding...

A sharp trill from the phone saved her, and she snatched up the receiver, seeing it as a lifeline back to sanity.

'Hi. This is Frank Collins, president of Summerland Combined Services Clubs. I don't suppose Harry's in.'

The outer door had just closed behind his back and, knowing he'd be as unwilling to return as she was to have him back right now, she didn't go after him.

'Sorry! He's in the hospital but not here right now. Can I take a message?'

'You surely can,' the cheery Frank told her. 'Could you tell him we've organised a free flight for his first island patient? He'll be arriving Tuesday of next week. We've accommodation arranged but we'll have to liaise with Harry on details. Could you ask him to phone me when he's got a minute?'

Steph jotted down the gist of the message, asked Frank for a phone number and was given three—work, home and mobile—then hung up and puzzled over the strange conversation.

The man had sounded excited—as if this patient was someone special.

From an island?

Steph was still thinking about it while she sorted through a ream of Health Department forms, filing them away in a bottom drawer in case they were ever needed.

The slight sigh the door made as it closed suggested Harry had returned, so she stood up, startling him as he reached the desk.

He was so close she could see the dark shadow beneath his newly shaven skin and the sheen of his hair where the light caught it. So close she could see unhappiness in his eyes and a grim set to the lips that were now featuring in all her dreams.

She wanted, badly, to apologise, but Martin's betrayal had bred distrust, which was strengthened by the fact that Martin's father now had some hold over Harry.

'There's a message,' she said, speaking quickly to break the tense silence. 'Frank Collins called—first patient arriving Tuesday. I wrote it all down and the numbers where you can contact him. He's at work at the moment.'

She pushed the message slip across the desk, watching Harry's face grow even grimmer as he read it.

'Hell and damnation! I should have called Frank to tell him about the delay. What's today?'

'Thursday,' Steph told him, as puzzled now by Harry's reaction as she'd been by the message. 'What's it all about?'

'And when's the official opening?' he demanded, ignoring her question completely.

'As if you didn't know!' Steph snapped. 'Saturday week.'

'Saturday week—we could operate the following Tuesday. We could do it, but it will be a rush—so much to organise.'

He looked up at Steph and she realised the old Harry had returned. Enthusiastic over something—excited to the point where his eyes sparkled with whatever challenge it was that lay ahead of him.

'It'll take work, Steph. We'll all have to pull together. You said something about Rebecca taking on the receptionist job here. When can you get her in? Today? Then see if you can get hold of a big whiteboard. Ideally, I'd like it in my consulting room, but that won't do for privacy reasons, so find a wall where we can put it. Somewhere we can sit and look at it, so we know where we are at any given time.'

He picked up the phone and started dialling, and when she hesitated he waved her away with an abrupt, 'I'll explain later. The number's ringing—can you switch it through to my room?'

Steph switched the call through, then checked the number of the office supply company with whom she'd set up an account. She was bemused, and puzzled, by the change in Harry, but pleased to have things to do.

Rebecca, she found, would be happy to start working for Harry, and could be in by lunchtime. The whiteboard was also installed by then, on the wall in the small tearoom—the only available space.

'Good idea,' Harry told her, when he returned from heaven knew where and came in to make himself a coffee. 'With it there it hits us in the face whenever we come in, so we can see if there's something we're missing.'

He slumped into a chair and stared at the blank whiteness.

'When's the official opening?'

'Saturday week.' He obviously wasn't aware he'd asked the question earlier.

'Ten days away. OK, write that in up the top so we remember it. Then, in a column down the side, we'll list all the support services we'll need. I've got two anaesthetists lined up and another two surgeons, but I've got to give them a definite date. The kid arrives Tuesday. We'll put him on a strong course of antibiotics immediately—'

'Wait!' Steph held up her hand. 'Stop right there. What kid? What operation are you doing that requires two anaesthetists and three surgeons?'

'Four—you'll assist as well,' he told her, then he ran his hand over his face and offered her a hesitant smile.

'I'm sorry. It came as such a shock to find the first patient arriving so soon—now I have to work out how I can get it all organised in time.'

'Go on,' Steph ordered.

'When I was in Paris, I met a French surgeon who spent part of each year in the Pacific islands. Children were brought in to the larger cities from neighbouring islands and he operated on them. But he told me of the operations he couldn't perform because of lack of facilities and expertise. Children, for instance, who'd had a broken jaw which went untreated, so the jaw healed but with the jawbones fused so the children were left unable to open their mouths.'

'But they'd have died of starvation,' Steph protested.

Harry's smile was better this time.

'No way! Their parents simply bashed in their two front teeth and fed them through a straw.'

'All their lives?' Steph asked, horrified by the idea.

'If necessary,' Harry told her. 'Which is where we come in. The French doctor had tried to organise to get some of these patients to Paris, but the logistics were too great, so before I came home I contacted a local service club who were interested in the project, then bargained with Bob for an occasional charity case in his hospital.'

'You bargained for a free bed in Bob's brand-new hospital?' Steph repeated, aware her disbelief was showing.

'Yeah, well...' Harry said, shrugging his shoulders as if it was nothing.

'No wonder he expected you to run his messages.' Steph barely breathed the words as understanding dawned. 'But you'll need more than a bed—you'll need theatre time, and presumably a post-op stay in Intensive Care for all these special patients, and who knows what other services.'

She gazed at him in awe.

'You talked him into all of this?'

Harry's smile lit up his eyes, then faded as he said, 'Well, I kept harping on the good publicity he and the hospital would get, and I thought he'd finally agreed because of that. But maybe, from the start, he saw I could be useful in other ways.'

'Like being the one to break the news about the name of the hospital—and asking me if Fanny could cut the ribbon?' Steph sighed, then nodded. 'Seems fairly petty—almost negligible—compared to helping a young man live a normal life.'

Shame at how she'd treated Harry swamped her, and she was wondering how to apologise when she realised he was no longer listening, his whole attention absorbed by notes he was writing on the board.

'You know, Steph,' he said, as if there'd never been a moment's antagonism between them, 'it was one thing talking about doing all of this, but now, out of the blue, it's all happening.'

'Except the hospital won't be open next Tuesday,' Steph protested.

'No, but we couldn't operate immediately anyway. We need X-rays and blood tests—need to take some of his blood to store for emergencies. And start him on antibiotics—there's likely to be many sources of infection already breeding happily in his mouth, given the restricted access to it he's had over the years.'

'So where will he stay? Can you organise all of this to be done without him being in hospital?'

'We have to,' Harry told her. 'Hence the whiteboard. I want everything charted on it so we can look at it all the time and know exactly where we are. He'll stay with one of the service club families both before and after the op, but we have to think about post-op problems and complications as well. He'll need physio to get his jaw working, and speech therapy to teach him how to talk and eat again.'

Harry watched Steph as she considered the magnitude of the task in front of them, and had to hide a smile as she straightened her shoulders. He knew she was accepting the challenge—and doubted whether there'd be any further arguments about her working with him in theatre.

'When will you operate?' she asked.

'Hopefully, the Tuesday after he arrives—that will be a couple of days after the official opening. It's going to be tight for us, but as far as other things go, it's working well as the hospital won't be up to full operating strength and we'll have more access to its facilities.'

'And Bob's gone along with all of this?'

The question made Harry feel slightly queasy.

Or maybe that was lack of sleep...

'He agreed the hospital would take two patients a year—and offered theatre time and all services free of charge.'

'But?' Steph said, no doubt hearing the uncertainty in his voice.

'I haven't actually told him about this patient yet. That he's coming so soon. I've spoken to the administrator—did that earlier this morning before I called the other surgeons who'd offered to donate their time—but whether Bob knows yet I've no idea. I suspect he doesn't, or he'd have been in to tell me it's too soon or make some other objection.'

Harry suddenly looked doubtful—and very, very tired. Steph longed to step towards him and put her arms around his shoulders—draw his head to rest against her body. But she knew where touching Harry led, so even an exhausted Harry represented danger.

'You admit Bob's in it for the publicity,' she said, hoping she could comfort him with words. 'And coming so soon after the publicity of the opening, it can only be good for the hospital.'

She hesitated, trying to gauge Harry's reaction—which wasn't exactly brimming with confidence.

'Can't it?'

Harry shrugged.

'Who knows?' he said, and Steph felt a tiny tremor of unease reverberate through her body.

Harry had offered her a job and guaranteed no strings attached, but Bob wasn't Harry—and anything he gave free would most probably have not strings but hefty hawsers attached to it.

'Perhaps when you speak to him you can tell him it's OK for Fanny to cut his stupid ribbon at the opening ceremony,' Steph conceded. 'But I won't have to be there, will I?'

'Wouldn't Fanny like you to see her in action?'

Steph nodded reluctantly.

'But it will be from right up the back—not as part of any official party. I know you've been invited to the dinner back at their place later—if they want Fanny at that, you could keep an eye on her for me.'

Harry recognised that she'd been pushed as far as she'd go.

'I'll do that,' he promised, then he took her hand. 'And thanks. Having something to sweeten Bob will certainly help when I spring this other surprise on him.'

He drew her towards him and kissed her gently on the lips, but it was a distracted kiss and she must have recognised it as such for she drew away, picking up a white-board pen and waving it in front of the board.

'So what do we write here?'

'Prophylactic antibiotics, X-rays, blood tests, blood retrieval. Let's just jot down things as we think of them, then put them in order and draw up a time line later. Jot down on the right-hand side speech therapist and physio—you might be able to find out who'll be working at the hospital and if they'd be willing to give some time to the patient. And find a dentist—he'll need dental treatment for sure. Then Steve Lowry, Jason Blunt—they're the two surgeons who'll assist—and Fred Carter, who'll bring his own assistant anaesthetist. Their phone numbers are on my desk. They'll need to be kept informed about what's happening.'

'How long will the operation take?'

'Max ten hours, I'd say.'

'Ten hours?'

He smiled at the astonishment in her voice.

'The idea of the operation is to give the patient a workable jaw so we need to drill out the fused bone from the sockets in the skull then fasten something to the rami—those two bits of bone that come off the mandible or jawbone to attach it to the skull—which will fit back into those sockets.'

Steph considered this bald précis of an operation that could take ten hours and saw the first problem.

'But you'll need cartilage to cushion whatever you insert into those sockets to attach the bones and provide movement. Hasn't the jaw fused because the cartilage in the joint either became diseased or broke down in some other way?'

'Exactly!' Harry told her. 'In some cases it's an infection but, according to Frank, in the patient we're expecting—his name's Ty, by the way—he was injured when he was a toddler. He was in a car accident. The car rolled and he was trapped with lateral pressure squeezing his jaw, which obligingly broke. Unfortunately, although the jaw was wired and immobilised, the X-rays taken at the time didn't reveal a dislocation of both sides of his jaw and by the time his jaw healed and the wiring was released, it was too late to fix the dislocation.'

'Too late?' Steph asked, remembering operations she'd seen where jaws had been broken and reset.

'Too late where he lived,' Harry replied. 'As far as I can make out, he was treated by a visiting doctor at a clinic on one of the bigger islands some weeks after the accident, so you can imagine the difficulty in reducing the damage at that stage! It may have been too late even then, but who knows? Anyway, the family took him back home with instructions on how and when to cut the wire. I suppose when he couldn't open his mouth after they'd removed the wire they assumed that was how he would be for ever. They're a very tolerant people, accepting of the troubles fate throws their way.'

'Hmm,' Steph said, wondering if Harry had made the point to remind her of her own intolerance. 'So what exactly do you do?'

Harry grinned at her.

'Can you picture the rib cage?'

She nodded assent. 'Sure! One, two, three, four, five and six ribs are attached on each side to the sternum, then seven, eight, nine and ten all join up and are attached by the same...'

'Light dawns? Attached by the same cartilage!' he finished for her. 'While eleven and twelve float free. In fact, the first six pairs are also attached to the sternum by cartilage which gives the rib cage the provision to expand when the lungs fill.'

A familiar excitement began to tingle along Steph's spine, only this time it had nothing to do with Harry Pritchard. It was the excitement of a new discovery—or new to her—in the medical field, the intense delight she had always felt when realising that now more people could have their pain eased or their illness treated more efficiently.

To be part of such a miracle—right there when the surgery was performed—seemed unbelievably exciting.

'You take costal cartilage to cushion the mandibular joints?' she asked.

'We do more than that,' he told her. 'We actually take a small piece of rib—about five centimetres—with some costal cartilage attached. The cartilage is shaped and fitted into the jaw socket with the bone, then the piece of bone is fixed with titanium screws into the patient's mandible.'

'And will it work?' Steph asked, while in her mind she was

picturing the different tasks required of the surgeons and the magnitude of what would appear to be a simple operation.

Harry, however, must have been confident, for he chuckled at the doubt in her tone.

'I haven't seen such an operation done, but the surgeon in Paris, who had assisted at one, assured me it will.'

'But the lad's facial muscles haven't worked for years,' Steph reminded him. 'Won't they have atrophied?'

'They'll have had a certain amount of involvement in the sucking movements but will certainly have diminished in size and strength. The good thing is that he's young—fourteen—so there's no reason the facial muscles can't be brought back into first-class working order. That's where you'll come in—supervising the post-op stages and making sure he sticks with his therapy schedule.'

The tingle of excitement she'd felt earlier was now suffusing her body.

'It's better than sex,' she said, beaming happily at Harry, then blushing as she realised what she'd said. It was the kind of thing she'd have said years back, when they'd been such close friends, and not thought twice about—but now…

'Actually—' embarrassment had her stumbling on '—it's been so long since I had sex I probably can't judge, but it is exciting, isn't it, Harry?'

He stared at her for a moment, then shook his head, though whether in disbelief at her burbling comments or at something else, she couldn't guess. With embarrassment deepening to mortification, she rushed to change the subject.

'I can understand a lengthy operation when you have to take bone from another site, but ten hours?'

Harry's scrutiny lasted a few seconds longer, then, as if acknowledging her change-the-subject tactic, he nodded.

'It's difficult because of the proximity of major blood vessels and nerves so close to where we'll be operating—to say nothing of maintaining a viable airway and transplanting four pieces of bone. The trickiest part will be removing the fused section of the jaw without compromising these, and then maintaining viable nerve paths, so post-operatively, messages will get through to the renewed area.'

He paused, then added, 'Jason's a neurologist. He'll handle that part. Steve will retrieve the bone and cartilage, and I'll reshape it. You'll handle mopping and clamping and whatever else needs doing. The other two will come down from Brisbane the night before, and we'll go over it in detail then. I've already emailed them suggestions as to how I think it will work, and they'll get back to me with suggestions.'

Thinking of the actual operation banished the remnants of Steph's embarrassment. Harry might have kissed her earlier, but it had been a thank-you kiss, nothing more. Right now his mind was concentrated on the job ahead, and she'd better get hers onto it as well.

'I'll talk to the theatre secretary about theatre staff. Maybe two shifts of nurses.'

Harry nodded.

'Unless any of them want to volunteer to do the whole job. Though this is only the first of many patients I hope eventually to see, shifts would mean more theatre staff get an opportunity to see what we're doing.'

'I'll talk to the secretary,' Steph promised, realising she'd need her own whiteboard—or perhaps a small notebook she could carry with her—to make sure all her tasks were done on time.

Then Harry looked up at her and smiled, and she realised the tingly feeling she'd experienced earlier—talking about the op—was nothing on what his smile could produce. But she could hardly take back her comment.

Or let him know how he affected her.

So she frowned, hoping it would look as if she was considering the operation—not Harry's smile.

'You're OK with all of this?' he asked, perhaps more misled than she'd intended by the frown. 'Happy to be part of it? It won't be a paid assisting job, you realise. All the specialists are donating their time.'

It was as if he'd thrown a bucket of cold water over her.

'Oh, Harry,' she whispered, her voice breaking as she said his name. 'Have I really changed so much you could ask that? Grown so bitter you see me as someone who's only out for money?'

She stood up and walked out the door, not stopping until she was out of the rooms and into the security of the staff washrooms, where she locked herself into a cubicle and cried.

One step forward and twenty-five steps back, Harry thought as he sat and studied the whiteboard. How had he come to say something so stupid and hurtful to Steph? Especially when she'd been so excited.

Actually, it had been because she'd been so excited, he realised. When she'd come out with her 'It's better than sex' statement his mind had fought the implications of the analogy for a split second, then had weakened and started thinking how pleasurable it would be to prove her wrong.

True, he'd managed to carry on his explanation of the operation—and hopefully had sounded more involved than he'd felt—but his body had been reminding him of the passion of her kisses and the sweet softness of her full breasts pressed against his chest.

He'd been stupid to think they could work together. She was so damn distracting he should have applauded her suggestion of a move to Brisbane—though maybe migration to Mars would have been better…

He groaned, then studied the mostly blank board in front of him. Today was Thursday and Ty arrived on Tuesday. Well, at least for the next few weeks he'd be too busy to be having libidinous thoughts about Stephanie Prince.

CHAPTER NINE

THE ARRIVAL OF the young man from the small Pacific island brought a buzz of excitement to the suite of rooms and seemingly to the hospital itself, as more and more staff moved in prior to the official opening.

'We're like guinea pigs for all the different departments,' Steph said to Harry early on Friday evening—the day before the official opening—when she'd returned to the rooms after her pregnant women's session to tie up some loose ends. 'Ty's are the first X-rays the X-ray department has taken, and his blood is the first taken in the new pathology lab.'

She was slotting the X-rays into viewing boxes in Harry's treatment room as she spoke, and he was standing close beside her, peering at the illuminated images.

'Blood tests today are clear of any infection, and the lab couldn't find anything that might suggest delaying the op,' she continued, bringing him up to date on the latest tests.

She stepped back, because being so close to Harry, even when he seemed utterly unaware of her presence, made her feel edgy—even unpredictable. It was as if she couldn't trust her body to believe this was neither the time nor the place to fling itself into his arms.

'And they certainly tried. They took about six vials of blood from the poor lad.'

Harry unclipped the X-rays and slotted them back into their envelope, turning towards her as he did so.

'You've seen more of him than anyone, apart from his host family. How do you think he's coping?'

'I'm guessing he must be apprehensive, but he hides it well. He's behaving like a typical teenager, eager to see everything at once—now! I've talked to him about the op itself, and the aftermath, but he brushes it all aside, saying he's too busy to think about it now. Well, that's what he's jotting down on notes to me, but you don't pick up intonations from notes, do you?'

She was looking puzzled, and a little anxious, as if, in spite of all she'd done in preparing Ty, it might still not be enough. Harry reached out and touched her shoulder, intending the gesture as nothing more than reassurance. But the tension that had been escalating through his body as they'd stood so close to study the X-rays sneaked into the gesture, so it became a caress that lingered too long.

Silvery grey eyes looked into his, asking questions, but telling him things as well.

'Our timing is atrocious,' he muttered, as he used only the minimum of pressure to draw her slowly towards him. 'Has been since I first came back.'

She was within kissing distance now, and hadn't resisted.

'But after this operation—when we know Ty's over it all—we'll be sorting this out. Understand?'

She was so close he could feel the warmth of the air breathed out from her lungs, and her wide-eyed gaze held apprehension as well as excitement.

It was the excitement that made him ignore the apprehension—the excitement that made him close that small gap between them and claim her lips in a kiss, remembering, too late, where other kisses had led.

But this time he stopped it before they went too far, gently holding her a little apart from him while they both caught their breath.

'We've a lot ahead of us over the next few days,' he said. 'Let's wait until it's over, then make time for ourselves. Time to really think about what this is between us—and whether it's strong enough to overcome everything that's happened in the past.'

Luminous eyes searched his face, and her lips, slightly swollen from the kiss, parted as if there were things she wanted to say. But in the end she simply nodded, then grinned at him.

'OK!' she said, finally putting her agreement into words. 'But shouldn't we have one last kiss to seal the bargain?'

Without waiting for his reply, Steph moved closer, putting her arms around his shoulders and holding his body hard against hers. Then she raised her lips and brushed them across his mouth, her tongue teasing for entry. Harry might not know it, but for her it was a kiss that sealed more than the bargain. It sealed the misery of the past away where it belonged, freeing the happy memories from the clouds of doubt and distrust that had hovered over them since Martin's death.

From now on, she'd remember friendship, and the things she'd really loved in Martin—his humour, his generosity—and she'd open up her heart to Harry so love, if it existed beyond the attraction they were both obviously feeling, could come in.

By three o'clock the following afternoon, she wasn't so sure all the old animosity had been shut away. In fact, if Harry had appeared, she'd have let fly at him though she knew it wasn't his fault Fanny was cutting the ribbon at the blasted opening ceremony. She just needed someone to bear the brunt of her own bad temper, caused by the unbelievably difficult task of dressing a nearly four-year-old for this special occasion.

The dress, presented to Fanny by Doreen the previous Sunday, was so frilled and flounced that Fanny looked like a doll from the top of a very expensively decorated Christmas tree. Steph thought it ridiculous, but Fanny obviously loved it. The first argument had been which shoes she should wear with it.

Steph's decree that only her good black patent leather shoes would do was met with a minor tantrum, Fanny thinking her purple plastic sandals would be far better. This overcome, they then argued over where to tie the sash, how to arrange her golden curls, whether or not four-year-olds could wear lipstick—Steph, 'Definitely not', Fanny, 'But Grandma lets me'—and how late Fanny could stay up on this, her first sleep-over at her grand-parents for more than two years.

Grumbling inwardly in frustration over the whole silly busi-ness, Steph finally reached the hospital where she handed her child over to an over-excited Doreen, ten minutes before the cer-emony was to begin. She waited while Doreen passed Fanny's little overnight bag to the hospital receptionist—doing double duty organising tour guides and acting as a cloakroom atten-dant—then she wished Fanny luck, kissed her goodbye and walked out the front door.

The podium was set up on the curving driveway in front of the main entrance, with seats, already filling with invited guests, in front of it. Beyond the chairs, staff and other interested ob-servers stood, and Steph found herself a place where she could see proceedings without anyone's head getting in the way.

Which was when she realised she'd forgotten the camera.

'Here! I've got to sit in a chair up front with the other rent-paying tenants. Would you take a photo for me?'

Harry's voice skidded up her spine, causing the little hairs at the back of her neck to prickle with awareness. Steph took the camera, enjoying the touch of his fingers as they tangled in the transfer, all animosity forgotten in the pleasure of just being near Harry again.

'Sure you won't come tonight?' he asked gently, and she knew by the concern in his eyes he was anxious for her—anxious about her mental state on this particular day.

'No, but I'm OK,' she told him. 'With Fanny doing this—with her staying at the Quayles. Even with the hospital name. Martin *was* their son and they loved him and there was a lot of Martin that deserved remembering.'

'Oh, Steph!' Harry breathed her name, and the love she saw shining in his eyes all but overwhelmed her. 'If you only knew how good it is to hear you say that.'

He leant forward and kissed her on the cheek, adding, 'I have to go or someone will pinch my seat, and I promised Fanny I'd be right there in the middle of the front row.'

'You promised Fanny?' Steph echoed.

'On Thursday when she was in the rooms. We had a talk about it and I promised I'd be there for her.'

He smiled and walked away, and Steph, who'd been wondering if things could get much better, realised they could—they had.

The ceremony went off without a hitch—Steph feeling inordinately proud of Fanny. But once the official party, including Fanny, left, the bulk of them heading for the Quayle mansion for a buffet dinner, Rebecca claimed Steph's company.

'My kids have gone to their father so it's girls' night out,' she said, when Steph protested about it. 'Besides, you've been working so hard you need a break before the real work of Ty's operation and post-op work begins.'

They had an early dinner at a restaurant in the centre of Summerland's tourist area, then, after discussing various movie options, decided a long walk on the beach would be far nicer than sitting in a stuffy movie theatre.

Steph arrived home a little after ten, to a house that felt curiously empty as Tracy had gone surfing with friends further down the coast and would be away until Monday evening.

The message light on the answering machine was blinking, and for once Steph felt no anxiety as the flashing red eye lit the darkness. Though it might be Fanny, ringing up to say goodnight.

She hit the replay button as she walked past, heading for the kitchen and a drink of water.

Not Fanny, but Harry.

'Steph, is Fanny with you? Did you pick her up from the Quayles'? Phone my mobile as soon as you get in.'

Cold dread seized Steph's heart, clutching like an icy hand and squeezing so tightly she couldn't breathe.

Telling herself not to panic, she rushed towards the phone and with fumbling fingers dialled Harry's mobile.

'Of course she's not with me!' she screamed into the phone. 'How long has she been missing? Have you called the police? Or did you just assume I had her and keep on partying?'

She slammed down the phone and rushed out the front door, car keys clenched in her fist because she couldn't trust her shaking fingers not to drop them. The car started, and she summoned every ounce of will-power in her possession and forced herself to drive, slowly and carefully, towards the Quayle mansion.

Police cars in the drive told her at least something was being done to find her daughter, but when a young constable tried to stop her parking behind them, her control cracked and she yelled at him, telling him to stay away from her—to get out and find her child.

'Steph!' Harry appeared from nowhere, but though he tried to put his arm around her, she dodged away.

The fear she'd held at bay as she'd driven to the house erupted in volcanic anger, and she turned on him, flinging accusations at him, blaming his return—his interference in her life—saying things that even in her terrified state she knew were unforgivable.

He stood back and took it all, bowing his head as if to acknowledge her right to this rage, then, when she'd wound down and anger had been replaced by gut-wrenching sobs, he put his arm around her and led her carefully up to the house.

'Are you sure this isn't another of Doreen's tricks?' she demanded, hesitating on the doorstep of the house she still hated entering. 'How could this have happened if she or Bob weren't involved?'

Harry heard the fear and grief that closed her throat, making her voice hoarse and scratchy.

'They are as upset as you, Steph,' he said quietly. 'Doreen had to be sedated and you only have to look at Bob to know he had nothing to do with it.'

He eased her through the door, carrying his own guilt like a weight around his shoulders, echoes of his own promise for Fanny's safety—'I'll watch over her'—hammering in his head.

Steph had let loose her rage on him, but she couldn't possibly berate him as much as he had blamed himself.

While as for any hope of a relationship after this...

One step forward, four hundred steps back, though his personal feelings were of no account right now.

'When did it happen?'

She was looking around the foyer as if she'd never been there before—never lived in this huge mansion.

'We don't know, Steph,' he answered. 'Not precisely. Doreen took her up to bed at eight, read her a story and tucked her in. She stayed until Fanny went to sleep at about eight-fifteen. Then Mrs Woods went up to check on her a little before nine.'

He paused, because his mouth was dry with the terrible tension he felt, just repeating what had happened.

'At first Mrs Woods thought she might be hiding, but when she couldn't find her upstairs, she alerted Bob and the dinner guests helped search the house.'

'Then, no doubt, Bob came up with the notion I'd taken her and you all relaxed,' Steph snapped, as her anxiety overflowed into anger once again so she had to strike out—to hurt someone as badly as she was hurting.

'I don't think we ever seriously considered that,' Harry said, aligning himself with the Quayles with that 'we'.

But at that moment Bob appeared, looking as if he'd aged twenty years since she'd seen him that afternoon.

'Stephanie!' he said—making a desperate plea of her name

and walking towards her with his hands outstretched in supplication.

Steph saw his pain—knew it mirrored her own—and took his hands, pressing them tight—comfortee turned comforter.

'I'm going back outside,' he said. 'I know I'm probably useless out there, but I can't bear to do nothing.'

Steph nodded, and watched him go, then she looked around the foyer with its high walls reaching up two storeys, and the grand staircase stretching to the upper floor. She needed something to do as well, because it seemed as if the walls were closing in on her. She bit back a scream of sheer frustrated terror.

Harry must have sensed she was close to collapse. Up to now, he'd been careful not to stand too close, but now he put his arm around her shoulders again, helping her towards the steps, talking calmly, though his voice was croaky with emotion.

'The police are undertaking another search of the house and gardens, while two detectives are in the library. They're taking the names and addresses of all the guests, questioning them about what they might have seen, then letting them go. The guests are in the living room, so you probably don't want to go in there. Would you like to sit here on the steps or go out by the pool?'

Steph shook her head.

'I can't just sit and wait—I need to look for her.'

'Where, Steph?' he said, and she shook her head, feeling the tears of utter helplessness sliding down her cheeks.

'Can I look at her room? Is her bag gone?'

'I'll ask someone,' Harry said, hovering by her side, within touching distance but again not touching.

A harassed-looking man, clad in faded jeans and a checked shirt, appeared at that moment.

'Is this Mrs Quayle?' he asked, coming towards them.

'Prince. My name is Prince,' Steph said. 'I'm Fanny's mother. What's happening?'

'Brad Drew, Summerland CID,' he said, putting out his

hand but obviously not expecting her to respond to the politeness. 'We're searching for your daughter—we've circulated her description. We've fingerprint experts coming to dust the bedroom, and we're questioning all the guests. Two television channels covered the opening of the hospital. We're arranging to get copies of all the footage they shot, so we'll know who was there.'

He paused for a moment, then added, 'I'll need to ask you some questions as well, ma'am. About where you were tonight and who was with you. And about who might want to harm you in any way.'

'No one,' Steph said, but the coincidence of the hospital opening and Fanny's disappearance had suddenly clicked in her mind. Horrified by her suspicions, she grasped the policeman's arm. 'The hospital opening? She was there on the podium, granddaughter of the owners. Could a sick mind think a hospital owner must have money? Could someone have taken her for ransom?'

She knew her fingers must be biting into his arm, for she'd felt him flinch, but the look he exchanged with Harry puzzled her. It was almost one of relief, as if kidnapping was a good option to explain her daughter's disappearance.

But neither man explained the look and she was too distraught to think more about it, asking again about Fanny's overnight bag and if she could see the bedroom.

'The bag is gone—Mrs Woods noticed that immediately. It's better if you don't go up there,' the policeman said. 'Not because the room's upset in any way, but the fewer people we have in that part of the house, the more chance there is of the scene-of-crime officers finding something helpful.'

Steph nodded, and felt her shoulders slump with helplessness.

'But I need to do something!' she said.

'Come into the kitchen and have a cup of tea,' Harry suggested. 'Brad needs to ask you questions—about friends and relatives, about Fanny herself and whether she'd go off with someone she didn't know. You need to put aside your anxiety for a little while and think about the answers.'

Harry's voice seemed to echo in a vast empty space inside her head, but when he put his arm around her shoulders and led her into the kitchen, she went. The way her knees were shaking, sitting down was definitely a good option, and she doubted whether she'd have found her way anywhere without Harry to lean on—Harry to lead her around.

Brad's questions began simply enough—name, address, details of where Fanny went to kindy. But as he persisted, Steph sensed some purpose behind them, but was too consumed with worry to work out what.

'And although your daughter was in the official party at the opening of the hospital—named after your husband—you weren't.' It was a statement, not a question, so Steph ignored it. Then Brad followed it up with a real doozy.

'You've a history of bad relations with your parents-in-law,' he said bluntly.

Steph looked from Harry to Brad, as the undertones she'd sensed in Brad's questions suddenly became clearer, but before she could protest, Harry exploded.

'Where Steph was tonight or why she wasn't in the official party are nothing to do with Fanny's disappearance,' he said, his voice not loud but deep with anger. 'There is no way she'd hurt a hair on Fanny's head, nor would she pull a stunt like this for attention, or revenge, or any other macabre reason your policeman's brain might throw up.'

'You know Dr Prince that well?' the policeman asked, and Steph looked at Harry, who'd turned towards her, his eyes full of worry and pain.

'I know her as well as I know myself. She had nothing to do with Fanny's disappearance, so why don't you get someone onto checking her alibi, if that's what you need to do, so we can move past this to more productive questions?'

Brad made some reply, but Steph didn't hear it as her head

was repeating the words Harry had spoken—'I know her as well as I know myself.' For some reason, she found comfort in that simple declaration, and they gave her the strength she needed to keep going a little longer.

By Monday morning, there was still no news in spite of the fact Fanny's picture had appeared in every newspaper and had been splashed across television screens throughout the country. Neither had there been a ransom demand, a bad sign now Steph had figured out what the look between Harry and Brad had meant. To them, kidnapping for ransom was a good option—the only other one being that some sick or perverted stranger had taken the child.

Even *she* knew that a kidnapped child had some hope of being returned...

'It wasn't as if it was a sit-down dinner. How could she possibly disappear from a house with fifty people wandering around the rooms on the ground floor?' Steph demanded of Brad, who was sitting in her living room, going over the situation yet again. Again asking questions in the hope some chance remark or response might reveal a motive for Fanny's disappearance. 'Why choose a time like that? When there were so many chances of being caught?'

Bob stopped pacing by the window and came to sit beside Steph on the couch.

'Whoever did it might have chosen a time like that deliberately,' Brad reminded her, while Bob put his arm around her shoulders, offering silent support and comfort.

Bob had rarely moved from Steph's side, he and Harry sitting out the long days and even longer nights with her. No one saying much as tortured thoughts were best left unspoken.

And though in her heart she knew she needed him near her, Steph had protested about Harry's presence. With Ty's operation only twenty-four hours away, there was so much he should be doing.

'I can postpone it,' he'd said earlier, when she'd practically had to push him out of the house to go up to the hospital to check on Ty's admittance.

'No way,' she'd told him. 'That boy's been building up to this—to postpone it would be cruel to him.'

She'd squeezed his hand and kissed his cheek.

'Go, Harry,' she'd said, and he'd gone.

But his departure had left her with a new sense of emptiness, one that made her think about how quickly Harry had found his way back into her life, breaking through the careful defences she'd built up to protect herself from hurt.

Not that any defence had protected Fanny...

Brad's voice brought her out of her dismal thoughts.

'I've got the films of the official opening from all the television studios,' he told them. 'Our men have been through it and spliced it together so you only have to watch one video. I can play it as many times as you like, but what I really need are the names of everyone who was there.'

He slotted the video into Steph's player and turned to Bob.

'With the help of the hospital admin staff, we've identified most of the invited guests and a lot of the staff, but there are a number of people—you'll see their faces ringed by white lines— we can't put names to. Harry went through it last night—'

'Harry went through it last night?' Steph echoed. 'When last night? He was here.'

Bob and Brad exchanged a look, then Bob shrugged.

'He phoned Brad and offered to take a look at it when you went to sleep last night,' he explained. 'He knew he might not be able to be here this morning and went across to the station at about eleven.'

'But he was supposed to be sleeping himself,' Steph protested. 'You both said you'd sleep if I agreed to take a sleeping tablet.'

'To get back to the video,' Brad interrupted. 'If you could both concentrate on the faces ringed in white.'

Steph nodded, and Brad used the remote to start the tape

rolling. She saw a shot of herself, and brushed away useless tears as her beautiful daughter cut the ribbon. The sound had been removed, but as she watched Bob make his speech, she remembered parts of what he'd said, and felt the heaviness of regret that it had taken so long for her to get over not Martin's death but his betrayal.

The first circled head was that of a man who seemed vaguely familiar. Brad stopped the tape so they could look at the fuzzy image.

'Kent Cross, one of the security men employed by my building firm. I had a few of them there to boost the hospital security numbers,' Bob told Brad, and Steph knew from the hopelessness in Bob's voice he was thinking how useless security had been.

Another man, and this one Steph knew.

'Bill Jackson—he's a local GP who works at the practice where I do a session on Fridays. I didn't see him there.'

Brad wrote down the name, and moved the film on.

Steph saw herself again, this time with Rebecca—head circled.

'That's my friend—Harry's new receptionist.'

'Of course,' Brad said. 'I should have recognised her. I interviewed her myself.'

Because you had—or still have—suspicions I might have taken Fanny myself, Steph thought as the agony of the situation swept over her again. She put her hands to her face, wanting to cry until she had no tears left, but Bob squeezed her shoulder, alerting her to the fact the tape was rolling again.

Another woman—again a sense of familiarity. Only this time the familiarity was accompanied by a feeling of nausea.

Steph shook the bad memories away and waited for the film to move on.

It didn't.

Brad was looking at her.

'You know that woman?'

Steph shook her head.

'She reminded me of someone, that's all. It brought back…'

Remembering what it had brought back, and Bob's presence right beside her, she didn't finish.

But Brad persisted.

'Bad memories? She's someone you don't like?'

'It couldn't possibly be her,' Steph said, angered by his persistence. 'And it's more than four years since I saw her and then it was only once, so I wouldn't recognise her well enough to positively identify her anyway.'

'Any tiny thing might help,' Brad reminded her. 'Anything slightly out of sync. Even someone you haven't seen for four or five years appearing in your life again.'

Steph closed her eyes, but images of the one and only time she'd seen the woman were imprinted in her mind, and now played back in vivid Technicolor.

'Who might she be, Steph?' Bob asked. 'Someone who could want to harm you or Fanny?'

'No!' Her protest was a cry of pain, and she began to shake. 'It's not her, and if it is, it's coincidence. It was all so long ago—I don't even know her second name.'

'If there's even a tiny chance she might know something about Fanny, we have to look into it,' Bob said, urging her to talk—not knowing why she didn't want to mention the woman's name, or her connection to the family.

'Harry thought it might be someone called Stella,' Brad said, and Steph, who'd thought things couldn't possibly get any worse, realised they could. It seemed as if the entire world was falling apart. 'Is that who you're thinking of?'

'Yes,' she said hoarsely, 'but I only met her once.'

Yet even as she said the words, she wondered. There'd been publicity about the hospital opening in the Brisbane papers as well as Summerland's local rag. Could Stella have seen it and been reminded of what might have been?

Brad, meanwhile, had moved away, and was talking on his mobile.

'Who is she?' Bob asked. 'Someone you both once worked with? Someone who knew Martin as well, so came to the opening of the hospital? But wouldn't that be natural? Not suspicious?'

Steph looked at Bob, then back to Brad, still busy on the phone. She took a deep breath. A choice between saving Fanny and hurting Bob was no choice at all.

'I'm sorry, Bob, I never intended you to know this,' she began, turning towards him so he could see how serious she was. 'But Stella was Martin's girlfriend.'

She shrugged as the burden of saying the words aloud landed, far too heavily, on her shoulders.

'I didn't know about her, but apparently they'd been involved before he married me. The relationship might have stopped for a while but, according to Stella, who visited me in hospital the day after Martin died, she was the only person he'd ever loved and they'd become lovers again within months of our marriage. In Stella's version of what happened, Martin only married me because he realised Harry was showing interest in me. While the three of us were just good friends, everything was fine, but when he thought Harry and I might get together, he felt he'd be cut out of the friendship.'

Aware Bob was staring at her like a man turned to stone, she shrugged again, then continued.

'I guess you should also know that, according to Stella, she wasn't the only woman he was playing around with. That's what hurt me so much when Martin died, Bob. The fact that he'd betrayed me, not just with Stella but with other women. And that he'd never really loved me! That hurt, too. I didn't tell you and Doreen because I didn't want to spoil your memory of him, but I couldn't live with you any more, or hear you talk about how wonderful he was, when I was hurting so much.'

She brushed at the tears now rolling down her cheeks.

'Stella hated me—blamed me for Martin's death. She told me

all of that in one short visit. But it was so long ago. Why would she wait till now to hurt me? It's impossible!'

'You say Harry knew this?' Bob's voice was as hoarse as hers had been, and Steph realised he was feeling the grief of losing his son all over again.

'Harry knew!' Steph said. 'I asked him about it when he visited later that day, and he admitted it. Said he'd kept quiet because he didn't want to hurt me, and Martin had kept promising to break off the relationship with Stella.'

She shook her head as the memories threatened to overwhelm her, adding more pain to the pain of Fanny's disappearance.

'This woman could be the one, then, if she hated you,' Bob said, turning to Brad and demanding to know what he was doing.

'We started tracking her down as soon as Harry mentioned her name last night,' Brad explained. 'I just phoned in to confirm Stephanie had recognised her as well. She's not at her flat at the moment. According to the hospital where she works, she's currently on leave. We've alerted all road patrols to look out for her car but, remember, she's only one of many people who were at the ceremony and we need to talk to all of them.'

He'd just finished explaining this when his phone rang again.

'I have to get back to the office,' he said, when the phone call was completed. 'I'll leave the video with you. If you could go through and put names to any of the other faces. Stella was number four, so just number them and write the name—or "unknown"—against the numbers. One of my men will call for the video and list later.'

He stood up, and Steph stood with him—wanting to be where the action was.

'No! There's nothing new. I'm wanted back there on another matter, but I'll keep in touch. We'll do this carefully.'

Was Stella a lead or a false trail?

Steph wasn't sure.

She made coffee for herself and Bob, then started the video running again. Together they identified four more faces as staff

members, and in the end had only two labelled as unknown.
Now, as the policeman hadn't arrived to collect the tape, she ran
it again, pausing on the face that might be Stella's.

Wondering whether or not to hope this woman was responsible for Fanny's disappearance.

On the hope side—surely someone who had loved him
wouldn't harm Martin's child…

On the down side—Stella's confrontation with Steph all those
years ago had been laced with such hatred she could harm Fanny
to strike out at Steph…

Then there was the possibility they'd confronted right from
the beginning—that a total stranger had taken her…

CHAPTER TEN

HARRY CHECKED HIS PATIENT, then talked to Ty about what they would be doing that day in preparation for the operation, and the following day during it. But his mind was only half on what he said, the rest of it desperate to discover a way to find Fanny, while on a deeper layer he agonised over what would happen to Steph if the unthinkable happened and they didn't find her beautiful child.

At this stage of his cogitation his lungs cramped, and he forced his mind back to his patient, explaining now what would happen in the days immediately after the op.

'Steph told me all about it. Have they found her little girl?'

Ty's note rekindled Harry's anxiety, but he fought it down and said firmly, 'No, but they will.'

Did positive thinking work? And how badly was it affected by the dread he also felt?

Once satisfied that Ty understood what was to happen to him, Harry checked that Rebecca was keeping things going in the office, then headed back to Steph's house, calling at the police station on the way for the most recent news.

'Did you know this Stella?' Brad asked.

Harry shrugged.

'Not well, but as a co-worker, yes, I guess so. She was a nurse in the O and G ward at the time Martin and I did a clinical term there. Steph was doing paediatrics at the time, I think.'

'Would she remember you?'

Harry frowned at Brad while he thought about the question.

'Yes, I suppose so. I mean, I recognised her, so maybe she'd recognise me—well, she would, if that *was* her at the ceremony, because all the specialists were introduced by name and we had to stand and kind of be acknowledged.'

'That could be useful,' Brad said. 'If we find her and there's a chance she has the child, she might be less freaked out by someone she knows.'

'Page me if you need me,' Harry told him, giving him the contact number for his pager. 'I'll call you back. That way we won't raise Steph's hopes unnecessarily.'

Brad nodded, then shook his head, and Harry knew what he was thinking. The longer this went on, the less chance there was of finding Fanny alive.

He left the building, and drove towards Steph's house, his heart heavy in his chest as he considered the situation. He'd come back to Summerland hoping he and Steph might stand a chance of finding happiness together. And once they'd met again that hope had become a possibility.

Oh, there'd been setbacks, but somehow he'd sensed he was getting closer to achieving his dream—that he, Steph and Fanny would somehow become a family. That he could make up for the hurt she'd suffered in the past and teach her to trust again.

But now?

Harry shook his head, thinking instead about Fanny—and Stella Spence, who'd been the cause of so much pain to Steph once before.

Could she be the cause again?

The day dragged on. Harry had returned at midday but with no news by late afternoon, he'd been paged and called away again, presumably to go to the hospital for the briefing with the other specialists involved in the operation. Steph thought of Ty, but couldn't feel her usual hope and apprehension for the young lad and what lay ahead of him. Her exhausted body and mind were so concentrated on Fanny's safety, an atom bomb exploding beside her would have failed to elicit a reaction.

At ten that evening, a young policeman arrived at the house.

'Brad sent me to tell you we've located Stella. She's in a motel near the beach at the southern end of Summerland. Long-range microphones have picked up television noise and what could be conversation masked by the TV. The motel owners thought she was alone when she checked in at about nine on Saturday night, but admit there could have been a child asleep in the car.'

Hope was hammering in Steph's heart as she heard the news, and she grasped the young man's arm, wanting to shake more information out of him.

'Apparently Stella told the owner she wanted to be left in peace,' he said. 'She explained she was a nurse on leave and all she wanted to do was sleep for a few days, but the owners have heard the television going most of the day, starting from children's programmes early in the morning.'

'If she checked in on Saturday evening, it fits. And Fanny loves TV, though I don't let her watch a lot of it,' Steph said, excited yet dreading that Fanny might not be with the woman. 'Why don't you just go in and see if Fanny's there?'

'Brad's watching the room. He's waiting until later. It's safer if we go in when Stella's asleep. I'm here to collect you. We'll leave as soon as I get a message to say the light has gone out in the unit. You can sit in the car so if Fanny is there, we can give her straight to you.'

'If Fanny's there alive,' Bob muttered brokenly, and Steph turned on him.

'Of course she'll be alive. We've got to believe that, Bob! We have to have faith.'

She ran into Fanny's room and grabbed her bear, still sporting his bright ribbon bow-tie from the day he'd been to kindy.

Then she picked up a blanket which had been on Fanny's cot when she'd been a baby. Clutching both these talismans, she returned to the living room.

'Let's go,' she said.

'It's too early,' the policeman protested.

'Then we'll sit outside. You must have other cars parked there, listening and keeping watch. We'll keep watch with them.'

She led the way to the car, the young man following, while Bob had the presence of mind to find her keys and lock the door behind them.

The motel was down a quiet side street, and on a Monday night had only two cars parked outside it. The lighting outside was dim, so the light shining from behind the curtain in the window of the fifth unit along threw a square of pale yellow on the path that ran along the front of the building.

'That's one of our cars ahead of us,' the policeman said, pointing to a car in the deep shadow of a huge fig tree. 'They'll wait about an hour after the light goes out,' he added, as Steph fought the urge to leap out of the car, race across the driveway, smash open the door and seize her daughter. Though tortured by anxiety, she still realised such an action could provoke Stella to harm her child.

If Stella had her child…

They sat in the darkness, seemingly for ever, while Steph's limbs grew chilled and heavy, matching the cold fear in her heart.

Then the square of yellow light disappeared, and she tensed.

'Soon,' the policeman said. 'They'll need to give her time to get properly to sleep.'

He turned to Steph.

'You realise she might not have Fanny.' He spoke soberly, reminding her this was an off-chance. 'She *could* be here on leave, tired after night duty, just wanting to sleep for a few days. And being in Summerland, maybe she just joined the crowd to see the opening of a hospital named after her lover.'

'I realise that,' Steph told him. 'But I feel this is right. I know it's stupid, but I can't help sensing Fanny's near.'

She squeezed Bob's hand.

'And alive.'

The next fifty minutes were interminable, then there was movement at the car in front, doors opening silently and dark figures walking in shadows towards the motel. Steph saw the black shadows of two back-up men move to the rear of the building, and two more figures, one a woman, fall in on either side of Brad.

The policeman had explained what they would do. Using a key he'd procured from the motel owner, Brad would unlock the door and turn on the light. Even if Stella woke immediately, the three policemen would be in the room, and if Fanny was there, she would be the main priority, the three law officers moving directly to cover her from any attack.

Steph didn't like to think about what form the attack might take, or about possible harm to the three people who would put their lives at risk to save her child.

If she was there...

As the threesome approached the building, light from the front office lit up their silhouettes.

'The tall one—that's not a policeman, it's Harry!' Steph gasped, as the shadows became people. 'Why's he there? What's he doing?'

She was clutching Bob's arm, and shaking with an unnamable dread, but before Bob could answer—if he'd had an answer—she saw the door of the unit they'd been watching open. As a light flashed on, it was Harry who went first into the room.

Steph closed her eyes and prayed, though for Harry this time, as well as Fanny.

The figures disappeared into the room, then she heard Brad's excited cry of, 'Bingo!'

It wasn't an arranged signal, but Steph knew what it meant. She was out of the car and racing across the driveway at the back of the motel, reaching the door of the unit as Harry came out, a small, blonde-headed bundle held snugly in his arms.

Steph snatched the burden from him, but even as she pressed Fanny close to her chest, she glared at the man who'd rescued her.

'You could have been killed,' she muttered angrily at him, then her gaze feasted on her child, scanning every inch of skin to assure herself it *was* Fanny and she was alive and well.

Fanny opened sleepy eyes and smiled.

'Oh, Mummy, you're back. I'm so glad. Stella is so boring. Did you see my picture on TV? Was it because I cut the ribbon they kept putting it on?'

She snuggled closer to Steph, who closed her eyes and gave thanks, not only for the safe return of her child but to Stella as well, who had somehow managed to make the whole ordeal boring rather than traumatic for her child.

Then the agony of the past few days caught up with her, and relief weakened her knees. She sagged and would have collapsed if Harry and Bob, both hovering by her side, hadn't caught her and helped her to the car.

The young policeman drove them home, where Bob picked up his car and departed, eager to tell Doreen the good news.

Determined to keep things as normal as possible for Fanny, Steph put her into her own bed, read her a story and watched her fall asleep before the first page was finished.

'Now, bed for you, too,' Harry said. 'I'll stay. I'll watch her.'

'You can't,' Steph told him, though she was now so tired she could barely talk. 'You have to sleep yourself. You're operating tomorrow.'

He reached out and grasped her shoulders, looking down into her eyes.

'I've asked someone else to do it,' he said.

'But you can't do that. You came home to do these operations—it was your dream, Harry.' Tiredness lifted enough for her to protest.

'Dreams don't mean much when you're faced with the reality we've all faced this last weekend, Steph,' he said gently, his dark eyes soft with anguish. 'It's a terrible thing for a man to realise he can't protect the woman he loves, but at least I could be here for you. I couldn't not do that. And I won't leave you now.'

He touched her softly on the cheek, then smoothed his finger between her eyebrows where she knew frown marks must be settling in.

'Don't worry. As soon as you're rested, I'll catch up on a bit of sleep, then take over from the primary surgeon this afternoon. We'd worked out we'd need to do shifts.'

Steph knew she was too tired for her thoughts to be making sense, but she certainly wasn't worrying about Harry's part in Ty's operation. In fact, she wasn't sure what she was worrying about—but it had begun when she'd seen him walk into that motel room...

She woke with a start, leaping off the bed and racing to Fanny's room, seeing not her daughter but a tousled, slept-in bed that reassured her the previous night's events hadn't been a dream.

Fanny was in the lounge, sitting on Harry's knee while he brushed her hair.

'I got dressed all by myself, but I couldn't do my hair,' Fanny announced, and Steph felt tears rush into her eyes. Fanny was all right!

She lifted her daughter into her arms and hugged her, then, as Fanny announced she could get her own breakfast and departed to the kitchen, Steph turned to Harry.

'Thank you,' she said, smiling for what seemed like the first time in months.

'I don't need thanks, Steph. You know that.'

Harry stood up and she saw the tiredness in the way he moved, but when he took hold of her shoulders she felt his quiet strength, and when he looked into her eyes she saw the love he felt for her.

'I know you need to spend some time with Fanny right now,'

he said gently. 'But when you're feeling more secure—when you've convinced yourself she's safe—would you take a little time to think about us? About you and me and whether there's a future for us—together?'

He sighed then kissed her gently on the lips.

'I know Martin betrayed your trust, and this horrific incident has put further dents in it. I'd love to promise you'd never suffer unhappiness again, but there are no guarantees in this world, Steph. All I can promise is, whatever happens in the future, I love you and will always be there for you.'

He turned away before she could think of a reply—before she could explain that she was so mixed up right now that love was the last thing on her mind.

But when she thought over what he'd said, she realised Harry must have known that. He'd told her how he felt and was leaving the rest to her.

Steph spent the week at home, knowing Fanny needed to get back into her normal routine but unable to be far away from her, even going so far as to sit in her car outside the kindy, watching over the child she'd so nearly lost.

Rebecca reported regularly on Ty's progress. The operation had been a success, he was out of the ICU and doing really well. The test would come when the bandages came off and the lad tried to move his jaw.

Harry was seeing patients—busier than he'd expected to be because once Fanny had been found Bob had turned his attention back to work and had milked the 'free' operation for all the publicity he could get.

Inevitably, some of this spotlight shone on Harry, and referrals for facial surgery were coming in at a steady rate.

But as Steph's stress levels dropped, and life began to fall back into its normal pattern, she began to wonder why Harry hadn't called or come to see them.

Because he left it up to you to make the next move, she reminded herself. He's offered you his love—and left you to decide if you want to take it.

Left you to decide if you trust that love...

She pondered it on the Friday—the first day she felt secure enough to leave Fanny at kindy and actually drive home. But not secure enough to get back into her work routine.

Brad had called on Wednesday evening. Stella had admitted seeing the publicity about the hospital opening. Apparently, she'd been four months pregnant by Martin when he'd died, but had lost the baby. The publicity brought back her pain and grief and loss, and with them an overwhelming sense of injustice.

She hadn't so much planned to kidnap Fanny as gone looking for an opportunity to do harm. She'd bought supplies so she could hole up in a motel somewhere, still thinking more of ruining the opening ceremony then getting away, not considering taking the child.

But Fanny had looked so like Martin that her control had broken. She'd followed the guests' cars to the Quayles' house, then had mingled with the guests. She'd stayed in the house with Martin many years earlier when his parents had been overseas, so knew her way around, and when she'd found Fanny sleeping, it had seemed so easy just to pick her up and carry her down the back stairs and out the door that led to the service gate.

Brad suspected she'd planned it more thoroughly than she admitted as her car had been parked near that exit, but she was adamant that taking Fanny had been a spur-of-the-moment decision.

In reply to Steph's question of what would happen to Stella now, Brad had shrugged, explaining it would be up to the courts, but he guessed they would recommend a psychiatric evaluation.

Steph, now Fanny had been returned to her, felt pity for the woman who'd been cheated of everything she'd ever wanted. And though she'd vowed to put her bitterness and anger towards Martin behind her, she couldn't help but lay the blame for Stella's actions at his door.

And thinking of Martin, she *had* to think of Harry. To think about 'us', as he'd put it.

Was she ready to put her happiness into someone else's hands—her own and Fanny's happiness?

Was she ready to trust again?

Forget Harry, think about a job, she told herself when no answer to her queries about that part of her future popped obligingly into her head.

But it was still too soon to consider going back to work. She was, with difficulty, giving up her post outside the kindy, but leaving Fanny while she went to work seemed too big a hurdle to contemplate just yet.

Maybe in a little while...

Bob arrived that afternoon as she was still pondering the options. He was more understanding now, and though he hadn't pushed her to return to live with them, today's offer wasn't that far off.

'Let me pay off the house for you and give you an allowance,' he said. 'Then you won't have to work.'

'But I enjoy work,' she explained to him. 'And I need to do something. I can't sit at home on my own all day, worrying about Fanny. As well as going nuts myself, I'd probably do her irreparable psychological harm by being an over-protective mother.'

'Will you go back to work for Harry?'

Steph shrugged.

'I don't know if the job's still on offer,' she admitted. 'And, to be honest, women with dependent children aren't the most dependable of employees. Surgeons can't back out of an operation at the last minute, but if Fanny was sick, I might have to do just that.'

Bob nodded.

'Though Doreen could pick up a lot of the slack at times like that if you let her. I know she's been a weak reed to lean on since Martin's death, but Fanny's disappearance has changed all that.

She hasn't touched a drop of alcohol, and she's doing volunteer work at the hospital.'

He touched Steph gently on the shoulder.

'She needs to be needed, Steph.'

This time it was Steph who nodded, but having Doreen available to mind Fanny if Tracy was at college made a range of jobs now possible.

Forget jobs and think about Harry!

In the end, she went to see him. Collecting Fanny herself from kindy then later leaving her with Tracy for the first time since her daughter's disappearance, Steph set off for the hospital.

First stop was the new, sparsely populated surgical ward to visit Ty, who was in good spirits and already moving his jaw experimentally, although it was still heavily bandaged.

Then on to Harry's rooms, where she hesitated before opening the door.

It was late enough for Rebecca and the new junior Rebecca had employed to have left, but the fact that the door was unlocked suggested Harry would still be there.

She hesitated outside the closed door of his consulting room.

'Harry?'

No answer, but she heard a shuffling sound, then the door opened and he was standing there.

'You look terrible,' she said, seeing the lines strain had etched in his face and the pain and tiredness in his eyes.

'Harry!' His name slipped out again, this time as a protest. 'What's wrong?'

He tried a smile but it was a dim, exhausted effort.

'It hasn't been the best week I've ever had, Steph,' he said, not moving to invite her in, not reaching out to touch her.

'Ty? Is it Ty? Are there complications?'

She was so anxious she reached out herself, grasping his forearm, feeling his muscles contract as if he'd flinched at her touch.

She took her hand away, then stared at it, wondering how a pale palm, four fingers and a thumb could cause offence.

Beyond Harry's shoulder she could see X-rays in the viewing boxes and, seeking a bit of normality in what had suddenly become an unreal situation, she stepped past him, saying, 'Are these Ty's? Are they the latest? Are you happy with the way things went?'

She knew he'd followed her into the room because the skin on her back was prickling with awareness of his presence.

'Very happy,' he said in a voice more suited to a funeral than a celebration of success. 'See here, where we pinned new bone, if you look closely you can see it's already starting to grow.'

He came closer to point to the section he wanted her to see, and her body throbbed with being so close, yet not close enough. Throbbed with uncertainty as well, because this Harry seemed completely oblivious to her as anything other than a fellow doctor.

She turned away from the films—she wasn't concentrating on what he was saying anyway—and rested her hands on his shoulders. Again she felt that stiffening, but she'd come to say things and wasn't going to be put off.

'Harry, I've thought about what you said—about us.'

'And?' he prompted, and she saw wariness in his eyes as if he feared bad news. 'Is there an us?'

'I think so,' she said softly, 'but it would help me be sure if you kissed me.'

She saw the veil of tiredness lift from his face and the glow of love light his eyes, then she was in his arms, clinging to him as if she'd been adrift on a wind-tossed sea for far too long.

Then his lips met hers and she gave in to the sheer bliss of being in Harry's arms—or kissing Harry.

A long time later they stopped for air, and she snuggled up against him.

'You're sure about this?' he said, his voice betraying a mix of awe and hope.

'Absolutely,' Steph said. 'That morning, after Fanny came back, you talked about guarantees. I'm not asking you for any guarantees. I've already figured out they're not possible. But loving you, and knowing you love me—that's enough for now. All last weekend, while Fanny was missing, I kept telling myself that getting her back would make my life complete. I thought it was all I could ever wish for.'

She studied Harry's face, so familiar—so dear.

'And getting her back was like a miracle. Even though I was still fearful, and obsessively over-protective, I could at least breathe normally again. Then, as the week progressed, I realised breathing wasn't enough. I was alive, but not really living, Harry. Believe me, I know the difference. I've been like that for nearly five years, and enough's enough.'

Harry's arms closed more tightly around her.

'There is one guarantee I can give, Steph,' he said, as his gaze roamed her face, feasting on the so-familiar features like a starving man on food. 'And that's my love. For you, for Fanny, for any other children we might one day have. My love is yours—I guarantee it.'

Then he bent his head and sealed the words with a kiss.

* * * * *

Midwife...To Mum!

Sue MacKay

Books by Sue MacKay

Doctors to Daddies

A Father for Her Baby
The Midwife's Son

The Family She Needs
A Family This Christmas
From Duty to Daddy
The Gift of a Child
You, Me and a Family
Christmas with Dr. Delicious
Every Boy's Dream Dad
The Dangers of Dating Your Boss
Surgeon in a Wedding Dress

Visit the Author Profile page
at millsandboon.com.au for more titles.

Dear Reader,

I'm so excited to have written one of the Midwives On-Call continuity stories set in Melbourne.

When Kiwis visit Australia we call it hopping across the ditch. In this case my story has hopped over there. It's fun to write a story set in a very different location from my usual haunts.

Flynn and Ally are made for each other—it just takes them time to work that out. But who could go wrong with love on the beautiful Phillip Island, which sits just below Melbourne and the Victoria coastline? Throw in the cutest little boy and a big friendly dog and life's a beach.

I hope you enjoy reading Flynn and Ally's story and seeing how it ties in with the other stories in this series.

Drop by my website, suemackay.co.nz, or send me an email at sue.mackay56@yahoo.com.

Cheers!

Sue MacKay

CHAPTER ONE

ALYSSA PARKER DROPPED her bags in the middle of the lounge and stared around what would be her next temporary living quarters. She could pretty much see it all from where she stood. Dusting and vacuuming weren't going to take up her spare time, like it had at the last place. She'd have to find something else to keep her busy after work. Take up knitting? Or hire a dog to walk every day?

Her phone rang. Tugging it from her jacket pocket, she read the name on the screen and punched the 'talk' button. 'Hey, boss, I've arrived on Phillip Island.' The bus trip down from Melbourne city had been interminable as she'd kept dozing off. It had taken the ferry crossing and lots of fresh air to clear her head.

'How's the head?' Lucas Elliot, her senior midwife, asked.

'It's good now. Who have you been talking to?' She and some of the crew from the Melbourne Midwifery Unit had gone out for drinks, which had extended to a meal and more drinks.

'My lips are sealed,' Lucas quipped. 'So, Phillip Island—another place for you to tick off on the map.'

'Yep.' Her life was all about new destinations and experiences. Certainly not the regular nine to five in the same place, year in, year out, that most people preferred.

'How's the flat?'

'About the size of a dog kennel.' Stepping sideways, Ally peered into what looked like an overgrown cupboard. 'It's an exaggeration to call this a kitchen. But, hey, that's part of the adventure.' Like she needed a kitchen when she favoured take-out food anyway.

'Ally, I forgot to tell you where the key to the flat would be, but it seems you've taken up breaking and entering on the side.'

She was Ally to everyone except the taxman and her lawyer. And the social welfare system. 'It was under the pot plant on the top step.' The first place she'd looked.

'Why do people do that? It's so obvious.' Lucas sounded genuinely perplexed.

Still looking around, she muttered, 'I doubt there's much worth stealing in here.' Kat, the midwife she was replacing temporarily, certainly didn't spend her pay packet on home comforts.

'Are you happy with the arrangements? I know you enjoy everywhere we send you, but this should be the best yet as far as location goes. All those beaches to play on.'

'It's winter, or haven't you noticed?' Ally shook her head. 'But so far the island's looking beautiful.'

His chuckle was infectious. 'I'll leave you to unpack and find your way around. You're expected at the medical centre at eight thirty tomorrow. Dr Reynolds wants to run through a few details with you before you get started with the Monday morning antenatal list.'

'Same as any locum job I do, then?' She couldn't help the jibe. She'd been doing this relief work for two years now. It suited her roving lifestyle perfectly and was the only reason she remained with the Melbourne Midwifery Unit. They'd of-fered her fixed positions time and again. She'd turned them all down. Fixed meant working continuously at the midwifery unit, which in turn meant getting too close to those people she'd work with every day.

The days when she set herself up to get dumped by anyone—

friends, colleagues or lovers—were long over. Had been from the monumental day she'd turned sixteen and taken control of her life. She'd walked out of the social welfare building for the very last time. It hadn't mattered that she'd had little money or knowledge on how to survive. She'd known a sense of wonder at being in charge of herself. Since then no one had screwed up her expectations because she'd been in charge of her own destiny. Because she hadn't allowed herself to hope for family or love again.

'I'm being pedantic.' Lucas was still on the other end of the line. 'I wanted to make sure everything's okay.'

Why wouldn't it be? She didn't need him fussing about her. She didn't like it. It spoke of care and concern. But Lucas did care about the people he worked with, which, despite trying not to let it, had always warmed her and given her a sense of belonging to the unit. Since she didn't do belonging, it showed how good Lucas was with his staff.

She told him, 'I'll take a walk to get my bearings and suss out where the medical centre is as soon as I've unpacked.' Tomorrow she'd collect the car provided for the job.

'Even your map-reading skills might just about manage that.' He laughed at his own joke. 'I'll leave you to get settled. Catch you in four weeks, unless there's a problem.'

Stuffing the phone back in her pocket, she headed into the bedroom and dumped a bag on the bed. At least it was a double. Not that she had any man to share the other half with. Not yet. *Who knows? There might be a hot guy at the surf beach who'd like a short fling, no strings.* Her mouth watered at the thought of all those muscles surfers must have. Winter wouldn't stop those dudes getting on their boards. There were such things as wetsuits.

After dropping her second, smaller bag full of books and DVDs out of the way in the corner of the lounge, she slapped her hands on her hips and stared around. Four o'clock in the afternoon and nothing to do. Once she started on the job she'd be fine, but these first hours when she arrived in a new place and moved into someone else's home always made her feel antsy. It wasn't her space, didn't hold her favourite possessions.

Except... Unzipping the bag, she placed two small silver statues on the only shelf. 'Hey, guys, welcome to Cowes.' Her finger traced the outlines of her pets. If she ever got to own a pet it would be a springer spaniel like these. Make that two spaniels. One on its own would be lonely.

She hadn't forgiven the Bartlett family who'd given her these on the day they'd broken her heart, along with their promise they'd love her for ever. She'd wrapped the statues in an empty chocolate box and tied it with a yellow ribbon, before burying them in the Bartletts' garden. The gift had been a consolation prize for abandoning her, but one dark day when she'd felt unable to carry on, she'd remembered the dogs *she'd* abandoned and had sneaked back to retrieve them. They'd gone everywhere with her ever since, a talisman to her stronger self.

Having the statues in place didn't make the flat hers, though. Again Ally stared around. She could do a lap of the cupboards and shelves, learning where everything was kept. By then it'd be five past four and she'd still not know what to do with herself.

This moment was the only time she ever allowed that her life wasn't normal. *Define normal.* Doing what other people did.

Standing in the middle of a home she'd never been in before, didn't know the owner of, always brought up the question of what would it be like to settle down for ever in her own place.

As if she'd ever do that.

What if it was with a man who loved me regardless?

The answer never changed. That person didn't exist.

She followed her established routine for first days in new towns. First, off came her new and amazing knee-high black boots, then she pulled on her top-of-the-line walking shoes.

Sliding on her sunglasses, she snatched up the house key and stuffed it and her wallet into her pocket and headed out. There had to be a decent coffee shop somewhere. Might as well check out the options for takeout dinners, too. Then she'd head to the nearest beach to do some exploring.

The coffee turned out to be better than good. Ally drained the paper mug of every last drop and tossed it into the next rubbish bin she came across. The beach stretched ahead as she kicked up sand and watched the sea relentlessly rolling in. Kids chased balls and each other, couples strolled hand in hand, one grown-up idiot raced into the freezing water and straight back out, shouting his head off in shock.

Ally pulled out her phone and called the midwifery centre back in the city, sighing happily when Darcie answered. 'Hey, how's the head?'

'Nothing wrong with mine, but, then, I was on orange juice all night.'

'You shouldn't be so quick to put your hand up for call.'

Darcie grumped, 'Says the woman who works more hours than the rest of us.' Then she cheered Ally up with, 'You can move into my spare room when you get back to town. As of this morning it's empty, my flatmate having found her own place.'

'Great, that's cool.' Darcie was fast becoming a good friend, which did bother her when she thought about it. But right this moment it felt good to have a friend onside when she was feeling more unsettled than usual at the start of a new assignment. Today she sensed she might be missing out on the bigger picture. This was the loneliness she'd learned to cope with whenever she'd been shuffled off to yet another foster home full of well-meaning people who'd always eventually packed her bags and sent her away.

'You still there?' Darcie asked.

'Did you get called in today?'

'I've just finished an urgent caesarean, and I'm about to get something to eat.'

'I'll leave you to it, then. Thanks for the bed. I'll definitely take you up on that.' After saying goodbye, she shoved her hands deep into her jacket pockets and began striding to the farthest end of the beach, feeling better already. Being alone wasn't so bad when there were people at the end of a phone. At least this way she got to choose which side of the bed she slept on, what she had for dinner, and when to move on to the next stop.

A ball came straight for her and she lined it up, kicked it back hard, aiming for the boys running after it. One of them swung a foot at it and missed, much to his mates' mirth at a girl kicking it better.

'Girls can do anything better.' She grinned and continued walking a few metres above the water's edge, feeling happier by the minute. How could she remain gloomy out here? The beach was beautiful, the air fresh, and she had a new job in the morning. What else could she possibly need?

The sun began dropping fast and Ally stopped to watch the amazing reds and yellows spreading, blending the sky and water into one molten colour block, like a young child's painting. Her throat ached with the beauty of it.

Thud. Something solid slammed into her. For a moment, as she teetered on her feet, she thought she'd keep her balance. But another shove and she toppled into an ungainly heap on the sand with the heavy weight on top of her. A moving, panting, licking heavy weight. A dog of no mean proportions with gross doggy breath sprawled across her.

'Hey, get off me.' She squirmed between paws and tried to push upright onto her backside.

One paw shoved her back down, and the dark, furry head blocked out all vision of the sunset. The rear end of the animal was wriggling back and forth as its tail whipped through the air.

'Sheba, come here.' A male voice came from somewhere above them. 'Get off now.'

Sheba—if that was the name of her assailant—gave Ally's chin a final lick and leapt sideways, avoiding an outstretched hand that must've been aiming for her collar.

'Phew.'

Her relief was premature. The dog lay down beside her as

close as possible, and farthest away from the man trying to catch her. One paw banged down on her stomach, forcing all the air out of her lungs.

Somewhere behind her a young child started laughing. 'Sheba, you're funny.'

The sweet childish sound of pure enjoyment had Ally carefully pushing the paw aside and sitting up to look round for the source. A cute little boy was leaping up and down, giggling fit to bust.

'Sheba. Sit now.' The man wasn't nearly as thrilled about his dog's behaviour.

Ally stared up at the guy looming above her. 'It's all right. I'm fine, really.' She even smiled to prove her point.

'I'm very sorry Sheba bowled you over. She doesn't understand her own strength.' As he glanced across at the child his annoyance was quickly replaced by something soft she couldn't read. 'Adam, don't encourage her.'

'But it's funny, Dad.' The boy folded in half, still giggling.

Ally clambered to her feet, dusting sand off her jeans, and grinned. 'What is it about kids and giggling? They don't seem to know how to stop.' Just watching the boy made her happy— especially now that the dog had loped across to bunt him in the bottom, which only made the giggles louder. Laughter threatened to bubble up from deep inside her stomach.

The guy was shaking his head, looking bemused. 'Beats me how he keeps going so long.'

Ally winced. Slapping the sand off her left hip just made it sore. Sheba must've bruised her.

'Are you all right?' the man asked, worry darkening his expression. 'Look, I apologise again. I hope you haven't been hurt.'

'Look,' she used his word back at him. 'I'm fine. Seriously. Sheba was being playful and if I hadn't been staring at the sunset I'd have seen her coming.' She stuck her hand out. 'I'm Ally. That's Sheba, and your boy's called Adam. You are?'

'Flynn. We've been visiting friends all day and needed some

fresh air before settling down for the night.' He looked at her properly, finally letting go the need to watch his boy and dog. 'What about you?'

'Much the same. The beach is hard to resist when the weather's so balmy.' He didn't need to know she'd only just arrived. Running her hands over the sleeves of her jacket, she smoothed off the remaining sand, trying to refrain from staring at him. But it was impossible to look away.

Despite the sadness in his eyes, or because of it, she was taking more notice of him than a casual meeting on the beach usually entailed. The stubble darkening his chin was downright sexy, while that tousled hair brought heat to her cold cheeks. If she played her cards right, could this be the man she had her next fling with?

She glanced downward, taking in his athletic build, his fitted jeans that defined many of his muscles. The sun glinted off something on the guy's hand and she had her answer. A band of gold. Said it all, really.

'Can I call you Ally?' Adam bounced up in front of her.

Blink, blink. Refocus on the younger version now that the older one was out of bounds. 'Of course you can.' As if they were going to see each other again. Though they might, she realised, if Flynn brought his son to the beach often. She'd be walking along here most days that she wasn't caught up with delivering babies and talking to pregnant mums.

Hopefully, if they ran into each other again, Flynn would have his wife with him. A wife would certainly dampen the flare of attraction that had snagged her, and which should've evaporated the moment she'd seen that ring. Flings were the way to go, but never, ever with a man already involved with someone else. She didn't do hurting for the sake of it, or for any reason at all, come to think of it.

Guess she'd have to keep looking for someone to warm the other half of that bed. *Whoa, Ally, you haven't been here more than an hour. What's the hurry?*

The thing was, if she was playing bed games there wouldn't be long, empty nights that had her dreaming of the impossible. She could shove the overpowering sense of unworthiness aside as she and a man made each other happy for a short while, and then bury her face in the pillow while he left. Every parting, even as casual as her relationships were, was touched with a longing for the life she craved, had never known, and was too afraid to try for.

Flynn Reynolds dragged his gaze away from the most attractive woman he'd met in a long while and focused on his son. Except Adam stood directly in front of her, talking nonstop, and Flynn's gaze easily moved across the tiny gap to a stunning pair of legs clad in skin-tight jeans. His breathing hitched in his throat. Oh, wow. Gorgeous.

The woman—*Ally, she has a name*—laughed at something Adam said, a deep, pure laugh that spoke of enjoyment with no hidden agenda. Very refreshing, considering most women he met these days seemed intent on luring him into their clutches with false concern about him and Adam. He hated it that many women believed the way to attract him was by being over-friendly to his son. What they didn't get was that Adam saw through them almost as quickly as he did.

What they also didn't get was that Flynn wasn't interested. Not at all. So why was his gaze cruising over the length of this curvy woman with a smile that had him smiling back immediately, even when it wasn't directed at him? Especially since he apparently didn't do smiling very much these days.

He looked directly at his son. 'Time we made tracks for home. The sun's nearly gone and it will be cold soon.' Any excuse to cut this short and put some space between him and Ally before his brain started thinking along the lines of wanting to get to know her better. He wasn't ready for another woman in his life. Certainly wouldn't have time for years to come, either.

'Do we have to?'

'Yes, I'm afraid so.'

What I'm really afraid of is staying to talk to Ally too long and ending up inviting her home to share dinner with us. If she's free and available. As if a woman as attractive as her would be seriously single. The absence of rings on her fingers didn't mean a thing.

He looked around and groaned. 'Sheba,' he yelled. 'Come here.'

Too late. The mutt was belly deep in the sea, leaping and splashing without any concern for how cold the water had to be.

Adam ran down to the water's edge and stood with his hands on his skinny hips. 'Sheba, Dad says we're going home. You want your dinner?'

Beside Flynn, Ally chuckled. 'Good luck with that.'

Glancing at her, he drew a deep breath. Her cheeks had flushed deep pink when the mutt had dumped her on the sand, and the colour still remained, becoming rosier every time she laughed. Which was often.

He noticed her rubbing her hip. 'You did hurt yourself.'

She jammed her hand in her pocket. 'Just a hard landing, nothing to worry about.'

'You're sure?' He'd hate it if Sheba had caused some damage.

'Absolutely.'

Adam and Sheba romped up to him. Then the dog did what wet dogs did—shook herself hard, sending salty spray over everyone. Now Ally would complain and walk away. But no. Her laughter filled the air and warmed the permanent chill in his soul. It would be unbelievably easy to get entangled with someone like her. Make that with this woman in particular.

He sighed his disappointment. There was no room in his life for a woman, no matter how beautiful. Not even for a short time. Adam and work demanded all his attention. Besides, how did a guy go about dating? He hadn't been in that market for so long he wouldn't know where to start. Was there a dating book for dummies? *I don't need one. It's not happening.* He gave himself a mental slap. All these questions and doubts because of a woman he'd met five minutes ago. He was in need of a break. That was his real problem. Solo parenting and work gobbled up all his time and energy.

'Let's go.' He grabbed Sheba's collar and turned in the direction of their street. 'Nice meeting you.' He nodded abruptly at the woman who'd been the first one to catch his interest since Anna had died two years ago. It had to be a fleeting interest; one that would've disappeared by the time he reached home and became immersed in preparing dinner, folding washing and getting ready for work tomorrow. Damn it all. It could've been fun getting to know her.

'Bye, Ally,' Adam called, as they started walking up the beach.

She stood watching them, both hands in her jacket pockets. 'See you around.' Was that a hint of wistfulness in her voice?

'Okay,' Adam answered, apparently reluctant to leave her. 'Tomorrow?'

'Adam,' Flynn growled. 'Come on.' He aimed for the road, deliberately stamping down on the urge to invite the woman home to share dinner. He did not need anyone else's problems. He did not need anyone else, full stop.

Anyway, she probably wouldn't like baked beans on toast.

Baked beans. He only had to close his eyes to hear Anna saying how unhealthy they were. They'd eaten lots of vegetables for lunch so he could relax the rules tonight. Beans once in a while wouldn't hurt Adam, and would save *him* some time. Who knew? He might get to watch the late news. Life was really looking up.

CHAPTER TWO

PLASTERING ON HER best smiley face the next morning, Ally stepped inside the medical centre, unzipping her jacket as she crossed to the reception desk. 'Hi, I'm Alyssa Parker.' Lucas always wrote her full name on her credentials when sending them to medical centres. It was a technicality he adhered to, and she hated it. 'Ally for short. I'm covering for Kat while she's away.'

A man straightened from the file he was reading and she gasped as the piercing blue eyes that had followed her into sleep last night now scanned her. Her smile widened. 'Flynn.' The buzz she'd felt standing by this man yesterday returned in full force, fizzing through her veins, heating her in places she definitely didn't need warmed by a married man. He was still as sexy, despite the stubble having been shaved off. *Stop it.* But she'd have to be six feet under not to react to him.

'Ally. Or do you prefer Alyssa?'

'Definitely Ally. Never Alyssa. So you're Dr Reynolds?' They hadn't swapped surnames the previous day. Hardly been any point when the chances of meeting again had seemed remote. Neither had she learned his first name when she was told about this job. She became aware of the receptionist glancing from her to Flynn, eyebrows high and a calculating look in her eyes.

Fortunately Flynn must've seen her, too. 'Megan's our office lady and general everything girl. She'll help you find files and stock lists and anything else you want.'

'You two know each other?' Megan asked her burning question.

Ally left that to Flynn to deal with and took a quick look around the office, but listened in as Flynn told the receptionist, 'We met briefly yesterday. Can you tell the others as they arrive that we're in the tearoom and can they come along to meet Ally?' Then he joined her on the other side of the counter. 'I'll show you around. You've got a busy clinic this morning. Three near full-term mums and four who are in their second trimester.'

'Three close to full term? Was there a party on the island eight months back that everyone went to?' She grinned.

'You'd be surprised how many pregnant ladies we see. Phillip Island's population isn't as small as people think. One of the women, Marie Canton, is Adam's daytime caregiver when he's not at preschool.'

So Adam's mum worked, too. Ally wondered what she did. A doctor, like her husband? 'Will Marie be bringing Adam with her?'

'I'm not sure.'

'What time's my first appointment?' she asked, suddenly needing to stay on track and be professional.

But Flynn smiled, and instantly ramped up that heat circulating her body, defying her professionalism. 'Nine. Was it explained to you that Kat also does high school visits to talk to the teenagers about contraception?' Flynn stood back and indicated with a wave of his hand for her to precede him into a kitchen-cum-meeting-room. 'You've got one on Thursday afternoon.'

'I didn't know, but not a problem.' What was that aftershave? She sniffed a second time, savouring the tangy scent that reminded her of the outdoors and sun and...? And hot male. She tripped over her size sevens and grabbed the back of a chair to regain her balance. 'I'm still breaking these boots in,' she explained quickly, hoping Flynn wouldn't notice the sudden glow in her cheeks. He mustn't think she was clumsy but, worse, he mustn't guess what had nearly sent her crashing face first onto the floor.

But when she glanced at him she relaxed. His gaze was firmly fixed on the boots she'd blamed. Her awesome new boots that had cost nearly a week's pay. His eyes widened, then cruised slowly, too slowly, up her thighs to her hips, up, up, up, until he finally locked gazes with her. So much for relaxing. Now she felt as though she was in a sauna and there was no way out. The heat just kept getting steamier. Her tongue felt too big for her mouth. Her eyes must look like bug's eyes; they certainly felt as though they were out on stalks.

Flynn was one sexy unit. The air between them sparked like electricity. His hair was as tousled as it had been yesterday and just as tempting. Her fingers curled into her palms, her false nails digging deep into her skin as she fought not to reach out and finger-comb those thick waves.

'You must be the midwife.' A woman in her midforties suddenly appeared before her. 'Faye Bellamy, part-time GP for my sins.'

Ally took a step back to put space between her and Flynn, and reached for Faye's proffered hand. 'That's me. Ally Parker. Pleased to meet you.'

'Pleasure's all ours. Darned nuisance Kat wanting time off, but I've read your résumé and it seems you'll be a perfect fit for her job.' Bang, mugs hit the benchtop. 'Coffee, everyone?'

Kat wasn't meant to take holidays? Or just this one? 'Yes, thanks. Where's Kat gone?'

Flynn was quick to answer. 'To Holland for her great-grandmother's ninetieth birthday. She's been saving her leave for this trip.' He flicked a glance at Faye's back, then looked at Ally. 'She could've taken two months and still not used up what she's owed,' he added.

'Europe's a long way to go for any less time.' Not that it had anything to do with her, except she would have been signed on here for longer and that meant more weeks—okay, hours—in Flynn's company. Already that looked like being a problem. His marital status wasn't having any effect on curtailing the reaction her body had to him.

She took the mug being handed to her and was surprised to see her hand shaking. She searched her head for something ordinary to focus on, and came back to Kat. 'Bet the trip's another reason why there isn't much furniture or clutter in the flat.' A girl after her own heart, though for a different reason.

'Morning, everyone.' A man strolled in. 'Coffee smells good.' Then he saw Ally. 'Hi, I'm Jerome, GP extraordinaire, working with this motley lot.'

Amidst laughter and banter Ally sat back and listened as the nurses joined them and began discussing patients and the two emergencies that had happened over the weekend. She felt right at home. This was the same Monday-morning scenario she'd sat through in most of the clinics she'd worked at ever since qualifying. Same cases, different names. Same egos, different names. Soon her gaze wandered to the man sitting opposite her, and she felt that hitch in her breathing again.

Flynn was watching her from under hooded eyes, his chin low, his arms folded across his chest as he leaned as far back in his chair as possible without spilling over backwards.

Ally's breathing became shallow and fast, like it did after a particularly hard run. The man had no right to make her feel like this. Who did he think he was? The sooner this meeting was finished the better. She could go and play with patients and hide from him until all her body parts returned to their normal functions. At the rate she was going, that'd be some time around midnight.

The sound of scraping chairs on the floor dragged her attention back to the other people in the room and gave her the escape she desperately needed.

But fifteen minutes after the meeting ended, Flynn was entering her room with a frightened young girl in tow. 'Ally, I'd like you to meet Chrissie Gordon.' He ushered the girl, dressed in school uniform, to a chair.

'Hi, Chrissie. Love your nail colour. It's like hot pink and fiery red all mixed up.' It would have lit up a dark room.

'It's called Monster Red.' Chrissie shrugged at her, as if to say, Who gives a rat's tail? Something serious was definitely on this young lady's mind.

Given that Flynn had brought Chrissie to see *her*, they must be about to talk about protection during sex or STDs. Or pregnancy. The girl looked stumped, as if her worst possible nightmare had just become real. Ally wanted to scoop her up into her arms and ward off whatever was about to be revealed. Instead, she looked at Flynn and raised an eyebrow.

'Chrissie's done several dip-stick tests for pregnancy and they all showed positive.' Flynn's face held nothing but sympathy for his patient's predicament. 'I'd like you to take a blood sample for an HCG test to confirm that, and then we'll also know how far along she is if the result's positive.'

It wasn't going to be negative with all those stick tests showing otherwise. 'No problem.'

Ally took the lab form he handed her and glancing down saw requests for WR and VDRL to check for STDs, antibodies and a blood group. She noted the girl's date of birth. Chrissie was fifteen. Too young to be dealing with this. Ally's heart went out to the frightened child as she thought back to when she'd been that age. She'd barely been coping with her own life, let alone be able to manage looking after a baby. Face it, she doubted her ability to do that *now*. Locking eyes with Flynn, she said, 'Leave it to me.'

His nod was sharp. 'Right, Chrissie, I'll call you on your cell when the lab results come back.'

'Thanks, Dr Reynolds,' Chrissie whispered, as her fingers picked at the edge of her jersey, beginning to unravel a thread. 'You won't tell Mum, will you?'

'Of course not. You know even if I wanted to—which I

don't—I'm not allowed to disclose your confidential information. It's up to you to decide when to talk to your mother, but let's wait until we get these tests done and you can come and see me again first, if that'll make it easier for you.' Flynn drew a breath and added, 'You won't be able to hide the pregnancy for ever.'

'I know. But not yet, okay?' The girl's head bowed over her almost flat chest. 'I'm afraid. It hurts to have a baby, doesn't it?'

Ally placed a hand over Chrissie's and squeezed gently. 'You're getting way ahead of yourself. Let's do those tests and find out how far along you are. After I've taken your blood I'll explain a few things about early-stage pregnancy if you like.'

'Yes, please. I think.' Fat tears oozed out of Chrissie's eyes and slid down her cheeks to drip onto her jersey. 'Mum's going to kill me.'

'No, she won't,' Flynn said. About to leave the room, he turned back to hunker down in front of Chrissie and said emphatically, 'Angela will be very supportive of you. You're her daughter. That's what mothers do.'

Yeah, right, you don't know a thing, buster, if that's what you believe. Did you grow up in la-la land? Ally clamped her lips shut for fear of spilling the truth. *Some mothers couldn't care two drops of nothing about their daughters. Some dump their babies on strangers' doorsteps.*

But when she glanced at Flynn, he shook his head and mouthed, 'It's true of Angela.'

Had he known what she'd been thinking? The tension that had been tightening her shoulders left off as she conceded silently that if he was right then Chrissie was luckier than some. A big positive in what must feel like a very negative morning for the girl. 'Good,' she acknowledged with a nod at Flynn. As for his mind-reading, did that mean he'd known exactly what she'd been thinking about him back there in the staffroom?

'Have you had a blood test before?' she asked Chrissie. She'd wasted enough time thinking about Dr Reynolds.

Flynn disappeared quietly, closing the door behind him.

MIDWIFE...TO MUM!

'Yeah, three times. I hate them. I fainted every time.'

'You can lie on the bed, then. No way do I want to be picking you off the floor, now, do I?'

She was rewarded with a glimmer of a smile. 'I don't weigh too much. You'd manage.'

It was the first time anyone had suggested she looked tough and strong. 'I might manage, but me and weightlifting don't get along. How heavy are you anyway?'

'Forty-eight k. I'm lucky, I can eat and eat and I stay thin. My mum's jealous.' At the mention of her mum her face fell and her mouth puckered. 'I can't tell her. She'll be really angry. She had me when she was seventeen. All my life she's told me not to play around with boys. She wants me to go to university and be educated, unlike her. She missed out because she had me.'

Handing Chrissie a cup of cold water and a box of tissues, Ally sat down to talk. Her first booked appointment would have to wait. 'I won't deny your mother's going to be disappointed, even upset, but she'll come round because she loves you.' Flynn had better have got that right because she didn't believe in giving false hope. It just hurt more in the long run.

'You think? You don't even know her.'

'True. But I see a young woman who someone's been making sure had everything that's important in life. You look healthy, which means she's fed you well and kept you warm and clothed. Your uniform's in good condition, not an op-shop one. You're obviously up to speed with your education.' She daren't ask about her father. It didn't sound like he factored into Chrissie's current situation so maybe he didn't exist, or wasn't close enough for it to matter. 'I'm new here. Where do you live?'

'Round in San Remo. It's nice there. Granddad was a fisherman and had a house so Mum and I stayed with him. He's gone now and there's just us. I miss him. He always had a hug and a smile for me.'

'Then you've been very lucky. Not everyone gets those as

they're growing up.' She sure as heck hadn't. 'Let's get those blood samples done.'

Chrissie paled but climbed onto the bed and tugged one arm free of her jersey and shirt. Lying down, she found a small scared smile. 'Be nice to me.'

Ally smiled. 'If I have to.' She could get to really like this girl. Pointless when she'd be gone in a month. Despite Chrissie's fear of what the future had in store for her, she managed to be friendly and not sulky, as most teens she'd met in this situation had been.

Ally found the needle and tubes for the blood in the top drawer of the cabinet beside the bed. 'Do you play any sport at school?' She swabbed the skin where she would insert the needle.

'I'm in the school rep basketball team and play soccer at the club. I get knocked about a bit in basketball because I'm so light, but my elbows are sharp.' The needle slid in and the tube began to fill. 'I'm fast on my feet. Learnt how to get out of the way when I was a kid and played rough games with the boys next door.'

Ally swapped the full tube for another one, this time for haematology tests. Flynn was checking Chrissie's haemoglobin in case she had anaemia. 'I see one of the beaches is popular for surfing. You ever given that a try?' All done.

'Everyone surfs around here. Sort of, anyway. Like belly-surfing and stuff.'

'You can sit up now.' Ally began labelling the tubes.

'What? Have you finished? I didn't feel a thing.'

'Of course you didn't.' She smiled at the girl, stopped when she saw the moment Chrissie's thoughts returned to why she was there, saw the tears building up again. 'You're doing fine.'

'I'm not going to play sport for a while, am I?'

'Maybe not competitively, but keeping fit is good for you and your baby.'

Chrissie blew hard into a handful of tissues. 'You haven't told me I'm stupid for getting caught out. Or asked who the father is, or anything like that.'

'That's irrelevant. I'm more concerned about making sure you do the right things to stay healthy and have an easy pregnancy. Have you got any questions for me?'

Chrissie swung her legs over the side of the bed and stared at the floor. 'Lots, but not yet. But can I come see you later? After school? You'll have the tests back by then, right?'

'The important one, anyway. But won't you want to see Dr Reynolds about that?' She was more than happy to tell Chrissie the result, but she had no idea how Flynn might feel if she did.

'He's going to phone me, but I might need to see someone and I don't want to talk to a man. It would be embarrassing. I'd prefer it's you.'

'That's okay.' Ally scribbled her cell number on a scrap of paper. 'Here, call me. Leave a message if I don't answer and I'll get back to you as soon as I'm free. Okay?'

'Thanks.' Sniff. 'I didn't sleep all night, hoping Dr Reynolds would tell me I'd got it wrong, that I wasn't having a baby. But I used up all my pocket money on testing kits and every one of them gave me the same answer so I was just being dumb.'

'Chrissie, listen to me. You are not dumb. Many women I've been midwife to have told me the same thing. Some of them because they couldn't believe their luck, others because, just like you, they were crossing their fingers and toes they'd got it wrong.' Ally drew a long breath. 'Chrissie, I have to ask, have you considered an abortion? Or adoption?'

The girl's head shot up, defiance spitting out of her eyes. 'No. Never.' Her hands went to her belly. 'This is my baby. No one else's. I might be young and dependent on Mum, but I am keeping it.'

In that moment Ally loved Chrissie. She reached over to hug her. 'Attagirl. You're awesome.' It would be the hardest thing Chrissie ever did, and right now she had no idea what she'd let herself in for, but that baby would love her for it.

'Have you ever had a baby?' Chrissie pulled back, flushing pink. 'Sorry, I guess I'm not supposed to want to know.'

'Of course it's all right to ask. The answer's no, I haven't.'

An image of a blue-eyed youngster bent over double and giggling like his life depended on it flicked up in her mind. *Go away, Adam. You've got a mother, and anyway I'd be a bad substitute.*

'So while I will tell you lots of things over the weeks I'm here, I only know them from working with other mums-to-be and not from any first-hand experience.' She would never have that accreditation on her CV. She would not raise a child on her own, and she wouldn't be trusting any man to hang around long enough to see a baby grow to adulthood with her.

Flynn appeared in the doorway so fast after Chrissie left that she wondered if he'd been lurking. She said, 'She's only fifteen and is terrified, and yet she's coping amazingly well, given the shock of it all.'

'You must've cheered her up a little at least. I got the glimmer of a smile when she came out of here.' He leaned one shoulder against the doorframe. 'I meant what I said about her mother. Angela is going to be gutted, but she'll stand by Chrissie all the way. From what I've been told, Angela's always been strong, and refused to marry Chrissie's dad just because people thought it was the done thing. Her father supported them all the way.'

Another baby with only one parent. But one decent parent was a hundred percent better than none. 'Aren't you jumping the gun? Chrissie didn't mention the father of her baby, but that could be because she's protecting him. They might want to stick together.'

'They might.' Flynn nodded, his eyes fixed on her. Again.

When he did that, her stomach tightened in a very needy way. Heat sizzled along her veins, warming every cell of her body. *Damn him. Why does he have to be married?*

'Right, I'd better see my first patient. First booked-in one, that is. I told Chrissie I'll talk to her later today. Is that all right with you?'

'Go for it. As long as she's talking with someone, I'm happy. You did well with her.' There was something like admiration in his voice.

She didn't know whether to be pleased, or annoyed that he might be surprised. 'Just doing my job.'

'Sure.'

The way he enunciated that one word had her wondering if he had issues with Kat and her work. But that didn't make sense after he'd been fighting the other woman's corner about using her holiday time. 'Being a filler-in person, I don't have the luxury of knowing the patients I see. Neither do I have a lot of time with them so I work hard to put them at ease with me as quickly as possible.'

'So why aren't you employed at a medical practice on a permanent basis? Wouldn't you prefer getting to know your mums, rather than moving on all the time?'

If he hadn't sounded so genuinely interested she'd have made a joke about being a wandering witch in a previous life and ignored the real question. But for some inexplicable reason she couldn't go past that sincerity. 'I get offers all the time from my bosses to base myself back at the midwifery unit, but I don't do settled in one spot very well. Yes, I miss out on seeing mothers going the distance. I'm only ever there for the beginning of some babies and the arrival of others, but I like it that way. Keeps me on my toes.'

'Fly in, do the job and fly out.' Was that a dash of hope in his eyes? Did he think she might be footloose and fancy-free enough to have a quick fling with him and then move on? Because she'd seen the same sizzle in his eyes that buzzed along her veins.

Then reality hit. Cold water being tipped over her wouldn't have chilled her as much. *Sorry, buster, but you're married and, worse, you're not even ashamed to show it.*

She spun around to stare at the screen in front of her. What was the name of her next patient?

'Ally, I've upset you.'

Of course he had. He only had to look at her to upset her— her hormones anyway. Flicking him a brief smile, she continued staring at the computer. 'Holly Sargent, thirty-five weeks. Anything I need to know about her that's not on here?'

When Flynn didn't answer, she had to lift her head and seek him out. That steady blue gaze was firmly fixed on her. It held far too many questions, and she didn't answer other people's enquiries about anything personal. 'Flynn? Holly Sargent?'

'Third pregnancy, the last two were straightforward. She's had the usual colds and flu, a broken wrist and stitches in her brow from when she walked through a closed glass slider. Full-time mum.'

Ally looked at her patient list. 'Brenda Lewis?'

'First pregnancy, took six months to conceive, family history of hypertension but so far she's shown no signs of it, twenty-five years old, runs a local day care centre for under-fives.'

Her anger deflated and laughter bubbled up to spill between them as she stared at this man who had her all in a dither with very little effort. 'That's amazing. Do you know all your patients as thoroughly?'

'How long have you got?' He grinned. 'Makes for scintillating conversations.'

Deliberately rolling her eyes at him, she said, 'Remind me not to get stuck with you at the workplace Friday night drinkies.'

'Shucks, and I was about to ask you on a date,' he quipped, in a tone that said he meant no such thing.

So he was as confused as she was. That didn't stop a quick shiver running down her spine. She'd love to go out with this man. *But hello. If that isn't a wedding ring, then what is it? He's obviously a flagrant playboy.* 'Sorry, doing my hair that night.'

'Me, too,' he muttered, and left her to stare at his retreating back view.

A very delectable view at that. Those butt muscles moved smoothly under his trousers as he strode down the hall, those shoulders filled the top of his shirt to perfection. A sigh trickled over her bottom lip. He would've been the perfect candidate for her next affair. *Flynn might be the one you can't easily walk away from.*

'Get a grip, man,' Flynn growled under his breath. How? Ally was hot. Certain parts of his anatomy might've been in hibernation for the past couple of years, but they weren't dead. How did any sane, red-blooded male ignore Ally without going bonkers?

'Flynn.' Megan beckoned from the office. 'Can you explain to this caller why she should have a flu jab?'

'Can't Toby do that?' The practice nurse was more than capable of handling it.

'Busy with a patient and...' Megan put her hand over the phone's mouthpiece '...this one won't go away.'

'Put her through.' He spun around to head to his consulting room. *See? You're at work, not on the beach with nothing more important to think about than getting laid.* Forget all things Alyssa. *Alyssa.* Such a pretty name, but it had been blatantly obvious no one was allowed to use it when talking to their temporary midwife.

'Dr Reynolds.' Mrs Augusta's big voice boomed down the line, causing him to pull the phone away from his ear. 'I've been told I have to have a flu injection. I don't see why as I never get sick.'

Except for two hits with cancer that had nearly stolen her life. 'Mrs Augusta, it's your decision entirely but there are certain conditions whereby we recommend to a patient they have the vaccination. Your recent cancer puts you in the category for this. It's a preventative measure, that's all.'

'Why didn't Megan just tell me that?'

'Because she's our receptionist, not a qualified medical person. It's not her role to advise patients.'

'All right, can you put me back to her so I can book a time? Sorry to have been a nuisance.' Mrs Augusta suddenly sounded deflated, all the boom and bluster gone.

'Pat, is there something else that's bothering you?'

'No, I'm good as gold, Doctor. Don't you go worrying about me.'

'How about you make an appointment with me when you come for your jab?'

'I don't want to be a problem, Doctor.'

That exact attitude had almost cost her life. By the time the bowel cancer had been discovered it had nearly been too late and now she wore a bag permanently. 'I'll put you back to Megan and you make a time to see me.' When he got the receptionist on the line he told her, 'Book Mrs Augusta in with me at the first opening, and don't let her talk you out of it.'

A glance at his watch on his way out to the waiting room told him he was now behind the ball as far as keeping on time with appointments. 'Jane, come through.' As he led the woman down the hall, laughter came from the midwife's room. Sounded like Ally and Holly were getting along fine. A smile hovered on his mouth, gave him the warm fuzzies. Everyone got along with their temp midwife.

Jane limped into his room on her walking cane and sat down heavily. 'I'm up the duff again, Flynn.'

Not even ten o'clock and his second pregnant patient of the morning. What had the council put in the water? 'You're sure?' he asked with a smile. Nothing ever fazed this woman, certainly not her gammy leg, not a diabetic three-year-old, not a drunk for a husband.

'Yep, got all the usual signs. Thought I'd better let you know so I can get registered with Kat.'

Now, there was something that did tend to wind Jane up. Kat's attitude to her husband. Kat had tried to intervene one night at the pub when he'd been about to swing a fist at Jane. Something Flynn would've tried to prevent, too, if he'd been there. 'Kat's away at the moment so you'll get to meet Ally.' Of course, there were nine months to a pregnancy, and Kat was only away for one, but hopefully Ally could settle Jane into things so that she'd be happier with Kat this time round.

'Is she nice?' Jane's eyes lit up.

More than. 'You'll get along great guns. Now, I'm surmising that we need to discuss your arthritis meds for the duration of your pregnancy.'

The light in those eyes faded. She accepted her painful condition without a complaint, but she knew how hard the next few months were going to be. 'I've cut back already to what you've recommended before. There's no way I'm risking hurting junior in there.' Her hand did a circuit of her belly. 'Can't say I'm happy with the extra pain, but I want this wee one. Think I'll make it the last, though. Get my bits chopped out afterwards.'

As he made a note to that effect in her computer file, Flynn tried not to smile. Her bits. He got to hear all sorts of names for vaginas and Fallopian tubes in this job. 'How far along do you think you are?'

'I've missed two periods. Should've come to see you sooner, I know, but that family of mine keeps me busy.' Jane wasn't mentioning the lack of money, but he knew about it. 'Anyway, it's not like I don't know what to expect. They haven't changed the way it's done in the last three years, have they?'

'Not that anyone's told me.'

After writing out prescriptions, ordering blood tests, including an HCG for confirmation of the pregnancy, and taking Jane's blood pressure, he took her along to meet Ally.

It wasn't until he was returning to his room and he passed Faye, who rolled her eyes at him, that he realised he was walking with a bounce in his stride and a smile on his face. All due to a certain midwife.

What was it about her that had him sitting up and taking notice? It had happened instantly. Right from that moment when Sheba had knocked her down and he'd reached out a hand to haul the dog off, only to be sidetracked by the most startling pair of hazel eyes he'd ever seen.

Whatever it was, he'd better put a lid on the sizzle before anyone else in the clinic started noticing. That was the last thing he needed, and no doubt Ally felt the same.

CHAPTER THREE

'FLYNN,' MEGAN CALLED from her office as he was shrugging
into his jacket. 'The path lab's on line one.'

'Put them through.' Damn, he'd just seen Ally head out the
front door for home. He'd intended talking to her before she left,
maybe even walk with her as far as Kat's flat, then backtrack
to home. Which, given he lived on the opposite side of town,
showed how fried his brain had become in the last twenty-four
hours.

For an instant he resented being a GP. There were never any
moments just for him. Like it had been any different working
as an emergency specialist. Yeah, but he'd chosen that career
pathway, not had it forced on him. So he'd give up trying to
raise Adam properly, hand him over to spend even more hours
with day carers? No, he wouldn't. The disgruntled feeling disappeared in a flash, replaced with love. His little guy meant
everything to him.

'Flynn?' Megan yelled. 'Get that, will you?'

He kicked the door shut and grabbed the persistently ringing
phone from his desk. 'Flynn Reynolds. How can I help?' *Could
you hurry up? I'm on a mission.*

'Doctor, this is Andrew from the lab. I'm calling about some
biochemistry results on William Foster.'

William Foster, fifty-six and heading down the overweight

path through too much alcohol and fatty food since his wife had died twelve months back. He'd complained of shoulder pain and general malaise so he'd ordered urgent tests to check what his heart might be up to. 'I'm listening.'

'His troponin's raised. As are his glucose and cholesterol. But it's the troponin I'm ringing about.'

He took down details of the abnormal results, even though Andrew would email them through within the next five minutes. Finding William's phone number, he was about to dial but thought better of it. Instead, he phoned Marie on the run. 'I'm going to be late.'

'I'll feed Adam dinner, then.'

Flynn sighed. 'I owe you. Again.'

Marie chuckled. 'Get over yourself. I love having him.'

Yeah, she did, but that didn't make everything right. For Adam. Or for him.

William lived ten minutes away and halfway there Flynn decided he should've rung first to make sure the man was at home and not at the club, enjoying a beer. William didn't know it yet, but beer would be off the menu for a while.

William opened his front door on the third knock, and appeared taken aback to find Flynn on his doorstep after dark. 'Doc, what's up?'

'Can I come in for a minute?'

William's eyes shifted sideways. 'What you want to tell me?'

The man was ominously pale. He hadn't been like that earlier. 'Let me in and we'll discuss it.' From the state of William's breathing and speech, Flynn knew there'd be a bottle of whisky on the bench. That wouldn't be helping the situation. 'It's important.'

With a sigh the older man stepped back, hauling the door wide at the same time. 'I haven't done the housework this week, Doc, so mind where you step.'

This week? Flynn tried not to breathe too deeply, and didn't bother looking into the rooms they passed. It was all too obvious the man was living in squalor. He wasn't coping with Edna's passing, hadn't since day one, and nothing Flynn or William's daughter had done or said made the slightest bit of difference. The man had given up, hence Flynn's visit. A phone call would never have worked. Besides, he needed to be with William as he absorbed the news.

In the kitchen William's shaky hands fidgeted with an empty glass he'd lifted from the table. He didn't look directly at Flynn, not even for a moment, but every few seconds his eyes darted sideways across the kitchen. Sure enough, an almost full whisky bottle was on the bench, as were three empty ones. How long had it taken for him to drink his way through those?

It would be too easy to tell the man some cold hard facts about his living conditions and his drinking, but Flynn couldn't do it. He understood totally what it was like to lose the woman he loved more than life. He suspected if it hadn't been for Adam and having to put on a brave face every single day, he might've made as big a mess of his own life after Anna had been killed. He still struggled with the sense of living a life mapped out by fate, one that held none of his choices.

Pulling out a chair, he indicated William should sit down. Then he straddled another one, not looking at the condition of the once beautiful brocade on the seat. 'William, your test results have come back. They're not good, I'm afraid.'

'Figured that'd be why you're here.'

'The major concern is that you've had a cardiac incident. A heart attack, William.'

Rheumy eyes lifted to stare at him, but William said nothing, just shrugged.

'You need to go to hospital tonight. They'll run more tests and keep an eye on you until they find the cause of the attack.'

'What else?' William wheezed the question.

'They'll give you advice on diet and exercise.' Things he'd have no inclination to follow. The same as with any advice he had given him.

'I meant what other tests were bad?'

He was about to add to the man's gloomy outlook, but couldn't see a way around it. All he could hope for was that he shocked his patient into doing something about his lifestyle before it was too late. 'Your cholesterol's high, which probably explains your cardiac arrest. You've got diabetes and your liver's not in good nick.'

'I hit the jackpot, didn't I?' The sadness in William's voice told how much he didn't care any more. 'I don't suppose you went on a bender when you lost your wife, Doc.'

Yeah, he had. Just one huge bender, when he'd almost killed himself. Big enough and frightening enough to put him off ever doing it again. But he knew he still might've if it hadn't been for Adam. 'I couldn't afford to, William.'

'I get it. Your boy.'

'You've got family who care about you, too.' Flynn tried to think of something that might interest William in getting his act together, but nothing came to mind, apart from his daughter and grandkids. That had been tried before and William hadn't run with it. 'Now, don't get upset, but I've ordered the ambulance to transfer you to hospital. It should be here any minute.'

'I don't need that. I can drive myself there.'

'What if you have another heart attack and cause an accident that hurts someone?'

There was silence in the kitchen. Not a lot William could say to that. He was a decent man, unable to cope with a tragedy. He wasn't reckless with other people.

'I'll wait here until you're on your way. Want me to talk to your daughter?' Working in the ED, he'd have phoned the cardiologist and had William wheeled to the ward, no argument. Patients were in the ED because someone recognised the urgency of their situation. Urgent meant urgent—not talking and cajoling. He missed that fast pace at times, but if he got William under way to getting well then he'd feel deep satisfaction.

'After I've left. Don't want her telling me off tonight.' William stared around the kitchen, brought his gaze back to Flynn. 'Don't suppose I can have a whisky for the road.'

By the time Flynn finally made it home Adam was in his pyjamas and glued to the TV. 'Hiya, Dad.'

'Hello, my man.' Tonight he couldn't find it in him to make Adam stop watching—an Anna rule or not. Instead, he turned to Marie. 'I appreciate you bringing him home.'

Marie was already buttoning up her coat, the gaps between the buttons splayed wide over her baby bulge. 'Have you decided who's going to look after Adam when my little one arrives?' Marie was determined to look after Adam right up to the last minute. She'd also sorted through the numerous girls wanting to take her place until she was ready to take Adam back under her wing and had decided on two likely applicants.

'Caught. I'll get onto it.' He pushed his fingers through his hair. 'Tonight?'

'Whenever.' She laughed. 'It's not as though you'll be left high and dry. Half the island would love to look after Dr Reynolds's boy. Not just because he's such a cute little blighter either. There's a family likeness between father and son.'

'Haven't you got a husband waiting at home for his dinner?' He wasn't keen on dating any of the island's females. Too close to home and work. Anyway, no one had caught his interest in the last two years. Not until Ally had got knocked over by Sheba, that was.

Ally wasn't answering when he phoned after putting Adam to bed. She wasn't answering her phone when he called at nine, after giving in to the tiredness dragging at his bones and sitting down to watch a crime programme on TV. She might've answered if he'd rung as he was going to bed at ten thirty, but he didn't want her to think he was stalking her.

But she sure as hell stalked him right into bed. As he sprawled out under the covers he missed her not being there beside him, even though she'd never seen his bed, let alone lain in it. He stretched his legs wide to each side and got the same old empty spaces, only tonight they felt cold and lonely. Make that colder and lonelier. In his head, hot and sexy Ally with those brilliant hazel eyes was watching and laughing, teasing, playing with him. How was he supposed to remain aloof, for pity's sake? He was only human—last time he looked.

Was this what happened when he hadn't had sex for so long? Should he have been making an effort to find an obliging woman for a bit of relaxation and fun? He yawned.

Did Ally know she'd cranked up his libido? Yeah, it was quite possible she did, if the way the air crackled between them whenever they came within touching distance was any indication.

So follow up on it. Have some fun. Have sex. Have an affair with her. It would only be four weeks before Ally moved on. He wouldn't disrupt Adam's routine too much or for too long.

Flynn rolled over to punch his pillow and instead squashed his awakening reaction to the woman in his head. The air hissed out of his lungs as he grinned. That had to be a good sign for the future, didn't it?

'Morning, Ally,' Megan called as she stepped through the front door of the clinic on Tuesday. 'I see you've found the best coffee on the island already.'

'First thing I do on any job.' She sniffed the air appreciatively just to wind Megan up.

Scowling happily at her, Megan lifted her own container then asked, 'What did you think of the movie?'

'It was great. Nothing like a few vampires to fill in the evening.' She'd bumped into the receptionist and her boyfriend as they'd been walking into the theatre. 'Seeing you there made me feel I'd been living here for a while.'

Megan laughed. 'Small towns are like that. Believe me, people around here will know what you had for dinner last night.'

'Then they'll be giving me lectures on healthy eating. Fried chicken and chips from Mrs Chook's.' It had been delicious, even if she should've been looking for a salad bar. In winter? Hey, being good about food could sometimes be highly over-rated. Anyway, she'd wanted comfort food because when she had gone back to the flat after work she'd felt unusually out of sorts. Arrival day in a new place, yes, that was normal; every other day thereafter, never.

This nomadic life had been one of her goals ever since she'd left school and become independent of the welfare system. Those goals had been simple—earn the money to put herself through a nursing degree then support herself entirely with a job that she could give everything to but which wouldn't tie her to one place. Along with that went to establish a life where she didn't depend on anyone for anything, including friendship or love.

So far it had worked out fine. Sure, there were the days when she wondered if she could risk getting close to someone. She had no experience of being loved, unconditionally or any other way, so the risks would be huge for everyone involved. She had enough painful memories of being moved on from one family to the next to prove how unworthy of being loved she was. At unsettled moments like this those memories underlined why she never intended taking a chance on finding someone to trust with her heart. Sometimes she wondered if her heart really was only there to pump blood.

In the midwife's room she dumped her bag and jacket, then wandered into the staffroom, surreptitiously on a mission to scope out Flynn, if he'd arrived. He must've, because suddenly her skin was warming up. Looking around the room, her eyes snagged with his where he sat on a chair balanced on two legs. She'd known he was there without seeing him. She'd felt an instant attraction before setting eyes on him. What was going on? Hadn't she just been remembering why she wasn't interested?

She took a gulp of coffee and spluttered as she burned her tongue. 'That's boiling.'

Concern replaced the heat in Flynn's gaze and the front legs of the chair banged onto the tiled floor as he came up onto his feet. 'You all right?' He snatched a paper towel off the roll on the wall. 'Here, spit it out.'

Taking the towel to wipe the dribble off her lips before he could, she muttered, 'Too late, I swallowed it instantly.' And could now feel it heating a track down her throat. 'I forget to take the lid off every time.' But usually she wasn't distracted enough to forget to sip first. 'Black coffee takes for ever to cool in these cardboard cups.'

'Slow learner, eh?' That smile should be banned. Or bottled. Or kissed.

It sent waves of heat expanding throughout her body, unfurling a need so great she felt a tug of fear. What if she did give in to this almost overwhelming attraction? Could she walk away from it unscathed? Like she always did? This thing with Flynn didn't feel the same as her usual trysts. There was something between them she couldn't explain. But they wouldn't be getting started. Staying remote would keep things on an even keel. *You're not lovable. Forget that and you're toast.*

'I called you last night to ask how you felt about your first day here.'

So much for remote. He wasn't supposed to play friendly after hours. 'That explains one of two missed calls. I went to a movie and switched it off for the duration.'

Flynn looked awkward. 'I rang twice.'

'Did I miss something?' Had one of her patients gone into labour? Or developed problems? Had Chrissie wanted to talk to her again? This wouldn't look good for her if she had.

'Relax. They were purely social calls.'

The way he drawled his words did everything but relax her. She managed through a dry mouth, 'That's all right, then.' Highly intelligent conversation going on here, but she was incapable of much more right now. He shouldn't be phoning her.

'Ally, I was wondering—'

'Morning, everyone.' Jerome strolled in. 'You came back for more, then, Ally?'

'Yes.' She shook her head to clear the heat haze. 'Missed the ferry back to the mainland so thought I'd fill in my day looking after your pregnant patients,' she joked pathetically.

Then Flynn asked, 'How was Chrissie when you talked to her after school?'

She wondered what he'd been going to ask before Jerome had interrupted. 'Resigned would best describe her attitude. But today might be a whole different story after a night thinking about it all.' Ally dropped onto a chair and stared her coffee. 'I hope she's going to be all right.' Chrissie still had to tell her mother. That'd be the toughest conversation of her young life.

'Like I said, Angela will be very supportive.' Flynn returned to his seat. 'Marie was happy with her new midwife, by the way.'

Marie was happy with her boss and his boy, with the impending birth of her baby, with her husband, with the whole world. 'I saw Adam for a few minutes when she came in. At least he'd stopped giggling.'

'Ah, you missed the standing in the dog's water bowl giggles, and the dollop of peanut butter on the floor right by Sheba's nose giggles.'

She could picture Adam now, bent over, howling with laughter. 'He's one very happy little boy, isn't he?'

Flynn's smile slipped. Oops. What had she gone and done? Sadness filtered into his eyes and she wanted to apologise with a hug for whatever she'd managed to stir up, but she didn't. Of course she didn't. Hugging a man she'd only met two days ago and who was one of her bosses wasn't the best idea she'd ever had. She sipped coffee instead—which perversely had turned lukewarm—and waited for the meeting to get under way.

'I see you had William admitted last night,' Faye said as she joined them.

Flynn looked relieved he'd been diverted from answering what she'd thought had been a harmless question. He hurried to explain. 'He'd had a cardiac event. Hardly surprising, given the way he's been living.'

'He'll be seen by a counsellor while in hospital. Maybe they can make him see reason,' Faye said. 'Not that we all haven't tried, I know.'

Flynn grimaced, his eyes still sad. 'I'm hoping this is the wake-up shock required to get him back on track.' He turned to Ally. 'William's wife succumbed to cancer last year.'

'That's terrible.' She shuddered. *See? Even if you got a good one, someone who never betrayed your trust, they still left you hurt and miserable.* No wonder Flynn looked sad. He seemed to hold all his patients dear.

Jerome spoke up. 'Ally, I believe you're doing house calls today. One of your patients is Matilda Livingstone. This is her first pregnancy. Be warned she's paranoid about something going wrong and will give you a million symptoms to sort through.'

Ally's interest perked up. 'Any particular reason for this behaviour?'

'She has a paranoid mother who suffered three miscarriages in her time and only carried one baby full term. She's fixated with making sure Matilda checks everything again and again. It's almost as though she doesn't want her daughter to have a stress-free pregnancy.' Jerome shook his head, looking very puzzled.

'Mothers, eh?' She smiled, knowing her real thoughts about some mothers weren't showing. Ironic, considering she spent her days working with mums—the loving kind. 'Thanks for the nod. I'll tread carefully.'

'You know you've got the use of the clinic's car for your rounds, don't you?' Flynn asked.

'Sure do. I'm hoping it's a V8 supercharged car with wide tyres and a triple exhaust.'

'Red, of course.' Flynn grinned.

Faye stood up. 'Time to get the day cranking up. There seems to be a kindergarten lot of small children creating havoc in the waiting room.'

'Toby's doing vaccinations. For some reason, the mothers thought it better if they had them all done at the same time,' Jerome explained. 'Seems a bit much, considering that if one cries, they'll all cry.'

Flynn stood up. 'Who's going to cry when they've got Toby? That man's magic when it comes to jabbing a child.' He turned to Ally. 'I heard that you're also no slug when it comes to drawing bloods. Chrissie was seriously impressed, even told Toby that he needs practice.'

'So Toby's magic doesn't extend to older children?' Chrissie was still a child in many ways, baby on the way or not. When they'd talked about her HCG result yesterday afternoon it had been difficult. One minute Chrissie had acted all grown up and the next Ally could picture her tucked up with her teddy and a thumb in her mouth as she watched cartoons on TV.

'Sure it does, just not Chrissie. Has she mentioned when she might apprise her mother of the situation?'

'I think never would be her preferred approach. But realistically she's preparing herself. She did ask if I'd be present.'

'How do you feel about that?' Flynn asked.

'Of course I'll do it if that's what she wants, but I'd have thought you, as the family doctor, should be the one to talk to Angela with her.'

Flynn didn't look fazed. 'If she's relaxed with you then that's good. I'm not getting on my high horse because she's my patient. What works for her works for me. Or we can both be there.'

'Thanks.' Why was she thanking him? Shrugging, she added, 'Guess I'd better get on the road. My first appointment's at nine and I haven't looked at the map yet.'

Flynn gave her that devastating smile of his. 'You're not in Melbourne now. Come here and tell me who you're visiting.' He closed the door behind Jerome and Ally felt as though the air had been sucked out of the room.

What was he doing? Here? At work? Any minute someone could walk in for a coffee.

'Here's the clinic.' Flynn tapped his finger on the back of the door. 'Who's first on your list?'

Ally's face reddened as her gaze took in the map pinned to the door. 'Um.' Think, damn it, peanut brain. 'Erika Teale.'

She watched in fascination as Flynn's finger swept across the map and stopped to tap at some point that made no sense whatsoever. Running her tongue over her lips, she tried to sound sane and sensible. 'That's next to the golf ranch.' Too squeaky, but at least she'd got something out.

He turned to stare at her. 'Are you all right? Is map-reading not your forte?'

'I'm better with drawing bloods.' No one could read a map when Flynn was less than two feet away. Even a simple map like this one suddenly became too complex. Taking a step closer to the map—and Flynn—she leaned forwards to study the roads leading to Erika's house. Truth was, despite moving from town to town every few weeks she'd never got the hang of maps. 'So which side of the golf place is she on?' Why did he have to smell so yummy?

'What are you doing tonight?'

Gulp. Nothing. Why? 'Eating food and washing dirty clothes.' Like there was a lot of those, but she had to sound busy. Saying 'Nothing' was pathetic.

'Have dinner with me. We could go to the Italian café. It's simple but the food's delicious.'

She gasped. *Yes*, her head screamed. *I'd love to. Yes, yes, yes.* 'No, thanks,' came from her mouth. Sanity had prevailed. Just. 'You're married.'

Flynn's mouth flattened, and his thumb on his right hand flicked the tell-tale gold band round and round on his finger. The light went out in his eyes. 'I'm a widower. My wife died two years back.'

Her shoulders dropped their indignant stance as his words sank in. 'Oh.' She was getting good at these inane comments.

'I'm so sorry. That must be difficult for you and Adam. But he seems so happy, you must be a great father.'

Shut up, dribble mouth.

But he's free, available.

Yeah. I'm a cow.

Guilt followed and she reached a hand to his arm, touched him lightly. 'I don't know what else to say. How do you manage?' The way he looked at that moment, he'd be retracting his invitation any second.

'Adam keeps me sane and on the straight and narrow. If it wasn't for him, who knows what I might've done at the time?' Sadness flicked across his face and then he looked directly at her and banished it with a smile. 'For the record, you're the first woman I've asked on a date in the last two years. The only woman I've looked at twice and even considered taking out.' Then his smile faltered. 'I guess it's not much of an offer, going to the Italian café, considering what you must be used to in the city.'

'Flynn, it's not about where I go but who I go with. I'd love to try the local Italian with you.' She meant every word. A wave of excitement rolled through her. A date—with this man—who set her trembling just by looking at her. What more could she want? Bring it on.

'Then I'll pick you up after I've put Adam to bed and got the babysitter settled. Probably near eight, if that's all right?' There was relief and excitement mingling in his expression, in those cobalt eyes locked on her, in the way he stood tall.

She was struggling to keep up with all his emotions. 'Perfect.' She'd have time for a shower, to wash and blow-dry her hair, apply new make-up and generally tart herself up. Bring it on, she repeated silently.

CHAPTER FOUR

SOMEONE SHOULD'VE TOLD the pregnancy gods that Ally had a date and needed at the minimum an hour to get ready. Seems that memo had never gone out.

As she slammed through the front door of the flat at seven forty-five, Ally was cursing, fit to turn the air blue. 'Babies, love their wee souls, need to learn right from the get-go to hold off interrupting the well-laid plans of their midwife.'

Baby Hill thought cranking up his mum's blood pressure and making her ankles swell was a fun thing to do a couple of weeks out from his arrival. Pre-eclampsia ran through Vicky Hill's family but she'd been distressed about having to go to hospital for an evaluation, and it had taken a while to calm her down. Jerome had finally talked to his patient and managed to get her on her way with her thankfully calm husband.

Ally suspected some of Vicky's worry was because she was dealing with a new midwife right on the day she needed Kat to be there for her. Ally had no problem with that. Being a midwife had a lot to do with good relationships and they weren't formed easily with her, due to the come-and-go nature of her locum job.

The shower hadn't even fully warmed up when Ally leapt under the water. Goose bumps rose on her skin. Washing her hair was off the list. A hard brush to remove the kinks from the tie that kept it back all day would suffice. If there was time. She'd make time. After slipping on a black G-string, she snatched up a pair of black, body-hugging jeans to wriggle her way into. The lace push-up bra did wonders for her breasts and gave a great line to the red merino top she tugged over her head.

The doorbell rang as she picked up the mascara wand. Flick, flick. Then a faster-than-planned brush of her hair and she was as ready as she was ever going to be.

She might not have had all the time she'd wanted, but by the look on Flynn's face she hadn't done too badly. His Adam's apple bobbed as his gaze cruised the length of her, making her feel happy with the hurried result.

'Let's go,' he croaked.

We could stay here and not bother with dinner. Or we can do both.

She slammed the front door shut behind her and stepped down the path. 'I'm starving.' For food. For man. For fun.

Flynn knew he should look away. Now. But how? His head had locked into place so that he stared at this amazing woman seated opposite him in the small cubicle they'd been shown to by the waiter. He hadn't seen her with her hair down before. Shining light brown hair gleaming in the light from wall sconces beside their table and setting his body on fire. He desperately wanted to run his hands through those silky layers, and over it, and underneath at the back of her neck.

'Excuse me, Dr Reynolds. Would you like to order wine with your meal?'

Caught. Staring at his lady friend. Reluctantly looking up, he saw one of his young patients holding out the wine menu. 'Hello, Jordan. How's the rugby going? Got a game this weekend?' He glanced down the blurred list of wines.

'It's high school reps this weekend. We're going up to Melbourne on Thursday.'

After checking with Ally about what she preferred, he ordered a bottle of Merlot, and told Jordan what meals they'd chosen. Then he leaned back and returned his attention to Ally, finding her watching him with a little smile curving that inviting mouth.

'How often do you get out like this?' she asked.

'Never. When I go out it's usually with people from work.' Comfortable but not exhilarating.

'Who's looking after Adam tonight? Not Marie?'

'No, she needs her baby sleep. Jerome's daughter came round, bringing her homework with her.' Better than having a boyfriend tag along, like the last girl he'd used when he'd had a meeting to attend. He'd sacked her because of that boyfriend distracting her so she hadn't heard Adam crying.

'So they know at work that you and I are out together?' Her eyes widened with caution.

'There's no point trying to be discreet on Phillip Island. Everyone knows everyone's business all too quickly, even if you try to hide it.'

The tip of her tongue licked the centre point of her top lip. In, out, in, out.

Flynn suppressed a groan and tried to ignore the flare of need unfurling low down. What was it about this woman compared to any of the other hundreds he'd crossed paths with over the last two years that had him wanting her so much? Admittedly, for a good part of those years he'd been wound up in grief and guilt so, of course, he hadn't been the slightest bit interested. His libido hadn't been tweaked once. Yet in walks Ally Parker and, slam-bang, he could no longer think straight.

The owner of the café brought their wine over and with a flourish poured a glass for Ally. '*Signorina*, welcome to the island. I am Giuseppe and this is my café. I am glad our favourite doctor has brought you here to enjoy our food.'

Ally raised her glass to Giuseppe. 'Thank you for your welcome. Is everyone on Phillip Island as kind as you and the medical centre staff?'

'*Si*, everyone. You've come at the right time of year when

there are very few tourists. Summer is much busier and no time for the small chat.'

Finally Giuseppe got around to filling Flynn's glass, and gave him a surreptitious wink as he set the bottle on the table. 'Enjoy your evening, Doctor.'

Cheeky old man. Flynn grinned despite himself. 'I intend to.'

Ally watched him walk away, a smile lighting her pretty face. 'I could get to like this.' Then the smile slipped. 'But only for a month. Then I'll have somewhere else nice and friendly to visit while I relieve yet another midwife.'

He wanted to ask what compelled her to only take short-term contracts, but as he opened his mouth the thought of possibly spoiling what was potentially going to be a wonderful evening had him shutting up fast. Then their meals arrived and all questions evaporated in the hot scent of garlic and cream and tomatoes wafting between them.

Ally sighed as she gazed at her dish. 'Now, that looks like the perfect carbonara.' This time her tongue slid across first her bottom lip and then the top one. What else could she do with that tongue? Lifting her eyes, she studied his pizza. 'That looks delicious, too.'

'I know it will be.' The best pizzas he'd ever tasted had been made right here. 'One day I'll get to trying a pasta dish, but I can't get past the pizzas.'

Sipping her wine, Ally smiled directly at him. 'Thank you for bringing me here.'

'It's the best idea I've had in a long time.' Had he really just said that? Yes, and why not? It was only the truth. Picking up a wedge of pizza, he held it out to her. 'Try that.'

Her teeth were white and perfect. She bit into the wedge and sat back to savour the flavours of tomato and basil that would be exploding in her mouth. As he watched her enjoyment, he took a bite. Ally closed her eyes and smiled as she chewed. 'How do you do that?' he asked.

She swallowed and her eyelids lifted. 'Here, you must try

this.' She twirled her fork in her pasta and leaned close to place it in his mouth.

The scent of hot food and Ally mingled, teasing him as he took her offering. The tastes of bacon and cream burst across his tongue. 'Divine.' Though he suspected cardboard would taste just as good right now.

They shared another wedge of pizza. Then Ally put her hands around her plate. 'Not sharing any more.'

Moments later she raised her glass to smile over the rim at him and let those sultry eyes study him.

Flynn sneaked his fork onto her plate and helped himself. 'You think you're keeping this to yourself?' Not that his stomach was in the mood for more food while she was looking at him like he was sexy. He felt alive and on top of his game, very different from his usual sad and exhausted state.

Her tongue ran around the edge of her glass, sending desire firing through his body heading straight for his manhood. *Pow.* 'You're flirting with me, Miss Ally.'

'Yes.' Her tongue lapped at her wine, sending his hormones into overdrive.

He placed the fork, still laden with carbonara, on his plate. 'Come here,' he growled. 'I've wanted to do this for two whole days.'

He placed his fingers on her cheeks to draw her closer. Pressing his mouth to her lips, all he was aware of was this amazing woman and the taste, the feel, the heat of her.

Finally, some time later—minutes or hours?—Flynn led Ally outside, only vaguely aware they'd eaten tiramisu for dessert, and hoped he'd had enough smarts to pay the bill before leaving. No worry, Giuseppe knew where to find him. In one hand he held the wine bottle, still half-full, while his other arm wrapped around Ally's waist as she leaned in close, her head on his shoulder, her arm around him with her hand in his pocket, stroking his hip, stroking, stroking.

Forget the car. He led her across the road and down to the

beach. It was cold, but he was hot. They didn't talk, and the moment they were out of sight of the few people out on the road, Ally turned into him, pressing her body hard against his. Her hands linked at the back of his neck and she tugged his mouth down to hers.

The bottle dropped to the sand as he slid his hands under her top. Her skin was satin, hot satin. Splaying his fingers, he smoothed his hands back and forth, touching more of her, while his mouth tasted her, his tongue dancing around hers. He wanted her. Now.

'Ally?' he managed to groan out between kisses.

Between their crushed-together bodies she slipped a hand to his trousers, tugged his zip down. The breath caught in his throat as her fingers wrapped around him.

'Ally.' This time there was no question in his mind.

She rubbed him, up, down. Up, down.

Reaching for her jeans, he pushed and pulled until he had access to her, trying—and nearly failing—to remain focused on giving her pleasure. She was wet to his touch, moaning as his fingers touched her, and she came almost instantly, crying out as she rocked against his hand. Her hand squeezed him, eased, squeezed again, and his release came quickly.

Too quickly. 'Can we do that again?' he murmured against that soft hair.

Ally had wrapped herself against him, her arms under his jacket, her breaths sharp against his chest. Her head moved up and down. 'Definitely.'

'Come on, we'll go home.'

Her head lifted. 'You've got a babysitter. We could go to the flat.'

His lips traced a kiss across her forehead and down her cheek. 'Are you always so sensible?' He'd fried any brain matter he had. 'Good thinking.'

'What are we waiting for?' Ally spun around and took his hand to drag him back up the beach to his car.

The flat was less than five minutes away. Thank goodness. He didn't know how he'd manage to keep two hands on the steering wheel for that long, let alone actually function well enough to drive.

The moment she shut the front door behind them Ally grabbed Flynn's hand and almost ran to the bedroom. That had been amazing on the beach, but it was only a taste of what she knew they could have. It had been nowhere near enough.

She laughed out loud. 'I want to wrap myself around you.' She began tearing clothes off. Flynn's and hers. 'I want to get naked and up close with you.'

'Stop.' It was a command.

And she obeyed. 'Yes?'

'Those knickers. Don't take them off. Not yet.'

So he was into G-strings. She turned and saucily moved her derrière, then slowly lifted her top up to her breasts, oh, so slowly over them, and finally above her head, tossing it into the corner.

Then turned around, reaching behind her to unclasp her bra. Flynn's eyes followed every move. When she shrugged out of the lace creation, his hands rose to her breasts, ever so lightly brushing across her nipples and sending swirls of need zipping through her. Once had definitely not been enough with this man.

Twice probably wouldn't be, either. This was already cranking up to be a fling of monumental proportions. Her time on Phillip Island had just got a whole lot more interesting and exciting. 'Flynn.' His name fell as a groan between them.

As he leaned over to take her nipple in his mouth he smiled. A smile full of wonder and longing. A smile that wound around her heart.

Back off. Now. Your heart never gets involved. Back off. Remember who, what you are. A nomad, soon to be on the road again. Remember. You take no passengers.

Flynn softly bit her breast, sending rationale out the window.

Her hands gripped his head to keep his mouth exactly where it was. His hands cupped her backside. Tipping her head back so her hair fell down her back, Ally went with the overwhelming need crawling through her, filling every place, warming every muscle until she quivered with such desire she thought she'd explode.

Flynn's mouth traced kisses up her throat, then began a long, exploratory trip downward. Back to her breasts, then her stomach and beyond. It was impossible to keep up with him, to savour each and every stroke. They all melted into one, and when her legs trembled so much she could barely stand, Flynn gently guided her onto the bed, where he joined her, his erection throbbing when she placed her hand around him and brought him to where she throbbed for him.

Ally rolled over and groaned. *Is there any part of me that doesn't ache?* A delicious, morning-after-mind-blowing-sex ache that pulled the energy out of her and left her feeling relaxed and unwilling to get up to face the day.

She was expected at work by eight thirty. *Yeah, tell that to someone who cares.* But she dragged herself upright and stared around. The bed was a shambles, with the sheets twisted, the cover skew-whiff and the pillows on the floor.

What a night. Really only for an hour, but for once she doubted she could've gone all night. Not with Flynn. He took it out of her, he was so good.

The phone rang. It wasn't on her bedside table or on the floor next to the bed. But it did sound as though it was in this room. She tossed the cover aside, shivering as winter air hit her bare skin. Lifting the sheets and pillows, she found her jeans, but not what she was looking for. 'Don't hang up.' What if it was one of her mothers having contractions? 'Where is the blasted phone?'

Picking up her top from the corner where she'd thrown it last night, she pounced, pressed the phone's green button. 'Morning, Ally Parker speaking.'

'Morning, gorgeous,' Flynn's voice drawled in her ear. 'Thought I'd make sure you're wide-awake.'

'And if I hadn't been?' The concern backed off a notch at the sound of his warm tone. 'You'd have come around and hauled me out of bed?'

'My oath I would.'

'That does it. I'm sound asleep.' What was wrong with her? Encouraging Flynn was not the way to go.

His laugh filled her with happiness. 'Unfortunately I have a certain small individual with me this morning and I know he'd love nothing better than to try and pull you out of bed.'

'So not a good look, considering I'm naked.' She'd left her brain on the beach. Had to have.

Flynn growled. 'I certainly wouldn't be able to fault that.'

Then she saw the time. 'Is it really eight o'clock? It can't be. Got to go. I'm going to be late.' She hung up before he could say anything else and ran for the bathroom. The left side of her left brain argued with the right side about what she was doing with Flynn.

'Only five minutes late,' she gasped, as she charged into the staffroom. A large coffee in a takeout mug stood on the table at the spot where she usually sat. 'Black and strong,' Flynn muttered, as he joined her.

'You're wonderful.' She popped the lid off.

Jerome and Toby sauntered in. 'What did you think of our local Italian?' Jerome asked with a twinkle in his eye.

'I'm hooked. Definitely going back there again.' Her knee nudged Flynn's under the table.

He pushed back as he continued to stare across at the other men. 'She's got Giuseppe eating out of her hand.'

I thought that was your hand. 'He's a sweetheart.'

'Ally.' Megan popped her head around the door. 'You've got visitors. Chrissie and her mum.'

Back to earth with a thud. Reality kicked in. 'Showtime.' Ally stood up, sipped her coffee, found it cool enough to gulp some down. No way could she start her day without her fix, especially not this morning. Her stomach was complaining about the lack of breakfast, but it'd have to make do with caffeine. 'Is it okay if I go and see Chrissie? Or would you prefer I stay for the meeting?'

'Don't worry about the meeting. One of us can fill you in later if there's anything you need to know,' Toby told her.

Flynn spoke up. 'If you need me, just call. But I'm sure you'll be fine.'

'Chrissie's mum would have to be dense not to know why her daughter has requested an appointment with a midwife, wouldn't she?'

Flynn nodded. 'And dense is not a word I'd use to describe Angela. She's probably cottoned on but could be denying it.'

Angela didn't deny it for any longer than it took for the three of them to be seated in Ally's room with the door firmly shut. 'You're going to tell me Chrissie's pregnant, aren't you?'

'Actually, I was hoping Chrissie might've told you.' She looked at the girl and found nothing but despair blinking out at her. Dark shadows lined the skin beneath her sad eyes and her mouth was turned downwards, while her hands fidgeted on her thighs. 'Chrissie, did you get any sleep last night?'

She shook her head. 'I was thinking, you know? About everything.' Her shoulders dropped even lower. 'I'm sorry, Mum. I didn't mean it to happen.'

'Now, that I can understand.' Angela might have been expecting the news but she still looked shocked. 'All too well.' She breathed deeply, her chest rising. 'How far along are you, do you know?' Her gaze shifted from her daughter to Ally and then back to Chrissie.

'Nearly twelve weeks.' Chrissie's voice was little more than a whisper. 'You're disappointed in me, aren't you?'

Angela sat ramrod straight. Her hands were clenched together, but her eyes were soft and there was gentleness in her next words. 'No, sweetheart, I think you're the one who's going to be disappointed. You had so many plans for your future and none of them included a baby.'

'But you managed. You've got a good job. You're the best mum ever.'

'Chrissie, love.' Angela sniffed, and reached for one of her daughter's hands. 'A good job, yes, but not the career I'd planned on.'

Ally stood up and crossed to the window to give them some space. They didn't need her there. Yet. Flynn had been right. This woman was a good mum. *Why didn't I have one like her? Why didn't I have one at all? One who loved me from the day I was born?*

Behind her the conversation became erratic as Chrissie and Angela worked their way through the minefield they were facing. At least they were facing it together.

'Do you regret having me?' Chrissie squeaked.

'Never.' A chair scratched over the surface of the floor and when Ally took a quick peek she saw Angela holding her daughter in her arms. 'Never, ever. Not for one minute.'

'I'm keeping my baby, Mum.'

Ally held her breath. This was the moment when Angela might finally crack. She fully understood the pitfalls of single parenthood. And the joys. But she'd want more for Chrissie.

Angela was strong. 'I thought you'd say that. I hope your child will love its grandmother as much as you loved your grandfather, my girl, because we're in this together. Understand?'

As Chrissie burst into long-overdue tears, Ally sneaked out the door, closing it softly behind her. In the storeroom she wiped her own eyes. Did that girl understand how loved she was? How lucky?

'Hey, don't tell me it was that bad in there.' Flynn stood before her, holding the box of tissues she'd been groping for.

'It was beautiful.' Blow. 'What an amazing mother Angela is. Chrissie will be, too, if that's the example she's got to follow.'

'Told you.' Did he have to sound so pleased with himself?

His finger tipped her chin up so she had to meet his kind gaze. 'Come and finish that coffee I bought you. We can zap it in the microwave.'

He'd be thinking she was a right idiot, hiding in the cupboard, crying, because her patient had just told her mother she was pregnant. 'I'll give them five minutes and then go and discuss pregnancy care and health.'

'Make it ten. You'll be feeling better and they'll have run out of things to say to each other for a while.' His hand on her elbow felt so right. And for the first time it wasn't about heat and desire but warmth and care.

More stupid tears spurted from her eyes. Her third day here and he was being gentle and kind to her. Right now she liked this new scenario. Thank goodness Flynn would think these fresh tears were more of the same—all about Chrissie and her mother, not about him. And her.

CHAPTER FIVE

THE MOMENT FLYNN saw the clinic's car turn into the parking lot on Friday night he couldn't hold back a smile. A smile for no other reason than he was glad to see Ally. Her image was pinned up in his skull like a photo on a noticeboard. More than one photo. There was the one of Ally in those leg-hugging, butt-defining jeans and the red jersey that accentuated her breasts. Then the other: a naked version showing those shapely legs, slim hips and delicious breasts.

There was a third: tearful Ally, hiding away and looking lost and lonely. What was that about?

The front door crashed against the wall as she elbowed it wide and carried her bag in. 'Hi, Flynn, you're working late. Had an emergency?'

Yep, two hours without laying eyes on you definitely constitutes an emergency. 'Do you want to join Adam and me for dinner? There's a chicken casserole cooking as we speak. Nothing flash, but it should be tasty.'

'A casserole's not flash?' Her smile warmed him right down to his toes. 'My mouth's watering already.'

'Is that a yes, then?' His lungs stopped functioning as he waited for her reply.

'Are you sure there'll be enough?' As he was about to answer in the affirmative, she asked, 'Shall I stop in at the supermarket and get some garlic bread to go with the meal? Some wine?'

'Good idea. I left the Merlot behind the other night. On the beach,' he added with a grin.

'You're too easily distracted, that's your problem.' Her mouth stretched into a return smile. 'Someone probably got lucky when they went for a walk that morning.'

A devilish look crossed his face and his eyes widened. 'I got lucky that night.'

'A dinner invitation will get me every time.' She swatted his arm. 'What's your address? Better give me precise directions if you really want me to join you.'

'The island's not too large and most people know where to find me.' Glancing at his watch, he added, 'I'll get home so Marie can leave.'

Flynn hummed all the way home, something he hadn't done in for ever. Even without Tuesday night's sexual encounters, the fact that Ally was coming to his place for a meal made him feel good. Mealtimes weren't lonely because Adam was there, but sometimes he wished for adult conversation while he enjoyed his dinner. He'd also like an occasional break from Adam's usual grizzles about what he was being made to eat. His boy was a picky eater. Just because his mother had wanted him to eat well, it didn't mean Adam agreed.

Flynn shook his head. Where did Adam come into this? This hyper mood had nothing to do with him. Try Ally. And himself. *Be honest, admit you want a repeat of Tuesday night's sex.*

Guilt hit hard and fast.

What was he thinking? How could he be having fun when Anna was gone? He didn't deserve to. It had been his fault she hadn't been happy with her life. He should've taken the time to listen to her when she'd tried to explain why it was so important to her to leave the city behind.

He'd loved his life in Melbourne, had thought he was well on the way to making a big name for himself in emergency medicine. Sure, he hadn't always been there for Anna and Adam, had missed meals and some firsts, like Adam saying 'Hello, Mummy', but they'd agreed before Adam had been conceived that he'd be working long hours, getting established, and that it would take a few years before he backed off so they could enjoy the lifestyle they both had wanted.

Anna had quickly forgotten their agreement once Adam had arrived, instead becoming more demanding for him to give up his aspirations and move to family-orientated Phillip Island. What he hadn't told Anna before she'd died was that he'd begun talks with the head of the ED to cut down his hours. It would've been a compromise. Too late. Anna had driven into an oncoming tram, and he and Adam had moved to her island full-time. Sometimes he had regrets about that—regrets that filled him with guilt. This was right for Adam. He should've done it for Anna while he could.

Turning into his drive, he automatically pressed the garage door opener and drove in, hauled on the handbrake and switched off the engine. He tipped his head back against the headrest. 'Anna, I miss you.'

A lone tear tracked down his cheek.

Is it wrong to want to have some fun? To want to move on and forge a new life for me and our boy? Adam misses his mummy so much I'm afraid I'm getting it all wrong. I try to do things as you'd want, but sometimes I feel I'm living your life, not mine.

The engine creaked as it began cooling down. Sheba nudged her wet nose against his window and Flynn dragged himself out of the car. He didn't have time to sit around feeling sorry for himself. Rightly or wrongly, Ally was coming to dinner.

After stopping off at the supermarket, Ally went back to the flat and had a quick shower, before changing into jeans and a clean shirt. She took a moment to brush her ponytail out, letting it fall onto her shoulders. If the way Flynn kept running his hands through it the other night was an indicator, he obviously liked her hair.

She checked her phone for texts. Nothing. Not even from Darcie. She quickly texted.

How's things?

The reply was instant.

The usual. What r u doing 2night?

Having dinner with hot man.

You're not wasting time.

Did I mention his 4-yr-old son?

Ally? That's different for you.

Ally slipped her phone into her pocket without answering. What could she say? In one short message Darcie had underlined her unease.

Swiping mascara over her lashes, she stared at her reflection in the mirror. Most of the day, even when busy with patients, a sense of restlessness had dogged her. Strange. Her first-day nerves weren't going away.

Get over it. Coming to a new job's nothing like starting over with a new family when you're scared and wondering if they'll love you enough to keep you past the end of the first week. Don't let the worry bugs tip you off track. You're in control these days.

She twisted the mascara stick into its holder so hard it snapped.

Thank goodness she had something to do tonight other than sit alone in that pokey lounge, eating takeaways and watching something boring on TV. She'd be with Flynn and his boy, and be able to have a conversation. What about didn't matter, as long as she had company for a few hours. It would be an added bonus if she and Flynn ended up in bed. But she wasn't sure if it would happen, with Adam being in the house, Flynn rightly being super-protective of him.

Then she laughed at herself. Since when did she put sex second to conversation? After one night with Flynn she hadn't stopped wondering where he'd been all her life. What was happening? Had her regular hormones packed their bags and taken a hike, only to be replaced with a needier version?

She froze, stared into the mirror, found only the same face she'd been covering with make-up for years. No drastic changes had occurred. The same old wariness mixed with a don't-mess-with-me glint blinked out of her eyes. And behind that the one emotion she hoped no one ever saw—her need to be loved.

Dropping her head, she planted her hands wide on the bathroom counter, stared into the basin and concentrated on forcing that old, childish yearning away.

Sex with Flynn and now this? Why now? Here? What was it about him that had the locks turning on her tightly sealed box of needs and longings?

She couldn't visit him. Throwing the mascara wand at the bin, she grimaced. She had to, then she'd see that he was just an everyday man working to raise his son and not someone to get in a stew over. If he was wise he'd never want a woman as mixed up as her in Adam's life.

A quick glance in the mirror and she dredged up a smile.

Attagirl. You're doing good. She kissed her fingertips and waved them at her image. But right now she'd love a hug.

Ally got her hug within seconds of stepping inside Flynn's house.

'Hey, there.' His eyes were sombre and his mouth not smiling as he wrapped her in his arms. Her cheek automatically nestled against his chest. Her determination to be Ally the aloof midwife wobbled. *Should've stayed away. At least until this weird phase passes.*

Then Adam leapt at her, nearly knocking her off her feet and winding his arms around her waist.

'Is this a family thing?' she asked, as she staggered back against the wall. She dredged up a smile for Adam.

'Easy, Adam, not so hard. You're hurting Ally.'

'No, I'm not,' he answered. Then he was racing down the hall to where light spilled from a room. 'Now we can eat.'

'There's an honest welcome.' Kind of heart-warming. 'I'm sorry if I've kept you waiting.'

Flynn shook his head. 'You're not late. You could've got here by midday and Adam would've been waiting for dinner. He's a bottomless pit when it comes to his favourite food.'

'I bought him a wee treat at the supermarket. I hope that's all right.' The house was abnormally quiet. No blaring TV, she realised.

'The occasional one's fine, but I try not to spoil him with too much sugar and fatty foods. His mother held strong beliefs about giving children the right foods early on to establish a good life-style for growing up healthy. Healthy body, healthy mind was a saying close to her heart.'

He was trying to implement his late wife's beliefs. 'Fair enough.' Ally had no idea what it must be like to be suddenly left as a solo parent to a two-year-old, especially while juggling a demanding career. 'Have you always worked on Phillip Island?'

'Only since Anna died.' Flynn found matching glasses and poured the Chardonnay she'd brought. 'I was an emergency consultant in Melbourne. Being a GP is relatively new for me, and vastly different from my previous life.'

'So you had to re-specialise?' Why the drastic change?

'It was a formality really as my specialty leant itself to general practice.' He lifted his glass and tapped the rim to hers. 'Cheers. Thanks for this.'

The wine was delicious, and from the way Flynn's mouth

finally tipped up into a smile after he'd tasted it, he thought so, too.

'Thanks for feeding me.' She pulled out a bar stool from under the bench and arranged herself on it to watch Flynn put the finishing touches to dinner. *Looking for the everyday man?*

As he chopped parsley he continued the conversation in a more relaxed tone. 'Anna grew up here and it had always been her intention to return once she had a family.' His finger slid along the flat of the knife to remove tiny pieces of the herb and add them to the small pile he'd created. 'I wasn't ready to give up my career in the city. I was doing well, making a name for myself, working every hour available and more. We lived in a big house in the right suburb, had Adam registered for the best schools before he was born. It was the life *I'd* dreamed of having.'

She sensed a deep well of sadness in Flynn as he sprinkled the parsley on the casserole and rinsed his hands under the tap. *Not quite the definition of an everyday man.* Hadn't he and Anna discussed where they wanted to live and work before they'd married? Before they'd started a family? 'Yet here you are, everyone's favourite GP, living in a quiet suburban neighbourhood, seemingly quite happy with it all. Apart from what happened to your wife, of course,' she added hurriedly.

She wanted to know more about him, his past, his plans for the future. She craved more than to share some nights in bed with him. *Leave. Now.* But her butt remained firmly on the seat and her feet tucked under the stool. She'd have to stay and work through whatever was ailing her.

Flynn's smile was wry. 'Odd how it turned out. It took Anna's death for me to wake up to what was important. Family is everything, and Adam is my family, so here we are.' He held cutlery out for her to take across to the table.

Did he add under his breath, 'Living the life Anna wanted for all of us?' If he did, then he'd pull the shutters down on any kind of relationship other than a fling. His late wife wouldn't be wanting him to have a woman flitting in and out of his life, and definitely not Adam's.

Relief was instant. She didn't have to fight this sense of wanting more from him. There wasn't going to be anything other than sex and a meal or two. *You're jumping the gun. He mightn't even want the sex part any more.* Except when she glanced across to where he was dishing up the meal, she knew he did. It was there in the way he watched her, not taking a blind bit of notice where he spooned chicken and gravy. When their gazes locked she was instantly transported back to the moment they'd come together on the beach. Oh, yes, there were going to be more bed games.

Games that didn't involve her heart and soul, just her hormones and body.

'What is there to do on the island during winter?' Apart from going to bed with sexy doctors. 'I read somewhere about a racetrack, but there's not going to be a race meeting this month.'

'Do you like watching cars going round and round for hours on end?' He looked bored just thinking about it.

'I've never been, but I'm always looking for new adventures.'

'So what do you do with your spare time?'

Not a lot. Her standard time-fillers were, 'Shopping, movies, sunbathing on the beach, swimming, listening to music.'

'That's it?' His eyebrows lifted. 'Seriously?'

'What's wrong with that? It's plenty.' *I don't have a child to look after. Or a house to clean and maintain. Or a partner who wants me to follow him around.*

Flynn shook his head. 'Don't tell me your life is all work and no play?'

She locked her eyes on him. 'No play? Care to rephrase that?' She'd done playing the other night—with him.

He grinned. 'How about we take you to see the penguins this weekend? It's something I can take Adam to with us.'

'Penguins?' Adam's head swivelled round so fast he should've got an instant headache.

'Big Ears always hears certain words.' Flynn shrugged.

'Can we really go, Dad? They're funny, Ally.' Adam leapt up from the table to do his best impersonation of a penguin, and Sheba got up to run circles around him. Next Adam was having a fit of giggles.

Ally chuckled. 'I love it when he does that. Okay, yes, let's go and see these creatures.' It would be something to look forward to. Going out with an everyday man and his child. Different from her usual pursuits. She bobbed her head at Adam and held her arms tightly by her sides as she shuffled across the floor.

Adam rewarded her with more giggles as they returned to the table.

'That's enough, you two.' Flynn looked so much better when he laughed. 'Sorry we're eating early, but Adam needs to have his bath and get to bed.' Flynn didn't look sorry at all.

'I understand you must have a routine. Don't ever think you have to change it for me. I'm more than happy being fed,' she said, before forking up a mouthful of chicken. 'This is better than anything I'd make, believe me.'

Adam pushed his plate aside. 'Are we having pudding, Dad?'

'I've chopped up some oranges and kiwi fruit. Just need to add the banana when we're ready.'

'Can I get the ice cream out of the freezer?'

'Yes, you can tonight since we've got a visitor.' Flynn winked at her. 'You'll get an invitation every day now.'

I wish. 'I'll clean up the kitchen after dinner.' A small price for a home-cooked meal.

While Flynn was putting Adam to bed, Ally cleared away the plates. Once she'd put the last pot into the dishwasher and wiped down the benches she approached the coffee machine and began preparing two cappuccinos. 'These things make decent frothy milk,' she commented as Flynn joined her. 'How's Adam?'

'Asleep, thank goodness.' He took the coffees over to the lounge.

Following, she asked, 'This your quiet time?'

'Definitely. Don't get me wrong, I love my boy, but to have a couple of hours to unwind from the day before I go to bed is bliss.'

Bed. There it was. The place she wanted to be with Flynn right now. But he'd sat down and was stretching his legs out in front of him. She remembered those legs with no clothing to hide the muscles or keep her hands off his skin. Skin that covered more muscle and hot body the farther up she trailed her gaze. *Stop it.* She sipped the coffee, gasped as it burned her tongue. 'I'm such a slow learner.'

He stood up to take the mug out of her hand and place it on a small table beside the chair. Then he reached for her hands and pulled her to her feet. His mouth was on hers in an instant; his kiss as hot, as sexy, as overwhelming as she remembered from the previous night. She hadn't been embellishing the details.

His arms held her close to his yummy body, his need as apparent to her as the need pulsing along her veins.

When he lifted his mouth away she put her hands up and brought his head back to hers. She liked him kissing her. More than any man before. *Scary. Don't think about what that means right now. Don't think at all. Enjoy the moment.* Her tongue slipped across his bottom lip, tasting him, sending enough heat to her legs to make them momentarily incapable of holding her upright without holding on to Flynn tighter.

'Ally, you're doing it to me again. Sending me over the edge so quickly I can't keep up.' Thankfully he returned to kissing as soon as he stopped talking.

So not the moment for talking. This was when mouths had other, better, things to do. Since when had kissing got to be so wonderful anyway? Or was it just Flynn's kisses that turned her on so rapidly? Before Flynn she'd thought they were just a prelude to bedroom gymnastics, but now she could honestly spend the whole evening just kissing.

Then his hands slid under her top to touch her skin and she knew she'd been fooling herself. She had to have him, skin to skin, hips to hips. Hands touching, teasing, caressing. Now. Pulling her mouth free, she growled, 'The couch or your bedroom?'

His eyes widened, then he shook his head. 'Bedroom. There's a lock on the door.'

She hadn't had to think about children barging in before. But why did Flynn have a lock on his bedroom door? Did he do this often? No, he'd told her she was the first since Anna died. Somehow she knew he hadn't lied to her. Whatever the reason it was there, she was grateful or Flynn wouldn't have continued with this even with Adam sound asleep.

He said, 'I'm hoping you've got more of those condoms in your bag.'

'That's what the pharmacy's handy for. Called in at the one farthest from the clinic on my way back from visiting a patient.' No point in creating gossip if she didn't have to.

Flynn laughed. 'You don't honestly think they won't know who you are already?'

Her fingers caught his chin and pulled that talkative mouth down for another kiss. 'Let's get back to where we were.'

'Now who's talking too much?'

They both shut up from then on, too busy touching and stroking, kissing, undressing one another as their desire coiled tighter and tighter. And tighter.

The phone woke Ally. It was a local number, though not one she knew. Seven o'clock on a Saturday morning. She might not know many people on this island, but it seemed someone always wanted to get her out of bed before she was ready. Or in bed, as with Flynn.

'Ally, is that you? It's Chrissie.'

'Hey, Chrissie, what's up?" Ally pushed up the bed to lean back against her pillow.

'I'm bleeding. I'm not losing the baby, am I?' Her voice rose.

'First of all, take a deep breath and try to calm down. I'll have to examine you to know the answer to that, but you're not necessarily having a miscarriage. Sometimes women do have some spotting and it's fine.'

'But what if I am miscarrying?' There were tears in Chrissie's voice. 'I don't want to lose it.'

Ally felt her heart squeeze for this brave young woman. 'How heavy is the bleeding?' Wrong question. To every pregnant mother it would be a flood.

'Not lots. Nothing like my period or anything.'

Got that wrong, then, didn't I? 'I'll come and see you this morning. Try to relax until I get there. This could just be due to hormonal changes or an irritation to your cervix after sex.' Had Chrissie been seeing the boy who'd had a part in this pregnancy? There'd still been no mention of the father and she was reluctant to ask. It wasn't any of her business, unless Chrissie was under undue pressure from him about the pregnancy and so far that didn't seem to be the case.

'Really?' Chrissie's indrawn breath was audible on the phone. Girls of this age didn't usually like talking about their sexual relations to the midwife. It was *embarrassing*. 'But that didn't happen before when I wasn't pregnant.'

'Your body is changing all the time now, and especially your cervix.' It sounded like they might have the cause of the spotting, but she needed to make absolutely sure. Ally got up and stretched, her body aware of last night's lovemaking with Flynn. Easing the kinks out of her neck and back, she used one hand to pull on a thick jersey and trackpants before making her way to the kettle for a revitalising coffee. 'Have you told your mum what's happening?'

'Yes. She said to ring you or Dr Reynolds.'

And I got the vote. Warmth surged through her. 'If I'm at all worried after the exam, you'll still need to see Dr Reynolds. He might want you to have an ultrasound. But first things first. I'll be at your house soon. Is that all right?' She wouldn't mention the blood tests she'd need samples for. Chrissie might've sailed through the last lot without a flinch, but she didn't need to be stressed over today's until the last minute.

'Thank you, Ally. That's cool. I'm sorry to spoil your day off.'

'Hey, you haven't. This is what being a midwife's about. You wait until junior is ready to come out. He or she won't care what day of the week it is, or even if it's day or night.'

'I'm going to find out if it's a boy or girl. I want time to think of a name and to get some nice things for it. I feel weird, calling the baby "it". Like I don't care or something.'

Talking about the scan was more positive than worrying she might be losing the baby. Ally sighed with relief. 'Catch you shortly.'

Four hours later Ally parked outside Flynn's house and rubbed her eyes. She was unusually tired. Her head felt weighed down—with what, she had no idea. Maybe the slower pace of the island did this to people. She'd noticed not everyone hurried from place to place, or with whatever they were doing. Certainly not the checkout operator at the supermarket, where she'd just been to stock up on a few essentials. The girl had been too busy talking to her pal she'd previously served to get on with the next load of groceries stacked on her conveyor belt.

Tap-tap on her window. Flynn opened her door. 'Hey, you coming in or going to sit out here for the rest of the day? Adam could run errands for you, bring you a coffee or a sandwich.'

'That sounds tempting.' The heaviness lifted a little and she swung out of the car. 'How's things in your house this morning?'

He ignored her question. 'You look exhausted. All that sex-ercise catching up with you?' He suddenly appeared genuinely concerned. 'You're not coming down with anything, are you?'

'Relax, I'm good. Just tired. I've spent most of this morning with Matilda Livingstone, trying to calm her down and make her understand that her pregnancy is going well, that she doesn't need to worry about eclampsia at this early stage, if at all.'

'Her mother's been bleating in her ear again, I take it?'

'Unfortunately, yes. Such a different outlook from Angela and Chrissie. I had an hour with Chrissie, as well. She had some mild spotting this morning, but hopefully I've allayed her concerns. We talked a lot about the trimesters and what's ahead for her and the baby. I'm amazed at how much detail she wanted to know.'

'Could be her way of keeping on top of the overwhelming fact that she's pregnant and still at school and hoping to go to university.'

Ally nodded. 'Yes, well, that plan of becoming a lawyer is on hold for a little while, but I bet she will do her degree. Maybe not in the next couple of years, but some time. There's a fierce determination building up in her that she'll not let baby change her life completely, that she's going to embrace the situation and make the most of everything.'

'That's fine until her friends leave the island to study and she's at home with a crying infant. That's the day she'll need all the strength she can muster.'

Ally shook her head at him. 'She'll love her precious baby so much she'll be fine.'

'Spoken like someone who hasn't had a major disappointment in her life.'

Spoken like a woman who's had more than her fair share of those, and has learned to try and see only the best in life by not involving herself with people so they can't hurt her.

'That's me—Pollyanna's cousin.' It shouldn't hurt that Flynn didn't see more to her than her cheery facade, didn't see how forced that sometimes was, but it did. Even if she cut him some slack because it had barely been a week since they'd met and outside work they'd only had fun times, she felt a twinge of regret.

What would it be like to have someone in her life who truly knew her? Where she'd come from. Why she kept moving from one clinic to the next, one temporary house to another. She'd thought she'd won the lottery with the Bartletts. She had come so close to belonging, had been promised love and everything, even adoption, so when it hadn't eventuated, the pain of being rejected for a cute three-year-old had underscored what she'd always known. She was unlovable. Letting people into her heart was foolish, and to have risked it to the Bartletts because they'd made promises of something she'd only ever dreamed of having had been the biggest mistake of her young life. So big she'd never contemplated it again.

Oh, they'd explained as kindly as they could how their own two children, younger than her, hadn't wanted a big sister. Being mindful of their children's needs made Mr and Mrs Bartlett good parents, but they should never have promised her the earth. She'd loved them with such devotion it had taken months to fully understand what had happened. They'd said she was always welcome at their home. Of course, she hadn't visited.

As she locked the car she watched Flynn with her bags of goodies striding up the path to his front door. Why did she feel differently about Flynn? Whatever the answer, it was all the more reason to remain indifferent.

Did his confidence come from having loved and been loved so well that despite his loss he knew who he was and why he was here? He wasn't going to share his life with her or another woman. It was so obvious in the way he looked out for Adam, in the balancing act he already had with his career and his son. She'd been aware right from the get-go that there would be no future for her here.

That's how she liked it, remember?

As Flynn stopped to look back at her she knew an almost overwhelming desire to run up to him and throw herself into his arms. So strong was this feeling that she unlocked the car. She had to drive away, go walk the beach or take a visit to the mainland.

'Ally? You gone to sleep on your feet?' The concern was genuine. 'I think you should see a doctor.' Then he smiled that stomach-tightening smile straight at her. 'This doctor.'

How could she refuse that invitation? There was friendship

in that smile. There was mischief, as in sex, in that smile. That was more than enough. That's all she ever wanted.

She locked the car again and headed inside.

Flynn watched Ally with Adam. She didn't appear to be overly tired, more distracted. By what? Was she about to tell him thanks, she'd had a blast, but it was over? Already?

He wasn't ready to hear that news. Not yet. They'd just got started. It had come as a surprise to find he wanted her so much, needed to get to know her intimately. He understood it had to be a short-term affair. Ally would leave at the end of her contract in three weeks—no doubt about that. For that he should be grateful. There wasn't room in his life for anyone else. Adam came first, second, and took anything left over from the demands of the clinic.

Anyway, he doubted whether Ally had room for him or any man in her life. She was so intent on moving on, only touching down briefly in places chosen for her by her bosses and circumstances, doing her job with absolute dedication and then taking flight again.

'Hey, Adam, what've you been doing this morning?' The woman dominating his thoughts was talking to his boy and scratching Sheba's ears.

'We went to the beach to throw sticks for Sheba. I chucked them in the water. That's why she's all wet.' Mischief lightened that deep shade of blue radiating out of Adam's eyes. *Here we go, another round of giggles coming up.*

'The water must've been freezing.' Ally smiled softly and ruffled his hair, which Adam seemed to like. And that simple show of affection put the kibosh on the giggles as he stepped close to Ally and patted the top of Sheba's head, too.

'Sheba likes swimming.' Adam looked up at Ally, hope in his eyes. 'Are you still coming to see the penguins with us?'

'That's why I'm here. You and I can do the funny walk on the beach, see if they want to be our friends.' She was good with him, no doubt about that.

Which set Flynn to more worrying. That look Adam had given her showed how much his boy already felt comfortable with Ally. Though, to be fair, he was comfortable with just about everybody. But was this a good idea, having Ally drop by for lunch and a drive around the island? His boy didn't need to lose anyone else in his life. It was only recently that he'd got past that debilitating grief after Anna's death. *He must not get close to Ally. He could not.*

'Flynn, you've caught the sleeping-on-your-feet bug.' Ally had crossed to his side and was nudging him none too gently in the ribs with her elbow. 'You with us?'

He relaxed. Let the sudden fire in his belly rule his head. 'You bet. Do you want to come back for dinner tonight?' *Afterwards we could have some more of that bedroom exercise.*

'Did you have anything else in mind for the evening? There's a wicked glint in your baby blues.'

'Dessert maybe.'

'With whipped cream?' Her tongue slid across her lips and sent heat to every corner of his body.

So this was what it was like to wake up after a long hibernation. Not slowly, but full-on wide-awake and ready to go. Making love with this woman had been like a promise come true. Exciting and beautiful. He wanted to do it again and again. *Making love as against having sex? Now, there's something to think about.*

'Can I have ice cream, too?' Adam asked, bringing them back to earth with a thud.

'We can get cones when we're out this afternoon.' How many hours before Adam was tucked up in bed fast asleep? How long until he could kiss Ally until she melted against him?

'Flynn,' she mock growled. 'We have plans for this afternoon. Let's get them under way, starting with lunch. My shout at a café or wherever you recommend near this penguin colony. The busier we are, the quicker the day will go by.'

'Can't argue with that.' She was so right he had to drop a kiss on her cheek as a reward. It would've been too easy to move slightly and cover her mouth with his. Thank goodness common sense prevailed just in time and he stepped back to come up with, 'I'm thinking of getting our flippers out of the cupboard in the garage so that you two human penguins can flip-flop along the beach.'

'Can we, Dad? Ally, want to?' Adam yelled, as he ran in the direction of the garage internal door.

Flynn waved a hand after him. 'Go easy on that cupboard door. You know what happened last time you opened it.'

'I'll help him.' Ally was already moving in the same direction, her fingers tracing the spot on her cheek he'd just kissed.

'Good idea. Things tend to spill all over the place when he starts poking through the junk on the shelves.' He relaxed. Adam was excited, and Ally was just being a part of that, helping make his day more fun. It wasn't like she'd moved in or would see him every day of the week. She'd be gone soon enough, and Adam would still have all his playmates and the many adults on the island who enjoyed spoiling and looking out for him. He'd be safe. He wasn't in danger of getting hurt.

Flynn paused. Neither was he. Despite being equally excited as his boy. Ally hadn't said anything about calling their affair— if that's what it was—quits yet, so he'd carry on for three more weeks and make the most of her company. It wasn't as though he'd be broken-hearted when she went, mad, crazy attraction for her and all. He'd miss her for sure. She was the woman who'd woken him up, but that didn't mean he had to have her in his life permanently.

CHAPTER SIX

'WHERE'S DAD?' ADAM bounced into the bedroom and jumped up on the bed, effectively ending any pretence of Ally sleeping.

Groaning, she rolled over to stare up at this little guy. Something warm and damp nudged her arm. Turning her head, she came eye to eye with Sheba. Another groan escaped her. So this was what it was like to wake up in a family-orientated house. Kind of cosy, though it would've been better if Flynn were here.

'Why are you here?' Adam asked, looking around as though he might find his father in the wardrobe or on the floor beside the bed.

'Dad had to go to work so I stayed to look after you.'

'Did someone have a crash?' No four-year-old should look so knowledgeable about his father's work.

'Yes, during the night.' The call had come through requesting Flynn's presence as Ally had been about to walk out the door to return to the flat. They'd agreed she shouldn't be there in the morning with him when Adam woke up. But when the call came Flynn had been quick to accept her offer to stay, so apparently he could break his own rules.

Jerome had picked up Flynn ten minutes later. Teens had been racing on the bridge in the wee hours of the morning after too much alcohol. Two cars had hit side on and spun, slamming into the side of the bridge, injuring four lads. Carnage, Flynn had told her when he'd phoned to explain he wouldn't be back until early morning as he was accompanying one of the boys to the Royal Melbourne Hospital.

'He doesn't like going to crashes. They're yucky.' Adam patted the bed and the next thing Ally felt the bed dipping as Sheba heaved herself up to join them.

'Is she allowed on the bed?' Ally shuffled sideways to avoid being squashed by half a ton of Labrador.

'Sometimes.'

'Right, and today's one of those times. Why did I not see that coming?' She chucked him under the chin. About to sit up, she stopped. Under the covers she wore only underwear. Definitely not the kind that decently covered all the girl bits. 'Adam, do you think you could take Sheba out to the kitchen while I get up?' Her clothes were in a tangled heap on the floor where she'd dropped them before climbing back into bed after Flynn had left.

'Do you want Dad's dressing gown? It's in the wardrobe. He never uses it.' Adam leapt off the bed, obviously unperturbed that she was there. Maybe he could explain that to his father. 'He walks around with no clothes on when he gets up in the morning.'

Too much information. At least while Flynn wasn't there and this little guy was. But she could picture Flynn buck naked as he strolled out to put the kettle on. Seriously sexy. 'I'd love the dressing gown.'

Adam had just dumped the robe on the bed when they both heard the front door opening. 'Dad's back.' He raced through the house, Sheba lumbering along behind him.

Making the most of the opportunity Ally slipped out of bed and into the dressing gown, tying the belt tightly around her waist. A glance in the mirror told her that as a fashion statement, an awful lot was lacking. Her face could do with a scrub, too. All that mascara had worked its way off her lashes and smudged her upper cheeks.

In the kitchen she plugged in the coffee maker and leaned

her hip against the bench, waiting for the males of this house to join her.

Flynn sloped into the kitchen, with Adam hanging off his back like a monkey. Sheba brought up the rear. 'Morning, Ally. Sleep well?'

Huh?

Then he winked and she grinned. 'Like a lizard.'

'Like your outfit,' he tossed her way.

'I'm not sure about the colour. Brown has never been my favourite shade of anything. Want a coffee?'

'I'd kill for one, but can you give me five? I want to leap under a very hot shower.' His face dropped and his eyes saddened. 'It was messy out there,' he said quietly.

She nodded, wanting to ask more but reluctant to do so in front of Adam. Instead, she reached a hand to his cheek, cupped his face. 'Go and scrub up. I'll have the coffee waiting.' *Cosy, cosy.*

'Ta. You're a treasure.' For a moment she thought he was going to kiss her. His eyes locked on hers and he leaned closer. Then he must've remembered Adam on his back because he pulled away. 'I won't take long.'

He returned in jeans and a polo-neck black jersey that showed off his physique to perfection. His feet were bare, his hair a damp mess. He couldn't have looked more sexy if he'd tried. It came naturally.

Passing over a mug of strong coffee, she picked up the container she'd found in the pantry. 'Feel like croissants for breakfast?'

'Croissants it is. I'll heat them while you have a shower if you like.' He didn't like her lounging around in his dressing gown? Then his eyes widened and she realised he was staring at her cleavage. An exposed cleavage.

Grabbing the edges of the robe, she tugged them closed. 'As soon as I've finished my coffee I'll get cleaned up.' Then what? Did she head home after breakfast? It would be fun to hang out with these two for a while. Talk about getting used to this cosy stuff all too quickly. Today she was simply ignoring the lessons learned and taking a chance. At what?

'We always go for a walk on the beach after breakfast in the weekends. You coming?' Flynn asked.

'Love to. Were you having a late breakfast when Sheba bowled me over last Sunday?' she asked around a smile, suddenly feeling good about herself. A chance at some normal, everyday fun that families all over the country would be doing. She wouldn't think about how often she'd stared through the proverbial window, longing for exactly this. She wouldn't contemplate next Sunday or the one three weeks away when she was back in Melbourne. Instead, she'd enjoy the day and keep the brakes on her emotions.

'No, two walks in one day. Makes up for the weekdays when she gets short-changed. I don't like dragging Adam out of bed too early. Marie walks her occasionally, but I think she's worried about being knocked over in her pregnant state.'

'Have you known Marie long?'

He nodded. 'Anna and Marie were school friends. They went their separate ways but kept in touch and Anna always talked about when they'd both be living back here with their families.' That sadness was back, this time for himself and his family.

Great. It was hard to compete with a woman who held all the aces and wasn't around any more to make mistakes. *You're competing now? What happened to your fixed-in-concrete motto— Have Fun and Move On?* That was exactly what she was doing. Having fun. And...in three weeks she'd be moving on. So none of this mattered. *Really?* Really. She tried for a neutral tone even when she felt completely mixed up. 'Marie must miss her, too.'

'She does, especially now her first baby's due.'

'What would Marie have to say if she knew about us?' Would she stick up for Anna or accept that Flynn was entitled to get on with his life? *Hello? What does any of that matter? You're out of here soon enough.*

'I have no idea.' Flynn looked taken aback. 'It's nothing to do with her.' But now that Ally had put the question out there he seemed busy trying to figure out the answer.

Am I trying to wreck this fling early? Because Flynn is sure to pull the plug now.

Placing her empty mug in the sink, she headed for the bathroom. The hot water could ease the kinks in her body, but it was unlikely to quieten the unease weaving through her enjoyment of being with Flynn. It was ingrained in her to protect her heart, but already she understood this wasn't a fling she'd walk away from as easily as any other. What worried her was not understanding why. She already knew she was going to miss Flynn.

But she would go. That was non-negotiable.

Sheba and Adam raced ahead of them, one barking and one shouting as they kicked up sand and left huge footprints. Flynn stifled a yawn and muttered, 'Where do they get their energy?'

'Perhaps you should try dry dog pellets for breakfast instead of hot, butter-soaked croissants,' a certain cheeky midwife answered from beside him.

'You're telling me Adam didn't eat a croissant with a banana and half a bottle of maple syrup poured on top? That was all for show and he actually scoffed down dog food?' Breakfast hadn't stacked up against Anna's ideas of healthy eating, but sometimes his boy was allowed to break the rules. Or *he* broke the rules and Adam enjoyed the result.

Ally's shoulder bumped his upper arm as she slewed sideways to avoid stepping on a fish carcass that had washed up on the tide. 'Yuk. That stinks.'

His hand found hers, their fingers interlaced, and he swung their arms between them. For a moment everything bothering him simply disappeared in this simple gesture. How much more relaxed could life get? He and Ally walking along the beach, hand in hand, watching Adam and the dog playing. Right now this was all he needed from life.

Then his phone broke the magic. 'Hello? Flynn Reynolds speaking.'

'This is William Foster's sister, Maisey. He's having chest pains again and refusing to go in the ambulance I called. Can you talk some sense into that stubborn head of his?'

'On my way. Can you hold on a moment?' He didn't wait for her reply. 'Ally, I've got to see a patient urgently. Can you take Adam home for me when you've finished your walk?' Asking for help twice in less than twenty-four hours didn't look like he managed very well. She'd probably be running away fast.

'No problem. Key to the house?'

'I'll need it to get my car out so I'll leave it in the letterbox.' He waved Adam over. 'I've got to see a patient. Ally's going to stay with you, okay?'

'Can we get an ice cream, Ally?' Hope lightened his face.

'No, you can't.' He wiped that expectancy away. 'Not after that enormous breakfast.' Bending down, he dropped a quick kiss on Adam's forehead. 'See you in a bit, mate.'

'You haven't said goodbye to Sheba.'

'I'm sure she won't mind.' Straightening up, Flynn looked at Ally, leaned in and kissed her cheek. 'Thanks, I owe you.'

Then he started to jog the way they'd come and got back to talking to Maisey. 'I didn't know William had been discharged.'

'He wasn't.'

So the old boy had taken it in his own hands to get out of hospital. 'He definitely needs that talking to, but I have to say I've already tried on more than one occasion and he's never been very receptive to anything I've said.'

'He's lost the will to live.'

That was it in a nutshell. 'I'll talk to his daughter again.' Not that he held out any hope. She'd had no more luck than anyone else.

Glancing over his shoulder, he saw Adam throwing a stick for Sheba, laughing and shouting like only four-year-olds could. *When he's older, will he fight for me if the need arose? I hope*

I am such a good parent that he will. Ally drifted into his vision as she chased another stick Adam had thrown, and he felt a frisson of longing touch him. Longing that followed him up and across the road and all the way home.

Longing that wasn't only sexual; longing that reminded him of lazy days with Anna and Adam, of friendship and love. Longing he had no right to explore. He'd been married to the love of his life. No one got a second whack at that. Anyway, as Anna had told him on the day she'd died, he hadn't been the perfect husband. He'd worked too many hours, putting his career before his family apparently. It hadn't mattered that the career had given them the lifestyle they'd had. Yeah, the one Anna apparently hadn't wanted. Not in the middle of Melbourne anyway. *Damn it, Anna, I'm so sorry we were always arguing. I'm sorry about so many things.*

He needed to scrub that from his mind and concentrate. William needed him urgently. Hitting the gas accelerator, he drove as fast as the law allowed—actually, a little faster.

Sure enough, the ambulance was parked in William's driveway. Maisey led him inside, where the paramedics had the heart monitor attached to William's chest. The reading they passed him was abnormal. He inclined his head towards the door, indicating everyone should leave him with his patient for a few minutes.

'Don't even start, Doc,' William wheezed the moment they were alone.

'You think you have the right to decide when you should clock out, do you?'

William blinked. 'It's my life.'

'From the moment you're born, it's not just yours. You have family, friends, colleagues. They all have a part of you, whether you care or not. Whether you love them or not.'

'I've lost interest in everything since Edna died. You know how it is, Doc.'

Yes, he sure did, but, 'Don't play that card with me, William. Look me in the eye and tell me Edna would want you ignoring your daughter's love? What about your grandchildren, for goodness' sake? What sort of example are you setting them with this attitude? You think teaching them to give up when the going gets tough is good for them?' Flynn sat down and waited. He wouldn't belabour the points he'd made. There was such a thing as overdoing it.

Silence fell between them. The house creaked as the sun warmed it. Somewhere inside he heard Maisey and the paramedics talking. He continued to wait.

William crossed his legs, uncrossed them. His hands smoothed his trousers. He stared around the room, his gaze stopping on a photograph of his family taken when Edna had still been alive.

Flynn held his breath.

William's gaze shifted, focused on a painting of a farmhouse somewhere on the mainland, then moved on to another of a rural scene. Paintings Edna had done.

Flynn breathed long and slow, hoping like hell his patient didn't have another cardiac incident in the next few minutes. What if he'd done the wrong thing? But he'd tried the soft approach. It was time to be blunt. They had to get William aboard that ambulance and manhandling him when he refused to go wasn't the answer—or legal. He had every right to say no. But he'd better not arrest, at least not until he was in hospital.

William had returned to that family photo, his gaze softening, his shoulders dropping a little from their indignant stance. Then one tear slipped from his right eye and slowly rolled down his cheek. He nodded once. 'I'll go. For my Edna.'

Good for you. 'I'll tell the paramedics.' And Maisey, who'd no doubt be phoning her niece the moment William had been driven away.

After Flynn had filled in some paperwork to go with his patient, he talked briefly to Maisey and then headed for his car. He was going home to Adam and Ally. They'd go for a jaunt round to San Remo. If only he didn't feel so drained of energy. Already tired after last night's emergency call-out, talking with William had taken more out of him than he'd have expected. He understood all too well how the other man felt; he also knew William was wrong. Hopefully, one day the old guy would acknowledge that, at least to himself if no one else.

The sunny winter's day had brought everyone out to San Remo to stroll along the wharves and look at the fishing boats tied up. The restaurants and bars were humming as the locals made the most of fewer tourists.

'What's your preference for lunch?' Flynn asked Ally, after they'd walked the length of the township's main street and had bumped into almost the entire register of his patients at the clinic.

'Fish and chips on the beach.' Then she smiled at him.

Her smiles had been slow in coming since he'd returned home, making him wonder if she felt he'd been using her. Which, he supposed, he had, but not as a planned thing. She'd been there when he'd got both calls and he hadn't hesitated to ask her. She could've said no. 'Good answer. There's a rug in the boot of my car we can spread on the sand.'

Had he used Ally by putting his work before what she might've wanted? *Just like old times.* But asking Ally to stay was putting Adam first, just not her. Turning, he touched a finger to her lips. 'Thank you.'

'What for?'

'Being you. I'm going to get lunch.'

'Adam and I will be over on that monster slide.'

'He's conned you into going down that?' Flynn grinned. 'Don't get stuck in the tube section.'

Yep, this felt like a regular family outing. Dad ordering the food, Adam wanting to play with Mum. Except Ally wasn't Mum, and never would be.

Which part of having a short affair had he forgotten? As

much as Ally turned him on with the briefest of looks or lightest of touches, no matter how often they fell into bed together, this was only an affair with a limited number of days to run. When was that going to sink in?

While he waited for his order he watched the woman causing him sleepless nights. She smiled sweetly at his son bouncing alongside her, said something that made him giggle. Then she rubbed her hand over his head, as she often did. How come Adam didn't duck out the way as he did with other people who went to touch him?

Flynn sighed. Should he be getting worried here? How would his boy react when Ally left them? Yes, he'd asked himself this already, and would probably keep doing so until he knew what to do about it. He'd have the answer on the day Ally left.

The real problem was that he didn't want to stop what he and Ally had going on. It was for such a short time, couldn't he make the most of it? Wasn't he entitled to some fun? If only that's all it was, and the fun didn't come with these conflicting emotions.

The fish and chips were the best he'd ever had, the batter crisp, the fish so fresh it could've still been flapping. The company was perfect.

Ally rolled her eyes as her teeth bit into a piece of fish. 'This is awesome. I'm going to have to starve all week to make up for it.'

As if she needed to watch her perfect figure. 'We'll eat salads every day till next Sunday.'

Surprise widened those beautiful eyes. 'Something you haven't talked to me about yet?'

It had only occurred to him at that moment. 'You might as well join us for dinner every night. I like cooking while you obviously have an aversion to it. Next Saturday we can visit the wildlife centre.' Once he got started, his plan just grew and grew. 'Fancy a return visit to Giuseppe's on Saturday night? It's band night.'

'Don't tell me. The old two-step brigade.' She grinned to take the sting out of her words.

'Way better than that. The college has a rock band that's soon going to compete in a talent show. Giuseppe's way of support- ing them is to hire them on Saturday nights. He says the music is crazy.'

'We can crazy dance, then. Yes to all those invitations. Thank you. You've saved me having to stock up on instant meals.' She wrapped up the paper their meal had come in and stood to take it across to a rubbish bin.

'Can we go to the wildlife park now, Dad?'

'Not today, Adam. You've already had a busy weekend, going places that you don't usually visit.'

'But, Dad, why can't I go? Now?'

'Don't push it, son. We're going home. I've got things to do around the house.' Flynn could feel that tiredness settling over him again, stronger this time. He yawned just as Ally sat down on the sand again.

'Can't hack the pace, eh, old boy?'

'I don't know anyone who can run a marathon first up after no practice for years.' Not that making out with Ally felt as dif- ficult as running a marathon. It all came too naturally.

'So that's why we do sprints.' Her grin turned wicked and the glint in her eyes arrowed him right in his solar plexus.

It also tightened his groin and reminded him of the intensity of her attraction. They'd be waiting hours before they could act on the heat firing up between them. Adam did put a dampener on the desire running amok in his veins.

'Dad, we're going to the school tomorrow.'

'What school? What are you talking about?' First he'd heard of it.

'Where the big kids go. Marie's taking me with the play group to see what it's like.'

He'd phone Marie when they got home. 'Are you sure?' This

sounded like something he should be doing. 'That's my job, taking you there. I'm your parent, not Marie.'

Ally put a hand on his forearm. 'Wait till you've talked to her. Adam might've got it wrong.' The voice of reason was irritating.

'I doubt it. Marie should've mentioned it. She knows that when it comes to the major parenting roles I'll do them. Not her or anyone else.' Now he sounded peevish, but he *was* peeved. 'I'm doing what Anna would've wanted. What I want. I'm not a surface parent, supplying warmth and shelter and avoiding everything else going on in Adam's life. No, thank you.'

She pulled her hand away, shoved it under her thigh. 'Has anyone suggested otherwise?' An edge had crept into her tone.

Had he come across too sharply? Probably. 'Sorry, but you don't understand.' Had she just ground her teeth? 'When Anna was alive she did most things with Adam. We agreed she'd be a stay-at-home mother, and when she died I wanted nothing more than to stay at home with him, but of course that's impossible.'

'How can you say I don't understand? What do you know about me? I might have ten kids back in Melbourne.'

'Perhaps you should try telling me something.' He drew a calming breath. This was crazy, arguing because Adam might be going to school with Marie tomorrow. It wasn't Ally's fault he hadn't known or that he felt left out. 'Have you had a child?' he asked softly after a few minutes. Had she been a teenage mother who'd had her baby adopted?

'No,' she muttered, then again, a lot louder. 'No. Never.'

'Got younger brothers and sisters, then?'

Now her hands fisted on her thighs. 'No.'

He backed off a bit, changed direction with his quest for knowledge about her. 'Why did you choose midwifery as your specialty?' Was that neutral enough? Or was her reason for becoming a midwife something to do with her past? A baby she wasn't admitting to?

'I wanted to be a midwife after helping deliver my foster-mother's baby at home when I was fifteen. The whole birthing process touched something in me. I'd never seen a newborn before and I knew immediately I wanted to be a part of the process.'

Flynn wanted to know how Ally had found herself in that situation, but he didn't dare ask. Instead, he said, 'Birth is pretty awe-inspiring.'

'You're saying that from a parent's perspective.' She stared out beyond the beach at who knew what. 'My foster-mother let me hold the baby and when she asked for him back I struggled to let him go. He was beautiful and perfect and tiny. And vulnerable.'

Flynn sat quietly, afraid to say anything in case she closed down.

'For the first time in my life I'd experienced something so amazing that I wanted to do it again and again.' Her fingers trailed through the sand. 'I felt a connection—something I'd never known in my life.'

The eyes that finally locked onto his knocked the air out of his lungs. The pain and loneliness had him reaching for her, but she put a hand on his chest to stay him, saying, 'Until that moment I'd supposed birth and babies were things to be avoided at all cost. My own mother abandoned me when I was only days old.'

He swore. Short and sharp but full of anger for an unknown woman. How could anyone do that? How could Ally's mother not have wanted her? But, then again, as a doctor he'd seen plenty of people who just couldn't cope. Drug problems, mental illness, abusive partners—sometimes bringing up a baby was beyond people when they couldn't even take care of themselves.

She continued as though she hadn't uttered such a horrific thing. 'There was something so special about witnessing a new life. New beginnings and hope, that instant love from the mother to her baby.' Ally blinked but didn't cry. No doubt she'd used up more than her share of tears over the years. 'It doesn't matter how many births I've attended, each one rips me up while also giving me hope for the future.'

'Yet you don't stay around long enough to get involved with your mums and their babies.'

'No.'

So Ally didn't believe in a happy future for herself.

Her laugh was brittle as she shifted the direction of the conversation. 'I had one goal—to become a midwife. Shortly after my foster-mother's baby arrived, I went back into a group home, but I enrolled for night lessons at high school and worked my backside off during the day. Finally I made it to nursing school and then did the midwifery course and here I am.' The words spilled out as though she wanted this finished. But she couldn't hide her pride.

'It must've been darned hard work.' Lots of questions popped into his head, questions he doubted she'd answer. Ally looked exhausted after revealing that much about herself. It obviously wasn't something she did often—or at all.

The drive home was quiet. Flynn's forefingers drummed a rhythm on the steering wheel as his frustration grew. He'd learnt something very important about Ally that had briefly touched on who she was, and yet it wasn't enough. There had to be so much behind what he'd heard, things she obviously kept locked up, and he needed to hear them. How else could he help her?

'Dad, stop. You're going past our house.'

Flynn braked, looked around. 'Just checking to see if you were awake.'

Ally stared at him like he'd grown another nose. 'It's dangerous not to concentrate when you're driving.'

Because she was right and he didn't want to tell her what had distracted him, he ignored her and pressed the automatic garage door opener.

Inside the house, Flynn reached for the kettle. 'What would you like to do now, Ally?'

She tensed briefly then shook her head. 'You know what? I'm going to head back to the flat. I've got a few chores that need doing.'

His heart lurched. 'Thank you for sharing some of your story.'

Her deliberate shrug closed him off from her. 'I'm just your regular girl. And this regular girl needs to do some washing and answer some emails before work tomorrow.'

He wanted to insist she stay and share a light dinner, watch a movie on TV with him, but for once he knew when to shut up. 'Okay. I'll see you in the morning, then.'

CHAPTER SEVEN

ALLY DROPPED HER keys on the bench and stared around Kat's flat. Not grand on any scale, but a cosy and comfortable bolt-hole for Kat at the end of her day, a place to kick off her shoes and be herself. A place to face the world from.

What had possessed her to spill her guts to Flynn? At least he'd understand why she wasn't mother material. But it was Adam's laughing face cruising through her mind, teasing her with hope when in reality she wasn't ready for a child, would never be. Ally caressed her two ornamental dogs, her mouth twisted in sadness. Real-life pets required stability in their lives. The idea of owning a home hadn't made it onto her list of goals for the next ten years. She faced everything the world threw her way by digging deep and putting on a mask. She didn't need bricks and mortar to hide behind. Honestly, she had no idea about setting up a home that she could feel comfortable in.

Would I feel more content, less alone, if I had a place I could call home? A place—the same place—to live in between jobs, instead of bunking with whoever has a spare bed?

Sweat broke out on her upper lip. Her stomach rolled with a sickening sensation. Thirty-one and she'd never had a home, not even as a child. Those foster-homes she'd lived in had been about survival, not about getting settled. She'd always tried so hard to please her foster-parents in the desperate hope they'd fall in love with her and adopt her, but that had never happened. The only time she'd believed she might be there long term had ended in tears and her packing her few possessions to take to the next stop in her life. She'd finally wised up to the fact—starting with her own mother—that no one cared for her enough to give her what she craved.

Don't go there. You've been over and over and over trying to understand why she left you on a stranger's doorstep. There is no answer.

Poking around in her bag, she found her music player, put the earbuds in and turned the volume up loud. Music helped to blot out the memories. Sometimes.

Then her phone vibrated against her hip and broke through her unease. Removing the earbuds, she answered the phone. 'Hey, Lilia, glad you rang.' Curling up on the settee she sighed with relief. A bit of girl talk would send those other thoughts away. 'What have you been up to?'

Lilia had refused to be pushed away while she'd been on a job in Lilia's home town, and they'd become friends despite her wariness.

'Just the usual. What about you? Having a blast on the island?'

'Yep, it's great.'

'Try to sound like you mean that,' Lilia said. 'Not like you've been sent to the middle of nowhere with no man in sight.'

That might've been boring, but it would've been safer. Flynn was sneaking in under her radar. She drew a breath and found some enthusiasm. 'Oh, there are men here. Even downright drop-dead sexy ones.'

'Ones, as in many? Or one? As in you're having fun?'

'One. Dr Flynn Reynolds. Do you know him? He used to work at one of Melbourne's hospitals, left about two years ago.'

'The name doesn't ring any bells, and I can't picture him. Is he a GP?'

'A GP, a widower and father of one. Perfect for a short fling.'

'Why do I hear a note of uncertainty?' Lilia suddenly laughed.

'Oh, my God, don't tell me you've gone and fallen for him? You? Miss Staying Single For Absolutely Ever? I don't believe it.'

'That's good because it's not true.' Not true. Not true. Her heart thudded so loudly Lilia probably heard it. Her fingers gripped the phone. 'We've been doing the leg-over thing, even taken the dog and kid for a walk, but that's as far as it's going.'

'Taken the kid and dog for a walk?' Lilia shrieked. 'That's Domesticity 101. You are *so* toasted.'

Panic began clawing through Ally, chilling her, cranking her heart rate up. 'Seriously.' She breathed deeply. 'Seriously, it's all about the sex. Nothing else.'

Lilia was still laughing. 'Go on, tell me some more. Is this Flynn gorgeous?'

'Yes, damn it, he is.'

'Good. Is he a great dad?'

'What's that got to do with anything?' The panic elbowed her. Adam was happy, but even if he wasn't, that had nothing to do with her. Unless she was contemplating having babies with the man. The phone hit the floor with a crash.

Slowly bending to retrieve the phone, she couldn't think of what to say to Lilia. She didn't know what to think, full stop.

Fortunately, Lilia had no such difficulty. 'What happened? You okay? I'm sorry if I've upset you. You know I mean nothing when I say these things.'

Swallow. 'Sure. I dropped the phone, that's all.' Another swallow. 'Lilia, what if I did like Flynn? I can't do anything about it. I know nothing about families or looking after kids or playing house.'

'Hey, girlfriend, go easy on yourself. You're so much better than you think. You're capable of anything you set your mind to. I know you haven't told me everything, but how you handled putting yourself through school and getting a degree shows that in bucketloads. Do you really like him?'

Unfortunately, it could be shaping up that way. It would explain her unease and sudden need to re-evaluate her life. But it was early days. She'd soon be out of here and so would whatever feelings she was dealing with. She'd settle back to her normal, solo life and forget Flynn. Easy. 'He's okay. So how's it going in Turraburra? Any interesting men coming your way?'

'That's why I rang.' Lilia got a giant-sized hint without having to be bashed over the head. 'You know Noah Jackson, don't you?'

'Enough to say hello to and swap a sentence or two about our weekends whenever I bump into him, which isn't often as I rarely see the surgical teams. Seems an okay guy, though.' She turned the tables. 'You interested in him?'

'I've heard he's starting here in a month or so, apparently.'

'He can't be. You've got the wrong guy. Noah doesn't do general practice. He's a senior surgical registrar, not a GP. Great guy he may be, but he's very determined to get to the top of his career—and that does not include sitting and talking to mothers and their colicky babies in a small town.'

Lilia sniffed. 'Nothing wrong with general practice.'

'I know that. But I can't see Noah fitting into it. Nah, you've got the wrong guy. The Noah I know wouldn't be seen dead in a place like Turraburra.'

'Well, I heard he'll be with us for four weeks. Perhaps it's a mistake.'

'Well, if he does turn up, the good news is he's a seriously good-looking dude and definitely sexy.' Didn't set her hormones dancing but plenty of women drooled over him.

No, her hormones got a kick out of a certain doctor living here on the island. She had to get a grip, put any stupid concerns behind her and get the job done. Three weeks to go. Twenty-one days. Couldn't be too hard to have some fun and not get involved with the source of that fun. Face it, Flynn no more wanted or needed anything more connected than she did. He definitely wouldn't want Adam getting too attached to her, and she felt exactly the same. More than anything, she couldn't abide hurting that cute wee boy because she understood more than most what it was like to be left behind or shunted on. And she certainly would never be moving into their home and becoming super-mum.

'You still with me?' Lilia interrupted her musings.

'All ears. When are you coming down to Melbourne next?'

After Lilia hung up, Ally went to tug on her running shoes and shorts. A good hard pounding of the pavement would help what ailed her and put everything back into perspective.

'You've got a busy morning stacked up,' Flynn greeted her the moment she walked into the medical centre the next morning. 'Seems word's out that we've got a great new midwife and everyone who's pregnant wants to meet you.' His smile was friendly, but there was caution in his eyes. Did he think she might start considering staying on?

Returning his smile, she shrugged. 'I won't be delivering most of them. Kat will be back before long.'

His smile dipped. 'The islanders are friendly, that's all it's about. Bet you get an invitation or two for a meal before the morning's out.'

'Cool. But I'm all booked up—most nights anyway.' She locked eyes with Flynn. He hadn't changed his mind on her joining him and Adam for dinners, had he? Of course, she should be backing off a little, but how when right this moment her body was bending in his direction in anticipation of being woken up again? *Back off.* Easy to say, hard to do.

'So you'll come to dinner tonight. I'm glad.' At last the caution disappeared. His smile widened, brought a different kind of warmth to her.

A warmth that touched her deep inside in that place she went when alone. A warmth she hadn't realised she'd needed until she'd walked in and seen him. She'd missed him overnight. Had reached out to hug him and come up empty-handed—empty-hearted as well. 'Babies withstanding, I'll be there at six. Is that okay?'

He leaned close, whispered, 'Bring your toothbrush.'

That warmth turned to heat, firing colour into her chilled cheeks and tightening her stomach. 'Think I'll buy a spare,' she whispered back, before entering the office to collect the notes in her tray.

Megan winked at her. 'Have a good weekend?'

How much had she heard? Ally bit back a retort. She and Flynn would have to learn to be far more careful. 'I went to San Remo.'

Megan laughed. 'Was that you I saw out running late yesterday?'

'Running?' Flynn looked surprised.

'As in putting one foot in front of the other at a fast pace.'

'That explains...' He spluttered to a stop as Megan's eyes widened. 'A lot,' he added lamely. 'Come on, meeting time.'

As she led the way to the staffroom, she wanted to turn around and wrap her arms around him. She wanted to feel his body against hers, his chest against her cheek, his shoulder muscles under her palms. She kept walking, facing directly ahead. She wouldn't be distracted by Flynn at work. She wouldn't. It was all very well for the others to know they'd had a meal out together, might even be aware they'd spent hours doing things over the weekend, but she couldn't show how her body craved his.

'Meeting's cancelled.' Faye barrelled out of her office. 'Flynn, we're needed at the school. Two kids on bikes have been hit by a car. Where's Toby?'

'Do you need me to come along?' Ally asked.

'No, we're sorted.' Faye sped to the back door and the car park, her medical bag in one hand.

Flynn glanced around, quickly dropped a kiss on Ally's mouth. 'See you later.' And he was gone.

Leaving her with her finger pressing her lips, holding that kiss in place. Yeah, she really had missed him all night. But she'd be seeing him tonight. The knot in her tummy loosened as she headed to her room and prepared for her first mum of the day.

Her relaxed mood stayed in place all day, and when she knocked on Flynn's door that night, she didn't hold back on her smiles.

'Ally, you came,' Adam swung the door wide, inadvertently letting Sheba out.

'Sheba, no,' Ally made a grab for her collar. 'Inside, you big lump.'

Sheba replied with a tongue swipe on her hand.

'Now the woman insults my dog.' Flynn stood behind Adam, grinning at her.

Were they both as happy to see her as she was them? Stepping inside, she closed the door behind her, shutting off the world and entering the cosy cocoon that was the Reynolds home. 'Sheba knows I think she's awesome.' Then she had a brainwave. 'I could take her with me when I go running.'

Flynn's eyebrows rose. 'She'd probably have a heart attack. Walks are one thing, but a run?'

'I'm not very quick. More of a snail.' She followed Flynn and Adam into the kitchen, suddenly very aware that by making that suggestion she'd committed herself to this little family for the rest of her stay. As she had that morning when she'd said she would be here for dinners. Nothing wrong with that, as long as she kept everything in perspective. As long as Adam didn't get too close and miss her when she left.

Flynn said, 'See how you go. You might find you just want to get on the beat and not have to swing by to collect her.'

Was he having second thoughts, too?

'Can I run, too?' Adam asked hopefully.

'No,' Flynn said emphatically.

As his little face began to crumple, Ally explained. 'It's usually very early when I go.'

'It's not fair.'

'Adam, you can't do everything just because you want to. Ally's told you why you can't go with her so leave it at that.' Worry filtered into Flynn's eyes as he watched his son stomp away. When Adam turned on the TV, Flynn growled. 'Turn it off, please.'

Ally glanced from Flynn to his boy's sulky face. 'Has he been naughty?'

'He's not allowed to watch TV often. Anna was against it.'

Ah, Anna's rules. 'Surely a little time watching kids' programmes can't hurt?' *Mind your own business.* 'Other kids don't turn out as delinquents because of it.' *Shut up.*

Flynn stared at Adam, not her. 'It's hard to let go. You know?'

No, she didn't. 'Fair enough. But Adam needs to fit in with his peers at times.'

'You have a point, I guess.' Then he changed the subject. 'How was your day? Angela called me, full of praise for the way you've handled Chrissie's crisis. She doesn't want you leaving before the baby's born.'

Sliding onto a stool and propping her elbows on the bench, she shook her head. 'Chrissie will be fine with Kat.'

Flynn nodded. 'Sure she will. It's just that with Chrissie being so young and this not being a planned pregnancy, she's taken a shine to you and won't be keen to start over. But it'll work out.'

'It has to.'

'It does, doesn't it?'

Ally stared at him. What did that mean exactly? 'I was never going to be here any longer than the month Kat's away.'

He locked his eyes with hers. 'I know. But sometimes I find myself wishing you were.'

Pow. That hit right in the solar plexus, and knocked her heart. Never in a million years would she have thought he'd say something like that. 'A month's long enough for a fling. Any longer and we'd have to start wondering just what we were doing.'

'You ever had a long-term relationship?' He picked up a wooden spoon and stirred the gravy so hard a glob flicked out onto the stovetop.

'No.' She reached for a cloth to wipe up the gravy.

'Never?'

'Never. I go for short flings. Makes leaving the job easier.' *Don't ask me any more.*

'Surely you haven't always moved around as much as you currently seem to do?' He'd stopped stirring, instead studying her as though she was an alien.

Compared to him and his normal family life, she probably was different to the point of being weird. 'I spent two years in Sydney while I went to school, then moved to Melbourne for the years it took to get my degree.' Which had seemed like for ever at the time. She wouldn't mention how often she'd moved flats during those years.

Reaching across to put her hand on his, she pushed the spoon around the pot. 'You're burning the gravy.' His hand was warm under hers, and she squeezed it gently. This was so intimate—in a way she'd never known before—that tears threatened. Tugging her hand away, she stood up and went to set the table.

Flynn watched Ally banging down cutlery on the table. She was hiding something. The answer hit him hard. *More of her past.* What was so bad that she couldn't talk about it? He wouldn't judge her, but maybe he could help her. From what little she'd disclosed about being abandoned, he'd surmised that she'd grown up in the welfare system. Had she gone off the rails as a teen? Asking her outright wouldn't get him any answers, more likely her usual blunt response of no or yes. Those tight shoulders showed the chance of learning anything tonight was less than winning the lottery and he never bought tickets.

He'd told her about Anna. *You call all of about five sentences spilling your guts?* He hadn't said he and Anna had been in love from the first day they'd met at university or all the promises he'd made about Adam at her funeral.

'When's dinner? I'm hungry.'

'Now, there's a surprise.' He saw Ally wink at his son and then Adam started showing off to her.

Yeah, Adam definitely liked her a lot. So did he. Enough to want more than this affair she was adamant was going nowhere? He began dishing up, thinking how he'd never once considered he might feel something for another woman. Anna had been his everything. Hard to believe he might want a second chance at love.

The pot banged onto the stove top. Love? Get outta here. No way. Too soon, too involved, too impossible.

'You all right?' Ally stood in front of him, studying him carefully.

Swallowing hard, he nodded. 'Of course. Here…' He handed her a plate and was shocked to see his hand shaking.

'You sure?' Her gaze had dropped to his hand. 'Flynn?'

'It's nothing,' he growled. 'Adam, sit up.'

Ally did that irritating shrug of hers and picked up Adam's plate just as he reached for it. Rather than play tug of war, Flynn backed off and headed for his seat at the table. As he gulped his water he struggled to calm down. It wasn't Ally's fault he'd just had a brain melt. But love? Not likely. He needed some space to think about this. How soon could he ask her to go home for the night? Guess she'd want to eat dinner first, though the way she was pushing the food around with her fork she wasn't so keen any more. 'Chicken not your favourite food?'

'I eat more chicken than anything.' She finally took a mouthful, but instead of her eyes lighting up she was thoughtful as she chewed. Swallowing, she asked, 'Do we have a problem? Would you like me to leave?'

Yes. No. 'Not really.' Damn it. 'Sorry. Please stay. For a while at least. I'd like to get to know you better and I can't do that if you're back at Kat's flat.' He'd taken a risk, but he had to learn more about her. Had to.

Her smile was wobbly. 'You want to know more about me? You are hard up for entertainment.'

Another diverting answer, but he wasn't going to be fobbed off any more. He'd start with something innocuous. 'What sort of books do you read?'

'Suspense and thrillers. The darker the better. You?'

'I'm more into autobiographies, especially of people who battle the odds to achieve their goals. Solo round-the-world sailors, mountain climbers, those kinds of people.' Definitely not dark, but it was staggering what a person could achieve if he was determined enough.

Her mouth curved deliciously. 'You're not a suppressed endurance man who wants to battle the odds, are you?'

He shuddered. 'Definitely not. I've got too much respect for my limbs to go off doing something that crazy. Quite happy to read about others' exploits, but that's as far as I go.'

'That's a relief. For a moment there I got worried. Think of that guy who recently tried to kayak from Australia to New Zealand. It must've been incredibly hard for his wife to have to wait for him to make it safe and sound.'

But you're not my partner, so why would you be worried? 'That's why I won't be letting Adam do anything remotely dangerous until he's old and decrepit.'

He leaned back in his chair as the tension eased out of him. They were back on safe ground and suddenly he didn't want to ask even about the weather in case he put her on edge again. He enjoyed her company too much to chance her leaving early.

'Good luck with that.' She chuckled.

Unfortunately, Ally was referring to Adam. Or so he thought until Ally came around to stand by him, putting a finger on his chin, pressuring him to look at her. She bent to kiss him, softly, sweetly, and still the passion came through fiery and urgent.

At last they'd moved past that earlier little conundrum. The last thing he wanted was to watch Ally walk out the front door tonight. The only place he wanted to be with her was in his bed, making love, tangling the sheets around their legs and holding her so close they'd be as one. He returned her kiss, hard and fierce, trying to convey his need for her.

When she stepped back her eyes were slumberous and that hazel colour had darkened. How soon could he insist Adam go to bed? Because they'd be heading down the hall the moment his son closed his eyes.

Tonight he'd make up for sleeping alone last night. He'd pleasure Ally so much she'd never contemplate a night without him again while she was on the island. Hopefully then this crazy, wonderful desire for her might calm down enough for him to make rational decisions about where they were going with their fling. Ally's word, not his.

Though maybe a fling was still all he needed, and the fact that sex had become alien to him over the last two years could be the answer to why he was reacting like a teenager who'd finally discovered sex.

Ally nudged him in his side. 'Can I read Adam's stories tonight?'

Adam shrieked, 'Yes.'

Flynn spanked her gently on the bottom. 'Anything to get out of doing the dishes.'

She wriggled her butt under his hand. 'Just speeding up the process.'

Of course, Adam had no intention of settling down and going to sleep after only one story. He must've caught the vibes playing between Flynn and Ally because he was wide-awake. 'He's hyper. Unusual for him,' Flynn muttered to Ally when he looked in to see what the delay was.

'It's all right. We're having fun.'

'I'll make coffee, then.' *Go to sleep, Adam. Please, please. Oh, damn it, just go to sleep. I'm going to explode with need any minute.*

He listened as Ally read on, and on, and on. And told himself off for wanting to deny Adam his time with her. Adam came first. First.

Finally, an hour later than he'd hoped, Flynn swung Ally up into his arms and carried her to his bedroom, locking the door behind them. He stood her on her feet and leaned in to kiss that mouth that had been teasing him all night. 'At last.'

Ally already had her shirt over her head, and was pushing those magnificent breasts into his hands. 'You talk too much.'

So he shut up and showed her how much he wanted her, and gave her everything he had.

CHAPTER EIGHT

THE DAYS FLEW by but the nights went even faster. Ally had never known a placement to be so engaging. Was that entirely down to Flynn? Yes, if she was being honest, Flynn owned it—made her dizzy with excitement, warmed her with everyday fun and laughter, distracted her to the point she caught herself wondering how hard it would be to stop in one place for ever.

These heady days hinted at what her childhood dreams had been made of—someone to love her unconditionally for the rest of her life, someone she could give her heart to and not have it returned when the gloss rubbed off. But reality had taught her differently. The only difference now was that she chose where she moved to, and not some overworked, underpaid bleeding heart sitting behind a desk in a dimly lit welfare office. She was no longer a charity case.

Unfortunately, a reality check didn't slow her enthusiasm for all things Flynn. Her body ached in every muscle, her lips were sore from smiling too much, her eyes were heavy from lack of sleep. But would she wish for quiet nights at Kat's flat with only her music and a book for company? No. Not even knowing that the day of reckoning was approaching made her want to change a thing. The complete opposite, in fact. She found herself needing to grab at more and more time with Flynn.

'Hey,' Flynn called as he walked past the medical storeroom.

Then he was in there with her, sucking up all the oxygen and leaving her light-headed. When he traced her chin with his forefinger she caught it and licked the tip, delighting in the sound of his quickly indrawn breath. 'This room's never been so exciting.'

'Are we all set for tonight?' she asked.

'The table's booked at the restaurant. The babysitter's organised. The warning's gone out that no one on Phillip Island is to have an accident.' He ticked the points off his fingers. 'I've put clean sheets on the bed and bought more condoms since we must've used up your supply.'

Her giggle was immature, but that's how she reacted these days. She was always laughing or coming out with mixed-up, stupid things. 'I go to the supermarket on a regular basis.'

'I was beginning to wonder why you had so many.' He grinned, looking as loony as she felt.

'Everyone on the island must be talking about us by now. In fact, the women are probably giving their men a hard time about how many condoms we're getting through.' She didn't care at all. Every night she raced home to change into something relaxed and less midwife-like, touch up her make-up and put the washing on, then drove around to Flynn's house. She wasn't tired of him at all.

Flynn grinned. 'I'm sure they've all got better things to do than talk about their GP and the midwife.'

'I hope so.' Her heart lurched. That grin always got her behind the knees, making her nearly pitch forward onto her face. For a casual fling Flynn was breaking all the rules and turning her to mush, making her heart skip when no one had done that to her before. 'Does Giuseppe know we're returning to his restaurant?'

'I spoke to him earlier. He's planning a special meal for us. Unless there's something you don't like to eat, we are to sit back and let the courses come.'

'Sounds wonderful.' She planned on wearing a dress tonight, a short black number that she'd found in one of the local shops during her lunch break yesterday. It looked fantastic with her knee-high boots and black patterned stockings. She wouldn't be wearing anything else, bras and knickers being expendable.

'Are you two going to spend the day in that room?' Faye muttered loudly as she stomped past the door. 'There are patients waiting for both of you.'

Guilt had Ally leaping back from Flynn. 'Onto it,' she called out. 'Seriously, Doctor, you should know better than to kiss the nurse at work.'

'I'll do it out in the open next time.' His finger flicked her chin lightly. 'I'll pick you up at seven thirty.'

'I can't wait.' It was true. She'd see him on and off all day and yet she felt desperate to be with him, just the two of them sharing a meal in a restaurant, no interruptions from Adam or the phone or Sheba.

Uh-oh. What was happening? This was starting to feel way wrong. Keep this up and she'd have difficulty leaving at the end of her contract.

'Ally,' Megan called urgently from the office. 'Ally, you're needed. Lisa Shaw's on the line, her waters have broken.'

Now, that was reality. 'Coming.' She picked up her medical bag and dashed to the office, Flynn sent to the back of her mind only to be brought back out when she wasn't helping a baby into the world. This was the real stuff her life was about. The grounded, helping-others kind of thing that gave her the warm fuzzies without asking anything of her heart.

'I'm going to be late.' Ally phoned Flynn at five o'clock when it became obvious Baby Shaw had no intention of hurrying up for anyone, least of all so his mother's midwife could go out to dinner with the local GP. 'I have no idea when Ashton will make his entry. Lisa's contractions slowed nearly two hours ago and so far don't look like speeding up.' Not very medically technical terminology, but he'd get the gist.

'You can't hurry babies.' Disappointment laced Flynn's words. 'Is it selfish to wish Lisa hadn't wanted a home birth?'

'Yes, it is. I'd better go. I'll call you when I know if we're still on for our date.'

An image of that black dress hanging on the wardrobe door flicked across her mind, and she had to suppress a groan.

Lisa was the only person allowed to groan around here, which she was doing with deep intensity right this moment. Scott held her as she draped her pain-ridden body against him and gritted her teeth.

Ally rubbed Lisa's back. 'You're doing great. Seriously.'

'I have no choice, do I?' Lisa snapped. 'Next time I have a dumb idea that having a baby would be wonderful, tell me to take a hike.' She glared at Scott. 'Or you have it.'

Scott kissed her forehead and wisely refrained from commenting.

Ally went for diversion. 'How long have you been married?'

'Two years,' Lisa ground out.

'We've been wanting a baby right from the beginning.' Scott grinned. 'Couldn't get it right.'

Ally chuckled. 'Babies are control freaks. They get conceived when it suits them, arrive when they choose, and they've hardly started. But you know what? They're wonderful.'

Under her hand Lisa's shoulders tensed as she yelled out in the pain of the next contraction.

'Lisa, breathe that gas in. You're doing brilliantly.'

The next hour passed slowly. Ally took observations regularly, noting them on Lisa's chart, occasionally going for a walk to the letterbox and back to give the couple a few moments alone, then returning to give Lisa more encouragement. Six o'clock clicked over on her watch. *There goes dinner with Flynn.* Even if Baby Ashton miraculously popped out right then, she'd be needed for a time. Guilt hovered in her head. Never before had she cared how long the birthing process took, she just loved being there with the mums, dads and their babies. But now she loved being with Flynn, too.

Her head jerked up. Loved being with him? Or loved Flynn, full stop?

'Ally, come quick. Lisa's pushing,' Scott called down the hall.

Good, focus on what's important. 'That's good, but we could be a while yet.' Though for Lisa's sake she hoped not. She was exhausted.

Examining her, Ally was happy to announce, 'Baby's crowning. When the urge to push comes, go with it. Don't try to hold back.'

'It's too damn painful to push,' Lisa yelled.

'Come on, Lisa. He's got to come out of there.' Scott reached for Lisa's hand and grimaced as she gripped him.

'Easy for you to say,' his wife snarled.

Ally had heard it all before. 'As soon as Ashton makes his appearance, you two will forget everything but your beautiful little boy.' This parenthood thing was awesome. Babies were amazing, so cute and vulnerable and yet bonding their parents in a way nothing else could.

Why hadn't her mother felt like that about her? Was her mother a freak? She was definitely the reason Ally would never have her own baby. What if the don't-love-your-own-baby gene was hereditary? There was no way on earth she'd chance having a child, only to dump her into the welfare system and disappear. And even if she did love her baby—which she was sure she would despite her past—she didn't know the first about raising one, about providing all the things a child needed, including loads of love. Her experience of babies stopped once she knew they were able to feed from mum's breast.

'Ally, I think he's coming,' Lisa broke into her thoughts, brought her back to the here and now, away from the daydreams of someone who should know better.

When Ashton slid into her hands, Ally felt tears prick her eyelids. 'Wow, look, Scott, he's lovely.' She lifted him to meet his parents. Her knees were shaky and her heartbeat erratic. 'He's the most beautiful baby I've seen.'

'Of course he is,' Scott whispered.

All babies were. She'd reacted the same way at that very first birth that had started her on the path to becoming a midwife. *Thank you, wee Lloyd, wherever you are now. Not so wee any more, I guess.* Mopping her eyes with her arm, she cleaned the mucus from Ashton and placed him on Lisa's breast.

Flynn picked her up a little after eight. She was tired and exultant. 'Another little baby safely delivered and in good hands.' She clicked her seat belt into place. 'Do you remember when you first held Adam?' That hadn't exactly changed the subject, had it? Darn.

'Everything about him—his scrunched-up face, his red skin, spiky black hair and ear-shattering cry. He hasn't changed much.' Flynn smiled with a far-away look in his eye.

'His face isn't red.' The love in Flynn's voice brought tears to her eyes and she had to look out the window at the houses they were passing until she got herself back under control. It was too easy to picture Flynn carefully cradling Adam wrapped in a blanket, like he was made of something so fragile he'd break at the slightest pressure. *I want that. No. I don't. I can't have it. It would be wrong for everyone.*

'Ally? Where've you gone?'

Suck it up, play the game. You know how to. 'I'm thinking pasta and garlic and tomatoes. It's been a long day and I forgot to buy my lunch on the way to work so missed out what with Baby Ashton stealing the show.'

'I'm sure Giuseppe will fix what's ailing you.' Flynn pulled up outside the restaurant.

'Good.' Pity there was no cure for what really troubled her. She could not, would not get too involved. Flynn had been hurt badly with Anna's death. So had Adam. She couldn't risk hurting them again. Forget involvement being a risk; hurting them would be a certainty. She was clueless in the happy-families stakes, and they so didn't deserve or need to be hurt by her. She shoved the door wide before Flynn had a chance to come round to open it for her. 'Let's go and have the night of our lives.'

'Ally.' Flynn's hand on her arm stayed her. 'You look absolutely beautiful tonight. More beautiful, I mean.'

'Thank you.' Her heart rolled. Talk about making everything harder. 'I went shopping yesterday.'

'I'm not talking about the dress, though you look stunning in it. It fits you like a second skin, accentuates all those curves I love touching.' He hesitated, breathed deep. 'But it's you that's beautiful—from the inside out.'

Nothing could've made her move at that moment if she'd tried. His words had stolen the breath out of her, liquefied her muscles, making them soft and useless. She was supposed to be having dinner with Flynn and then going back to his house and bed. He was not meant to be saying things that undermined her determination to stick to her rules—no deep, attaching involvement.

'Ally? Did I go too far?'

Yes, you did. Way too far. You're frightening me. Forcing a smile, she laid her hand over his. 'Thank you. That was a lovely compliment.'

'A heartfelt one. Now, let's enjoy ourselves and I'll stop the sentimental stuff since it seems to be upsetting you.' He hopped out of the car and strode around the front to her side.

She'd let him down. But what was a girl supposed to do? She couldn't take in what he'd said and start believing. That would be dangerous, but at the same time she couldn't walk away from Flynn tonight, or tomorrow, or any time during the next two weeks. No, she couldn't. Pushing out of the car, she laced her fingers through his and walked up the path to the welcoming door of the restaurant. 'I see the tide's farther in tonight. We won't be having our wicked way on the beach.'

Grinning, Flynn held the door wide and ushered her inside, whispering as she passed, 'You give up too easily.'

Did she? 'I'm not going to ask what's on your mind. I want to eat first.' She ran a hand over his delectable butt before turning to follow the same young waiter they'd had last week.

Giuseppe was there before they'd sat down. 'Welcome back, Ally. I'm glad you enjoyed our food enough to return.'

'Come on, Giuseppe, how could I not?' She kissed her fingertips. 'That carbonara was superb.'

'The carbonara or the company you were keeping?' the older man asked with a twinkle in his eye. 'By the way, you might be wanting this.' He held up the half-full bottle of Merlot they'd left on the beach.

Flynn laughed loudly. 'You old rascal. Who found that?'

'I go for a walk along the beach every night after I close the door for the last time.' Giuseppe kept the bottle in his hand.

Uh-oh. What time had he closed the restaurant last Friday? Ally glanced across at Flynn, saw the same question register in his eyes. Had Giuseppe seen them making out? She croaked out, 'Thank you. It seemed a waste not to have finished a good wine.'

Giuseppe nodded, his eyes still twinkling, leaving her still wondering what he'd seen, as he said, 'Tonight you will try something different. Something I recommend to match the meal I have arranged. This half-finished one you can take with you when you leave.'

Ally watched as he walked away, pausing at other tables to have a word with his guests. 'Do you think he knows?'

'That we made love on the beach? Yes, I suspect he does.' Flynn reached across and took her hand in both his. 'You know what? I couldn't care less.'

'Then neither do I.' And she wouldn't worry about anything else tonight either.

The meal was beyond superb and the wine excellent. The company even better. Flynn made her laugh with stories from his training days and she told him about going to school as an adult. It was a night she'd remember for a long time. It was intimate, almost as though they had a future, and she refused to let those bleak thoughts refuting that spoil anything.

'Here.' She twined her arm around Flynn's, their glasses in their hands. 'To a hot night under the stars. Tide in or out.'

Flynn smiled, a deep smile that turned her stomach to mush and her heart to squeezing. 'To a wonderful night under the bright stars with a special lady.'

But when they stepped outside there were no stars. A heavy drizzle had dampened everything and was getting heavier by the minute. 'You forgot to order the weather.' Ally nudged Flynn as they hurried to the car.

'Never said I was perfect.' He held the car door while she bundled inside.

No, but he wasn't far off. Leaning over, she opened his door to save him a moment in the rain. 'How long will it take you to drop off the babysitter?'

'Ten minutes.'

'That long?'

'You can warm the bed while I'm away.' Flynn laid a hand on her thigh. 'Believe me, I'll be going as fast as allowed.'

Heat raced up her thigh to swirl around the apex between her legs, melting her. 'Pull over.'

'What? Now? Here?' The car was already slowing.

'Right now and here.' She was tugging at his zip. Under her palm his reaction to her move was more than obvious.

'I haven't done it in a car since I was at high school.'

'Hope you can still move your bones, you old man.'

He growled as he nibbled the skin at her cleavage. 'Just wait and learn.' His hand covered her centre, his fingers did things that blanked out all the doubts and yearnings in her mind and made her cry with need, followed with release.

Flynn rolled onto his side, his arm under his head and his gaze fixed on the beautiful woman sleeping beside him. He was addicted to Ally Parker. There was no other word for what he felt. Addiction. He'd never known such craving before. The more he had of her, the more he wanted. His need was insatiable. If it wasn't so damned exciting it would be frightening. Frightening because it was filled with pitfalls.

He'd loved Anna beyond reason and had still failed her. If he hadn't been so damned determined to follow his career the way he'd wanted it she wouldn't have been in Melbourne that day and the accident wouldn't have happened. If he'd listened to her wishes, instead paying them lip service, his boy would still have his mother. That, more than anything, he could never forgive himself for. Every child deserved two parents, and especially their mother, to nurture them as they grew up.

And this had what to do with Ally? Ally already enjoyed being with Adam, didn't treat him as a pawn to get to his father but rather as an individual in his own right. She'd nurture and mother Adam if they got together.

A chill lifted goose bumps on his skin. He withdrew his arm and rolled onto his back to stare at the ceiling. They could not get together. Firstly, Ally didn't do settling down. That was so clear he'd be a fool not to acknowledge it.

He glanced across at her sleeping form. 'What happened that you can't stop in one place for more than a few weeks? Who hurt you so badly that you're prepared to miss out on what life's all about?' he whispered. 'Someone other than your mother?' That would be enough to knock anyone sideways for ever. But he had this niggling feeling he hadn't heard it all.

As the chill lifted and his skin warmed back to normal he ran a hand over her hair, rubbed a strand between his fingers. 'I would never hurt you, let you down.'

Huh? Hadn't he just reminded himself of how badly he'd let Anna down? Yep. And Adam. Adam. The crux of the matter. He'd do anything for his son. Anything. Which meant not getting too close to Ally, not seeking the answers to those questions in case they drove him on to making her happy, not sharing his life with her.

Ally rolled over, blinked open her eyes and smiled in a just woken up and still sleepy way. 'Hi,' she whispered.

'Hi, yourself.' He leaned in to place a light kiss on her brow, then her cheek, her chin, her lips. Two weeks. *Make the most of them. Stop analysing the situation and enjoy what's left.*

As he reached for her, the door flew open.

'Dad. Why was the door shut?' Adam shouted, loud enough for the whole island to hear as he pushed it wide.

'Good morning to you, too.' Flynn smiled and pulled the bedcovers up to Ally's chin. 'Hope you're okay with this,' he whispered to her. 'I forgot to relock the door after I went to the bathroom.'

'Not a problem, unless he wants to get in here with us,' she whispered back. 'Hello, Adam. How long have you been awake?'

'A long time. I've been watching cartoons.' Adam started to climb onto the bed.

Hell, Ally was buck naked. Adam was used to seeing him in the nude, but not a woman. 'Adam, can you pass Ally my robe? She's getting cold.'

'She should wear pyjamas to bed.'

How did Adam know she hadn't? Distraction needed. 'Let's have pancakes for breakfast.' That'd get his attention, pancakes being his all-time favourite breakfast food. *Unhealthy. Tough.*

'Ally, are you coming for a sleepover every night now?'

Flynn mentally threw his hands into the air. If pancakes didn't work, then he had to get serious. 'Adam, go out to the lounge while we get up.'

Ally shook her head as though trying to make sense of everything. 'Sometimes when it's late I don't go home, but not every night. I've got my own place to go to.'

Adam nodded. 'I thought so. But if you want to stay every night we don't mind, do we, Dad?'

Which part of 'Go out to the lounge' hadn't he got? 'I guess not. Adam, we want to get up.'

'Okay. Are we having maple syrup and bacon on the pancakes?' Adam didn't look like he had any intention of moving this side of Christmas.

'We won't be having pancakes at all if you don't leave us.'

Under the covers Ally touched his thigh and squeezed it. 'Bacon, syrup *and* bananas. But I want to shower first and the longer we lie around, talking, the longer we're going to wait for our yummy breakfast.'

Adam nodded again. Where had this new habit come from? 'I'll get everything ready.'

'Great. See you out there soon.' Ally nodded back with a smile. 'But promise me you won't start cooking anything.'

'I don't know how to mix the flour and stuff.'

As Adam ran out of the room Flynn stared after him. 'He listens to you.'

'I'm a novelty. You're Dad.' Her hand stroked where a moment ago it had been squeezing.

'Keep that up and breakfast will be postponed for hours.'

She instantly removed her hand. Damn it. 'Hours? Talk about bragging.' She grinned at him. Then slid out of bed and wrapped herself in the too-large robe. 'I'm going to look so good sitting down to breakfast in my little black dress. Why didn't I think to bring a change of clothes?'

'You should leave a set here for the morning after.'

'If I did that, I wouldn't have many clothes left at the flat.'

She travelled light. Very light. 'Go shopping. Get some gear to keep here. In the meantime...' he swung his legs over the side of the bed, dug into his drawers for a sweatshirt and pair of trackpants '...try these for size.'

'I already know they'll be too long and loose around the waist, but my hips might hold them up.' She took the clothes and hugged them to her breasts. 'Who's first in the shower?'

'You go. I'll keep an eye on proceedings in the kitchen. Today could be the day Adam decides to try mixing the batter and that would be messy, not to mention uncookable.'

'You're not fair. He's got to have a go at these things. How else is he going to learn to look out for himself?'

'But it's so much quicker to do everything myself.'

Her face tightened and her chin lifted. 'In the long run you'll save heaps of time because Adam will be able to do these things for both of you.'

Ouch. She'd gone from Fun Ally to Serious Ally in an instant. She'd also had the nerve to tell him how his parenting sucked. 'Go and have that shower,' he ground out through clenched teeth.

He didn't want to start an argument by saying she should leave this to him, but it had nothing to do with her. Even if she might be right, Ally wasn't the one constantly working with a time deficit.

For a moment she stood there, staring at him. Was she holding back a retort, too? Or formulating a whole load more criticisms? Or, heaven forbid, was she about to explain why she felt so strongly about his son learning to cook?

Not likely. She'd never do that. Ally was a closed book when it came to herself. Except for that one time of sharing her past hurts, what drove her, and what held her back, her past was still blurred. He needed to remember that—all the time. But right this minute he had to get back onside with her. They were spoiling what had been a wonderful night and should be a great day ahead. 'Ally, please, go and get cleaned up. Let's not waste the morning arguing.'

Her eyes widened. Then her stance softened, her shoulders relaxed. 'You're right. We've got pancakes and a morning at the wildlife centre to enjoy. And we'll need to stop at the flat on the way so I can put on some proper clothes.'

He'd dodged a slam dunk. 'Proper clothes? Since when weren't trackies and a sweatshirt proper?'

'Since fashion became important. In other words, since the

first time a woman put on an animal hide.' She grinned and his world returned to normal.

His new normal. The one with Ally Parker in it. The normal that would expire in two weeks' time.

CHAPTER NINE

TUESDAY, AND ALLY parked outside the bakery just as her phone vibrated in her pocket. 'Hello?'

'It's Marie. I'm in labour.'

Her due date was in three weeks, but technically speaking Marie wasn't having her baby too early. Two weeks before due date was considered normal and nothing to be concerned about. 'I'm on my way. After I examine you we'll arrange to get you over to the mainland and hospital.'

'I doubt I'm going anywhere. The contractions are already coming fast.' Marie's voice rose with every word. 'Hurry, will you?'

'On my way. Try to relax. I know, easy for me to say, but concentrate on your breathing and time the contractions.' Great. The last thing Marie had said to her was that she never wanted to have a home birth. A friend of hers had had one last year and there'd been complications that had nearly cost the baby her life.

With a wistful glance at the bakery she jammed the gearshift in Reverse and backed out into the street.

Adam opened the door the moment she parked in Marie's driveway. 'Ally, Marie's got a tummyache. She's holding it tight.'

Adam was there. Of course he was. It was a weekday. He wasn't going to be anywhere else in the afternoon. 'Does Flynn know you've gone into labour?' she asked Marie the moment she stepped inside.

'No. I needed a midwife, not a doctor.' Marie glanced in the direction Ally was looking. 'Oh, Adam. He'll be fine. Anyway, what can Flynn do? Take Adam to the surgery for the rest of the day?'

'Surely Flynn's got someone he can ask to look after him?'

Marie's face contorted as a contraction gripped her. She held on to the back of a chair and screwed her eyes shut.

'Breathe deep. That's it. You're doing good.' Ally stepped close to rub her back and mutter inane comments until the contraction passed. Then she got down to business. 'Let's go to your bedroom so I can examine you. Adam, sweetheart, Marie is having her baby so I want you to be very good for her. Okay?'

'She's having a baby? Really? Why does it hurt her?' His little eyes were wide.

'It's baby's way of letting everyone know it's coming.'

'Can I tell Dad?'

'Soon. I'm going with Marie to her bedroom.' His eyes filled with expectancy and she quickly stomped on those ideas. 'I want you to help me by getting things I need, like water or cushions or towels. But not until I ask you, all right?'

'Yes, I'll be good. Can I bring them into the bedroom?'

'No, leave them outside the door.' Hopefully Marie was wrong about her baby coming quickly and she'd soon be on her way to hospital. 'Why don't you watch TV until I call you?'

'I want to help.'

'I know, but first I have to check the baby, then I'll know what you can do for us.' If Marie was heading to hospital she'd drop Adam off at the medical centre. Flynn would sort out childminding. He must have made alternative arrangements for this eventuality.

Adam's mouth did a downturn, but he trotted off to the lounge and flicked on the TV.

'Thank you, Adam,' she called, before hurrying to Marie's

bedroom and closing the door behind her. 'Have you called your husband?'

Tears welled up in Marie's eyes. 'My call went straight to voice mail. He's at sea on the fishing boat. This wasn't supposed to happen. He's booked leave for when the baby's due. He can't get here for days,' she wailed.

Ally gave her a hug and a smile. 'Well, in the meantime it's you and me. Unless you've got a close friend you'd like here, or family?' Someone familiar would make things work more smoothly.

'My family all live on the mainland and my girlfriend would be hopeless. Faints if there's the hint of blood or anyone's in pain.' Marie sank onto the bed as another contraction gripped her. 'I don't think I'm going anywhere. These contractions are coming too fast. I seriously doubt I've got time to get to the hospital.' Her voice was strained.

Ally glanced at her watch. She'd already begun timing the contractions. 'Four minutes. You're right, they're close.' She held Marie's hand until the current contraction passed. 'If you lie down I'll see what's going on.'

Marie flopped back onto the bed. 'I feel this pushing sensation, but I don't want a home birth. What if something goes wrong?'

'We have doctors only five minutes away. But you're jumping the gun. Baby might just pop out.' Ally mentally crossed her fingers as she snapped on vinyl gloves and helped Marie out of her panties. She wasn't surprised at the measurement she obtained. 'You're ten centimetres, fully dilated, so, yes, baby's on its way.' She calmly told her patient, 'Sorry, Marie, but hospital's definitely out. There isn't time.'

Marie's face paled and her teeth dug deep into her bottom lip. The eyes she lifted to Ally were dark with worry.

'Hey.' Ally wrapped an arm around her shoulders. 'You're going to be fine. I'll phone the surgery to tell them what's going on.' One of the doctors would be on notice to drop everything and rush here if anything went wrong.

'Sorry, I'm not good at this.' A flood of tears wet her cheeks.

'Find me a mother who is. This is all new to you. Believe me, no one pops their baby out and carries on as though nothing has happened. It's an emotional time, for one. And tiring, for another.' She sat beside Marie. 'Take it one contraction at a time. You've done really well so far. I mean it.'

Marie gripped Ally's hands and crushed her fingers as another contraction ripped through her.

'Breathe, one, two, three.' Finally getting her hands back and able to flex her fingers to bring the circulation back, Ally said, 'I'll get the gas for you to suck on. It'll help with the pain.'

'That sounds good. But I do need to push.'

'Try to hold off until I'm back. Promise I'll hurry.' She dashed out of the room and nearly ran Adam down in the hallway. 'Oops, sorry, sweetheart, I didn't see you there.'

'Is the baby here yet?'

'No.' But it wasn't too far away. 'Can you fill two beakers with water and leave them outside the door?' She had no idea if Marie wanted one, but giving Adam something to do was important.

His little shoulders pulled back as pride filtered through his eyes. 'I'll put them on a tray, like Dad does sometimes.'

'Good boy.' Out at the car she dug her phone out of her pocket and called the medical centre. 'Megan, it's Ally. Can you put me through to Flynn?'

'He's with a very distressed patient and said not to be interrupted unless it was an emergency.'

Define emergency. She guessed a baby arriving early didn't quite fit. 'When it's possible, will you let him know that I'm with Marie and she's having her baby at home? There isn't time to transfer her to hospital. Also mention it to Faye and Jerome in case I need help.'

'That's early. Tell her good luck from me. When Flynn's free

I'll talk to him, but I suspect he's going to be a while. His patient is really on the edge.'

'Thanks, Megan, that'd be great.' She cut the receptionist off. Marie needed her. She gathered up the nitrous oxide tank, a bag of towels and another bag full of things she'd need.

'I'm still getting the water,' Adam called as she closed the front door.

'Good boy.' Back in the bedroom the temperature had dropped a degree or two. Sundown was hours away, but outside she'd noticed clouds gathering on the horizon. 'Marie, how are you doing?'

'Okay, I guess.'

'Here, suck on this whenever the pain gets bad.' Ally handed over the tube leading from the nitrous oxide tank. 'Have you got a heater we could use? I don't want baby arriving into a cold room, and I'd prefer to warm these towels as well.'

'There's an oil column one in the laundry. Adam knows where it is and can push it along on its wheels. It'll be perfect for what you're wanting.'

'Onto it.'

Outside the door Adam was placing the beakers ever so carefully on a tray he'd put on the floor earlier. 'Can you bring me the heater out of the laundry? Or do you want me to help?'

'I can do it. Do I have to leave it out here?'

'Yes, please.'

His little shoulders slumped. 'Why can't I see Marie?'

Ally knelt down and took his small hands in hers. 'When women have babies they don't like lots of people with them, watching what's happening. They get shy.'

'Why?'

'Because having a baby is private, and sometimes it hurts, and Marie wouldn't want you to see her upset.' *Sometimes it hurts?* Understatement of the century.

'No, she only likes me to see her laughing. I'll knock when I've got the heater.'

For a four-year-old, Adam was amazingly together about things. Nothing fazed him. But then he had lost his mother so he wasn't immune to distress, had probably learned a lot in his short life. He coped better than she did. He did have a great dad onside. 'Then you can play with all those toys I saw in a big box in the lounge.'

'But I like playing outside. Marie always lets me.'

'Today's different. I need you to play inside today, Adam.' She held up a finger. 'Promise me you won't go outside at all.'

'Promise, Ally.'

Her heartstrings tugged. What a guy. As she gave him a hug a groan sounded from inside the bedroom. 'You're a champ, you know that?' *Now, please go away.*

'What's a champ?' Adam didn't seem to have heard Marie.

'The best person there is.' The groan was going on and on. 'I've got to see Marie.' *Please, go away so you don't hear this.* Nothing was wrong but that deep, growling groan might frighten him, or at least upset him.

Thankfully Adam had his father's sensitivity and recognised a hint when it came. He raced down the hall towards the laundry and Ally let herself back into the bedroom.

'Hey, how's it going?' The pain on Marie's scrunched-up face was all the answer she needed. 'Feel like pushing some more, I take it.'

'How can you be so cheerful?'

So they were at the yell-at-anyone stage. 'Because you're having a baby and soon you'll forget all this as you hold him for the first time. Can you lie back so I can examine you again?'

'Examine, examine—that's all you do.' But Marie did as asked.

Kneeling on the floor, she gently lifted Marie's robe. 'The crown's further exposed. Baby's definitely on its way.' She stood up and dropped the gloves into a waste bag. 'Have you tried to get hold of your husband again?'

'His name's Mark and, no, I haven't. He's not going to an-

swer if he's on deck, hauling in nets. They don't have time.'
Tears tracked down her face. 'Anyway, I want him here, not on
the end of a phone.'

Ally picked up Marie's phone. 'How do we get hold of him?
Can we talk to his captain?'

Marie stared at her like she'd gone completely nuts. Then she
muttered, 'Why didn't I think of that?'

'Because you're having a baby, that's why.' Ally handed her
the phone. 'Go on. Try every contact you've got.'

Just then another contraction struck and Marie began pushing like her life depended on it, all thoughts of phone calls gone.

'That's it. You're doing well.' Ally again knelt at the end of
the bed, watching the crown of the baby as it slipped a little farther out into the world.

Knock-knock. 'I got the heater,' Adam called.

'Thank you. Now you can play with those toys.' She gave
him a minute to walk away before opening the door and bringing the heater in. Plugging it in, she switched it on and laid two
towels on top of the columns to warm for baby.

'Hello?' Marie yelled at someone on her phone. 'It's Marie,
Mark's wife. I can't get hold of him and I'm having our baby. I
need to talk to him.'

Ally held her hand up, whispered, 'Slow down, give the guy
a chance to say something.'

Marie glared at her but stopped shouting long enough to
hear a reply. 'Thank you so much. Can you hurry? Tell Mark
to phone back on the landline so I can put him on speaker.' A
moment later she tossed the phone aside, grabbed the edges of
the bed and pushed again.

The phone rang almost immediately. Ally answered, 'Hey,
is that Mark? This is Ally, Marie's midwife.'

'Hello, yes, this is Mark. What's up? Is she all right? The
baby's not due for weeks.'

'Marie's fine. You can be proud of how she's handling this.
Baby has decided today's as good as any to arrive.'

Marie snatched the phone out of her hand and yelled, 'Why aren't you here with me? I need you right now.' Then she had to drop it and clutch her belly.

Ally pressed the speaker button and Mark's voice filled the room. 'Hey, babe, you know I'd be there if I'd thought this would happen. How're you doing? Come on, babe, talk to me, tell me what's going on.'

'I'm having a baby, and it hurts like hell. It's nearly here and I can't talk any more. I've got to push.'

'Babe, I'm listening. Imagine me holding you against my chest like I did when you dislocated your shoulder. Feel my hands on your back, rubbing soft circles, whispering how much I love you in your cute little ear. Can you feel me there with you?'

Ally tried to block out this very personal conversation, pretend she was deaf, but those words of love touched her, taunted her. These two had a beautiful relationship. If Mark was a deep-sea fisherman, he was no softy, would definitely be a tough guy, and yet here he was speaking his heart to his wife when she needed him so much.

Marie cried out with pain, and pushed and pushed.

'Hey, babe, you're doing great. I know you are. You're a star. I'm not going anywhere until you have our little nipper in your arms, okay?'

Ally blinked back a tear and slipped out the door for a moment to get herself sorted. It wouldn't do for the midwife to have a meltdown in the middle of a birth. Not that that had ever happened but Marie's birth was affecting her deeply, more so than any other she'd attended. Leaning back against the wall, she took deep breaths to get her heart and head under control. *What was it like to have a man love you that much?* She could take a chance with a man like that. Even if she screwed up he'd be there to help her back onto her feet.

I want what Marie's got. Shivers ran through her and her skin lifted in goose-bumps. *No. I can't, don't, won't.*

Straightening up, she slapped away the tears and returned to her patient. Marie was still talking to Mark and didn't seem to notice her return. Had she seen her leave?

Then Marie was pushing again and this time there was no relief. Baby was coming and Ally prepared for it. 'The head's out. Here come the shoulders. That's it. Nice and gentle now.' She spoke louder so Mark could hear everything. Her hands were under the baby's head, ready for any sudden rush as the baby slid out into its new world. And then, 'Here he is, a beautiful boy. Oh, he's a sweetheart.'

Her heart stuttered. She'd called Adam a sweetheart earlier. It was one thing to say that about a baby she wouldn't be seeing much of, but Adam? He was wriggling into her heart without trying and soon she'd have to say goodbye.

'Can I hold him?' Marie asked impatiently, reaching out.

'In a moment. The APGAR score's normal.' Ally gently wiped away vernix, mucus and blood spots from his sweet little face.

'Give him to me, give him to me. Mark, we've got a boy. He's gorgeous. Looks like his dad.'

Ally rolled her eyes as she placed the baby on Marie's swollen breasts. 'I need him back in a moment to weigh him.'

Mark was yelling out to his crewmates, 'It's a boy. I'm a dad.' And then he was crying. 'Wish I was with you, babe. Tell me everything, every last detail. Are we still going to name him Jacob?'

'Well, I can't name him after our midwife so I guess so. I think it suits him.' Marie was laughing and crying and drinking in the sight of her son lying over her breast.

'Here comes the placenta.' Ally clamped it and cut the cord. 'I need to examine you once more, then I'll cover you up and let you talk to Mark alone for a bit.' Adam would be getting lonely out in the lounge. She'd make him a bite to eat, poor kid.

Her examination showed a small tear. 'You need a couple of stitches. Nothing major,' she added when worry entered Marie's eyes. 'It often happens in fast deliveries.'

'Right.' Marie went back to talking to Mark, the worry gone already.

Ally quietly went about retaking Jacob's APGAR score. His appearance and complexion were good. Counting his pulse, she tried not to listen in to the conversation going on between Jacob's parents, concentrating on the sweet bundle of new life. Her heart swelled even as a snag of envy caught her again. She could have it all if only she found the right man. Flynn instantly popped up in her head. Losing count, she started taking Jacob's pulse again, this time totally concentrating and pushing a certain someone out of her skull.

'Pulse one hundred and ten. Good.' She flicked lightly on Jacob's fingers, watched as he immediately curled them tight. 'Reflex good, as is his activity.' His little legs were moving slowly against his mother's skin, and she couldn't resist running a finger down one leg. He hadn't done more than give a low gasp but his chest was rising and falling softly. So his respiratory effort was okay. Ally wrote down her obs and then dealt with the tear while Marie carried on talking.

She found Adam in the lounge, despondently pushing a wooden bulldozer around the floor. He leapt up the instant he saw her with the rubbish bag. 'Ally, has the baby come?'

'Yes, and it's a little boy.'

Adam stared up at her. 'Can I see him now?'

'I can't see why not.' She took his hand and walked down to Marie's room, saying to the new mum, 'You've got your first visitor.' And then her heart squeezed.

Marie was cuddling her precious bundle and trying to put him on the breast. 'I hope Jacob takes to this easily.'

'Don't rush. It takes time to get the hang of it.' She went to help position Jacob.

Marie smiled down at her boy. Then looked up. 'Hello, Adam, want to see Jacob? Come round the bed so you can see his face. Isn't he beautiful?'

'Can I hold him?' Adam hopped from foot to foot and Ally saw the hesitancy in Marie's expression.

'Not today. He's all soft and needs careful holding. But tomorrow you can. He'll be stronger then.'

Adam stood close to Marie and stared at the baby. Slowly he placed one hand very carefully on his tiny arm and stroked it. His mouth widened into a smile. 'Hello, baby.'

Ally's eyes watered up. She'd never forget this moment. Adam's amazement, Marie's love, Jacob so tiny and cute. She'd seen it before, often, but today it was definitely different. Not because she'd begun to see herself in Marie's place, holding her own precious bundle of joy. Definitely not because of that.

She stood there, unable to take her gaze away from the scene, unable to move across to the towels that needed to be put into a bag for the laundry company. Just absorbing everything, as though it was her first delivery. The incredible sense of having been a part of a miracle swamped her. *Could I do this? Give birth myself?* Having a baby wasn't the issue. She'd be fine with that. But everything after the moment she held that baby in her arms—that was the problem. Did she have mothering instincts? Or had she inherited her mother's total lack of interest when it came to her own child, her own flesh and blood?

She couldn't afford to find out. It wouldn't be fair on her baby if she got it wrong.

'Marie, you certainly don't waste time when you decide you're ready to have your baby.' Flynn strode into the room and came to an abrupt halt. 'Adam, what are you doing in here?'

CHAPTER TEN

'DAD!' ADAM JUMPED up and down. 'Marie's got a new baby. I think it hurt her.'

'What?' Flynn spun around, his face horrified, and demanded, 'How does he know that?'

Ally stepped up to him. 'Adam did not see the birth, if that's what you're thinking.'

'Then explain his comment.'

Ally backed away from the anger glittering at her. 'He asked why he couldn't come in here and I said that having a baby is private and sometimes it hurts a little.' She had not done anything wrong.

Marie was staring at Flynn like she'd never met him before. 'For goodness' sake. Do you think either of us would've allowed him in here while I was giving birth? Seriously?'

Flynn shoved a hand through his hair, mussing it up, except this time that didn't turn Ally on one little bit. 'I guess not.'

'Dad, I helped Ally. I got water and the heater.'

Flynn's mouth tightened.

Ally told him, 'Adam left everything outside the door. The closed door.' Why can't he see the pride shining in his son's eyes? She ran a hand over Adam's head. 'My little helper.'

Flynn flinched. 'Sorry for jumping to conclusions, everyone.' He was starting to look a little guilty. 'I never did do anything about making alternative arrangements for this eventuality.' He gave Marie a rueful smile. 'Now can I meet Jacob?'

Reluctantly Marie handed the baby over. 'Only for a minute. I don't like letting him out of my arms.'

Ally watched Flynn's face soften as he peered into the soft blue blanket with its precious bundle, and felt her heart lurch so hard it hurt. There was so much love and wonder in his expression she knew he was seeing Adam the day he'd been born. It was a timely reminder that she didn't have a place in his life.

Spinning around, she shoved the baby's notes at Marie. 'I'll make that coffee I promised.' Like when?

Marie was quick, grabbing her hand to stop her tearing out of the room. Her eyes were full of understanding. 'White with two sugars.' She nodded and let Ally go.

Thank you for not outing me.

Flynn was oblivious anyway, so engrossed in Jacob that it was as though no one else was in the room.

When she returned with three coffees he was reading the notes and only grunted, 'Thanks,' at her. Guess he'd finally worked out where his loyalties truly lay, and they weren't with her.

Ally asked Marie, 'Is there anything you want me to do? Washing? Get some groceries in?'

Flynn answered before Marie could open her mouth. 'No need. Marie's mother will be here soon.'

Marie gaped at him. 'Tell me you didn't phone her.'

Colour crept into Flynn's cheeks and another dash of guilt lowered his eyebrows and darkened his eyes. He was having a bad afternoon. 'With Mark at sea for another week, you need someone here. Who better than your mother?'

'You know the answer to that,' Marie growled. 'Ring her back and tell her to turn around.'

'You don't think this is an opportune time to kiss and make up?' Flynn asked. 'Estelle sounded very excited about the new baby.'

Ally looked from Marie to Flynn. What was going on here? They knew each other well, but for Flynn to be telling Marie to sort her apparent problem with her mother could be stretching things too far. Time for a break from him. Taking Adam's hand, she said, 'Come on, let's get you some food. I bet your tummy's hungry.'

'It's always hungry.'

She glanced at Flynn as she reached the door and tripped. He was staring at her with disappointment in his eyes. 'What?' she demanded in a high-pitched voice.

He shook his head. 'Nothing.'

Hadn't she been telling herself what she and Flynn had going was only a short-term fling? If she needed proof, here it was.

In the kitchen Ally put together enough sandwiches for everyone. She got out plates and placed the food on them. Next she put the kettle on to make hot drinks all round. All the while she was trying to ignore that look she'd seen in Flynn's eyes.

Adam chomped through two sandwiches in record time.

'Slow down or you'll get a tummyache.'

'No, I won't. My tummy's strong.' He banged his glass on the table.

Ally smiled tiredly at the ring of milk around his mouth and ignored the tug at her heart. 'Wipe your face, you grub.'

Flynn strode into the kitchen and picked up one of the sandwiches, munched thoughtfully.

'Dad, can I see the baby again?'

'Of course you can. But be very careful if you touch him. He's only little.' Flynn watched his son run down the hall, a distant gleam in his eyes making Ally wonder what he was thinking. When Adam disappeared into Marie's room he closed the kitchen door and she found out. 'Marie's very happy with how you handled the birth. Said you were calm and reassuring all the time.'

'I'm a midwife, that's what we do. It's in the job description.'

'What I don't condone is my son's presence in the house at

the time. He shouldn't have been with Marie from the moment she went into labour. Why couldn't you have gone next door to see if Mrs James could look after him?'

'One, there wasn't a lot of time. Two, as I don't know Mrs James, I'm hardly going to leave a small boy with her. Your small boy at that. You could've arranged for someone to come and collect him. You did get my message?' Two could play this game.

'Why didn't you get Megan to arrange someone?'

'It's not my place to make demands of your receptionist.'

Flynn didn't flinch. 'What was Adam doing while you were occupied with Marie? You weren't keeping a proper eye on him, were you?'

'You know what? Adam isn't my responsibility.' She was repeating herself, but somehow she had to get through that thick skull. Except she suspected she was wasting her time. Maybe shouting at him might make him listen. But as she opened her mouth her annoyance faded. She didn't want to fight with him.

'But you were here. You could've taken a few moments to find a solution. Marie's baby wasn't going to arrive that quickly.'

Maybe he had a point, and she had made a mistake. 'I'm sorry. I got here as soon as I could after Marie phoned to say she'd gone into labour. Everything was hectic and Adam was happy watching TV.' But she should've thought more about Adam. Just went to show how unmotherly her instincts were. 'I did my best in the situation. I explained to Adam what was happening and he was happy to bring towels and water to leave outside the bedroom door. Not once did he see anything he shouldn't.'

'He's a little boy.' Flynn wasn't accepting her explanation. 'He'd have heard her cries and groans. It's not a massive house.'

'He was safe. I didn't put him in a position where he'd be scared, and I honestly don't think he was.' Her guilt increased. She should've thought more about Adam's age, should've tried harder to find a solution. He might've heard things a young child was better off not hearing. What if he had nightmares about it? But he'd been excited to see Jacob, not frightened of the baby or Marie. But there was no denying she'd got it wrong. Apparently she should've seen to Adam before Marie.

Ally shivered. Forget thinking she might have her own baby. She wasn't mother material. Having never had the parental guidance that would've made her see how she should've cared for Adam had shown through this afternoon. One thing was for sure, she wouldn't be any better with her own.

At least she could be thankful that she'd had a reminder of that now and not after she'd given in to the yearning for her own baby that had begun growing inside her. She would not have her own children. That was final. She squashed that hope back where it belonged—in the dark, deep recesses of her mind, hopefully to stay there until she was too old to conceive.

Flynn waited until Marie's mother arrived before he took Adam home. *Talk about being a spare wheel.* Ally and Marie talked and laughed a lot, getting on so well it reminded him of Anna with Marie. Ally had fussed over the baby while his mum had taken a shower, but handed Jacob back the moment Marie returned to her bedroom. She hadn't been able to entirely hide the longing in her eyes.

Flynn had tried to deny the distress he'd seen in Ally's face earlier. The distress that had changed to bewilderment and lastly guilt—brought on by him. The guilt had still been there whenever she'd looked at him, which was probably why she'd kept her head turned away as much as possible. He'd become the outsider in that house. Marie and Jacob and Adam had got all her attention. And he'd hated that. So he'd taken Adam and left. *Like a spoilt child.*

Now at home he swore—silently so Adam didn't pick up any words he'd then be told off for using. Then he deliberately focused on his son and not the woman who had his gut in a knot and his head spinning. He really tried. *Adam, my boy. I love you so much I'm being overprotective. But that's better than not caring.*

If ever there was a woman he could've expected to look out for Adam it was Ally. Not to mention Marie. He'd seen that stunned look on Marie's face when he'd given Ally a hard time. Of course Marie would know how unusual it was for him to lose his cool.

He cracked an egg and broke the yolk. 'Guess that means scrambled eggs and not poached.' He found a glass jug and put the pan away. Broke in some more eggs, whisked them into a froth and added a dash of milk. 'Adam, want to put the toast on?'

'Okay, Dad.' His boy stood on tiptoe at the pantry, reaching for the bread. 'Why isn't Ally sleeping over?'

Because your father's been a fool. 'She's tired after helping Jacob be born.'

'I like Jacob.'

Adam sounded perfectly happy, as if being around while a birth was going on was normal. And why wouldn't it be? Ally had made sure Adam wasn't affected by seeing anything untoward.

Flynn put the eggs into the microwave. *Ally, I'm so sorry for my rant. It was my responsibility to look out for my son, not yours, or anyone else's.* Ever since Anna's death he'd been determined to be the best dad he could to make up for Adam not having a mother. Hell, that's why they lived on the island and he did the job he did. Yet today he'd been quick to lay the blame right at Ally's feet for something that bothered him.

Sheba rubbed her nose against his thigh and he reached down to scratch behind her ears. 'Hey, girl, I've made a mess of things.' Picking up his phone, he punched in Ally's number. His call went straight to voice mail. 'Ally, it's Flynn. I'd like to talk to you tonight if you have a moment.'

But he knew that unless she was more forgiving than he deserved, she wouldn't call. Action was required.

'Adam, want to go and see Ally?'

The shout of 'Yes!' had him turning the microwave off and picking up his keys. 'Let's go.'

Despite the absence of the car in Kat's drive, Flynn still knocked on the front door and called out. 'Ally? Open up.'

Adam hopped out and added his entreaties but Ally wasn't answering.

Flynn doubted she'd be hiding behind the curtains. That wasn't her style. Ally wasn't at home.

Back on the road Flynn headed to town to cruise past the restaurants and cafés. 'There.' He pointed to a car parked outside the Chinese takeaway and diner.

'Yippee, we found her.' Adam was out of the car before Flynn had the handbrake on.

'Wait, Adam.' Though Ally was less likely to turn away from his son, he had to do this right or there'd be no more nights with her in his bed, or meals at Giuseppe's, or walks on the beach. *There aren't going to be many more anyway. She leaves at the end of next week.* He wouldn't think about that.

She sat in a corner, looking glum as she nodded her head to whatever music was playing through her earphones.

'Ally, we came to see you.'

Her head shot up when Adam tapped her hand. 'Hey.' She smiled directly at his son. 'Are you here for dinner?' Did she have to look as though she really hoped they weren't?

Flynn answered, 'Only if it's all right with you.'

Her eyes met his. No smile for him as she shrugged. 'I only need one table.'

'We'd like to share this one with you.' He held his breath.

Adam wasn't into finesse. He pulled out a chair and sat down. 'What can I have to eat, Dad?'

Flynn didn't take his gaze off Ally, saw her mouth soften as she glanced at his son. He said, 'I apologise for earlier. I was completely out of line.'

She didn't come close to smiling. 'Really?' Her gaze returned to him.

He took a chance and pulled out another chair. 'Really. I should've had something in place for today—for whatever day Marie had her baby. Adam is my responsibility, no one else's. It's been on my list to arrange another sitter but I never got around to it.' Much to his chagrin. He twisted the salt shaker back and forth between his fingers. 'I was angry for stuffing up, and I took it out on you. I apologise for everything I said.'

Ally pushed the menu across the table, a glimmer of a smile on her lips. 'I only ordered five minutes ago.'

That meant she accepted his apology, right? 'Adam, do you want fried rice with chicken?'

'Yes. Ally, are you coming for another sleepover tonight?'

Flynn's stomach tightened. *Too soon, my boy. Too soon. We need to have dinner and talk a bit before asking that.*

Ally shook her head. 'Not tonight. I need to do some washing and stuff.' She was looking at Adam, but Flynn knew she was talking to him.

Two steps forward, one back.

She hadn't finished. 'Besides, I'm always extra-tired after a delivery and need to spend time thinking about it all.' Her voice became melancholy, like she was unhappy about a bigger issue and not just about what he'd dumped on her earlier.

He gave the order to the woman hovering at his elbow and turned to lock eyes with Ally. 'What's up?' How could he have been so stupid as to rant at her? Now she wasn't staying the night, and who knew when she'd be back at his house, in his bed? Actually, he'd love nothing more than to sit down with a coffee or wine and try some plain old talking, getting to know each other better stuff. When she didn't answer he continued, 'What does a birth make you think about?'

'Everything and nothing. That whole wonderful process and a beautiful baby at the end of it. Like I told you the other day, I find it breathtakingly magical.' Her finger was picking at a spot on the tabletop. 'Yet I'm the observer, always wondering what's ahead for this new little person.'

'Do you want to have children someday?' Didn't most people?

The finger stopped. Ally lifted her head and looked around the diner, finally bringing her gaze back to him. 'No.'

'You'd be a great mother.'

Silence fell between them, broken only when Ally's meal arrived. But she didn't get stuck in, instead played with the rice, stirring and pushing it around the plate with her fork.

Adam asked, 'Where's my dinner?'

Flynn dragged his eyes away from Ally and answered. 'We ordered after Ally so it will be a few more minutes.'

Ally slid her plate across to Adam. 'Here, you have this one. It's the same as what you ordered.'

'You sound very certain—about no children of your own,' Flynn ventured.

'I am.'

'That's sad.'

'Believe me, it's not. If I'd had a child, that would be sad. Bad. Horrible.' The words fell off her trembling lips.

He couldn't help himself. He took her hand in his and was astonished to feel her skin so cold. 'Tell me.'

'I already did.' She'd found a point beyond his shoulder to focus on.

While he wished they were at home in the comfort and privacy of his lounge, he kept rubbing her hand with his thumb, urging her silently to enlighten him, let out what seemed to be chewing her up from the inside. 'Only that you were abandoned. Doesn't that make you determined to show yourself how good you'd be?'

Their meals arrived and they both ignored them.

'My mother didn't want me. I grew up in the welfare system. Moved from house to house, family to family, until I was old enough to go it alone.' Her flat monotone told him more than the words, though they were horrifying enough.

'Your father?'

'Probably never learned of my existence—if my mother even knew who he was.'

'You know,' Flynn said gently, 'your mother may have done what she did because she *did* love you. If she wasn't in a safe situation, or wasn't able to cope, it might have been that giving you up was her way of protecting you. Haven't you ever worked with women in that position?'

'Yes,' Ally admitted slowly. 'But if it was love, it didn't feel much like it to me.'

Flynn hated to think of Ally as a kid, adrift in the foster-care system without a steady and loving upbringing. It wasn't like that in all cases, he reminded himself. Anna's brother and sister-in-law had two foster-children that they loved as much as their own three. But look at Ally. Adorable, gorgeous, kind and caring. What's not to love about her? Was that his problem? Had he fallen for her? Nah, couldn't have. They'd only known each other a little more than two weeks. Hardly time to fall in love, especially when they knew nothing about each other. Except now he did know more about Ally than he would ever have guessed. And he wanted more. He could help her, bring her true potential to the fore.

Ally tugged her hand free, picked up her fork. 'See? You're speechless. It's shocking, but that's who I am, where I come from, what I'll always be. Now you know. You were right. I shouldn't have been in charge of Adam, even if by proxy. I know nothing about parenting.'

No. No way. Flynn grabbed both her hands, fork and all. 'Don't say that. I'd leave Adam with you any day or night. Today was me being precious. Since Marie and I are friends, I felt a little left out. Plain stupid, really.'

Ally tried to pull free, but he tightened his grip.

Finally she locked the saddest eyes he'd ever seen on him. 'Are we a messed-up pair, or what?' she whispered.

I'm not messed up. I get stuff wrong, but I think I've done well in moving on from Anna's death and raising our son.

'I am determined to do my absolute best for Adam, in everything.'

'You're doing that in spades.'

'So why do I feel guilty all the time?'

Her brow furrowed. 'About what?'

About Adam not having his mother in his life. 'I try to raise him as his mother wanted.' This was getting too deep. He aimed for a lighter tone. 'Eating raw vegetables every day and never having a sweet treat is too hard even for me, and I'm supposed to make Adam stick to that.' *But it isn't always what I want, or how I'd bring my boy up.*

Her fingers curled around his hands. 'That's not realistic. Even if you succeed at home, the world is full of people eating lollies and ice cream, roast vegetables and cheese sauces.' At last her eyes lightened and her mouth finally curved into a delicious smile that melted the cold inside him.

The smile he looked for every day at work, at night in his house. 'Like Danish pastries, you mean.'

'You've got it.' Her shoulders lifted as she straightened her back. Digging her fork into her rice, she hesitated. 'I haven't known you very long, but it's obvious how committed you are to your son, and how much you love him. Believe me, those are the most important things you can give him.'

Said someone who knew what it was like to grow up without either of those important things. He answered around a blockage in his throat, 'Thank you. Being a solo dad isn't always a level road. Scary at times.'

'It's probably like that when there are two parents. Come on, let's eat. I'm suddenly very hungry.'

'Something you and Adam have in common. You're always hungry.' The last hour being the exception.

She grinned around a mouthful of chicken and rice.

His stomach knotted. He loved that grin. It was warm and funny. But now he understood she used it to hide a lot of hurt. Hard to imagine her childhood when he'd grown up in what he'd always thought of as a normal family. Mum, Dad and his brothers. No one deliberately hurt anyone or was ungrateful for anything. Everyone backed each other in any endeavours. When Anna had died he'd been swamped with his family and their loving support to the point he'd finally had to ask them to get back to their own lives and let him try to work out his new one.

'Dad, can I have ice cream for pudding?'

Ally smirked around her mouthful.

'Gloating doesn't suit you.' He laughed. 'Yes, Adam, you can. Ask that lady behind the counter for some while Ally and I finish our dinner.'

As Adam sped across the diner, probably afraid he'd be called back and told to forget that idea, Flynn watched him with a hitch in his chest and a sense that maybe he was getting this parenting stuff right after all.

'Good answer,' said Ally.

'Would you change your mind about a sleepover?' Might as well go for broke. After being so angry with Ally, then getting the guilts, all he wanted now was some cuddle time. Yeah, okay, and maybe something hotter later. But seriously? He wanted to be with Ally, sex or no sex.

Her smile stayed in place. 'I meant it when I said I get exhausted after a delivery. And I do like to think it all through, go over everything again.'

Huge disappointment clenched his gut but he wouldn't pressure her. 'Fair enough. But if you decide you need a shoulder to put your head on during the night, you know where to find me.' Huh? What happened to no pressure? 'If you want company without the perks, I mean.' He smiled to show he meant exactly what he'd said, and got a big one in return.

'You have no idea how much that means to me. But this is how I deal with my work. I'm not used to dumping my thoughts on anyone else.'

'You should try it. You might find it cathartic.' Next he'd be begging. 'Tell me to shut up if you like.'

She took his hands in hers, and this time her skin was warm. Comfort warm, friendly warm. 'I'm not used to being with a man every night of the week. I'm used to my own company and like my own space. Don't take it personally, it's just the way I am.'

Sounded awfully lonely to him. 'I'll cook you dinner tomorrow night.' When would he learn to zip his mouth shut? 'If you'd like that.'

'It's a date. I'll bring dessert. Something Adam will love.'

'You're corrupting my kid now?'

'You'd better believe it.'

CHAPTER ELEVEN

'YOU LOOK WORSE than the chewed-up mess my cat dragged in this morning,' Megan greeted Ally the next morning when she walked into the surgery. 'Not a lot of sleep going on in your bed?'

'No. I tossed and turned for hours.'

'Haven't heard it called tossing and turning before, though I see the resemblance.' Megan laughed.

'Trust me, I was very much alone. Is everyone here yet?' Was Flynn here? He mightn't have kept her awake in the flesh, but she'd spent hours thinking about him. Hours and hours. Nothing like her usual night after a birth.

'I think they're all in the tearoom.'

Ally looked at the list of her appointments for the morning. 'At least there's no chance of falling asleep at my desk with all these women to visit.'

In the tearoom a large coffee from her favourite coffee shop was set at what had become her place. 'Thanks,' she muttered, as Flynn nodded to her. He was the only one in there.

'I was out early visiting Marie and Jacob so Adam and I had breakfast at the café.'

Ally chuckled. 'Now who's spoiling him?' Then wished the words back as his smile dipped. 'Spoiling's good. Who's looking after Adam today?'

'A friend on the other side of the island. She's had him before when Marie needed to go somewhere little boys weren't welcome.' Flynn pulled her chair out.

Sinking onto it, she lifted the lid on her coffee and tentatively sipped the steaming liquid. 'That's so good. Caffeine's just what I need. If I hadn't been running late I'd have stopped for one myself.' So Flynn had lots of friends he could call on. Lucky man. But friends also meant staying in touch, being there when needed, opening up about things best left shut off. *Has he changed how he feels about me now that he knows the truth?* 'Is Adam happy to go to this lady?'

'Absolutely. He gets to take Sheba so they can go for walks in the park with Gina's two spaniels.'

Cosy. Did the woman have a husband? *Down, green monster, down. You have no right poking your head up.* So far her night-time lectures to herself about falling in love with a man who was out of reach didn't seem to have sunk in. Slow learner. *Flynn is totally committed to Adam and his job. There is no room for you in his life.* She repeated what she'd said over and over throughout the night. And again it didn't make a blind bit of difference. Try, *There's no room for Flynn and Adam in your life. They live in the same place every day of the year. You move somewhere new so often you're like a spinning top.*

'Morning, Ally.' Faye strolled into the room. 'I hear Marie's baby arrived in a bit of a hurry.'

'He sure did. And he's absolutely gorgeous.' She couldn't wait to visit this morning.

'Humph. Babies are all the same to me. Cry and poo in their nappies a lot. Very uninteresting at that age.'

Ally blinked. Had she heard right? 'You haven't had your own children?' All babies were beautiful, even if some were more so than others.

'Got three of the blighters. Love each and every one, but that doesn't mean I thought they were cute when they arrived.'

What a strange lady. But at least she was there for her kids and probably did a lot with them. 'How was Marie this morning?' She looked at Flynn.

'Arguing with her mother about who was bathing Jacob.' He grinned like he'd been naughty. Which he had. If not for him Marie's mother wouldn't be there. 'But at least they're talking, which is a vast improvement.'

Jerome joined them and the meeting got under way. Thankfully it was short as Ally was itching to get on the road and go visiting patients, to get away from that distracting smile of Flynn's. As she headed to the door and her car, he called, 'You still on for tonight?'

'I'm buying the dessert after my house calls.' She shouldn't join him for the whole night, but she couldn't resist. This had been a fling like no other she'd ever had. This time she dreaded finishing it and heading away. Not that she wanted to stay put on Phillip Island for however long the fling took to run its course either. But there was this feeling of so much more to be done, to share with Flynn, to enjoy with his son.

For the first time in her adult life she didn't want to move on. For the first time ever a person had got under her skin, warmed her heart in a way it had never been warmed. It made her long for the impossible—a family she could truly call her own.

She should've said no, that she'd be staying home to wash her hair.

But there was no denying the liquid heat pouring through her body just at the thought of a night with Flynn. So—how could she leave next week without shattering her heart?

It's too late. Might as well grab every moment going. It'd be silly to go through the rest of my time here staying in the flat, being miserable. Miserable would come—later, back on the mainland.

'Chocolate Bavarian pie.' Ally placed the box she'd bought in the supermarket on Flynn's bench. 'It's defrosted and ready to go.' She bent down to scratch Sheba's ears. 'Hey, girl, how're you doing? Recovered from that run yet?'

Lick, lick. Yes or no? Sheba had struggled a bit as they'd loped along the beach early yesterday morning.

Flynn slid a glass of red wine in her direction. 'Merlot tonight. Goes with the sausages I'm cooking.' He grinned that cheeky grin that got to her every time. 'They're beef.'

'Beef and red wine. A perfect combination,' she said with her tongue firmly in her cheek. That navy striped shirt he wore with the top button open to show a delectable V of chest was also perfect. Just enough visible chest to tantalise and heat her up in places that only Flynn seemed able to scorch. She winked. 'What time does Adam go to bed on Fridays?'

'Half past nine,' Flynn told her, straight-faced.

She spluttered into her glass. 'Half past nine? You've got to be kidding me.' Three hours before she could get her hands on the skin under that shirt? She'd combust with heat.

'Yep, I am.' Then he grinned again. 'You're so easy to wind up.'

'Phew. For a moment there I thought I'd have to lock him in the lounge with Sheba and race you down the hall for a quickie.'

Desire matching hers flicked into his eyes. 'Now, there's a thought.'

This banter she could do. It was easy and fun and how flings were run. 'Guess I'd better stick to wine for now.'

'We're invited to Jerome's tomorrow night for an indoor barbecue, along with the rest of the staff. But he specifically asked us as a couple.'

The air leaked out of her lungs. This might be something she couldn't do. It hinted at something more than a casual relationship, like a date involving his colleagues and friends. Colleagues and friends who'd read more into the situation than was there. Was Jerome playing matchmaker? 'That's nice.' Well, it would be under other circumstances.

'You're not happy?'

She shrugged. 'I'm sure it will be fun, but maybe I'll give it a miss.'

A furrow appeared between his eyes. 'I accepted for both of us.'

'Then you'll have to *un*accept.' What had happened to consulting her first?

'Why? You've been working with everyone for three weeks so what's the big deal?' Then that furrow softened. 'I get it. The *couple* word. That's what's got your knickers in a twist, isn't it?'

'So what if it has? We're not a couple. Not in the true sense. We're having an affair. Next weekend it will be over. How do you face your colleagues then, if they're thinking we've got something more serious going on?'

How do I look Megan in the eye next week and say of course we're only friends. Even friends with benefits doesn't cover it. I'm falling for you and I need to be pulling back, not stepping into a deeper mire.

'Ally, relax. Everyone's aware you're moving on and I'm staying put. Jerome thought it would be more comfortable for you to go with me as there will be others there you haven't met. That's all there is to it.'

'You're ignoring that *couple* word.' Didn't it bother him? Because he was so comfortable in his life that he thought it ludicrous to even consider he was in a relationship?

Flynn set his glass carefully on the bench and ran his fingertip over her lips. 'Sure I am. It was the wrong word to use. We've spent a lot of time together since you turned up on the beach that first day. You've given me something special, and I'm going to miss you, but we've both known right from that first kiss that whatever we have between us would never be long-term. I don't care what anyone else thinks. It's no one's business.'

Where was the relief when she needed it? Flynn had saved her a lot of hassle by saying what they had going was a short-term thing. But the reality hurt. A lot. In her tummy, especially in her heart. Her head said the best thing for everyone was that she'd be leaving. Her heart said she should stay and see if she could make a go of a relationship with Flynn and his son.

'Ally? Would you please come to the barbecue with me as my partner for the night?' When she didn't answer he added, 'People know we've been seeing each other—going out for meals, taking Adam to the beach and other places. It's not as though this is going to be a shock for them or the source of any gossip.' He drew a breath and continued. 'I want this last week with you.' His smile was soft and yet determined. It arrowed right into her chest, stabbed her heart.

And made everything even more complicated.

How could she say no when she wanted it, too? In the end it was Flynn who'd be left to face any gossip. In the end it would be agony to leave him whether she went out with him again or not. She had to grab whatever she could and stack up the memories for later. 'I'd love to go with you,' she said quietly.

The days were flying by and Ally was withdrawing from him. Flynn hated it. Sure, she still came home with him for the night, but there seemed to be a barrier growing up between her and them as a twosome. She'd already begun moving on in her mind. There, he'd said it. He'd started denying the fact she would be leaving soon, even when it was there in black and white on the noticeboard in this office. Kat would return home on Friday—tomorrow. She'd take over the reins on Saturday and Ally would leave the island and head for her next job. He knew all that. He'd signed the contract with Ally's employers.

But knowing and facing up to what her leaving truly meant were entirely different. He refused to admit the other half of his bed would be cold and empty again. Wouldn't contemplate sitting down to an evening meal with only Adam for company. Daren't think how he'd fill in the weekends without her laughter and eagerness for fun pulling him along.

'That needs photocopying so the hospital in Melbourne have

records.' Ally dropped a file beside Megan. 'Hey, Flynn, got a minute?'

'Of course.' *Always got hours for you.* Had he been hasty in thinking she was putting space between them? Did she have a plan for what they might do on her last nights?

'I'm concerned about Chrissie.'

So much for plans and hot farewells. 'Come into my office.' He nodded at the patients sitting in the waiting room.

Ally got the message. 'Sure.' The moment she stepped inside his room she spun to face him. 'Chrissie's doing great physically. But she's got attached to me already and that's not good. She says she doesn't want to see Kat.'

'Strange. Kat gets on with everyone.' Like Ally. 'Did she give a reason?'

'Something about Kat's sister and Chrissie being rivals at school.' Ally shrugged those shoulders he'd spent a long time kissing last night. 'I was wondering if you could see her, maybe talk sense into her. I've explained that Kat would never tell her sister a single thing about the pregnancy, but Chrissie's not wearing it.'

'I'll talk to Chrissie, maybe with Angela there.' But he wondered how much of this had to do with Kat and how much was due to the way Chrissie had taken to Ally. 'You handled the situation very tactfully and sympathetically at a time when Chrissie was beside herself with worry. This could be about her not wanting you to leave.' He didn't want her going. Adam wouldn't, either.

A soft sigh crossed Ally's lips. 'There's not much I can do about that. I am going.'

'I know.' All too well. 'Do you ever get tired of moving on?'

Her eyes met his and she seemed to draw a breath before answering. 'No. It's how I live and there's a certain simplicity to not owning a house or a truckload of furniture or even a carful of clothes.' She looked away.

Flynn couldn't read her. He wanted to know if she felt sad

about leaving him, or happy about another job done and their affair coming to an end. But as he started to ask his heart knocked so hard against his ribs he gasped. *I love her. I love Ally Parker. I'm not wondering any more. I know.* Asking her about her feelings just became impossible. She might ask some questions in return, questions he still wasn't ready to answer.

So he continued to study her while not being able to lock gazes with her, and he thought he saw no regret in her stance, her face or her big eyes. So Ally hadn't come to love him in the way he had her. Pain filled him, blurred his vision for a moment. Rocked him to the core. How could he have fallen in love with Ally? He'd never believed he'd love again, and yet it only taken a few short weeks. Had it happened that first day when Sheba had dumped her on the beach?

Ally's soft voice cut through his mind like a well-honed blade. 'I'd better get a move on. I'm going to weigh Jacob this morning.'

He watched her retreating back, his hands curled into fists to stop from reaching after her. So much for thinking she might reciprocate his feelings. It wasn't going to be at all difficult for her to walk away.

Ally stayed in the shower until she heard Flynn and Adam leave for their walk on the beach with Sheba. She'd cried off, saying she had a headache. That was no lie. Behind her eyes her skull pounded like a bongo drum. Her hands trembled as she towelled herself dry. Her knees knocked as she tried to haul her jeans up her legs. It was Saturday.

'Goodbye, Flynn.' She hiccupped around the solid lump of pain in her throat. 'Bye-bye, Adam. Be a good boy for your dad.' *I will not cry. I don't cry. Ever.*

Reaching out blindly, she snatched a handful of tissues and blew her nose hard, scrubbed at her eyes. One glance at her hands and she knew it'd be a waste of time trying to apply make-up. 'Go plain Jane today.' What did it matter anyway? It wasn't as though she'd be seeing Flynn.

Tears threatened and she took as deep a breath as possible. 'Suck it up, be tough, get through the day. Tomorrow will look a whole heap better.'

Now she'd taken to lying to herself. But if it got her out of the house and on the road before Flynn and Adam returned, then it was the right thing to do.

Yesterday she'd packed up her few possessions and the bags sat in the boot of the medical centre's car. The key to Kat's flat was back under the flowerpot on the top step, her contact details written on a pad inside in case she'd left anything behind. Now all she had to do was drive to the surgery to dump the car and be on her way.

But she turned the car in the direction of Marie's house. 'One last cuddle with Jacob.' So much for leaving unobtrusively. But she couldn't bring herself to turn away yet.

Marie opened her front door before Ally had time to knock. 'Hey, you're out and about early.'

'Yeah, thought I'd see everything's okay with you.'

'Come in. Want a coffee?' Marie headed for the kitchen. 'Jacob's just gone down.'

'Then I probably should carry on.'

There was already a mug of steaming coffee on the bench and Marie poured another without waiting to see if Ally wanted it. 'We had a good night. Jacob only woke four times.' She grinned.

'How do you manage to look so good after that?' Ally paced back and forth.

'Mark's coming home today.' Marie slid the mug in Ally's direction. 'Excuse me for being blunt but *you* look terrible. What's up?'

'Nothing.' She tried to shrug, but her shoulders were too heavy.

'Ally, I don't know you well, but something's not right. Has Flynn done something wrong?'

'No. Not at all.' She'd gone and fallen in love with him, but that didn't make him a bad man. She was the fool.

'Good, I'd have been surprised. He thinks the world of you and would do anything for you. Apart from that hiccup the day Jacob was born.'

Coming here had been a mistake. 'I'd better go. I've to be somewhere. Thanks for the coffee.' Which she hadn't even tried. 'I'll see myself out.'

'Don't go,' Marie called.

Ally shut the door behind herself and ran to the car.

A taxi dropped her off at the ferry terminal half an hour later. Once on board she found an empty seat out of the way of the happy hordes and pushed her earbuds in, turned up the music on her music player and pretended all was right with her world. Except it wasn't, as proved by the onset of deep sobs that began racking her body as the ferry pulled out. Her fingers dug into the palms of her hands and she squeezed her eyes tight against the cascade of tears.

Someone tapped her knee. 'Here. Have these.' An older woman sitting opposite handed her a pack of tissues.

'Th-thanks,' she managed, before the next wave of despair overtook her.

Flynn. I love you so much it's painful.

Flynn. What I wouldn't give to feel your arms around me one more time.

Flynn. I had to go. It wouldn't have worked.

For every wipe at her face more tears came, drenching the front of her jersey. 'I love you, Flynn Reynolds,' she whispered. Shudders racked her body from her shoulders all the way down to her feet.

This was terrible. The last time she'd cried when moving on had been the day she'd left her favourite foster-family—the Bartletts.

The woman opposite stirred. 'We're docking.'

Ally blew her nose and swiped her eyes once more, drew a breath and looked up. 'Thank you again.'

'You'll be all right?'

'Yes, of course.' Never again. With one last sniff she inched forward in the queue to disembark and headed for her real life; the one she'd worked hard to make happen and that now seemed lonely and cold.

Flynn felt a chill settle over him the moment he turned into his street. Ally's car was gone. Somehow he wasn't surprised but, damn it, he was hurt. How hard would it have been to say goodbye?

Spinning the steering wheel, he did an about-turn and headed for Kat's flat to say to Ally the goodbye she hadn't been willing to give him.

But it was Marie's car outside Kat's flat, not the one Ally had been using. As soon as Flynn pulled up Marie was at his window. 'Do you know where Ally's gone?'

'I hoped she'd be here.' He was too late.

'She came to my place about an hour ago. She was very upset. I tried to find out why, but she left again. In a hurry, at that. That's why I came around here.'

Flynn's mouth soured. Ally was upset? Why? *Did you want to stay on? With me? No, that was going too far.* 'I'd say she's on the ferry, heading home.' Except she didn't have a home to head to. Just a bed she borrowed on a daily basis.

'Flynn, what's going on? Why's Ally upset? As in looking like she was about to burst into tears?' Marie's voice rose.

Ally and tears didn't mix. He'd never seen her close to crying. *Duh.* There hadn't been any reason for it. His gut clenched. If Ally was crying, then he wanted to be with her, holding her, calming her down and helping sort whatever her problem was. 'She's finished her contract with us, but from what I've learned about her that wouldn't be the reason for her being unhappy.'

Marie clamped her hands on her hips. 'Unhappy? Broken-hearted more like. Downright miserable.' She stared at him. 'A little bit like how you're looking, only more so.'

'I look miserable? Broken-hearted?' Here he'd been thinking

he could hide his feelings. But, then, most people didn't know him as well as Marie did.

Marie's stance softened. 'You love her, don't you?'

Ouch. This might not go well, Anna having been Marie's best friend and all. 'You don't pull any punches, do you?'

'Have you told Ally?'

He shook his head.

'What's held you back? Anna? Because if that's the case, you have to let her go. The last thing Anna would've wanted would be for you to be on your own for the rest of your life.'

Flynn growled, 'Since when did you become my therapist?'

She smiled. 'Just being a good friend. So? Spill. Why haven't you talked to Ally about this?'

'All of the above. And Adam. I'm totally focused on giving him everything he needs in life and I don't know if there's room for Ally. But, yes, I love her, so I guess I'll be making space.' Over the past weeks he'd begun to feel comfortable living here, enjoying his work more. Without Ally, life wouldn't be as much fun.

'I hope you come up with a more romantic approach when you tell Ally all this.' Marie leaned in and brushed a kiss over his chin. 'Adam adores Ally, and vice versa. What's more, he needs a mother figure in his life. You're not so hot on the soft, womanly touch.'

'Thank goodness for that.' Flynn felt something give way deep inside and a flood of love and tenderness swamped him. *Ally, love, where are you?* 'She's afraid she isn't mother material.' When astonishment appeared on Marie's face, he hurried to add, 'She's a welfare kid, lived in the system all her childhood.'

'Oh, my God. Now I get it. She was running from you. She doesn't want to make things any worse for you.'

'Yep, and I let her go.' Actually, no, he hadn't. He'd fully expected Ally to be waiting when he and Adam had got back. He should've known better. If he hadn't diverted to the vet's to pick up dog shampoo, would he have been in time to see her before she'd left? 'Marie, thanks, you're a treasure. Now, go home to that baby of yours and tell your mother to leave before Mark gets here.'

'On my way. What are you going to do?'

'Adam and I are taking a trip.'

CHAPTER TWELVE

'THE COFFEE'S ON,' Darcie said as she buzzed Ally into the apartment building.

'Hope it's stronger than tar,' Ally muttered, as she waited for the lift that would take her to the penthouse. She was wiped out. All those tears and that emotional stuff had left her exhausted. No wonder she tried so hard not to get upset.

The apartment door stood wide open as Ally tripped along the carpet to her latest abode, and she felt a temporary safety from the outside world descend.

'Hey, how's things?' Darcie appeared around the corner, took one look at her face and said, 'Not good. Forget coffee. I think this calls for wine.'

A true friend. 'Isn't it a bit early? It's not quite eleven yet.'

'It's got to be afternoon somewhere in the world.'

Good answer. 'I'll dump my bags.' And dip my face under a cold tap. But when Ally looked into the bathroom's gilt-edged mirror she was horrified at the blotchy face staring back at her. 'Who are you?' she whispered.

Cold water made her feel a little more alive but no less sad. She found her make-up and applied a thick layer in a misguided attempt to hide some of the red stains on her cheeks. Quickly brushing her hair and tying it up in a ponytail, she went out to Darcie. 'Sorry about that. I needed to freshen up a bit.'

Darcie immediately handed her a glass of Sauvignon Blanc. 'Let's go out on the deck. The sun's a treat for this time of year.'

She followed, blanking out everything to do with Phillip Island and Flynn, instead trying to focus on what might've been going on at the midwifery centre while she'd been away. 'Tell me all the gossip. Who's gone out with who, who's leaving, or starting.'

Sitting in a cane chair, Darcie sipped her wine and chuckled. 'You won't believe what's happening.'

Ally sprawled out on the cane two-seater, soaked up the sun coming through the plate-glass windows, and tried to relax. Darcie was very understanding. She'd wait to be told what was going on in Ally's life. And if Ally never told her she wouldn't get the hump. A rare quality, that. Exactly what Ally needed right now. 'Great wine.' She raised her glass towards Darcie. 'Cheers.'

At some point Darcie got up and made toasted sandwiches and they carried on talking about the mundane.

It was the perfect antidote to the tumultuous emotions that had been gripping Ally all morning. There was nothing left in her tanks. She'd given it all on Phillip Island, left her heart with Flynn and his boy. Thank goodness she had tomorrow to recover some energy and enthusiasm for work before turning up at the midwifery unit on Monday.

Then Darcie spoilt it all. 'Who's this Flynn you keep mentioning?'

Ally sat up straight. 'I don't.'

Darcie held her hand up, fingers splayed. 'Five times, but I'm not counting.'

I can't have. I would have noticed. 'He's one of the doctors I've been working with.'

'Yet I don't recall you mentioning any of the others. Guess this Flynn made an impact on you.'

You could say that. 'Okay, I'll fess up and admit to having a couple of meals with him and his wee boy.'

Darcie said nothing for so long Ally thought she'd got away with it and started to go back to her relaxed state.

Until, 'Ally, what else do you do when you're not being a midwife?'

That had her spine cracking as she straightened too fast. 'Isn't that enough? I'm dedicated to my career.' Apart from shopping for high-end clothes and getting in the minimum of groceries once in a while, what else was there to do?

'Your career shouldn't be everything. Don't you ever want a partner? A family? Your own home? Most of us do.'

'I'm not most of you.'

'What about this Flynn? Do you want to see him again?'

Yes. But she wasn't about to admit that. 'No,' she muttered, hating herself as she lied.

'You haven't fallen in love with him, have you?'

And if I have? Ally raised her eyes to Darcie and when she went to deny that suggestion she couldn't find the words. Not a single one.

'I see. That bad, huh?' Darcie leaned back in her seat. 'I don't know what's gone on in your life, Ally, and I'm not asking.' She paused, stared around her beautiful apartment before returning her gaze to Ally. 'Sometimes we have to take chances.'

Ally shook her head. 'Not on love,' she managed to croak.

'Loving someone can hurt as much as denying that love. But there's always a chance of having something wonderful if you accept it.'

There really wasn't anything she could say to that so she kept quiet.

The buzzer sounded throughout the apartment, its screech jarring. Darcie stood up. 'That's probably Mary from the ward. We're heading out to St Kilda for a few hours. Want to join us?'

Ally shook her head. 'Thanks, but, no, thanks. I've got a couple of chores to do and then I'm going to blob out right here. But with coffee, not wine.'

She tipped her head back and closed her eyes, pulled off

the band from her ponytail and shook her hair free. Her hand kneaded the knots in her neck. What was Flynn doing? Had he taken Adam around to see Jacob? Her heart squeezed. *I miss you guys already.*

'Hello, Ally.'

She jerked upright. 'Flynn?' Couldn't be. Her imagination had to be working overtime.

'Ally, we came to see you.' No mistaking that excited shriek. Or the arms that reached for her and held tight.

Not her imagination, then. Adam was here. *Flynn* was here. Meaning what? Lifting her head, she stared at the man who'd stolen her heart when it was supposed to be locked away. The man she'd walked away from only hours ago without a word of goodbye or a glance over her shoulder—because any of those actions would've nailed her to the floor of his home and she'd still be on Phillip Island.

Adam tightened his hold. 'I'm missing you, Ally. You didn't wait for us.' Out of the mouths of babes—came the truth.

Her head dropped so her chin rested on Adam's head. 'Adam, sweetheart.' Then her throat dried and she couldn't say a word. Finally, after a long moment of trying not to think what this was about, she raised her eyes to find Flynn gazing at her like a thirsty man would a glass of cold water on a hot day. The same emotions she'd been dealing with all day were glittering out from her favourite blue eyes. 'Flynn,' she managed.

'Hey.' He took a step closer. 'The house didn't feel the same when we got back from our walk. Kind of empty.' Flynn didn't sound angry with her, but he should. She had done a runner.

She owed him. 'I'm really sorry but I couldn't wait.' *If I did I'd never have left.* Her heart seemed to have increased its rate to such a level it hurt. 'It's an old habit. Get out quick. Don't look back.'

Bleakness filled his gaze, his tongue did a lap of his lips. 'I see.'

Adam wriggled free of her arms and sat on the floor beside her.

Flynn didn't move, just kept watching her.

Suddenly Ally became very aware that this was the defining moment in her life. Everything she'd faced, battled, conquered, yearned for—it all came down to now and how she handled the situation. She loved Flynn. Before— *Gulp.* Before she told him—if she found the courage—she had to explain. 'It's an ingrained habit because of all those shifts I made as a child. I learned not to stare out the back window of the car as my social worker took me away from my latest family to place me in the midst of more strangers.'

Flynn crossed to sit in the chair Darcie had been using earlier. He still didn't say a word, just let her take her time.

Her chest rose and fell as she spoke. 'I know it's not the same as what I did today, that you do care about me and never promised me anything that you haven't already delivered, but I come pre-conditioned. I'm sorry.'

'You were waiting for one of those families to adopt you.' Flynn looked so sad it nearly brought on her tears.

Adam, who shouldn't be taking the slightest notice of this conversation, stared up at her and asked, 'What's adopt mean?'

'Oh, sweetheart. It's when people give someone else a place in their family, share everything they've got, including, and most importantly of all, their hearts.'

'Don't you have a family?' He'd understood far too much.

'No, Adam, I don't.'

'We can adopt you. Can't we, Dad?'

Ally's mouth dropped open. Her stomach tightened in on itself. Her hands clenched on her thighs. What? No. Not possible. He didn't understand. It wasn't that simple.

She leapt up and charged across to the floor-to-ceiling window showcasing Melbourne city. Her heart was thudding hard, and the tears that should've run out hours ago started again.

'Ally.' A familiar hand gripped her shoulder.

She gasped. 'You've taken your ring off.' Could she start believing?

He tugged gently until she gave in and turned around. But she couldn't look up, couldn't face the denial of Adam's silly statement if it was staring at her out of Flynn's eyes. 'Ally, look at me. Please.'

Slowly she raised her head, her eyes downcast, noting the expanse of chest she'd come to know over the last month, the Adam's apple that moved as Flynn swallowed, that gorgeous mouth that had woken every part of her body and could kiss like no other man she'd known. Expelling all the air in her lungs, she finally met Flynn's gaze. There was no apology there, no *It's been nice knowing you but we don't want to know you any more.* All she found was love. Genuine love, deep love that spelled a bond and a future if she dared take it.

'Flynn,' she whispered. 'I have to tell you something.' The breath lodged painfully in her chest, but if she was going to gamble, then she had to start by being honest. 'Today was different. For the first time ever I didn't want to go. That's why I ran.' Tremors rippled through her. This was way too hard. But there was a lot to lose—or gain. A deep breath and she continued. 'I've fallen in love with you. Both of you.' And then she couldn't utter another word as tears clogged her throat.

His arms came around her, held her loosely so he could still watch her face. 'This is the last time you're walking away. You're not on your own any more. You have me, us. We are your family.' His mouth grazed hers.

'You want to adopt me?' she croaked against his lips, being flippant because she was afraid to acknowledge what he'd said for fear his words would vaporise in a flash.

'Try amalgamate. We want to bring you in with us, make us a threesome, a family.'

'Amalgamate? Sounds like a business deal.' But the warmth lacing his voice was beginning to nudge the chill out of her bones. 'I'll bring two bags of clothes and my music player and you'll supply a home.' She smiled to show she wasn't having a poke at him. Then she gasped and dashed to her bag to pull out the dogs. 'Plus these two. I take them everywhere. This time when I put them on the shelf they'll stay there so long they'll gather dust.'

Flynn looked ready to cry. 'That's the closest you've got to owning a pet?' His arms came around her again.

'Bonkers, eh?'

He stepped back, shoved his hand through his hair. 'You have no idea how much I mean every word. I love you so much it hurts sometimes.'

She gasped. Had Flynn said he loved her?

He hadn't finished. 'I could've told you that days ago, but I got cold feet. I put Adam before everything else. Which I have to do, but I used him as an excuse not to let you know where my feelings for you were headed. I didn't want you to leave, yet I didn't know how to tell you that. I think I was kind of hoping you'd just hang around and that would solve my dilemma.'

She stared at him as a smile began breaking out across her lips, banishing the sadness that had dominated all day. 'You said you love me.'

'Yes, Ally, I did. I mean it. I love you.'

'No one's ever told me that before.' Oh, my goodness. Flynn loved her. But it wouldn't feel so warm and thrilling and wonderful if she didn't love him back. 'I've never loved anyone before.' There hadn't been anyone to bestow that gift on. 'This love is for real, I promise.'

'Hey, I can see it in your eyes. It's been there for days if only I'd known what to look for.'

'Adam, look away. I'm going to kiss your father.'

'Why?'

'Because I love him.'

'Do you love me?'

'Absolutely.' She bent down to press a kiss on his forehead. 'Yes.' When she straightened Flynn was waiting for her, his arms outstretched to bring her close. His head lowered and his mouth claimed hers.

This kiss was like no other they'd shared. This was full of promises and love and life.

'How long are you going to kiss Dad?' Adam tapped her waist.

'For ever,' she murmured against Flynn's mouth, before reluctantly pulling away. She was afraid to let him go. She needed to keep reassuring herself he'd always be there.

Flynn took her hand and laced their fingers together. 'Want to come home with us for the rest of the weekend?'

'I can't think of anything I'd rather do.'

'Thank goodness.' Until he'd relaxed she hadn't realised how tense he'd become.

'I have to be back here on Monday.'

He nodded. 'But now you have a home to go to when you're not on a job.'

Her heart turned over. 'You're not expecting me to give up working for the midwifery unit, then?'

'You'll do that when you're good and ready. We've got all the time in the world to learn to live together and for you to feel right at home on the island. I won't be rushing you, sweetheart.' Then he really stole her heart with, 'When I say I love you, I mean through the best times and the worst, through summer, winter and Christmas and birthdays. I'm here for you, with you, Ally, for ever.'

'But what if I fail? This will be new for me.'

'You won't fail, Ally. You'll make mistakes.'

'Fine. What happens when I make these mistakes?' she asked, her heart in her mouth.

'We sort them and we move on. Together.'

Her heart cracked completely open. Could she do this? 'Can I do this? Really?' She locked her eyes on the man who'd turned her world on its head.

'Your call, sweetheart. But I believe you can do anything you set your mind to.'

Was Flynn not as scared as she was? For all his understanding, maybe he didn't get it. But looking into those eyes she'd come to trust, she saw nothing but his confidence in her. He trusted her to look out for Adam to the best of her ability, even if that ability needed fine-tuning along the way. He trusted her to love him as much as she'd declared. Her mouth was dry. Finally she managed to croak, 'Let's go home.'

'Yes.' Adam jumped up and down, then ran circles around the lounge. 'Yes, Ally's coming back home with us.'

Flynn reached for her, his smile wobbly with relief. 'Home. Our home. The three of us.' Then his smile strengthened. 'And the dogs.'

Eighteen months later...

Ally laid baby Charlotte over her shoulder and rubbed her tiny back. 'Bring up the wind, sweetheart, and you'll feel so much better.'

Flynn grinned. 'Look at you. Anyone would think you'd been burping babies for ever. Charlotte is completely relaxed lying there.'

Ally's heart swelled with pride and happiness. 'Seems I got the mothering gene after all.'

Flynn's grin became a warm, loving smile. 'Ally, I was never in doubt about that. I've seen you with Jacob, with Chrissie's Xavier and half the other new babies on the island. You're a natural when it comes to making babies happy.'

She blinked back a threatening tear at his belief in her. That belief had helped her through the doubts that had reared up throughout her pregnancy, had meant he hadn't hovered as she'd learned to feed and bath and love her baby. And Adam. Well. 'Adam's been complaining this morning. Apparently I should've made a boy so he had a brother to play football with.'

'He'll have to wait a year or two.'

'We're having more?'

'Why not?'

She blinked. That told her how much he believed in her. In her chest her heart swelled even larger.

The bed tipped as Flynn sat down beside her and reached for his daughter. 'Hello, gorgeous.' He laid Charlotte over his shoulder and held her with one hand.

'Hello,' said Ally, her tongue in her cheek.

He leaned over and kissed her. 'Hello, gorgeous number one. Did you get any sleep last night?'

'An hour maybe.' Charlotte had had colic and nothing had settled her. But Ally had been happy, pacing up and down the house, cuddling her precious bundle, kissing and caressing. Just plain loving her baby. She'd known what to do, hadn't had any moments of doubt when Charlotte wouldn't settle. And this morning she was being rewarded with a contented baby.

Yep, she did have the right instincts. When Charlotte had been born three weeks ago she'd been stunned at the instant love and connection she'd felt for her baby. It had been blinding in its strength. For the first time ever, Ally realised how hard it must have been for her mother to give her up. She might have desperately wanted to keep her baby but had been too scared, troubled or unable to support herself. Now, as a mother, Ally knew it wasn't a decision any woman would make lightly. She'd never know the reason her mother had left her on that doorstep. But now at last, with Flynn by her side, she was moving on, making a loving life for her family and herself.

'Flynn.' She wrapped her hands around his free one. 'I love you so much. I'm so lucky.'

'You and me both, sweetheart.'

'Let's get married.' She hadn't thought about it. The words had just popped out, but she certainly didn't want to retract them.

His eyes widened and that delicious mouth tipped up into a

big smile. 'That's the best idea you've had since we decided to get pregnant.'

'I thought so.' Her lips kissed the palm of his hand, and then his fingers. Life couldn't get any better.

* * * * *

Keep reading for an excerpt of
The Rancher's Return
by Maisey Yates.
Find it in the
The Carsons Of Lone Rock anthology,
out now!

Chapter One

Welcome to Lone Rock...

He hadn't seen that sign in years. He wasn't sure if he felt nostalgic or just plain pissed off.

He supposed it didn't matter. Because he was here.

For the first time in twenty years, Buck Carson was home.

And he aimed to make it a homecoming to remember.

"You look like you want to punch somebody in the face."

"You look like you got in a fight with your own depression and lost."

"You look like someone who hasn't learned to successfully process his emotions and traumas."

Buck scowled, and glared at his three sons, who were only just recently *legally* his. "I'm good," he said, as his truck continued to barrel down the main drag of Lone Rock, Oregon, heading straight to his parents' ranch, where he hadn't been since he'd first left two decades ago.

"Are you?" Reggie asked, looking at him with snarky, faux teen concern.

"Yes, Reg, and I wouldn't tell you if I wasn't, because I'm the parent."

"I don't think that's healthy," Marcus said.

"I think that somebody should've taught you not to use therapy speak as a weapon," Buck said to his middle son.

"You're in luck," said Colton, his oldest, "because I don't use therapy speak at all. Not even in therapy."

"Yeah, the therapy hasn't taken with you," Marcus said.

"Hey," Reggie said. "Leave him alone. He's traumatized. By having to go through life with that face of his."

"*All right*," Buck said.

It wasn't like he hadn't known what he was getting into when he'd decided to adopt these boys. But becoming an instant father to fifteen-, sixteen- and seventeen-year-old kids was a little more intense than he had anticipated.

When he'd left Lone Rock he'd been completely and totally hopeless. He'd been convinced he was to blame for the death of his friends, and hell, the whole town had been too.

After everything his family had already been through, he hadn't wanted to bring that kind of shame to their door. So he'd left.

And spent the first few years away proving everything everyone had ever said about him right. He had been drunk or fucked-up for most of that time. And one day, he had woken up in the bed of a woman whose name he didn't know and realized he wasn't living.

His three best friends had died in a car accident on graduation night, driving drunk from a bonfire party back to their campsite. He had also been drunk, but driving behind them in his own car. He had made the same mistake they had, and yet for some reason, they had paid for it and he hadn't.

They'd only been at the party because of him. All upstanding kids with bright futures, while Buck had by far been the screwup of the group. Their futures had been cut short, and for some reason, he had gone ahead and made his own future a mess.

That day, he woke up feeling shitty, but alive.

And when he had the realization that he still drew breath, and that he wasn't doing anyone any favors by wasting the life he still had, he had gotten his ass out of bed and gone into a rehab program.

But in truth, he had never been tempted to take another drink after that morning, never been tempted to touch another illicit substance. Because he had decided then and there he was going to live differently.

Because he'd found a new purpose.

After completing the rehab program, he had limped onto New Hope Ranch asking for a job. The place was a facility for troubled youth, where they worked the land, worked with animals and in general turned their lives around through the simple act of being part of the community.

Buck had been working there for sixteen years. Those kids had become his heart and soul; that work had become his reason why. And five months ago, when he had been offered the position of director, he had realized he was at a new crossroads.

There were three kids currently in the program who didn't have homes to go back to. And he had connected with them. It had been yet another turning point.

But that's when he had seen himself clearly. He had a trust fund he hadn't touched since he left Lone Rock. He had been living on the ranch, taking the barest of bare minimum pay. He had no possessions. He was like a monk with a vow of poverty, supported by the church. Though the ranch was hardly a church.

He used his paycheck for one week off a year, where he usually went to some touristy ski town, stayed in reasonable accommodations, found a female companion whose name he *did* know and spent a nice weekend.

But otherwise… He didn't have much of anything.

And he could.

He considered taking all his money and donating it to the ranch, but it was well funded by many organizations and rich people who wanted to feel like they were doing good in the world while getting a write-off on their taxes.

And then he remembered he had a unique resource.

His family.

He could give Reggie, Marcus and Colton a family. A real family.

Yeah, he was an imperfect father figure, but he had found that made it easier to connect with the kids at the ranch. Additionally, he had a mother and a father, six brothers and a sister. And they were all married with children of their own. He could give these boys a real, lasting sense of community.

And that was when he had decided to adopt those boys, buy a ranch in Lone Rock and reconnect with his parents. They had met on neutral ground, at various rodeo events over the summer.

His dad had been angry at first; his mom never had been. But he had explained what he had been through, what he had been doing and why he had been absent for so long, and ultimately, they had forgiven him. And welcomed him to come back home. He also knew they had done some work priming his brothers and sister to accept his presence. Or at least, the presence of the boys.

But...

He also had the sense all was not forgiven and forgotten when it came to his siblings.

Even so, he was looking forward to today's reunion.

At least he was pretty sure the sick feeling in his stomach was anticipation. And maybe some of the anger that still lived inside of him. At this town, at himself.

Well. Hell.

He supposed he didn't have a full accounting of all his emotions.

There was nothing simple about the loss this place had experienced all those years ago. His friends should be thirty-eight years old. Just like him. But they were forever eighteen.

He looked at his sons, sitting on the bench seat of the truck, with Marcus in the back.

It wasn't a coincidence that he had adopted three of them, he supposed. A more obvious mea culpa didn't exist. But then, he had never pretended he wasn't making as firm a bid for redemption as he possibly could.

Yeah. Well.

It was what it was.

"So we're meeting your whole family today?" Marcus asked.

"Yeah. For better or worse."

"You haven't seen them in twenty years," Colton said.

"No."

"God, you are so old," Colton said.

"Yeah. Really ancient," Buck said. "And feeling older by the minute around you three assholes."

"I do think you have more gray hair since you adopted us," Reggie said.

"I'll probably just pick up more girls with it," Buck said.

That earned him a chorus of retching gags, and genuinely, he found that was his absolute favorite part of this parenting thing.

Driving the kids nuts.

It was mutual, he had a feeling.

But he took it as a good sign that they felt secure enough to mess with him. They all definitely had their own trauma. Marcus didn't mess around using therapy speak by pulling it out of nowhere. He'd spent a hell of a lot of time sitting on a therapist's couch, that was for damn sure.

He turned onto the long driveway that was so familiar. But he knew everything else had changed. His parents had built a new house in the years since he had left. His siblings had been kids when he'd gone.

They were entitled to their anger, his siblings. They had already lost their youngest sister when they lost him too. And life had proven to be even crueler after that. So maybe his running off had been part of the cruelty, rather than the solution. Sobriety and maturity made that feel more likely.

But at the time, he had simply thought everybody would be better off without him. Hell, at the time that had probably been true. That was the thing. He had self-destructed for a good long while. He was pretty sure he would've done that even if he hadn't left.

So whether his family wanted to believe it or not, he really did believe that in the state he'd been in then, it had been better that he wasn't around. And then he had been afraid to go back. For a long time.

But his dad hadn't cut him off. His trust fund had still come available to him when he turned thirty. He supposed that should have been a sign to him. That he was always welcome back home.

But he'd left it untouched. Maybe that was the real reason he hadn't used it till now. He had felt on some level that he would have to reconnect with his family if he took any family money.

And it was the boys who had given him a strong enough reason to do that.

He followed the directions his mother had given him to the new house. It was beautiful and modern. With big tall windows designed to make the most of the high desert views around them.

"I didn't realize this place was a desert," Marcus said. "I thought it rained all the time in Oregon."

"In Portland maybe," he said.

"There's nothing here," Reggie added.

"There's plenty to do."

"Doesn't look like there's plenty to do," Colton said.

"You'll be fine."

"How come there aren't any cactuses?" Marcus asked.

He gritted his teeth. "Not that kind of desert."

"Are there at least armadillos?" Marcus, again.

"Still not that kind of desert," he said.

"What a rip-off," Marcus replied.

"I don't think you want armadillos, from the sounds of things. They're nuisances. Dig lots of holes in the yard."

Then, talk of armadillos died in the back of his throat. Because he was right up against the side of the house. He got out of the truck slowly, and the kids piled out quickly. And it only took a moment for the front door to open.

His parents were the first out. His mother rushing toward him to give him a hug. She had been physically demonstrative from the first time they had seen each other again.

"Buck," she said. "I'm so glad you're here."

"Me too."

"Hey," his old man said, extending his hand and shaking Buck's.

"You must be Reggie, Marcus and Colton," his mom said, going right over to the boys and forcing them into a hug as well. "You can call me Nana."

He could sense the boys' discomfort, but this was what he was here for. For the boys to have grandparents. To have family.

"You can call me Abe," his dad said.

And that made the boys chuckle.

He heard a commotion at the door and looked up. There were all his brothers, filing out of the house: Boone, Jace, Chance, Kit and Flint. Buck was about to say something, when a fist connected with his jaw, and he found himself hurtling toward the ground as pain burst behind his eyelids.

"Boone!" He heard a woman's shocked voice, though he couldn't see her from where he was lying sprawled out on the ground.

"Oh *shit*!" That, he knew was Reggie.

"Fair call," Buck said, sitting up and raising his hand in a "hold on" gesture. "Fair call, Boone."

"Violence isn't the answer, Boone," came a lecturing teenage voice.

"Sometimes it is," returned an equally lecturing different

teenage voice. "Sometimes a person deserves to get punched in the face."

"Maybe not right now," the angry female voice said.

Buck stood up. And looked his brother square in the face.

"Good to see you again, Boone," he said.

"Don't think I won't hit you again," Boone said.

"Hey," said his brother Jace, moving over to Boone and putting his hand on Boone's shoulder. "Why don't you guys punch it out on your own time."

"I don't have anyone to punch," Buck said. "And I'll take one. Maybe two. But no more than that."

Chance and Kit exchanged glances, like they were considering getting in a punch of their own. For his part, Flint looked neutral.

For the first time, Buck got a look at the woman who had defended him.

"I'm Wendy," she said. "I'm Boone's wife."

And he had a feeling the two lecturing teenage girls were Boone's stepchildren. His mother had filled him in on everybody's situation, more or less.

Right then, another woman came out of the house with a baby on her hip.

Callie.

His baby sister. Who had been maybe five years old when he'd left. He knew it was her. She was a mother herself. He had missed her whole damn life.

He was sad for himself, not for her.

There hadn't been a damn thing he could've taught her. He hadn't been worth anything at the point when he'd left. But he sure as hell felt sorry for himself. For missing out.

"Buck," she said. Her eyes were soft, no anger in them whatsoever.

"Yeah," he said, "it's me."

And he realized this whole reunion was going to be both more rewarding and more difficult than he had imagined.

Because his family wasn't a vague, cloudy shape in the rearview mirror of his past anymore. His family was made up of a whole lot of people. People with thoughts and feelings about this situation. About him.

Hell. He had spent a little bit of time with the therapist himself.

"Why don't we go inside?" his mother said. "But no more hitting."

"Yes, ma'am," Boone said, looking ashamed for the first time.

This didn't have to be easy.

Buck was used to things being hard.

But he was home.

For better or for worse.

He was home.

Subscribe and fall in love with a Mills & Boon series today!

You'll be among the first to read stories delivered to your door monthly and enjoy great savings.